I0678264

Also by Gene Lazuta

Bleeder
Blood Flies
Forget Me Not
Happy Cage (as Daniel Raven)
The Shinglo (as Alex Kane)

The Bill Hawley Undertakings (as Leo Axler)
Final Viewing
Double Plot
Grave Matters
Separated at Death

VYRMIN
GENE LAZUTA

ISBN-13: 978-0-9980679-0-2
ISBN-10: 0998067903

READ UNTIL YOU BLEED!

VYRMIN

by Gene Lazuta

This book, like every book,
is for my wife, Sue.

CONTENTS

There's wolves in the woods,
my girl, my girl.
There's wolves in the woods,
my dear.

But come the full moon,
see the blue moon.
And there's wolves in the house,
and the mirror.

- Children's rhyme (circa 1800)

PROLOGUE

JANUARY 7, 1963

"Your father says you have bad dreams," an invisible doctor said from behind a bouncing ball of blinding white light.

The boy nodded sheepishly, rubbing his hands over his naked knees and squinting as the light moved from his left eye to his right, describing phantom capillaries in a sulfurous glow that burned away the last of his sleepy confusion. He was fully awake. He didn't know where he was. It was almost two o'clock in the morning.

"Tell him," his father's voice commanded angrily from the antiseptic smell behind the glare. "Tell him who it was this time!"

"Mr. Norris, please," the doctor said, snapping off his penlight. "There's no need to frighten the child."

"He's my kid, and I'll frighten him all I want!" his father slurred, jutting his face forward and watching the boy with that same, wary expression he'd worn when he'd wrenched him from his bed, driven him down anonymous, snow-covered streets, and pounded on an unlit door. It was the same expression he'd worn as he'd whispered hoarse apologies to this frizzle-haired doctor who yawned and rubbed his chin while the boy shivered, shoeless, in a strange, amber-tinted alcove. And it was closely related to the gnarled mask of panic that had popped the sinews in his neck when he threw his hands into the air and cried, "There's something wrong with his goddamn head, and I gotta know what it is *tonight*!" in a voice that made the boy wince and the doctor unlock his examination room.

The shrillness of that pronouncement made the boy feel as

if salt had been poured into the hollow center of his spine. It sucked the life out of him, so that he dangled like a puppet when he was undressed. It festered in his mind, sensitizing him to the static charge of urgency hanging in the room. And it shrank his self-image into a tiny, vulnerable seed.

"Perhaps you should have a seat outside," the doctor suggested, skillfully gathering up the man's drunken protests and escorting him to the door. "I'll call you when I'm through."

"I know he's the one doin' it!" the man shouted as he was herded into the front room. "He denies it, but there's something in his brain...something in his head! It makes him see things...makes things *happen.* Whatever it is, you gotta get rid of it, Doc. You gotta cut it out before he can do it again!"

The door slammed, the room was cold, and the night outside was absolute.

The doctor, who was tall and lean, had a bristling grey beard, hard black eyes, and a nervous, birdlike way of holding his head that was absurd and disturbing. He terrified the boy with his every move. And just the idea of his long white fingers touching his skin tingled his groin and quivered his lower lip.

"So," the doctor said, then smiled, covering the distance between the door and the examination table in three flowing steps. "You're only five years old, and already your father is afraid of you. Isn't it a shame that such a weak man should be blessed with a son like you?"

The boy was trembling from head to foot.

Why did his dad do this to him? he wondered guiltily. What did he do that was so bad that it would make his father want to bring him to places like this, night after night, where men poked and prodded, jabbed him with needles, and took his blood, pee and spit? What did he do that made his father want to leave him with strange old men who did things to him...things that he couldn't even talk about later, when his dad would drive them home in silence? His dad knew about the things the doctors did—he knew how bad they were—but he acted like they were the boy's fault.

But they weren't!

Just like the dreams weren't his fault!

The dreams scared him.

He was scared of just about everything anymore. He was especially scared now that his father had left the room. But instead of displaying his fear, he straightened his spine, stuck out his jaw, and locked his fingers protectively over his crotch, producing a profile that would one day characterize the essence of his adult personality.

"Don't be afraid," the doctor said—like the doctors always said.

The muscles around the boy's mouth twitched.

"I'm not going to hurt you."

He knew that that was the signal that he was about to be hurt, and his hands reflexively clenched.

"Now, watch me..."

Then the doctor did something that no doctor had ever done before: he put his hands behind his back.

"Okay?" he asked, bending forward at the waist so that his hairy head loomed huge and close in the boy's vision. "There'll be no touching tonight. Do you understand?"

Tiny, twin reflections of a shivering child were drifting freely within the black depths of the doctor's eyes. Watching those phantom shapes, the boy coiled his muscles in hopeless preparation as his first whiff of the man's scent did something to him.

It was a warm, brown smell, a rich muskiness that seemed to place images in his mind, pictures that teased at his thoughts and made him blink. In his head he saw horses, and sparkling water, swirling spirals of wood-smoke, and twisted iron wheels rusting in the sunshine of rippling, grassy fields.

"You can feel it," the doctor said. He smiled, displaying remarkably white, unnaturally long teeth that were pointed, perfect, and...

Sharp.

He has teeth just like a dog, the boy thought flatly.

"Just let it happen, my son," the doctor added, and there was a babble like water running somewhere deep behind his words: cool, soothing, and deceptively inviting. "I know that you secretly want it to happen, because I know what you dream."

"You do?" the body couldn't help but ask—when he spoke, his tongue felt a little numb.

"I do. Now, watch..."

There was something in the doctor's eyes—something big. Gazing into those eyes, the boy felt trepidation and fear trickle from his system as a warm sensation of peace eased his thoughts and lowered his mental defenses. His hands were limp on his lap, his mouth dropped open a little, and his breathing slowed to a steady, gentle rhythm that was as shallow as a promise.

In the doctor's eyes, children floated...small, naked and distorted by perspective so that their foreheads bulged over swollen brows.

"I've been waiting for you," the doctor whispered lovingly, his lips forming the words with hypnotizing precision. "There've been others of your kind. But none of your breed. I've not seen a prince in three hundred years. Hail to thee, bloody prince. Hail to thee for thine kin."

His face was closer now, and around his eyes, wrinkled skin puckered over twitching muscle. His words played on the boy's sensitive cheek in hot, meaty puffs. And when he reached to cup the child's chin, he let him.

"Sometimes at night, you see things that make you scream," the doctor said, moving his head appraisingly back and forth. "Your father fears your screams and the things you tell him of your dreams. His fear is great enough to motivate his misguided search for a cure."

He laughed: one brutish grunt.

"A cure for the sun."

The boy nodded his agreement, unsure if it was he or the man who made his skull bounce.

The doctor smiled again.

"Sometimes, when you close your eyes, you float over your bed and you see yourself sleeping. That's when you see the things that your father is so worried about: the things that frighten you so badly. Isn't that so?"

The boy nodded…he couldn't help but nod. There was something about the way the doctor moved his head, slowly, back and forth, that made him want to tell nothing but the truth.

"Tell me what you see," the doctor urged. "When your spirit roams the night."

The boy hesitated, suddenly aware of his voice, coming not from his throat, but from the figure he was watching, awash in the darkest dark he'd ever seen. Somewhere in that dark behind his reflection, there were vague forms that seemed to drift shapelessly, swirling like mist and watching all that transpired.

"Tell me," the doctor prompted in a voice that was not to be denied. "I know of your pain…and your loneliness. I know of the men who've *examined* you at night. Tell me about your dreams, and I promise that no one will ever bother you again."

"Places," the boy offered hopefully, gazing into his reflection's eyes so as not to see the things that seemed to be peering at him from inside the doctor's head—the animal things. The things that looked so old, and so ugly.

"Go on."

"And people."

"I'll not ask you again, boy. Continue!"

The fear was back now. But this time, it wasn't simply physical. This time, it was a creeping sensation of dread that had nothing to do with the boy's body, and everything to do with his soul.

"Speak!" the doctor's voice pronounced, and the boy was instantly certain that if he didn't, something far worse than any touching would happen.

"I see people and places, far away," he said, meekly, his voice pitifully small. "I go up into the sky, or somewhere like the sky, and I see things happen—bad things happen—to people I don't know."

"And are you alone in the sky?"

"No. While I'm there I can feel...something. I don't know what it is, but it's big...maybe bigger than the sky is big. It watches me. I think it always watches me, but I can only really feel it for sure when I'm in the sky."

"And do you know what that something big is?" the doctor asked, pointedly.

"No."

"Would you like to know?"

"No! I want my daddy!"

"Silence!"

The boy felt himself flinch.

"I'm going to tell you about it, boy. I'm going to tell you, and you're going to keep it hidden until again we meet, many years from now. You're going to lock it away in your mind. You won't speak of it, or think of it, or remember it until the day I summon you unto myself. On that day you'll remember...*and you'll come.* No resisting will prevent it. You will come. And together, we'll change the world. Now, listen:

"The man who brought you here tonight isn't your father, and the place you live isn't your home. You are of the trees and the valleys. Your nature is green, and your essence earthen. You are of the holy places, where silver water is bejeweled with moon glow, and the gods breathe music through the sacred stillness as rustling leaves and singing rain. In your heart there is no concrete or steel, but forests and open skies. In your soul resides the flame of freedom, lost to all but a precious, dwindling few.

"For you are Wild.

"There are others of the Wild, but you…oh, you will be their prince, because you have been born a Sender! Your dreams will be the key to the future of your kin. *Your* gift will open *their* gate. And as the emancipator, you will be revered!

"Among your fellows you will be as a stallion is to a plowing nag. Your coming of age will herald the dawning of a new Dark Time for the unharried Flock that has passed so many a restful night without having its blood chilled by the Singing or spilled by the Law.

"In you, it all begins again. In you, it *is* again. In you…"

His voice trailed off, and his eyes picked up where the abandoned emotion of his words stained the air.

His eyes…

His deep, terrible eyes.

They mesmerized the boy, entranced and entangled him in a web of threat and enticement that made his heart pound and the tiny, inner voice of his thoughts scream, *He's not a man! He looks like a man, but inside…he's big! And old! And strong!*

He's not a man!

He's…

He didn't have the words to continue.

As if the doctor had heard his thoughts, a crackle of lightening sparkled in his eyes. In an instant his hands let go of the boy's chin and shot up before his face. With dreadful fascination, the boy watched the long white fingers curl into a fist. As they tightened, a terrible knot formed in his throat, and he gagged.

"That thing that watches you in the sky is me," the doctor said, squeezing his fist a little tighter as a tendril of hair crawled snakelike over his forehead. "I watch over you, and all others like you, wherever they are—as I've always done...since the start of it all."

The boy heard the words, but he didn't care what they meant. His throat was gorged, full and hard, his breath backed up hotly in a bloody bubble that trapped his racing heart. And his eyes were locked on a thing that had just appeared, in a corner, barely visible over the doctor's shoulder.

"When I call for you, will you come, *Blood Prince?*" the doctor asked, shaking his fist.

Everything inside the boy quivered. In horror he felt warmth on his leg and heard dribbling on the floor. As he peed, he felt every contact his young life had ever established with what he had been taught was "real" slip from his mind's fingers and shatter on the hard floor of events.

There was a monkey in the room—a monkey, here, in a doctor's office. It was grey and black, and it had sharp, dark eyes that blinked and stared and sparkled. It was only about three feet tall and had very long arms that it wound out before itself as if they were boneless. It was grinning, and watching him struggle, watching him squirm. At first he had thought that it was sitting on a shelf on the wall, but now he saw that it was just hanging there, sticking to the whitewashed plaster...

With its wings folded up on its back.

And with a running brown streak of shit crawling down the wall beneath it.

"Will you?" the doctor hissed, and the sound seemed to

bruise the air. Within the depths of his stare were sparkling pinpoints that gleamed like the eyes of hidden animals, cloaked by night. "The world is not as you perceive it, boy," he added, curling his lip savagely and turning his fist to reveal the pig-like bristles on the back of his hand. "Will you promise to remember the trees?"

The boy could feel himself drifting inside himself, and he experienced a profound sense of disassociation of spirit from body.

The monkey on the wall was jabbering now; clattering its jaws together in a rapid-fire staccato that was both maddening and mean.

"Will you swear to remember the earth?"

The boy's eyes felt as if they were about to split.

"Will you pledge yourself to the Wild?"

The monkey wanted him—he could see that in its eyes.

The monkey wanted his body…

And the doctor wanted his soul.

"*Will you swear?*"

Briefly, he wondered which would hurt less to give. But seeing the monkey's dripping teeth when it spread its lips made his decision easy.

"*Swear!*"

And he did…not as a word, but as a thought. He didn't voice it…he became it with every drop of blood and ounce of will he possessed. Inside his head he exploded, screaming, throwing out his soul's arms to embrace the very essence of the word…

"*Yes!*"

He swore, giving himself up to the vow.

"*Yes!*"

He raged, his body melting beneath his mind.

"*Yes!*"

He bled, signing a pact he could never understand with an

evil it would take him years to even recall.

And, with a smile, the doctor said, "Thus is our agreement sealed."

Before his eyes the man's fist unfolded, like the misty clouds at the eye of a hurricane, relaxing simply, and breaking the thunderhead that had amassed inside his skull. Breath rushed first up, and then out, chocking him with a gale of phlegm. Then it rushed in, and down, drowning him in a dizzying, uncontrollable gulp. His head reeled, his eyes rolled, and his world fell away.

"Now, sleep, Blood Prince," the doctor said, waving his hand. "Sleep until the wolf in thine heart is born."

And he did.

His legs kicked an instant before his head hit the table with a dull *thunk*. His eyes closed. He didn't want them closed. He wanted them open. He wanted to see what was happening as the examination room door opened. He could hear it, and he could hear his father's heavy steps.

"Watch out, Daddy!" he wanted to scream. "Watch out for the bad man and the monkey! The monkey's bad—so, so bad!"

But instead of screaming, he listened to the crumpling of money as it was withdrawn from his father's wallet. And the doctor's breathy sighs. He could hear it all, but he couldn't see any of it because he couldn't open his eyes.

"I gave him something to make him sleep," the doctor said.

"*No!*" the boy howled in his head—because he couldn't move his mouth.

"So what's wrong with him?" his father asked. "He says he sees people die in his dreams. He says that he sees people die, and sometimes, when I look in the paper the next day, the story's there, just like he said it'd be. What's wrong with him,

Doc? I been all over, and nobody can tell me what's wrong with my boy!"

"There's nothing wrong with him," the doctor said, and the boy protested again in his mind. "He's perfectly normal. He has the same nightmares a lot of children his age have. People die every day. It's inevitable that his dreams should mirror reality at least once in a while. There's nothing unnatural, or even supernatural about it. Mr. Norris, it's just coincidence."

"But tonight he dreamed that it was me that's gonna die!" his father cut in. "He said that he saw me with my head split open!"

"Mr. Norris, please. They're just a little boy's dreams," the doctor lied, gently. "They don't mean anything."

No!

Don't believe him!

They mean everything!

"Take him home," the doctor concluded. "He'll grow out of it. People nowadays think that doctors can cure the little inconveniences that our more primitive forebears knew were simply the unpleasant facts of life."

"Then I'm not going to die?" the boy's father said, the relief almost palpable in his voice.

"No. You're not going to die," the doctor promised.

So his father scooped up the boy's limp body, bundled him off to the car, and took him home.

On the way, he drunkenly swerved their station wagon into the path of an oncoming truck, and died when his head hit the windshield—just as his son had dreamt he would earlier in the evening, when his terrified screams had prompted their visit to the doctor.

The boy was unconscious when a sheriff's deputy named Conway pulled him from the burning wreck, and he stayed that way for three days. When he awoke, he didn't remember anything about the doctor he had seen, or his dream of his father's death, or even why they had been out riding around at three in the morning.

All he knew was that the people who told him that his father was dead were lying to him.

That's what he told his brother:

"Dad's not dead. Mom's wrong."

His brother didn't understand.

And, in truth, the boy didn't understand either. But his conviction was complete. A doctor—a psychologist—who couldn't seem to take his eyes off his mother said that his denial of his father's death was "natural" and that it would pass.

But it never really did...not all of it.

For the next twenty-five years, even after the psychologist had married his mother, he felt a nagging suspicion that his *real* father was waiting, out there, somewhere in the trees, for him to grow up. He was waiting, as he'd always waited, for the day that they two, father and son, would do something big...

Something important...

Something Wild.

I

HARPERSVILLE, OHIO
1987

ONE

1

The day Sheriff H.W. Conway was summoned out to Lefty Zimmer's farm by an urgent phone call, he thought the emergency had something to do with a "calf."

"I'm tellin' ya, H.W., it's the damnedest thing I ever seen," was how Lefty explained it on the phone.

"Leave it be 'till I get there," was the sheriff's only reply.

Horrence Wiggens Conway—"H.W." to his friends, and not even his wife knew what the "W" stood for—was a fifty-two-year-old, soft-spoken, steely-eyed American institution of a walking-cliché small-town sheriff.

At least on the outside.

He wore his khaki uniform casually, with his shirt's top button undone, his sunglasses dangling by one arm from his left front pocket. The well-oiled Colt .45 in his holster was the one he had carried in Korea. And when he spoke—with a southern twang that got even twangier when he was dealing with tourists—he stood with his legs crossed and his right hand resting on the weapon's butt.

Seeing him for the first time, strolling slowly up to the side of your car with his belly sticking out just a bit and his cowboy boots grey with road dust, it wasn't hard to imagine him spitting chaw while he looked your northern ass up and down and wondered how much money was in your wallet…

Which was just the reaction he was looking for.

Why, there had actually been times when he first got on the department that he had stood in front of his bathroom mirror and practiced saying things like, "Yo in a heep'a trouble, boy," just to perfect that vocally menacing edge that made the camper kids with their boom boxes and designer drugs piss in their fashionably ragged jeans.

But in real life, Conway wasn't like that at all. He was a good guy, friendly with everyone in town, looking out for folks and their property, cruising around in his big old Ford and knowing when a window on a house two miles off the last road before Mist County should be opened or closed. He played the redneck when he needed to, but the rest of the time he was just plain old "H.W.—Come on in and have a cup of coffee—Conway," county sheriff, and mailman part-time on the side when Don Wooster's gout acted up and he couldn't walk his route.

What Lefty Zimmer was doing with calves was a mystery. He hadn't done any actual farming since Sunoco found oil on his back ninety, punched in a couple of wells, and started sending him checks once a month. A lot of folks up on the north side had wells like that, and nobody there seemed to do much of anything anymore.

Lefty was waiting by the fence down near the gravel road when Conway pulled up. His face was a little pale, even in the stiff wind blowing up from the valley, and his eyes locked on the sheriff's the instant he climbed from his car. Lefty was a small, furtive man, forty years old and a drinker—like most of the men, and even a few of the women, up on this end. He looked haggard, and something else: he was trembling.

"'Bout time, H.W.," he said, practically pulling Conway through the gate. "It's out back, near the Retreat."

The Retreat, as it was called by the locals, was a steep, craggy five-mile drop of woods that separated the Killibrook Valley—the largest single area of untouched wilderness left in the state of Ohio—from the township of Harpersville. In some places, the ground simply ended, forming sheer cliff faces of stone up to a hundred feet deep, while in others it leveled off into flat, oasis-like outcroppings that offered splendid views of the Valley floor. Populated by raccoons, opossums, and stray dogs that conducted nightly raids on the town's garbage cans before hiding on the slope by day, the Retreat was hard and uncomfortable. And when winter made food scarce, it became dangerous. Children weren't allowed to play near its edge after the first snow for fear that some starving mongrel might grab somebody; like in the old woodcut prints many town residents—who were of predominantly German decent—had seen of wolves carrying children back to the Black Forest in their grandparents' terrifying storybooks.

It was in one such book that Conway had seen the picture that always haunted him when the first animal of the winter was killed.

The wolf in that picture was a striking beast, with massive jaws, sharp, jutting ribs, and thick, wild hair. Its eyes were cruelly human, and its form was rendered in a stylized, Germanic way that made it appear as if its fur were really flames, and its paws the hands of a man. In its mouth it clutched a tiny bundle of rags that gave no outward clue as to its contents. But the horrified expressions worn by the frantic, club-waving men and women running behind left no question as to the object of the animal's crime.

Frozen forever in this pose: the wolf inches from the safety of the trees, and the town's people a hopeless ten paces behind, that woodcut was symbolic—in Conway's mind at least—of the adversarial relationship between man and nature. The artist who had created it must have understood this relationship too, because, as the sheriff found out years later—for his grandmother had called the German text of the story "to disturbing," and had therefore refused to read it to him—the account to which this particular picture was attached was not that of a fictional wolf, but of a real-life wild-man named Jean Grenier, who lived in France in the early 1500s.

Grenier—as it turned out—was a cannibal.

"I told ya it was somethin'," Lefty said.

And Conway blinked.

He was standing not more than twenty yards from the tree line. At his back was the Zimmer farm: flat, grey, awaiting the first snow of the year on this late November morning. Before him lay the Retreat: from where he stood just a wall of trees. Beyond that, though invisible, he knew there was the Valley: that immense bowl gouged into the earth by God knew what, that, even on a sunny morning like this, would have a wispy shroud of mist hanging over it that wouldn't burn off until noon. The cool air betrayed a hint of ice. And when the wind whistled up from the valley to balloon the back of his tan vinyl jacket, he imagined Old Man Winter, with his icicle beard and frosted hair, grinning in the distance.

Sighing, he pursed his lips and examined the thing at his feet.

"Christ Almighty," he said, his right hand going automatically to his gun. "I thought you said 'calf'."

Lefty shook his head.

"Half," he muttered, sullenly.

"And you didn't hear *nothing*?"

"I told you that already."

"Well, Jesus, Lefty..."

"I know it! Why'd you think I called so quick?"

"I didn't even know you had horses."

"I don't...I mean, I didn't, at least not 'till a couple of days ago. My girl, Linda, she turned sixteen last week and she's been chewing on me for six months to get her one. It was a birthday present. Got her Friday. Traded the thresher. Wasn't using the thing, so I traded it on the mare. Named Ginger. Only been here two days. Prettiest damn thing you ever saw. Had one blue eye. Never saw a horse like that before...with one blue eye."

His words trailed off and his attention drifted to the ground.

"It's them goddamn Indian Diggers!" he suddenly snapped, his head jerking back up and his eyes flashing blearily. "Tell me I'm wrong! Go ahead...you tell me."

The sheriff squinted as he wordlessly stepped between Lefty and Ginger's carcass.

The horse was chestnut brown and had white bracelets over the hooves on her hind legs. Her tail was a satiny black, and there was a white splotch shaped roughly like the state of Florida on her rump.

She'd been cut in half just behind her forelegs, and her front quarters were gone.

Conway felt a little nauseous as he squatted and thought, *They must'a used a chain saw.*

The insides of the animal had been pulled out and were scattered before it in a hideous array. The soft, muddy ground was churned up all around, and Conway estimated that there were at least six separate sets of tracks—maybe more, but six at least—all boots, and all stomped around from every direction. Turning his head, he noticed that there was a line of hoof prints leading from the barn, which was about fifty yards south, and that nearly blocked his view of the back of Zimmer's house, to this spot. Alongside the horse's tracks, there was a single line of human prints.

He stood up.

"Somebody led her back here to where the rest were waiting."

Lefty nodded.

"What time'd you go to bed?"

"Midnight. . .a little later, maybe."

"How 'bout Linda and her mom?"

"They went up to see Sophie's brother in Columbus. Left yesterday morning and won't be back 'till Sunday, thank God."

That explains your red eyes, Conway thought. *Wife's away, and you been really tying it on. Probably explains why you didn't hear anything out back either: sozzled to the gills and dead to the world.*

"You been having company?" he asked, sliding his hands into his jacket pockets.

"Nope."

"Where's your dog?"

Lefty seemed startled by this question, and instead of answering, simply blinked.

The sheriff glanced back down at the carcass and forced himself to study the thing that had been done to the hind quarters that turned his stomach even more than the gaping maw of the animal's midsection.

"Folks that done this are some pretty sick bastards," he said, absently. "Let me use your phone."

"What for?" Lefty asked with a start.

"What's the difference?"

"Well, phone is out is all," Lefty said, rubbing his chin with his hand.

And for the first time, Conway noticed that the man was wearing gloves. As a matter of fact, he was dressed from head to foot, stocking cap and all. It was chilly out, but not cold enough for a country-born man to bundle up this way.

Suddenly a funny zip ran through Conway's guts. He took one involuntary step back, and shrugged.

"Didn't pay the bill," Lefty mumbled, half smiling with embarrassment. "Nothin' so strange 'bout that."

"It's okay," Conway said, the zip in his belly pealing into a full-scale alarm bell. "I'll ride back into town and take care of things. You just leave Ginger be 'till I get back. Understand?"

Lefty nodded. "Just didn't pay the goddamn bill's all," he added, as if to himself. "Ain't nothing so strange about not payin' a bill. Don't see what you need a phone for anyway since it's them Indian Diggers what done this, plain as day."

And Conway forced himself to walk slowly back to his care.

2

"Emil?" he said into the phone at Shaft's, a dry goods store two miles up the State Route.

Betty Shaft, the grocery's bored, overweight, middle-aged widow owner was eyeballing him from behind the counter, shamelessly hanging on his every word.

"Meet me at Ruggle's place in half an hour," he continued, hunching his shoulder up close to his mouth. "No. I don't wanna have a beer over lunch. It's business. Tell Samuels you ain't gonna be back the rest of the day. Maybe tomorrow too. Yeah. And Emil, bring along a couple of dogs, okay?"

Emil Lockner was Conway's deputy, and just about the best hunting-dog breeder in the state. He worked as a cop part-time since there really wasn't enough for a full-time deputy to do, and the town couldn't afford to pay him that much anyway. The rest of the time he did odd jobs at Sister Samuel's funeral home while Sister—which was Mr. Samuel's real first name, and had caused him just no end of grief, especially in the Army—tottered around town, easing through the last of his seventy-nine years and hoping that no one would die and spoil his day. Emil lived upstairs at the mortuary, which was part of his pay. He kept a kennel out back at his folks' farm.

At thirty-four years old, he was a great, hulking man, who was still the closest thing that Harpersville High School had ever had to a football star. Making All-State tackle in the Columbus *Dispatch* three years' running, he had gone on to Ohio State with high hopes, only to have his chimes rung and his knee broken in this first semester. He finished two years, gave up in disgust, came home, and got his high school sweetheart pregnant.

Now, while minding his three kids, that ex-sweetheart, present wife, answered the Samuel's Funeral Home phone with a sweetness in her voice that her husband rarely heard.

"Somebody led that horse out back and butchered it sometime after midnight," Conway said over the din of a noisy lunchtime crowd in Lester Ruggle's bar. As he spoke, Emil sat across from him, shoveling mashed potatoes into his mouth. "Looks like six men. Maybe more."

Conway wasn't eating. He was making a lunch of his fifth cup of coffee.

"When they were through, they dragged off her head and forelegs, shoulders and all. Lefty's German shepherd didn't bark when I drove up. And he hasn't seen her around. Men who cut horses in half kill dogs too, I imagine."

"So what you want me to do?" Emil asked.

"Take a couple'a hounds out there and see if you can't get a line on which way they went with that head. And while you're there, kinda keep an eye on Lefty."

"What for?"

"He's acting a little peculiar."

Emil laughed abruptly, almost spitting potatoes. "That's 'cause he *is* peculiar," he said, wiping his lower lip on his shirt sleeve.

"He wouldn't let me use the phone," Conway mused, distractedly watching something over Emil's shoulder. "Didn't pay the bill, he says. So where'd he call me from this morning? And why would his daughter up and go visiting for a week out of town the day after her daddy gets her the horse she's been wantin'?"

Emil noticed the sheriff studying something behind him and began following his eyes.

"Don't turn around," Conway ordered, quickly. "One o'

them Indian Diggers just came in...the one with the beard."

"Green?" Emil asked, leaning forward over his plate.

"Uh-huh."

"Now *that* fella's peculiar."

The Indian Diggers, as they were called by the locals, had started drifting into town about a week before. There were twenty of them around by the time Ginger was killed. And their leader was a man named Green.

They were "scientists," or so they said, though they didn't look like any scientists anyone had ever seen before. Ranging in age from nineteen to sixty-two, they were about equally balanced male to female and wore mostly jeans, big hiking boots, and expensive down jackets. Why they had come in November—right before the first snow would fly—to dig up some old Indian burial grounds that hadn't moved in like nine hundred years, and that would therefore more than likely still be around in the spring (when it was warm), was beyond most folks who took the time to care. But of all the groups that had come nosing around for Indian artifacts over the years, this was the first that had ever purchased all their shovels and kerosene lanterns from the Monroe Hardware Store. So that was something.

"And you know what else?" Conway said after Mr. Green took a seat in a booth near the back of the bar. "There weren't no animal prints 'round that body. There was half a horse layin' out in a field, but I didn't see one set of dog tracks, or bird marks, or nothing. Scavengers don't leave meat alone like that...not in November. Not ever."

Emil laid down his fork and smiled. "Well, if it's a mystery that needs solvin', you got the right man on the job."

He was about to stand when Conway put his hand out and placed it on his arm.

"I want you to be extra careful out at Lefty's," he nearly whispered. "I didn't tell you the rest of what was done to that horse 'cause you were eatin'. But what we got here's a real situation."

"What you talkin' 'bout?" Emil asked, his eyes narrowed.

"I don't know, for sure. But whoever killed that horse not only cut it in half, they took a tree branch—I'm talkin' a good five foot long, thick as your wrist—and shoved it up that animal's ass."

Emil frowned.

Conway nodded.

"We're got us some sicko bastards here, son. So I want you to be extra careful. Keep all this under your hat until we can figure out what's goin' on. And while you're doin' it, you watch your own ass too."

Emil promised that he would.

And Conway followed him out of the bar, ignoring Mr. Green's sticky-sweet smirk of greeting, which was the same expression he always seemed to wear. It was an infuriating look. . .one filled with secret knowledge that left a person feeling that the man making it was just waiting for something to happen that only he knew was coming.

3

"Hello?" Emil called as he pushed open the gate and stepped onto the Zimmer farm. "Lefty? You home?"

Absolutely nothing moved anywhere he could see. The sky had gone heavy with an even wash of battleship grey that made it appear solid, and ominously dark. A chilling mist that wasn't exactly rain because it didn't seem to fall so much as hang, thickened the air. And there were no lights on up at the house.

The place felt dead.

The big deputy sighed.

He'd half expected Lefty to be waiting for him at the fence, but he should have known better. Folks always treated Sheriff Conway like some kind of dignitary: shaking his hand, offering him pie and big, dopey smiles, inviting him over for dinner and thanking him up and down for any little thing he did as if doing things for people wasn't a part of his job.

But Emil...he was another story.

How many times had he answered the station phone only to have some yahoo say that he'd call back when the sheriff was in? As if the deputy couldn't handle such complicated questions as, "What time's the Lion's Club meeting tonight?" or, "Does my boy's learner's permit mean I gotta ride on the back of his motorcycle too?" The sheriff had said a thousand times that folks wanted to talk to him personally because they were his friends. But Emil knew the truth: everybody still saw him as that "dumb ox who couldn't cut it up at the college," the same way they would, probably, for the rest of his life.

So, since there was no sheriff in the truck, there was no Lefty at the gate, and Emil shrugged, thinking, "Fuck him," as he opened the Hop-Cap on his little Isuzu.

Inside stood Rachel, Marge and Buster, three of his best bloodhounds. They were perfect animals, so dark a shade of saddle tan as to almost appear as if they had each been carved from an enormous block of aged mahogany. Any one of them could have taken Best in Show at any contest Emil might have chosen to enter. But in his mind, dog shows were bullshit and his hounds were the best because they knew how to hunt, not because they were pretty, even though they were—the prettiest goddamn dogs in the world. Six intelligent eyes gleamed in the dark, and three black shapes waited for their master to say that it was okay for them to get out.

"Come on," Emil said.

And the dogs came.

But they didn't come right.

Usually they bounded out, barking and prancing around his legs in excited circles that would have instantly wrapped him in leashes, if he believed in tying his dogs, which he didn't. But today they climbed down as slowly as cats, their tails limp and their eyes wide as they looked over the flat, grey land and moved in close to Emil's side.

"Kinda creepy, huh?" he asked, snapping his fingers and heading for the gate.

Ruefully, the hounds fell in at his heels.

"Let's do what we gotta do and get you back in the truck 'fore this rain gives you the rheumatism," he added, unsnapping the flap on his holster.

But when they reached the horse's remains, he had to coax the hounds toward it. After five minutes of prodding, the male, Buster—the biggest and most aggressive of the three—still wouldn't go near the body. And Marge and Rachel sniffed at it halfheartedly before they looked up as if to ask, "Now what?"

Emil, feeling a little sick to his stomach, simply said, "Go find it!"

And his dogs sat down.

A cold breeze whipped up from the Valley with a moan, driving a sheet of real rain across the field with a rustle like wings.

The deputy drew his gun.

The figure was probably twenty-five or thirty yards away, but it still sent chills running up and down his spine. It was just standing there, at the tree line, or maybe back a few paces into the woods.

And it was watching him.

The dogs didn't bark, or whine, or move. Emil glanced at them and they were sitting, side-by-side, staring into the woods, their bodies rigid, their hair prickling like quills. They were simply petrified. He'd never seen anything like it in his life. They were too terrified to move, and suddenly he realized that their fear was contagious.

When he glanced back at the trees, the figure was closer. He hadn't seen it move. It just was…

Closer.

About thirty feet away.

And then he heard the first snarl.

Low.

And mean.

He'd have recognized Buster's voice anywhere. The big hound had a particularly deep, bassy sound to his bark that resonated in his chest and throat. When he growled, which was so rare as to be next to never, the tone he produced was dark, smooth, and blood-chilling.

Emil's first reaction was pride in his animal's coming to his master's defense.

And then he realized that Buster was growling at *him.*

The incongruity of it—the gut-twisting absurdity of Buster turning even a lick of anger his way—tore his attention to the animal's eyes. What he saw there, in a face that was normally sad, expressive, and full of affection, was a terrible rage that seemed to seethe up from the great dog's soul. Buster's eyes were red, hot and staring; his body was lifted into a crouch that trembled like a rattrap ready to strike; his lips were curled back over curved, wicked teeth that dripped with oily, bubbling spit.

"*Buster*!" Emil snapped, using his command voice, to which Marge responded by following the big male's lead and growling in her place.

Between the two snarling dogs, Rachel, the smallest and arguably most intelligent of the three, sat still, staring blankly, her entire body atremble and her brows working thickly over her eyes. She seemed at odds with herself, as if some internal struggles were tearing at her mind.

"You did this!" Emil shouted, throwing out his hand and aiming his gun at the figure he'd seen come from the trees. He almost expected the man to be closer again...maybe right on top of him. But he was still thirty feet away, and Emil got his first, really good look.

Which sent him running.

"*No*!" his mind roared as the world reeled, the tree line tilted in a dizzying rush, and Buster exploded into a snarling, insane lunge that sent him tearing at the deputy's throat.

Through it all were imprinted the details of a face on Emil's mind...a face of such portent that even as Marge leapt to join Buster in his traitorous attack, and Rachel—sweet, sweet Rachel—snapped out of her lethargy and threw herself into Buster, knocking him into a furious, struggling ball, the only thing that seemed important, the only thing that seemed *real*, was the haunting, timeless features of a being that laughed with delight when dogs turn on their master.

He was as old as the sky, Emil knew in that instant. He

was as old as the moon, and understood the dogs better than the dogs understood themselves. His flesh was an almost silver pale, and so deeply etched with leathery folds that his eyes were nearly lost when he smiled. His teeth were long, perfect, and sharp...

"He has teeth like a dog!" a voice said in the deputy's mind, God knew why.

And there was thick grey hair everywhere, hanging in a tangled mat that was his beard, cascading over his shoulders in ragged sweeps, sprouting in bristling patches over his black, black eyes.

There were bones in that hair...tiny bones, wrapped in hair, thousands and thousands of bones.

Somewhere, Buster was screaming.

Not barking, or snarling, or whining...he was screaming, and in a blur of rusty amber, Rachel moved from his rolling body and Emil saw that her jaws were slick with foaming blood.

Marge leapt to meet her, and the sound of their struggles was horrible as they entwined like two squid in a fast, liver-colored tangle.

Emil fell forward.

He had wanted to run but his legs were rubbery and his spine weak. There was something in his way...something in his eyes...and something in his mind that made it hard for him to think.

When Marge limped into view there were things hanging from her belly.

"Such wonders!" the man from the woods said with uplifted arms in words that resounded over the Valley.

And Emil started crawling toward the barn.

He didn't know why he was doing it, but at least he was doing something. All he knew was that he had to get away from this...had to escape. He was an outsider here...because he was a man. A man didn't belong where the dogs lost their senses. A man didn't belong where *he* raised his arms and made wonders appear. A man didn't belong...a man would die...a man always died when *he* came from the woods and the dogs started fighting.

The sound of screaming echoed through his skull; the barn was far away, and something with bones in its hair was laughing and filling the air with rain.

He wished to God he knew why he wanted to get up and dance.

A part of him wanted to do that.

Not all of him.

Just a part.

A small part...

So he didn't do it.

But a part of him wanted to...

And then the barn door swung open, and it was Emil who was screaming in the rain.

4

"It was his eyes that done it," he said later from the gloom in a corner of Lester Ruggle's bar. "He come right outta the woods with eyes so black that they made Lefty and my dogs go crazy. They almost made me go crazy too. But I guess I'm not of the Blood, so I'll be among those to die when they come again…like they will…like they always do. World without end, amen. That's what my grandma used to say, and she was right…dead or not."

He paused, took a deep draft of beer from his glass, and lit a cigarette.

Sheriff Conway leaned to the man next to him and whispered, "I've read about shit like this. But I never thought I'd see it."

And the rest of the crowd huddled near Emil's table waited for more.

At noon the day after he went out to Lefty's farm, Emil stumbled back into town, dazed and bloody. He'd walked all the way back—*walked*—after leaving his truck in Lefty's driveway. His clothes were smeared with mud, one of his shoes was missing, and he had his gun in his hand.

God only knew where he had spent the night.

Behind him a dozen children followed, grinning and twirling their fingers near their temples until adults pulled them off the sidewalk. The big deputy didn't acknowledge any of the nervous greetings offered as he worked his way to Ruggle's bar, but stared straight ahead, his eyes glassy and his mouth hanging open. Moving directly to a table in the corner farthest from the door, he leaned his back to the wall, ordered a pitcher of beer, drank it, ordered another, and started talking…first to the empty air. And then to a small knot of curious men. And finally to a steady stream of folks drawn into the bar as news of his condition spread.

Conway had spent the night at the Zimmer farm, watching the volunteers put out the fire that had consumed the house, barn and toolshed. The fire had been set, that much was obvious—even in the stiff breeze blowing up from the Valley the smell of gasoline was everywhere. Emil's truck sat by the fence, the charred remains of three dogs lay blackened in the field, and one of the deputy's shoes was found by the barn. Lefty Zimmer's burned corpse lay near that shoe, but there was no sign of the big man anywhere, and Conway hadn't slept, wondering what the hell had happened that would make him kill an old drunk and burn down his farm.

When he heard that Emil had reappeared, he rushed straight over to Ruggle's and found a crowd at the door. Men and women were waiting patiently in line, and others were silently emerging into the street, eyes cast down, faces grim. Emil's story was already spreading through town, and, after listening to it once, the sheriff decided, right then, to call the Division of Behavioral Comparison—the "Church"—for help.

He'd gotten the number the previous day from a friend who was the sheriff up in Rogers County. He'd called the man for some advice, describing Ginger's carcass and the tree branch—which was really the kicker as far as he was concerned—finishing up by saying that he suspected that a cult of some kind might have "violated" the animal.

"Satanists?" the Rogers County sheriff cried. "Like on Geraldo? Hot damn! Then you oughta call the Church. I used 'em a couple of months back on that Fenner thing, and they sure got the market cornered on weird shit, far as I can tell."

Calling the DBC had been one of the hardest things

Conway had ever done; but he couldn't think of a better place to call than the Church when you wanted to beat the devil.

So Detective Michael (call me Mike) Cooper arrived at a little after three that afternoon, and Conway took him straight to Ruggle's.

"Read about shit like what?" the detective asked during the silence through which Emil studied his cigarette.

"This," Conway whispered, motioning forward with his head. "The crowd. Quiet and hypnotized while the 'witness' tells a story that they've all gotta hear for themselves. It's exactly how the history books say it used to happen in the Middle Ages: the whole village would come, and the witness would tell his story over and over, for as long as it took for everyone to hear it directly from his lips. When *he* comes, that person who sees him first is supposed to look just like Emil does now: shell-shocked and empty...like his life's been sucked dry."

"When who comes?" Cooper asked, a bit too loudly.

And Emil raised his head, parting the crowd so that a corridor was formed between the table and the spot where the detective was standing.

"The Man in the Woods," he said with low, sincere emotion and red-rimmed, haunted eyes. "When the Man in the Woods appears to a mortal witness, it's a sign that the moon will soon be filled with its killing glow."

Cooper frowned.

The crowd seemed to hold its breath.

And Emil related his tale...again, for probably the hundredth time, as he had repeated it in his monotonous, broken-record way all day.

"There's wolves in the woods!" he said, moving his eyes appraisingly across the group.

A red and white neon Budweiser sign shaped like an electric guitar glowed fuzzily on the dark wall over his head.

"There's wolves in the woods…and in the house! Right here, right in this room. We just don't know who they are yet, so take care…and watch your neighbor. Take care, and watch your mirror!"

Slowly, he lifted himself to his feet, and when he did his voice grew a little louder.

"Lefty was one…and the Man in the Woods showed him how to make the belt. Lefty had it on when I saw him. Two o' my dogs went crazy, but the third, Rachel, she stayed true. She tore the throat outta one and ripped the guts out the other before I knew what was happening. But I still had to shoot her 'cause they tore out her eye and she was dyin'.

"Nearly killed me, havin' to shoot that dog.

"Nearly killed me…but that come later.

"When the Man in the Woods appeared, he made my whole world turn upside down. While my dogs was fightin' I tried to crawl away, but the barn door opened, and Lefty come out…naked. Painted up a bunch's colors. With blood runnin' down his legs.

"He made the belt from his wife. I found her in the basement. He took the skin off her back in three strips ant braided 'em around his waist so's the blood would drip down his legs. His arms were singed black up to the elbows from the fire. And his face…oh, sweet Jesus, his face. He had nails punched through his skin, runnin' all along the line of his upper lip. The heads made a row under his nose, and the points all stuck through so that when he opened his mouth to growl or bark, they pointed down, like fangs.

"The paint come from some cans in the barn—he'd drawn circles and crosses all over himself.

"And there was something riding on his back. Something little…with real long arms that pointed things out to him.

"When I saw him, I was on my hands and knees and the

ground was rolling beneath me. That face on his back was gibberin' and clatterin' its jaws while it pointed my way…lookin' like a black monkey…but with wings."

He stopped and raised his arms in an eerie, almost pagan imitation of the posture of a priest over an altar: palms upraised, elbows slightly bent, back straight.

"What was around me didn't come from the woods that we know," he said, his voice booming now. "Not from our Valley, not from our trees. What was around me came from the jungle of Hell itself, called up from the pit by that ancient thing that walks on moonbeams and moves through the night in silence and safety. It was *him:* that demon in the trees, that silver devil who feeds on shadows and bathes in blood. It was him! The same as our ancestors saw! The same as made the monsters we can still name after three hundred years: Jean Grenier, Peter Stubb, de Sade!

"Werewolves all!

"And how many more?

"Werewolves?

"Killers; eaters of man flesh; beasts!

"The Man in the Woods showed them how to make the belt of human skin, and they blessed it in the blood of something tamed so that they might follow him into the woods of their souls. He instructed them in the ways of the Wild, and they carved his name into the flesh of history: Satan! Lozella! Vennaltiza! A thousand titles for that which roamed the Garden of Eden itself, walked the earth while Pharaoh built his tombs, and slept in the shadow of Jesus' cross.

"He's waited, and he's watched, since the start of it all, since the beginning of time. *And now, he's come again!*"

"Je-sus Kee-rist," Conway heard Detective Cooper whisper as Emil stepped around the table and into the gauntlet of silent, staring listeners.

"That thing on Lefty's back," the deputy shouted,

pointing a huge index finger Cooper's way. "Them eyes in the bushes, them black shapes in the trees...the way the sky dulled over and the sun seemed to go cold...the horse's blood and shit on the ground... they all add up to the same thing. There's wolves in the woods! There's wolves in the house! And there'll be wolves in the mirror!

"This is my warning!" he roared, inches from where the detective stood his ground. "I'm the witness. As it's happened before, so shall it happen again, world without end!

"World without end!

"World without end!

"Amen," the crowd said in the gloom.

"I killed the belted one and burned his lair. But he was only the first. The Man in the Woods has come, and with him servants to his will. The passing of dry centuries has left him weak, and for now he walks in the shape of a man. But this will soon change, for a Prince has been born who will renew the Law and rekindle the Hunt. The Man in the Woods knows of this Prince and has watched over him with love and anticipation. His coming will herald a new Dark Time. His flesh will be as a belt around the world. The Wild will rise again!

"So said the belted one!

"'Hail to the Blood Prince!'

"So spoke the flesh-eater before he died.

"'Hail to the Blood Prince!'

"And so is my warning.

"Listen:

"Into the village of man will come a wolf, disguised as one with the Flock. Shun him, and drive him out, for he will bring ruin upon all he sees. He is the gate through which the Wild will come. He is the path down which the Wild will run. He is the key to the lock on the soul of the hateful ones...the secret ones. . .the Vyrmin!

"He will make others to drink of your blood.

"He will make others to eat of your flesh!

"He will make others to desecrate your graves!

"But never will he do these things himself, for he is the Prince of the Blood, and the Man in the Woods will use him to stir the Vyrmin to their rise.

"Be aware: there's wolves in the woods!

"Be aware: there's wolves in the house!

"Be aware: there's wolves in the mirror!

"The Blood Prince comes. . .known as one of us, remembered from our past. But he is a pest, a plague, and a wound. He is evil, and because of him, *we will kill!*"

"Okay, Emil," Conway said, reaching past Cooper and presenting his open hand to the sweating, trembling, nearly hysterical bear of a man shadowed in the gloom. "Each of us has heard."

"Then I can rest," Emil said, his voice dropping in tone and pitch so abruptly that it sounded as if he'd been deflated by a single shot. "The witness shall speak until each has heard—only that can the witness do. No more. . .and no less. The witness shall speak until each has heard, and then he shall rest until his flesh is ruined for his words."

"You've earned your rest," the sheriff said, producing, as if by magic, a pair of handcuffs which he snapped first around Emil's right wrist and then his left.

The big deputy nodded, allowing himself to be led from the bar. The crowd shuffled behind, wide-eyed and stern. Behind them followed Mike Cooper, frowning and grim.

"I've earned my rest," Emil said vacantly, hanging his head. "We must all rest before the Prince arrives. For once he comes, there'll be no rest for any in the Flock again."

5

"Any in the Flock!" Cheryl Lockner, Emil's wife, mimicked sardonically under her breath as she watched Sheriff Conway lead her husband through Ruggle's front door. She was hanging back in the crowd, sticking to the shadows along the back wall, dressed in a sack-like, flower-print dress and a frumpy, knee-length grey overcoat that had started its life as her Sunday best, only to end up looking like something out of a bag lady's shopping cart. Her right index finger was nervously twirling a tendril of jet black hair. Her left arm was folded over her small breasts. And her darkly circled blue eyes were flickering from Emil to the sheriff and back…

Suddenly the outside door opened, silhouetting the two men and making her squint as she headed for the bar's rear exit. She hit the alley at a trot, paused, and took a deep breath of the cool afternoon air.

It was dark here.

And cold.

The alley was narrow, tall, and lined on both sides by garbage cans. From overhead, tiny specks of snow swirled between the bar and the building next door. The rain that had fallen for most of the day now glistened on dirty brick as ice. And even the slightest gust of wind produced a soft, moaning howl that seemed to come from somewhere deep inside her head.

"Told them…" she mumbled, aloud. "Told them all!"

The alley didn't answer as the door banged shut behind her. There was no way out of this little courtyard. It was a dead end.

"The Flock…" she said, her eyes scanning the shadowy

jumble of swirling papers and heaped mounds of black plastic trash bags. "He saw it, and he *told!*"

She paused.

From inside her came a sudden rush of that same sensation that had been coming to her in one form or another most of her life. She thought of it as the "sexy feeling." It was like the charge she felt when she thought about a man—any man—since high school; only this time, it was better.

"He told..." she hissed, stepping deeper into the gloom. "And now they *know*!"

Sex was her favorite thing. She dreamt of it at night and fantasized about it during the day. She visualized it in her mind, from all different angles, and in all kinds of positions, with men of all ages, colors and types. She'd married Emil not because he had gotten her pregnant, but because he was a great fuck. Not just good...but great!

She married Emil.

And now he'd...

"Told!"

The sexy feeling was like vertigo, tingling her stomach and lightening her head. It came and went every day, all the time, and the goofiest things could bring it on. It was fun, and it was as much a part of her personality as was her temper, which was explosive...especially when she had her period and Emil wouldn't come near her, like now. The sexy feeling could make her crazy sometimes, and for the past couple of weeks, its stirrings had been nearly intolerable.

The swirling papers on the ground made dry, rustling sounds as they puffed up in brief flashes of white in the dark. They seemed to be reacting to some whirlwind...some whistling current of air that spiraled invisibly down in chilling, foul-smelling breaths. They seemed to be blurring as the wind moaned and a shape made of darkness formed in the center of rushing bits of light.

When that figure spoke, it made her hold her breath...the feeling was that good.

When the figure spoke, it asked, "Why have you come?"

And she didn't know...

Or care.

The words were like silk on her skin, and when she heard them she froze in her place, ran her tongue over her upper lip and hugged herself with both arms with an "Mmmmmmmm" that was sultry and wanton.

The darkness seemed pleased by this.

"Are there words for it?" it inquired.

And Cheryl Lockner closed her eyes.

She could feel herself drifting inside herself...as if she had fallen instantly asleep and her spirit were riding the warm waves of her most secret passions.

Fuck the words! She thought.

Fuck the world!

Fuck it all!

The darkness seemed pleased by this as well.

So pleased, in fact, that it reached out and took her arm: warm flesh on hers.

She opened her eyes.

And the man was tall and lean. His flesh was smooth, white and so, so warm. He had long hair and a beard. He was naked in the gloom...just standing there, naked: muscular, naked, and touching. He exuded an aroma that thrilled her. It seemed to climb right through her nostrils and into her brain.

She didn't speak.

Fuck the words! she thought, making the man smile.

Fuck it all!

Within the man's eyes was an emptiness so deep that it seemed to go on forever. When Cheryl Lockner gazed into that blackness, it was like falling into the sky.

6

After locking Emil in his cell, Conway and Cooper went to look at what he had done. They started at the Zimmer farm and ended at Samuel's Funeral Home, which served as the county's morgue since it had a cooler. The fire had destroyed a great deal of evidence, but because of the rain, and the speed with which the volunteers had arrived, it had not obliterated Lefty's "lair," as the deputy had obviously hoped that it would. As a result, they were able to sift through the ashes—so to speak—and reconstruct a scene that in many respects served to verify much of Emil's account.

Two of his hounds had indeed been torn apart. And the third had a hole in its chest, and a bullet in the ground beneath it.

"Put her head in my lap and shot her in the heart so's she wouldn't see the gun," Emil had explained from his cell, his face slack and his voice flat—a total change from the hellfire and damnation posture he had assumed at the bar not an hour before. "I didn't want her to see the gun. She knew what a gun was, and I didn't want her to have to look at it."

Much of the barn was demolished, the fire having spread quickly through the hay, old kindling wood, and rows of paint cans lying everywhere. But behind the scorched building, a curious arrangement of gardening tools had remained intact. Set like the skeleton of a tiny tepee over the smoldering mound of a campfire, two shoves and a rake served to suspend a stainless-steel kitchen pot on the end of a bicycle chain. Fused to the bottom of that pot, in a crust of blackened goo, was the cracked and fleshless skull of what look to be a German shepherd dog.

Lefty's burned body actually did have nails lining its upper lip—he'd been lying face-down on the ground when Emil poured gasoline on him, so his front was not too terrible damaged.

His wife's body had been skinned—and in a frying pan on the stove in the house was one of her severed hands, next to a bottle of Wesson oil.

"Eaters of man flesh," were the words Emil had used.

During the course of their tour, Conway and Cooper didn't really talk much. They walked, side by side, each studying the other as much as the crime scene, or anything else. The sheriff wasn't sure about this young man from the city yet, and the detective didn't seem all that certain about this redneck sheriff.

By seven that evening, they had seen enough, and together they stopped at the Thunderbird Café right across the street from the jail, where Conway drank yet more coffee, Cooper ate greasy meat loaf, and a heaviness hung between them that was almost visible.

Finally, as Conway sat studying the glowing yellow window of his office, Cooper pushed his empty plate away and said, "Okay, Sheriff. Let's have it."

Conway frowned.

And Cooper said, "Who's the Man in the Woods?"

The sheriff sighed, long and hard. "The devil," he said simply, his voice very serious. "Or at least he is as near as I've ever been able to figure."

Cooper waited.

And Conway looked at him. "Do you see this kind of thing often, Mr. Cooper?" he asked, his brown eyes betraying only a hint of the tension he was feeling in his chest. "I mean killings...for no real reason. Crazy shit. Stuff that makes your skin crawl."

Cooper nodded in response. "Yes, I do, Sheriff. I see it a hell of a lot more often than you'd probably think."

"I don't know how you do it," Conway said, softly. And then, as if the thought had just occurred to him, he added, "If we work this thing through, who makes the arrest?"

"Why, you do, of course."

"You sure? No red tape rules at the end gonna take it away from me? No bureaucratic baloney from the state gonna let the governor waltz in and take the credit?"

"I promise," Cooper said, earnestly. "I'm here to consult. That's my job. I go from one situation to the next, cataloguing the crimes of some very sick people in a database. I don't tell the local authorities how to run their business. And I don't tell them what to think. I'm not interested in credit—I solve problems."

"And now you wanna hear a fairy tale about the Man in the Woods?"

"No. I want to hear what you know. If you recognized something, you've got to let me in on it, because we're not going to move this thing along until we're both on the same footing. Crazy or not, anything familiar might be important."

Conway cleared his throat and thought, *There's something strange about this guy. He's just a little too calm. A little too willing to sit down and talk. He came her knowing something already, but he's playing it close to this chest.*

Finally, he said, "Okay. Yeah. I recognized a few things. As a matter of fact, I recognized a lot. Everything that Emil says he saw out at Lefty's farm, and everything that happened at the bar afterwards, lines up, step by step, with the stories my old German grandma got from her even older German grandma, who probably saw 'em carved on the wall of a cave somewhere. The whole thing supposedly started with the moon...it's that old. It's a legend. And all us children of immigrants down here know how it works."

Conway heard himself talking, but could barely believe what he was saying.

"Everybody," he began, seriously, as his grandmother might have done. "Or almost everybody, anyway, has got the evil in 'em. That's what my grandma used to say: 'Everybody's got some o' the evil; and everybody's got some o' the good. Only the saints are all one way; and only the Vyrmin are all the other.' The rest of us are stuck somewhere in between. But every once in a while, the edges come loose, the Vyrmin get out, and the Dark Times return.

"That's when the Hunt goes on—when mankind, which is the Flock that the Shepherd Jesus is supposed to protect, is threatened by the wolves, called Vyrmin. The Vyrmin look like normal, everyday people on the outside. But inside, their souls are black. Any good they do is for the sake of their disguise. They're the wolves in sheep's clothing, the hidden germ in the system. They live out their lives, day to day, sometimes unaware of what they are themselves. But when the time comes, and the Hunt begins, they come out."

"And that's what you think those people were doing when they slaughtered that horse?" Cooper asked, his eyes on Conway's face. "Their surface motive was to perform some ritual that would magically transform a human being into an animal?"

"Believe it or not," the sheriff said. "And, lookin' at the same stuff we looked at today, anybody who was raised in this area would tell you the same thing."

"Okay," Cooper said, scooting forward in his seat, his eyes sparkling. "Explain the components. Why the horse, the nails, and the belt?"

Before answering, Conway thought, *This son of a bitch is enjoying this*! Then he sighed. "Well… lemme see. I don't know everything, but what I do know, I wanna get right. A Vyrmin—in this case, Lefty, I guess—can turn himself into an animal, or at least he thinks he can, by wearing a magic belt made of human skin and anointed with the blood of an animal that's had its wildness beaten out of it; an animal that's been tamed, in other words. To get a belt like that, he or she has to entice the Man in the Woods into appearing in physical form, which means that they have to make a sacrifice."

"And that explains the dog's head in the pot?" Cooper cut in.

"Probably," Conway said. "Or the horse. I don't know which."

"Go on."

"Now, the Man in the Woods is a spirit, a forest nymph or, more accurately, a being sent down from the moon. He's been a part of European folklore since, Christ, I don't know. Supposedly the moon was once this free-roaming entity that saw the earth just after it was created, and liked it. But somehow, it felt that something was missing...which were trees. So it sent the Man in the Woods down to spread himself over the planet and make the forests outta his body, and the animal outta his soul. The moon is the eye of evil, the dark twin of the sun, which symbolizes goodness. And at night, when the moon dominates the sky, evil, in the form of the roamer in the trees, dominates the earth.

"And there he is: the Man in the Woods. His body, or skin, encircles our planet, and his master, our moon, watches us from the sky at night. He's been known as Pan, Lozella, Satan, and God knows how many more names in God knows how many languages. And he's always represented that sense of savage freedom that's both attracted and repelled mankind since the beginning of what we'd call civilization. Over the centuries, there've been those people who've sensed his presence strongly enough to want to actually summon him up from the trees so they can make that final jump from human to animal, like Jean Grenier, who Emil mentioned.

"As a matter of fact, Grenier's a good example. My grandma had him in a storybook when I was a kid. And I've been carryin' him with me most of my life. He was a seventeen-year-old who cannibalized five or six children in some French village in the early sixteenth century. The particulars are a little different, but the chronology of that story's just about exactly the same as the one we have here.

"See, this kid had a magic belt and was runnin' around pretty much like Emil says Lefty was—naked, all painted up, the whole nine yards—when, one day, he attacked a girl in a field. She became the 'witness' for her village, ran home, and told everybody what she'd seen. The men in town hunted the kid down, make him confess to being in league with the devil, and locked him in a monastery, where he died three years later, crawlin' around on all fours and barkin' at the moon."

"So this time, Emil's our 'witness'," Cooper said, smiling.

"Uh-huh," the sheriff agreed. "And here's the Christian part, since now we're followin' the middle European version. Supposedly, God sends a witness to the flock to announce the coming of the Dark Times. Since Satan—the Man in the Woods is called Satan now—is 'Lord of This World,' God doesn't interfere with his temptations of mankind. He just makes sure that we have a figntin' chance. So, for the time it takes the witness to tell his story, God fills him with knowledge that disappears when he's through. The people who hear God's word can believe it or not, just like everything else in the Christian faith.

"But the problem for the witness—and I'm sure that this is why Emil looked so worried when we locked him in his cell—is that God doesn't seem to think that the messenger warrants any special favors. Once his story's told, the witness just goes back to being an ordinary person. And from then on, his life ain't worth a shit. The Vyrmin know what he did, and hate him for it. Traditionally, the witness is always the next to die."

"Wow!" Cooper grinned, clapping his hands and shaking his head. "This is a *good* one!'

"What's so good about it?" Conway asked, consciously keeping his voice free of emotion.

"Oh, I'm sorry," Cooper said with a self-deprecating chuckle. I don't mean to sound insensitive. It's just that you're so well informed! You're a walking werewolf encyclopedia, and that cuts the work I'll have to do right in half."

Conway's eyes narrowed.

And Cooper reached out and put his hand on his arm, saying, "Now let me explain something to you, Sheriff. Normally I look like an ass-wipe to the people who call me in because the Church is almost always used as a last resort. The local cops stumble on a crime scene, monkey around with it for a few days, and then, when they can't make heads of tails out of the thing, they call me. In the meantime, the unsub responsible is a thousand miles away. Invariably, I end up with my thumb up my ass saying, 'I don't have the slightest idea what happened here,' so the local cops can use me as an example: if an 'expert' can't work out this case, how can they be expected to do it? Which is stage one."

Lifting his hand, he leaned forward and pointed his index finger at the sheriff's nose. "But stage two is very different. After the circus part is over, I go to work. While the cops on the scene add yet another mystery to their 'unsolved' file, I dig in, record what I've found, compare it with everything else I've got, study it, turn it upside down and inside out, lock it in my head, and sleep with it every night until I win. It might take me weeks, months, or years, but while those bozos who used me to justify their own ineptitude forget all about it, I'm quietly working my way right up to the spot they said no one could ever find. And in the end, I win. In the end, I *always* win."

"You take this personal," Conway said.

And Cooper rose from his seat, still smiling that broad, seemingly genuine smile that was so out of place with the emotion in his voice that the sheriff was suddenly filled with the impression that he was watching not a police officer discussing a case, but an evangelist thumping his stump.

"Sure I do!" he said, stepping up to the window so that, from where Conway sat, he saw the man's dark figure clearly defined by the amber light glowing in the jail across the street.

Between the two, snow was falling steadily in bright specks that flashed silver before spinning away in the dark.

"Sure I take it personally. And that's why this is such a good one. Usually the motivations of someone who could do a thing like this are so cryptic, convoluted, and tangled around some event, fixation or delusional construct that they have to be inferred from the logic of his behavior. Sometimes the root of that disturbance—or what he thinks he's achieving by doing the things he does—will stem back to a series of traumatic episodes that he's spent a lifetime weaving into a fabric of violent compulsions. Sometimes it's a sexual obsession or paranoid fantasy. And sometimes it's just plain old shit for kicks. But no matter what it turns out to be in the end, I'm lost going into it. That's my life. They throw me into a fucking ocean of blood and expect me to swim straight home, over and over again. But this time, I've got *you!* This time we apparently know quite a lot about the delusional structure. Or at least we've got a pretty fair idea of where it came from: old European werewolf legend! *Bang!*

"Step by step you laid it out. Now we can start running with it! In the end it won't turn out to be that simple. It never does. But just saying the word, 'werewolf,' is the kind of thing that could normally take me months to figure out. We already have a nucleus of fresh evidence, a working hypothesis, and a time frame that doesn't preclude the possibility that our suspects might still be in the area. We could actually solve this one on the scene, Sheriff Conway! We could actually make a bust, hands on, you and me

"You just don't know how exciting that is; you can't imagine how satisfying it would be for me to nail these fuckers, dead to rights. No bullshit, just snap on the cuffs and 'read 'em their rights.' You just don't know."

And that was true. Conway didn't know, because he wasn't listening anymore. He was staring through the window past the young detective into the street. His mouth was open, his skin was clammy, and a chill had just run the entire length of his spine and settled like a bowling ball in his gut.

What he was seeing happen in front of the jail flew in the face of every other experience he had ever had in his life. And, as he sat there, paralyzed for a heartbeat, his brain was busily denying what his eyes were so convinced was true.

In the glow of a single streetlight, beneath a swirl of blowing snow, a figure dropped into view from the inky darkness above. It just descended, floating down quickly, with smooth, effortless movements that kicked up little puffs of snow as it came to rest on the pavement as gently as if it were settling itself on the sandy bottom of some dim and lifeless ocean.

And then, as he stared, the creature's image burst into hideous, mind-numbing focus, overpowering his mental defenses with the simplicity of its presence, and reaching into that hidden corner of his mind populated by his most private nightmare specters.

He gasped, thinking, It's impossible! as the thing, or things—for it was actually two figures that he was seeing, and not, as he had first imagined, a single beast, with...wings—ran straight up the jailhouse steps.

Wings!

The fucker had wings!

And the woman was naked!

It must have been a week that he sat frozen in that chair. At least he felt as if it took him a week to sort things out well enough to get himself moving. In reality it was probably only a second or two before his legs jerked his body out of its seat, sending his chair clattering across the linoleum and turning every head in the place his way as he shouted, "Holy shit!" and pointed to the now empty street through the glass.

Only a second or two, in reality…

Reality?

Ha!

What reality?

What kind of reality is it that contains a thing like what he had just seen flutter down from the sky like some vile, black snowflake? Where in reality does an awful, hairy thing with long arms and short, crooked legs come from? Where do gibbering monkey faces and wide, leathery wings naturally fit together into one wicked little beast that couldn't have been more than three feet tall but that could dangle a full-grown woman beneath it and fly—with its fucking wings…oh, God, its fucking grey wings with the ribs and veins and bulging pockets of sinewy muscle…

What reality?

Sweet Jesus!

What fucking reality was there left?

"Sheriff?" Cooper asked, stepping forward and bumping their little table so hard that it too went crashing over, spilling dishes and breaking glass that crunched underfoot as he stumbled in clumsy pursuit.

But Conway didn't hear. He was plunging through a

weirdly distorted bubble of stupid, gape-mouthed faces and insane, bouncing door frames as a voice, a wondrous, all-knowing voice—that he would later privately identify as his grandmother's voice—said, over and over again in his mind, "The witness is the next to die...to die! The witness is the next to die!"

And by the time he hit the street, the witness was screaming inside the cage that Conway himself had locked up tight.

7

When the first bullet hit, it knocked Lefty Zimmer right on his ass. And that wasn't surprising considering that Deputy Emil Lockner carried a .357, long-barreled Magnum Python that he'd picked up at a sportsman's show in Dallas a couple of years back. Sheriff Conway had been kidding him about that gun ever since he got it, calling him "Dirty Harry"(even if Dirty Harry had carried a .44, not a .357), and his "big shot deputy." But when that cannon shuddered in his hand and Lefty took his dive, every bit of kidding he'd endured went up in smoke.

Emil's heart was pounding, and his bowels were juicy. That's how scared he was. And he had every right to be. Lefty would have scared anybody the way he exploded out from that barn, jumping around and screaming like a maniac, waving his arms and charging straight ahead with a row of goddamn carpenter's nails waggling under his nose so that the plum-colored puff of his upper lip bulged and bled and his own blood ran down his chin. His eyes were vacant and terrible. His hands were curled into black, fire-charred claws. And his dick was hard.

Maybe that's what scared Emil the most.

Maybe that's why he just pulled his gun and fired.

There wasn't any hesitation in this movement. Something in his head just said, "This is bad. The whole scene. It's bad. I mean really. There's no telling what he'll do when he gets here, so just do it…grease him. Do it now!"

And Emil did.

Ka-pow!

And down Lefty went, his legs lifted comically as smoke swirled everywhere and dogs snarled in the rain. He lay there for a moment, and then, to Emil's amazement, he got back up...grinning, bleeding, with a pencil-sized hole in his chest and pieces of himself lying in the grass behind him. The hole in his back where the bullet had exited must have been really something to leave that much bloody shit on the ground.

And that's when Emil pissed himself, because, by rights, Lefty should have been dead.

Without even thinking he fired again, and this time Lefty didn't get up. The bullet hit him high on the forehead, taking off his skull cap and blasting his brains out in a quick pink spray that hung like a halo as he spun to his left, his knees buckling and his eyes crossed as he turned his face up as if trying to see where his brains had gone.

When he landed, a thunderclap rolled up out of the Valley, and the Man in the Woods disappeared. Through the ominous grey clouds that boiled overhead, a brief break formed and a single shaft of sunshine shown down to where Emil stood with his wet trousers and smoking gun.

And...

Pretty much the next thing he remembered after that was Sheriff Conway slamming his cell shut and turning the key. There were vague, blurry images in his head of people gathered around him, listening to something he said. And there was a weird, droning echo of a voice he knew to be his own weaving crazy sentences in the depths of his skull. But his only vivid, substantial thoughts were the sound of that key turning in the lock on his cell door...

And his wife's voice calling his name.

It was right then that Emil Lockner knew he was going to die.

He was standing with both hands on the bars when the jail's outside door opened and Cheryl came in, saying,

"Hellloooo, Eeeeemmiiiiiiil?" in a weird, catlike whine. Crouching beneath a swirl of darkness and snow as wings flapped, teeth jittered, and the ground jerked underfoot, she was worse than Lefty had been—partly because she was his wife, but also because she was farther along the path to the final change than Lefty had ever had time to achieve.

Her eyes were big black slits that shone like silver dollars when the light caught them just right. Her teeth were crooked, veined, and sharp…bulging her lips and distorting the line of her mouth into a twisted, perverse grin. Her skin was milky—almost translucent under the harsh, fluorescent tubes—and there seemed to be something dark curled beneath it, like hairs that had not yet broken the surface. As if all the juice had been sucked from them with a hypodermic needle, her breasts hung flaccidly on her chest. And on her back was riding that… that…thing, that hellish creature with the human eyes and tiny fingers that he'd seen pointing from Lefty's shoulder as it leaned over and whispered in his ear.

For a moment time seemed to stop, and a tiny, almost imperceptible flicker sparkled in Cheryl's eyes. Maybe it was one final, tepid nod of human affection for her husband. Maybe not. But whatever had caused it passed, and a new and hideously wicked gleam spread up like a flame to take its place.

As the thing on her back beat its wings and lifted itself into the air, Cheryl Lockner cocked her head in an oddly animal way, reached over, and killed the lights.

Suddenly the room changed. All reason left Emil's mind and he staggered back…

Going where?

Straight for the concrete-block wall behind him.

Why?

To escape…of course!

It didn't make sense. But crying didn't make any sense

either, and he was doing that. Big, fat tears were rolling down his cheeks as the air-blasted black around him and the window over the sheriff's desk exploded into a white, hovering rectangle. Wings were fluttering as something small and fast shot past the window once, and then again, dangling its tail—with the heart-shaped, spatula end—and rushing aimlessly in quick, unclear silhouettes.

"I didn't mean it!" he bellowed, crashing into the wall behind him and bumping his head so hard that stars cascaded around the arched periphery of his vision. "It was the light! It came down from the sky and *made* me do it!"

"You're too tame, Eeeeemmmillllll!" his wife purred from the darkness in a voice obscenely thick with sexual expectation. "You're a gooooood man—goooood enough to eat"

And then, as if something had suddenly pumped twice as much air into the room as the place could hold, a new and overpowering sense of presence filled the darkness and Emil knew that all the evil in the world had just come in—however a thing like that could happen—up from the Valley, down from the sky, and in from that terrible, shadowland place in the corners of reality that God forgot to check when he sent the earth spinning on its way like a child releasing a ball into water. The evil just came.

It was here!

As leathery wings crackled, Emil's fingers spidered their way over invisible concrete and his sphincter let go, filling his cell with the smell of terror. As the sound of tiny human voices shouted on the street—ten million miles away, at least, and apparently in another language for as much as they mattered now—an intelligence took hold of the night and animated the very air, laying claim to the dark and exerting a new and irresistible pressure on the boundaries of sanity, the limitations of hope. For one hideous moment there was total silence. And then, with an *Ooooooowwwwwweeeeeeee* screech of tearing steel that testified to the power of this hellish presence, the bars on the cell's door were ripped apart and...

It was totally dark—both inside the room and within Emil's mind.

The light from the window, the lamps, and the sky—even the shining blade of gleaming warmth that had seemed so pure and elemental when the clouds had parted over his uplifted face—all of it, all light and every memory of light, paled before this total, ancient blackness.

It was heavy, thick and as familiar as breathing. It was the same darkness that had pressed around the campfires of huddled, terrified men when men were new, and the fire they could make even newer. It ran like swamp water into Emil's mouth and down his throat, smothering the light in his mind and erasing even his vaguest memories of reason, leaving him hysterical, desperate, and as alone with the night as his most distant ancestors had ever been when the sounds of animals...out there...in the dark...growled their hunger and approach...

Those same animals were growling in that same darkness now. And Emil did the same thing men have been doing in the dark since darkness was all there was....

He screamed.

8

Sheriff Conway was almost halfway across the street when he heard that scream, and the sound of it nearly killed him. He was running, his external posture perfect, eyes set, legs pumping, gun drawn...but his brain felt like a frog doing flip-flops in his skull, and at any moment he knew that he was fully capable of leaving a trail of fresh coffee and stomach acid on the cold concrete.

He'd seen a demon—an honest-to-Christ demon, like out of one of his grandmother's books—drop straight out of the sky, bat wings and all. That wasn't the kind of thing he normally dealt with around town. What was he going to do when he got to the jail and the thing was squatting on his desk, jabbering old Latin invocations to Satan, or whatever the fuck demons did? Say, "Put up your wings. Anything you conjure can and will be used against you in a court of law?"

Even worse, what was he going to do when he got to the jail and the thing wasn't there? "Ooops! My mistake. Excuse me while I call the happy house and see if they've got a shuttle bus running this late in the day."

What was he going to do?

What the hell has happening?

Ahead, the jailhouse looked like the one in the old Andy Griffith show, except that instead of Floyd's barbershop next door, there was a Laundromat. The two absurdly antique parking meters out front were leaning at odd angles, broken since nobody ever used them because parking up the street was free. And overhead, the town's only traffic signal was still stuck on yellow, as it had been for two days without anyone really noticing.

Conway saw all these things in careful detail, all at once and distinct. It was as if, subconsciously, he had made the decision to study his old world and imprint its specifics on his mind because, as his grandmother's voice was saying in his head, "Whatever makes a man scream like that'll change your world too, sonny-boy. You're gonna be a different man…and it's gonna be a different town."

He burst into the jail and searched for the lights.

Later, he would swear that it came with a noise—a *foom!*—that sucked the air right out of his lungs. He felt certain that someone had just hit him in the stomach with a battering ram.

Cooper was still running behind him, not yet there to see…

Which would soon cause them both some problems.

But Conway wasn't thinking about that.

He wasn't thinking at all…

He was stunned.

And it was in that instant that his eyes locked with those of the thing Cheryl Lockner had become.

She was inside the cell and Conway saw her through a tangle of chipped, yellow-painted steel bars that had been bent into a hole big enough to drive a car though. She was crouched over the body of her husband, naked, her hair hanging over her face and her arms working as she did something—he could see the muscles corded in her neck squirm beneath her skin as she worked. When her head snapped up in the light, her eyes were blackly luminescent, freezing him in his spot and making his skin crawl as Cooper ran right into him from behind. As he struggled to keep his view clear, Cheryl Lockner pulled a squirming, bloody snake out of the wound she had gouged into her dead husband's back and tied it around her waist, making the sky explode and the stars fall.

Pop-pop!

Pop!

Went three fluorescent tubes overhead, and Conway glanced up just in time to see a flood of falling glass and glowing retinal residue sparkle down at him as a dark, flapping shape fluttered around the last fixture.

Pop!

"Jesus!"

More glittering snow.

And Conway fired his gun in the dark.

The explosion was deep and concussive. Its flash seared his optic nerve and left it vibrating with vivid blue images long after the bullet ricocheted off concrete twice, shattering something...God knew what.

"Get outta my way!" an angry voice hissed hotly into his left ear as rough hands pushed him, and his gun, to one side.

He could hear Cooper's inept steps in the dark. He could also hear the slapping of bare flesh on linoleum as...

The force of the blow was incredible. It slammed him straight on, and even more stars sparkled in his eyes.

A light came on somewhere...on his desk...it was Cooper...Cooper with a light...standing over his desk and holding a glowing gooseneck lamp that made the room perform a weirdly improvised series of dips and curves while something strong disappeared through the door.

"Hey!" the detective shouted, dropping the lamp. "Hey you, stop!"

The sheriff hit the floor.

He didn't see it, Conway thought from where he sat, his back propped against the open door, his face pointed into the yawning darkness of the cell in which Emil Lockner lay so still.

Detective Cooper had been fumbling around, and he didn't see the blood smeared around her lips, and the lumps dripping down her chin as she raised her head up from where she was hunched and snarled, or grinned, or both, savage, triumphant, insane beyond the description or capability of rational thought. He didn't see the snake—at first a snake—but that was only sheriff's mind trying to identify the unknown with something familiar because it wasn't really a snake, it was skin: a length of bloody flesh peeled right off her husband's back. She picked it up and tied it around her waist and Cooper was fumbling around and that thing with its leathery wings was flying up at the lights and breaking the tubes and...

God!

She tied it around herself...

And she *changed!*

Goddamn it, he'd seen it!

It wasn't a story...

It wasn't a legend.

It wasn't, as the detective had said it was, "the product of sick minds, deluding themselves into believing that some ancient magic actually works, here, in this day and age of microwaves and AIDS."

It was *real!*

Cheryl Lockner tied that belt around herself, and in that split second before a tiny, hairy demon with human eyes and wings like a bat smashed the life out of four fluorescent tubes set into a ceiling almost twenty feet over the floor, Sheriff H.W. Conway—fifty-two years old, rational, reasonable, level-headed protector of the laws that balance society's protection with the freedom of the individual—saw a woman's face *change.*

It wasn't like in the movies. No fangs growing up from her lower jaw, or hair sprouting, or nose turning into a little black button. No pointy ears or whiskers. No, it wasn't like in the movies. It was like in hell. It was a turning completely animal, completely wild, of denying the humanity that had made her familiar, and expelling it, right then, before his eyes.

She's had an orgasm.

He'd seen it happen.

She'd tied the belt around herself and, in that very instant, her body shuddered, the muscles around her eyes flickered uncontrollably, and in a lurching, bucking movement she'd snarled and twisted, slavering like a beast...

He could have sworn that he'd seen something behind her as she ground her pelvis and growled out the death of her humanity. In that instant before the lights when out, he could have sworn that he'd seen something there, something invisible with its hands on her hips, pushing her, pushing...pushing, invisible, but there.

He could have sworn.

But then there wasn't any light, and she bounded through the dark as Conway fired at where she had been—not at her, but at the invisible thing—and she hit him so hard that he was amazed that he was still awake...if he in fact was still awake. And then it was completely dark until Cooper turned on the light and chased her.

Was he crazy?

Yes!

He realized suddenly, in a burst of insight that he didn't really want. The son of a bitch was nuts! He'd have to be to go charging off into the night chasing what Cheryl Lockner was now.

But he hadn't seen it!

He hadn't seen the change!

God help him.

And then something moved, and every nerve in Conway's body tingled.

Slowly he lifted his face to the ceiling and saw it: darkly hanging upside down with its head twisted back so that its tiny black eyes were pointed his way.

It stopped his breath, and very nearly his heart. It seemed to contort reality itself so that the bruise it created in the air extended all the way down and swept him away, making him a part of the madness, making him *responsible* for the madness—as if nothing would be wrong if it weren't for his presence to see it.

Slowly, Conway lifted his gun and perched the tiny, blurred spot of darkness directly over the tip of his .45's barrel. He still wasn't breathing, but his heart had picked up a little steam, sounding like a bed sheet being rhythmically torn, a foot at a time, right between his ears. He thought about what would happen when he pulled the trigger…about the flash, and the noise, about the bullet ripping into the face of that awful, impossible creature, and in something that was very much like despair, he let his finger relax on the trigger.

He couldn't do it.

He didn't want to do it

He didn't want to give that obscenity the legitimacy of death by being responsible for its wounds. He didn't want its body lying at his feet, bleeding green goo or whatever onto his floor and leaving a stain that others could see, even if, like in the movies, the creature should fizzle, or smoke, or disintegrate into a pile of ashes or dust. He didn't want there to be any proof. He didn't want there to be any evidence. He just wanted it to go away. He wanted Cheryl Lockner and this fucking thing on the ceiling to get the hell out of his world, so that he could just go back to what he had known before.

Or try to go back…

Though he knew that that was crazy.

"Go back to hell!" he hissed.

And the thing on the ceiling spread its wings and fluttered to the ground.

But it didn't land.

Something else did.

And that something was a woman.

It was at that very instant that a profound and substantive change occurred in Sheriff Conway. It was a positively inevitable thing, really. Being confronted with what he was seeing, his mind, and the personality that dangled so precariously from the safety line of sanity provided by the store of familiar objects and natural laws that he called reality, could literally choose one of two mutually exclusive courses.

One was to give up and shut down; to just roll over in that great basket-weaving field in the sky where mental daisies blew and the world spun along its buttercup path a zillion miles away. It was to make "Fuck it! I thought I knew, but I guess that I was wrong, so if you need me I'll be in the bar with Napoleon…where's my hat?" your answer to the world's trickiest questions. And it was tempting.

The other was a simple, "Wow!"

No judgments, arguments, or stiff-upper-lip-certain impossibilities. No more, "That can't be," or, "There must be a logical explanation."

Just, "Wow: there are more things in this world than are known to the careful observer, and buddy, that ain't you. So sit back, shut up, and watch the show. Look out, ego, here we go…"

And in his mind, Conway did one world-class, gold-medal-winning swan dive of a Wow! that reached right down to his shoes and pulled his crumbling psyche up by the laces. It was an act of utter acquiescence, a recognition of possibility, a desperate "rope-a-dope" crouch that protected his chin and left his eyes wide open to see…

A beautiful blond girl with bare feet and a flowing white gown simply float the last few feet from the air and settle gently on the floor next to his desk.

In her eyes was the essence of the expression he'd seen on Cheryl Lockner's face, condensing into a single, focused glare of sensuous desire. Her entire being radiated a voluptuous, nearly ridiculous need that was so physical in its power that Conway found himself responding despite his fear, confusion, revulsion and Wow! Almost instantly he achieved an aching erection, and his knees went weak. He could feel the muscles in his back and legs twitching beneath his skin, working independently and starting the back-and-forth motion that would thrust his pelvis should this woman give him even the slightest opportunity.

He wanted her…

Or, more accurately, his *body* wanted her.

As if it were trapped in a machine over which it had lost all control, his mind seemed to watch from the cockpit behind his eyes as his limbs jerked him up off the floor and into an absurd, knock-kneed peacock shudder that carried him inexorably toward the woman in white…the glorious, promising creature with the fire in her breast and blackness in her eyes who held out her long arms to welcome him to her, into her, into…

"Demon!" he cried, his own arms lifted, elbows stiff. "I know thee, Satan!"

For Satan was the word he knew…

"What the fuck is happening?" a voice inside his head screamed, while another voice, equally strange, though unarguably his own, used his mouth to pronounce, "To hell with thee, bitch! Whore! Slut!"

His body quivered and rocked. A wave of coldness washed up from the floor and killed his erection flat. A weird, sickening sensation of threat seemed to bleed outward, starting in the very center of his chest as a sharp, needling pain and ending at the extremity of his flesh as a blanketing electric prickle that all but crackled in the dark.

The source of all his fear stood before him in the midst of hideous flux. Responding to his words—if *his* words they were—the woman in white reacted with an exaggerated look of rage that began as a simple change in her expression, but that ended as a metamorphosis of her very being.

Those black eyes that, until this instant, had been pulling him forward suddenly spewed fire in a flash that exploded outward in a blood-red sparkle, obscuring her face for an instant that ended with a new and sinister rearrangement of the classically European, human beauty that had called so eloquently for the sheriff's body.

In quick succession, he saw a dog's snarling lip, a cat's eye, a tiger's teeth, a reptile's tongue, a diabolical line of gleaming horns, and a flash of bitter silver as a claw slashed from nowhere, all in a swirling hail of impressions that made his head reel and his mind scream for some familiar patch of ground upon which to land.

This was madness.

It was hell.

It was all...so...wonderful!

His erection was back, as was the woman in white, a raging gleam in her eye and an expression of unabashed lust on her face.

"Herr Kunneval!" a voice mocked from above, taunting, insinuating, hinting at deep knowledge that dwarfed any human's most sincere attempt at deception. *"The lady is for thee! Take her!"*

"No!" Conway whispered, shaking his head in revulsion at even the suggestion, and noticing for the first time that the area of the woman's white gown over her crotch was stained a deep and spreading crimson.

"Take her!" the voice repeated.

And the sheriff forced his eyes from the woman, whose

figure was now wavering, hovering over the floor, arms outstretched, flesh gaping in running ribbons of raw, steaming cuts that had begun to resemble individual, naked slits.

"Sweet God!" he gurgled.

"Take her!" the voice demanded.

"NO!" the sheriff roared, and suddenly both doors on the front of the jail blew open and the speaker was there, standing in the night beyond the...the...thing, where it hung over the floor, little more than a smear of flowing white.

The speaker was in the doorway.

And he had, more or less, the attitude of a man.

But he was more.

As Emil had described him, the Man in the Woods stood with upraised arms, his face nearly hidden beneath his hair and beard, his own robes rippling in the swirling wind and blowing snow, his eyes aflame. There seemed to be a light radiating out from his body, creating a shimmering pool of silver that boiled with snowy specks. Outside that pool, eyes sparkling and bodies black in flat silhouette, stood a ring of the creature's followers.

Conway fell to his knees before it. There just wasn't any question but that was what he was supposed to do. In the face of such a wonder as this, there was nothing for a mere mortal but supplication, worship, and awe.

When it spoke again, Conway realized that the words were German. He also realized, although he could not have explained how, that they were not for him.

"Come!" it pronounced, almost regretfully. *"He's their dog!"*

In response, an immediate rush of wings clustered within the blurred patch that was the blond woman burst angrily up in a swirl until Conway was sure that the thing would hurl some nameless monster his way to avenge his rebuke. How many humans had denied the advances of this beast? And how many who had, had lived?

As he watched, the distorted creature's form coagulated back into the bat-winged thing that had borne Cheryl Lockner down from the sky, clattering and flapping its way twice around the room before dipping into a graceful arc that led through the door and up, into the night.

Conway was trembling, and something was very wrong with his eyes: they weren't connected to his brain anymore. He was seeing things, but they weren't registering any impression. His head felt empty.

The Man in the Woods said, "Until tomorrow, Herr Kunneval..."

Kunneval was Conway's family name. His great-great-grandfather had brought it over from Europe with him nearly a hundred years before. The sheriff hadn't heard it since he was a child.

And then two things happened that, in concert as they were, combined to destroy Conway's equilibrium, resulting in the most violent, gut-wrenching gush of vomit he had ever experienced.

The first was that the Man in the Woods expanded, fast, his body filling the doorway and drawing back in a rush that made the sheriff's head swim.

And the second, happening almost at the exact same time, was that a thick, dripping darkness swallowed everything.

For a split second before he bent his head and spilled his guts, Conway saw the moon overhead become a single, open eye, surrounded by a silhouette that defined a being so vast that it could have easily held the Earth in its hand. It filled the sky, overhung the world. And dwarfed the planet. It was immense, towering, and black. The moon was its eye, and the sky its skin, and everyone and everything that had ever been or would ever be, all taken together, would combine as a speck of dust before it...

It was that big.

It was unbound.

It was a god.

And in an instant it sent a physical wave of darkness down from above that dripped over the outside of the building like a rain of ink, puddling on the station house floor, dribbling over streetlamps, and replacing all sight with a perfect void into which Conway sent the sounds of his stomach's revolt...

Three short gasps.

Then four.

And done.

9

When Cooper hit the pavement in pursuit of Cheryl Lockner, it was, for him, the absolute best of all sensations he'd ever experienced, rolled into a single, glorious instant. He had his gun—a .38-caliber Policeman's Special that his father had given him when he first got out of detective training—gripped firmly in his hand. And he was actually "in hot pursuit," just him and the suspect, one-on-one, and not a single computer terminal or telephone hookup in sight.

He'd solved a lot of crimes in his day, but never once—or at least not since he had spent his obligatory six months as a beat cop before moving into his office on the seventeenth floor downtown—had he actually made an arrest. Even during his days on the street, he'd been assigned cake duty so that the department wouldn't end up wasting four years of post-graduate schooling and two years' special training on a guy who, because of an assignment mistake, was destined to walk into a bullet trying to break a domestic dispute.

This was real!

This was big-time!

This was what it was all about, and hitting that pavement was like stepping through the curtain onto a brilliantly lit Broadway stage. All he needed was a fanfare. He could almost hear the applause.

But the elation was short-lived, because no sooner had he caught sight of his suspect than he realized that he was really going to have to work for this one...no shit. God! Could she run or what?

It had taken him two seconds, four maybe, tops, to leap

over the sheriff's prone figure, and already that crazy broad—he didn't even know her name— had a good three-storefront lead on him. He could see her naked ass shining in the dark, and for an instant he hesitated, blinked, and duck-shuffled because…

She ran weird…kind of loping, half on two legs and half on four, like a dog. It was physically impossible for a human being to run like that, but she—he blinked—had disappeared down an alley.

Move it! his body demanded.

And he did.

The street was perfectly empty, but there were shapes watching from a few lit windows. He thought it was lucky that the hicks down here rolled up the sidewalks at nine, because, should he have to use his gun, he didn't have any pedestrians at risk.

Sliding a little on the icy concrete, he skittered around the corner and stopped, dead, at the mouth of the alley down which the woman had turned. It was wide and perfectly dark—a single tunnel of blackness, with the pale moon hanging overhead in a strip of night sky, that emptied onto a street about thirty yards ahead.

He listened, heard nothing, and stepped forward, his eyes adjusting ever so slightly so that he found only the barest hint of garbage cans and rubbish lining the walls on either side. There wasn't a sound in the air; just flecks of snow that seemed to enter the alley from above and disappear.

His heart was hitting pretty hard in his chest, and his mouth was parched. He'd seen blood in the jail. He hadn't seen enough to get a real handle on just what she had done to the deputy in his cell, but he'd seen a streak of red when the woman ran through the door, and that was enough to tell him that there was blood on her hands, and maybe—Christ

Almighty, if it was true—on her mouth as well.

Oddly enough, even with his heart hammering, the detective still felt calm.

The gravity of his situation hadn't sunk in yet, he supposed. According to everything he had been told by the old-timers on the department back in Cleveland, the biggest component of any chase was fear.

"If you ain't scared," a grizzled old sergeant had once admonished after Cooper had pulled the most unforgivably stupid stunt of his life, which was approaching a car they had stopped on the street without his gun, "then you're either crazy or dead. And being the first is the fastest way I know of getting to be the second."

But Cooper wasn't scared. He hadn't been back then, and even now, alone in the dark looking for a woman who may have had blood smeared on her face, he still wasn't scared.

Excited maybe.

Tingling from head to foot, for sure.

But scared…never.

Maybe he *was* crazy.

But God! This was living.

At least it was until he reached the end of the alley, and then it almost became dying.

He hadn't been thinking. That was probably the worst part. He'd been daydreaming, savoring the excitement of his first confrontation more than he was paying attention to the gravity of the thing, and, as a result, he hadn't even seen the bitch crouching in the gloom to his left. He'd walked right past her and she'd taken the opportunity to strike. She could have let him go by and sneaked back out the way he had come in. But that wasn't what she wanted. She wanted to take him, and the alley had been a trap.

Like an animal, she growled as she leapt, which gave him just enough time to produce a startled, "Huuhh?!" and begin his turn. But instead of using his gun, he reached out to grab her, thinking she wanted to run past him.

He was wrong.

With one perfectly liquid motion, she grabbed his throat with one hand and simply lifted him off the pavement. His gun clattered, his head spun, there wasn't a lick of air in his lungs, and his brain—that perfectly reasonable, self-confident, highly analytical organ of his—all but announced to the rest of his body that it was all over.

"We fucked up, guys," it seemed to say. "See ya on the flip-flop!"

The woman grabbed his crotch with her free hand.

And then…

The pain was fabulous.

Actual sparkles of light dazzled him when she squeezed. He stiffened where he hung and tried to scream, but her iron grip had closed his throat so he writhed there as she smiled, grinned, and finally howled out her delight by throwing back her head and producing a plume of steam from her mouth.

Her smell was evil.

Her touch, foul.

The pain almost put Cooper out, but somehow he held on long enough to see a gleam start in her eye and her teeth, like retractable cat's claws, slide out to four times their length as she turned him sideways, brought her head toward his stomach...

And…

She bit me! his mind screamed, just before the lights went out.

She bit me and made me blind! he just had time to think before he fell.

In absolute darkness, he hit the ground, rolled, and groaned pitifully as pain charged up and down his legs from where his knees had cracked concrete. His hands sparkled with a thousand hot needles of impact. And he was choking.

Then he stopped, lay still, caught his breath, and, in the dark, forced himself to listen.

There were sounds, but none were close.

He was trembling.

He was alone.

Where the woman had gone, he couldn't imagine. How she had run like a dog, hidden so well, and lifted him over her head so easily—all were beyond him. How she had disappeared in the dark, leaving him to fall six feet straight to the ground as if she had simply dematerialized beneath him, he didn't care. All that was important was that he was alone, and…

He was bleeding!

Germs!

Spit!

Disease!

AIDS!

Rabies!

Blood!

Spit!

Disease!

AIDS! AIDS! AIDS! AIDS!

His mind whirled.

His hands were on his stomach and he could feel the wet, feel the warm, feel the blood.

AIDS!

No pain.

It didn't hurt a bit, even when he touched it, and that, more than any act of conscious self-control, interrupted the roll of hysteria building in his head.

It didn't hurt?

He sat up.

It was still dark.

Feeling with his fingers, he found his shirt torn, everything around his gut wet, and a series of rough, fleshy patches near his navel. Absorbed, he probed, actually inserting a fingertip into what he assumed was a puncture wound, without producing the slightest bit of discomfort, and thinking, Vampire bats can do that. They've got something in their spit that anesthetizes the wound.

Vampire bats?

Jesus!

He needed a doctor!

Climbing to his feet, he swayed, stumbled, and banged into a brick wall, a clattering trash can, and finally a mound of something that crinkled like plastic. He looked up, but the moon was gone. So were the stars. He looked around, but there was no light at either end of the alley. Feeling his way, he followed the wall until he emerged onto a street, where he paused, blinked, and tried to make out at least a ghost of the town. But the darkness was impenetrable. It was as if a sheet had been drawn across his vision. As if a blanket had been thrown over the earth.

But without his eyes to distract them, his ears became acute, and, frozen with his hand still on the corner of the building, he listened as a radio-theater mental picture of the street formed in his mind.

A fairly large group of people were running, starting out together and then splitting up, so that the sound of their heavy footsteps on icy pavement seemed to disintegrate like the wings of pigeons, rising from the ground en masse. Some ran very close to him, and he reached out, only to snatch his hand back as an unbidden image of the woman's terrible teeth rent it to a stump.

Overhead something rustled, fluttered, and fell.

A car door slammed.

And the last sound, that of a car starting, was so abrupt

that it made him gasp. In the dark it sounded like a rocket engine, nearly drowning the crunch of tires on dry snow as he craned his neck and tried to force the darkness away.

And then a light came on.

Yellow.

He blinked at it, thinking for a moment that the moon had fallen very low before realizing that this amber eye was a traffic signal hanging over the street. He had followed the alley back the way he had come and was now facing the jail from a spot just to the left of the Thunderbird Café. The light was weak, but when compared to the depth of darkness form which he had just been sucked, it virtually exploded in his vision, filling his eyes with glorious yellow that defined exactly enough of the street for him to see the black shape of a car crawling away from the jail, heading south on Main.

There were two people inside: a woman in the passenger's seat, and a man who was driving.

As the car moved, more lights came on. Exactly as it would pass a spot, a light—in a window, on a pole, over a doorway—would snap, creating a flowing, liquid impression of motion behind the vehicle, as if the car were rolling back the darkness, or taking it along, out of town. As each light came on, the back of the car became more visible, and Cooper studied it from where he stood, leaning on the café wall, squinting for a license plate, a model, or a make, some distinctive feature until…

"Wood…" he burbled, trying to call out but finding his tongue uncooperative.

The car was getting away, picking up speed, heading south. Overhead, the stars were twinkling back, also in time with the…Pinto—he could see it now—the Pinto's advance.

"Woodie!" he croaked, his voice coming as if unwillingly from his throat.

He took a wavering step forward.

"Woodie Norris!" he shouted out at last, his voice thin and shrill. "Woodie, come back!"

And then he noticed a form hanging in the doorway of the jailhouse, arms akimbo, legs wobbling. It was looking not at the car, but at him, and it was Sheriff Conway, hardly able to stand, but watching him nonetheless. Watching, and, Cooper knew suddenly, listening.

Then Woodie's Pinto disappeared around a corner.

The moon flashed back on overhead.

And Sheriff Conway stepped into the street, moving through the puddles of light thrown by streetlamps—bright to dark to bright in a dozen steps. His short grey-blond hair was wild, his eyes glaring and focused, the entire front of his uniform covered with puke, and his gun—a big, old, Korean war-vintage Colt .45—dangling at his side. In a flash he crossed the street, grabbed Cooper's collar, and dragged him away from the alley and into the glare of a streetlamp, pointing his gun at his face and snarling, "Take off your shirt!"

Cooper reflexively drew the front of his overcoat tight around his stomach, glanced around, and noticed that, despite all the commotion, not one curious citizen had poked his or her head out to see what was happening. In truth, there were fewer lights on then there had been just a moment before. And curtains were being drawn. It was as if he and the sheriff had the town to themselves... as if Woodie's Pinto had taken more than the light with it when it drove away.

"Take it off!" the sheriff commanded, drawing the hammer back on his gun with his thumb and producing a threatening, no-nonsense click.

Cooper allowed his coat to open.

And Conway lunged, spinning him around as he yanked and pulled and finally threw the coat to the ground before he tore the man's shirt off his back and left him standing, shivering in the cold, while he cursed, "Damn you!" through clenched teeth.

It was at that instant that Cooper decided that it might be a good idea to ask what the hell was going on, so he raised his hand to get the sheriff's attention and said, "It's…"

To which Conway responded by thrusting out his gun and demanding, "Silence!"

Which Cooper gave him.

Still holding his gun, the sheriff stepped forward and, with the heel of his boot, traced a rough circle in the snow around where Cooper stood. When he was finished, he moved back about six feet, looked down at the detective's feet, made the sign of the cross, and said, "Take two steps toward me. Two steps, and no more."

Cooper didn't move.

"*Now!*" Conway roared.

Two steps…and not an inch farther.

Conway looked into his eyes sadly, sighed, and said, "May God have mercy on your soul."

TWO

10

"But I need a goddamn doctor!" Cooper bellowed over and over again as Conway sat behind his desk and made a series of phone calls that took him nearly an hour to complete. Ignoring Cooper's pleas, he dialed each number by memory and said, "The witness is dead. Come if you'll do no harm," before replacing the receiver and doing it again. Once he said more, but the detective didn't hear the particulars. And once, he used the phone in a back room and talked for quite a long time, privately. After what seemed an eternity, he finished and, folding his hands on top of his desk, said, "Mr. Cooper, you've got to calm down."

But Cooper couldn't "calm down." He was practically hysterical. He'd worked himself into a lather, roaming the office, back and forth from the desk to a full-length mirror on the back of a closet door, wringing his hands and trembling until he finally planted his feet and shouted, "See this!" with both his index fingers pointing to his stomach. The wound was a bitter oval of purplish bruises that culminated in a row or real punctures on either end. The entire area had gone a sickly yellowish color and had puffed up a little, forcing a couple of the punctures to leak when he breathed. "I'm hurt. I need a doctor. . .a hospital!"

Conway shook his head.

"No doctor in the county'll touch you."

"Then I need one from out of the county."

"Be a waste of time. That's no natural wound, so no ordinary medicine will heal it."

"Oh-God-oh-Christ-oh-God!" Cooper cursed, running both his hands over his face. "At least let me have my car keys."

"Nope," Conway said with a sad shake of his head. "I can't have you runnin' around loose. You'll stay right here..."

"And die of infection!" Cooper screaming, slamming his hands down on the desk.

Conway was unfazed. Without so much as a blink, he said, "We can only hope you'll be that lucky."

It was useless and Cooper knew it. He couldn't get through to the sheriff, and he couldn't leave. He felt like a bug in a bottle, and his rage was so complete that everything he saw seemed to be tinted pink—as if his eyes were coloring his world bloody out of spite. He ended up sitting on a bench, covered with a blanket from one of the cots in a cell, drinking from a bottle of gin and mumbling about "hicks" and "fucking, redneck ignorant bastards," while Conway made coffee and rifled through the briefcase that Cooper had brought with him from Cleveland. When the door opened and a man walked in, the detective ignored him by hunching himself up and staring at the floor, while Conway silently indicated a chair for the man to take.

In half an hour, there were twenty others in the room, and finally the sheriff asked, "Did you bring it, Billy?"

To which a weird little guy in bib overalls and a canvas coat responded by nodding and handing over a mayonnaise jar that Conway opened and sniffed.

"Okay," he answered loudly.

And the tone in his voice made Cooper look up.

Despite his anger, he was a little surprised by what he saw. He'd been fuming in his place, and consciously blotting out sound and motion from his attention for fear that it would spark an explosion that would send him screaming for somebody's throat. So when he saw so many men, sitting on folding chairs, on benches, and cross-legged on the floor in a group before him and the sheriff, he wondered where the hell they had all come from. They looked like every stereotype of every hillbilly ever created, all rolled into a single, motley bunch.

Dim the lights and you'd have a Klan meeting, he thought. *Turn them off and you'd have a lynching.*

When the sheriff turned, the Klan looked his way and Cooper rose, the blanket sliding off his shoulders and the gin bottle suddenly heavy in his hand.

They were about three feet apart, the sheriff and the detective. All eyes were on Cooper's stomach, and self-consciously he kind of danced his fingers over the area, halfheartedly trying to hide the wound but knowing it was impossible. The expression on the sheriff's face was a mixture of regret, pity, and revulsion, and with a tone of resigned authority in his voice, he said, "Just so you'll all know," as he flipped the mayonnaise jar Cooper's way, sending its contents out at him in a quick, brown arch.

When the liquid hit, Cooper stared down at himself for probably fifteen seconds before the gin bottle crashed to the floor...

And then he screamed.

It hadn't hurt before...the wound. It hadn't hurt when he'd gotten it, explored it, probed it, and disinfected it with straight alcohol out of the sheriff's first-aid kit. It hadn't hurt at all...until Conway dumped whatever was in that jar on it, and then it did hurt...Christ Almighty!

It *HURT!*

"What was that?" he cried, doubling over and clutching

his arms over himself without actually touching his—*Christ!*—his *steaming* flesh. Sprayed out across his abdomen in a repulsive flower pattern were countless rivulets of burning skin, blackened and bubbling, sending tiny wisps of vapor up in nauseating, smelly tendrils until he thought just the stench alone would drive him mad. Where the liquid ran down his legs he could feel the flesh there burning. And on his crotch. Everywhere it touched burned like…

"*Acid!*" he hissed.

"Wolfsbane tea," the sheriff corrected, turning back to the group and adding, "Did ya'll see it?"

"Wolfsbane?" Cooper's mind pronounced giddily as in an act of remarkable self-control he forced himself to ignore the pain for a moment, looked at his body as objectively as possible, and noticed for the first time that, remarkably, his skin was the only thing reacting to the "tea" Conway had hurled his way. His pants, the floor, the bench, everything else it touched, all simply got wet. Only he was burned, only he was marked, only he screamed at the wolfsbane kiss.

In amazement he looked up and felt suddenly low, base, repugnant. In his mind was an image of himself as he must have appeared at that instant, and it was ugly.

"Better?" Conway asked.

Cooper nodded, dumbly.

"It'll ache for a while, but not long. There'll be some scars, but the holes'll close so they won't bleed no more. You ain't outta the woods yet, but it's the best we could do for now."

"Thank you," Cooper whispered, returning his attention to his stomach and sitting down.

As the sheriff had predicted, the splashed tea had created a star-shaped mass of scar tissue that glowed a livid and angry pink. But the holes, the teeth marks, were closed.

"Why?" he mouthed, almost inaudibly.

"You stepped out of the magic circle left foot first," came

the sheriff's response.

Cooper looked back at him, dumbfounded…

Wolfsbane?

Magic circle?

Silently his lips moved, but for the life of him, he couldn't decide what words he was trying to say.

"It's happened!" the sheriff suddenly proclaimed in a voice apparently intended for someone sleeping in a building across the street. He turned and confronted the men before him—who were all on their feet, leaning forward to study Cooper's scars. "But you already knew that, or you wouldn't have come when I called you. Now, listen…there's a Norris in town."

It was as if the sheriff had announced the nuking of the White House. Every eye in the place looked at Cooper, then at the bloody sheet covering Emil's body, and finally at the weirdly bent jail cell bars, twisted inward and broken by something that must have been incredibly strong.

Before anyone could speak, the sheriff continued.

"We all knew something was up soon's we saw them Indian Diggers. Especially that Mr. Green."

"Green?" Cooper whispered, snapping his attention up to the sheriff's face.

Conway met his look with an expression of quiet sympathy.

"We all knew something was up," he continued. "But how were we supposed to guess what it was? If it wasn't for Mr. Cooper, here, we probably still wouldn't know. Even with the 'witness.' Mr. Cooper brought this"—he lifted a black notebook for everyone to see—"and it explains a lot about Woodie Norris. It seems that the boy went and got himself involved with a pretty unusual group up north…but that's our Woodie; that's the way he is. Turns out Mr. Cooper's a friend of his, and as a favor, Woodie asked him to use his police connections to do a little studying on our Valley. What he found out is all in this notebook. To anybody else it'd probably just be a bunch of numbers: statistics showin' how, in the year 1884, there was a sudden increase in the number of people attacked by wild animals 'round the county. And how that number grew, year after year, 'till folks started sayin' how there was something wrong with Harpersville; that the woods down here were bad, and dangerous.

"To a stranger, that's all Mr. Cooper's statistics would explain. But we ain't strangers. And we already know 'bout them killings. We already know what folks thought about 'em, and what they think about 'em now. We know that those who could, moved far away from here, while the others, who had relatives in Europe, spent all their money bringing those relatives over right before the First World War 'cause they didn't have no other choice but to do it that way. We know how, when those newcomers arrived, one of the first things they did was to start into tellin' stories about the old country; stories full of werewolves, and weird little towns on the edge of the Black Forest with names like Vultenhallen and Bachrect—names that made certain, really old-timers go pale, and that they started associating with Harpersville almost soon's they got here. With Harpersville and a certain immigrant family named Nurrenvelt that came over in 1884: a husband who made shoes, and a wife who made one baby before she died of infection from a wildcat bite."

He dropped the folder and it made a harsh pop as its plastic covers slapped his desk.

"The Nurrenvelt family had a reputation in Europe," he continued more softly, scanning the mute group with his eyes. "Maybe what's why the old man Americanized his name to 'Norris' almost as soon as he got here. But as folks arrived fresh off the boat, they brought the family's reputation with 'em so that soon, Mr. Norris was known as Herr Nurrenvelt again, right up to the time he died, in 1921: a seventy-seven-year-old widower who most folks wouldn't so much as speak to for fear of...well, of something awful that he had carried over the Atlantic with him like a disease. He left a son named Matthew, and because of who he was, that son had to move outta town for three years before he could find himself a wife.

"'Ya know what Mr. Cooper's statistics show about the years 1927 to 1930, when Matthew Norris was out girl shoppin'?"

The group's answer was an uneasy stillness.

"They say that nobody died in the woods during that entire time."

The group made no response.

"Matthew Norris came back in 1931, his pregnant wife in tow, and the killin's not far behind. The next year, 1932, he had a son, who some of us older folks knew as Robert. And two years after that, in 1934, he died. It was funny how it happened. Had something to do with moonshine liquor and a couple of boys from the hills. I've seen the sheriff's report on that particular disappearance, and it don't strike me that anybody tried very hard to find out how old Matthew met his end. For all we know, he just went up into the woods one day and never came back. His body weren't never found.

"But for the next fourteen years, till his son, Robert Norris, was sixteen years old, the woods slept again, and almost nobody died."

The sheriff pushed a lock of short blond hair from his forehead nervously, and pulled himself up to his fullest height, which wasn't very imposing by itself, but that, right that second, with everyone's attention focused on him as it was, seemed to make him about ten feet tall.

"Ya see what I'm gettin' at here?" he asked rhetorically, as he raised a finger for emphasis. "Every time there's been an adult male Norris living in town, there've been killing in the woods. Every time they leave, or they ain't grown to at least sixteen years, the killings stop.

"Robert Norris had two boys, which is the other thing: looks like there ain't been nothing but boys in that family for at least three generations, and for all we know, even more. Anyway, Robert Norris was killed in a car accident in 1963, and I remember the night it happened 'cause I was a deputy on the scene. Was a horrible thing, let me tell ya. Me and him was roughly the same age, so it was really hard. I knew his wife, I knew him a little too. Small town. He hit a truck head-on, and it was hard on me. Coulda been worse, though, I suppose, 'cause his son was ridin' in the passenger's seat. Fuckin' three o'clock in the morning and he had his kid with him, out ridin' around, drunk as hell. Coulda been worse, but it was a miracle—least that's what we said at the time. It was a miracle 'cause the boy lived.

After the accident, his mother, who was a real pretty thing, ended up marrying one of the doctors that took care of the boy while he was gettin' over the crash. The whole family up and moved down to Mist County not long after that, and since then, the Valley's been asleep again."

"'Till now," a voice from near the back of the group cut in.

And the sheriff nodded glumly.

"'Till now," he concurred. "They say the Nurrenvelt family's been a line of bad blood forever. They say they're Vyrmin…"

He paused, as if expecting some outcry at the mention of the word. When none came, he nodded.

"They say they're Vyrmin of the worst kind…and have been since the beginning. They say that of all the original Vyrmin families with bloodlines stretchin' back to the very start of time, or so it goes, the Nurrenvelt clan, from the heart of the Black Forest, was always the worst—always the most loved by the Man in the Woods. Just havin' a Nurrenvelt around is supposed to make the magic work and bring the evil out in others. That's why the old man came to this country in the first place: he was runnin' for his life. He had to find a place where nobody knew what he was and what he could do. When he came, his presence brought the wilderness out in the animals around where he lived, and in the people around him too.

"And now they're back! Woodie Norris brought it back! Emil said so. He was the witness, and he said, 'The Blood Prince comes, and tomorrow the moon is full!'"

It was at the instant of this proclamation that the jailhouse door burst open, and a snow-covered man stumbled in, eyebrows frosted to twice their normal size, and face flushed a deep vibrant red.

"Gone!" he half shouted, hanging on the door as snow whipped around him in wicked licks of frigid wind. "The whole bunch! Gone! Their rooms...oh God! Straw on the floor, and shit smeared on the walls and...oh God! Like animals. And the smell..."

Cooper had had enough: the story, the legends, the twisting of his statistics, the meaningless mumbo jumbo that these hicks had been reading into what he thought of as *his* case—it was enough. It was too much!

"Who?" he demanded, rising unsteadily to his feet and feeling the thick layers of new scar tighten on his stomach as he straightened his spine. "What the hell's going on here?"

Conway turned, looked him in the eye, and said, "Mr. Green's Indian Diggers have left the house they've been renting. It looks like now that Woodie's here they're gonna do whatever they came to do. God help us."

Cooper blinked.

The group tensed as one, studying the sheriff's face.
The telephone rang.
And events slipped inexorably out of control.

11

"I'm not even supposed to be here this late, that's the real bitch of it," Luther thought as he crouched beneath the window and inched just the very top of his head over the sill. In his right hand he held a hammer, and in his left, the telephone receiver. He'd just called the sheriff because, *Goddamn!* and *Jesus Christ!* there were fucking, honest-and-for-true, in-the-flesh grave robbers running around his cemetery. And that shit was too much!

The phone rang twice before Sheriff Conway picked it up. When he did, Luther Van Dussen whispered out a hoarse and indignant call for help, describing how, from where he was kneeling, he could see the forms of what had to be ten or fifteen people gliding between the tombstones behind his caretaker's shack. They were carrying lanterns that seemed to be muted with some kind of shading arrangement so that their light was thrown directly down at the ground. They were all carrying shovels. And they were obviously looking for one particular grave.

"Indian Diggers!" he barked, his mouth close to the receiver. "There's strangers in my graveyard!"

And I'm not even supposed to be here this late, that's the bitch of it! he added mentally.

He'd been home when the snow started falling, and strangely, a terrible premonition of something being amiss with his cemetery had compelled him to take a walk back and have a look around. Luther lived about a mile down the road from the "Holy Ghost Garden of Peace." And he thought of the cemetery as his own, personal possession, even though he was only the sexton—a job that paid about nine thousand dollars a year, and that mostly required him to cut a little grass, dig a hole with the sputtering old backhoe every once in a while, and just generally hang around.

Good duty, if you could get it.

His wife worked at the Laundromat, so—at least by his modest standards—there was always plenty of money. And Luther, who wasn't known as a powder keg of ambition, didn't have anybody looking over his shoulder all day—a situation he'd found particularly disturbing when he had tried his hand as a clerk at the hardware store out of high school. He was just twenty years old, and already a father, twice. He didn't like most people, and most people didn't like him. They thought he was spooky because he liked his cemetery—and everybody in it—so much. But since he took over as sexton two years before, the place had never looked so good.

And now someone was going to dig up one of *his* graves, and he was furious. He didn't know how he had known there was something wrong, but during *Wheel of Fortune*, he'd just gotten a feeling, so here he was: crouched on the floor and grunting for the sheriff to, "Come in one goddamn big hurry 'fore I kill some son of a bitch with my hammer!" while trembling in his boots.

Really trembling.

He sounded pissed, but in truth he was scared half out of his skin because what was happening outside his window looked like something in *The Texas Chainsaw Massacre* or *Night of the Living Dead*, two movies he had seen once apiece, and the likes of which he would never subject himself to again.

"We're on our way," the sheriff said, reassuringly, and Luther hung up.

Click.

Silence.

Alone.

The cemetery was located about six miles from town, but with the new-fallen snow drifting across the roads it could be twenty minutes or more before the sheriff would arrive. In the meantime, he was determined to stay put. He wasn't going near anybody goofy enough to go tramping around a cemetery, toting lanterns and shovels, in full dark, on the night after Emil Lockner had slipped his gears and scared everybody in town half to hell and back with stories of werewolves and Vyrmin and the Man in the Woods and…

Holy shit!

He dry-swallowed a lump in his throat and dug his fingertips into the windowsill on either side of his chin.

"Hey!" he whispered, his eyes gone wide. "What the hell?!"

The cemetery was flat before him, just a smooth patch of ground, neatly tended before the inevitable dip in the Retreat and the bristling wild of the Valley trees below. Though the sky was heavily clouded, the moon illuminated the horizon, backlighting it a moody silver-grey that seemed to be peeling into eddying white snowflakes. Tombstones, some as high as twelve feet, leaned at every odd angle, blackly jutting up from the featureless ground and briefly swallowing the silhouetted shapes of moving people, only to spit them out again for another stone to consume. Within that maze of shadows, one figure caught his attention and held it…

It looked smaller than the rest.

And it was struggling.

One particularly large figure was practically dragging it along, holding it from behind with a hand on each of its wrists. The smaller shape was fighting like the devil, kicking up dark puffs of snow and squirming its arms around and around when…

Every form in the cemetery suddenly froze as someone to Luther's left waved for attention. Like robots, the group began converging on that spot, some actually skipping with enthusiasm, while the captive figure began its struggles again, with renewed energy and…

"It's a girl," Luther whispered, fingering the handle on his hammer. "She's just a kid."

There were more shapes coming up from the woods now, rising blackly from the ground as if emerging from beneath it.

Shovels were moving and dark clumps of earth began to fly.

When Luther opened the door on his tiny shack and stepped outside, the first thing he heard was a weird, whooshing sound, like a train approaching from a very long way off, emanating from the Valley to rise and fall in time to the wind whipping the snow around his face. The second was a stifled scream, muffled by distance and cut off, as if by a hand over a mouth. That scream, and the way it simply stopped, overruled his better judgment and compelled him into his graveyard, even though he had promised himself he wouldn't move from the window. It brought out the hero in him…Christ, he really had the makings of a hero inside him somewhere. How about that? And it made him move despite the movie scenes he was seeing on the mental screen in his head: the Leatherface chainsaw carnage and the bloody knife attacks that were Hollywood's shock stock-in-trade.

He headed out just as a car pulled up at the shack.

Something in his head told him to hide. He knew by the sound of the tires that this car was smaller than the sheriff's Ford, so he jumped behind a nearby stone and watched as a Pinto stopped and two people got out—a man and woman from what he saw in the brief flash of interior light, which died when the doors slammed.

Two more nuts.

And these were a couple of beauts!

The man had long hair and was skinny as a rail. The way he moved, so ineptly that he looked as if he'd keel over any minute, made Luther think that he was drugged. The woman, on the other hand, was different, and it was she that held his notice as the couple moved to join the rest at the digging.

Her hair was blond, long, and luxurious. Her eyes were black, even in the pale moonlight. And her dress was strange, to say the least. A flowing white gown that billowed when she stepped so that, in the dark, she seemed to float over the ground draped itself sensuously over her fine shoulders, intimating at the loveliness of her body and painting out glimpses of her catlike line. When he saw her, Luther felt almost instantly warm. . .almost horny.

At a time like this? he thought, shaking his head. *What the Hell's wrong with me?*

But there wasn't any doubt about it: the lady in white was a siren. All she needed to do was say his name and Luther just knew that he'd throw himself at her feet.

Blinking, he took a deep breath and felt the feeling pass when the woman disappeared amid the stones.

But his relief was short-lived because, as he rose to follow the couple to the cemetery's edge, he noticed a new and eerie glow pulsating up in a silver haze from where he knew the group had gathered. His hand resting uncomfortably on the frozen stone of the monument behind which he had hidden, he felt a liquid sensation of dread moisten his guts as that light grew to a true blaze that illuminated the figures around the grave.

His hammer dropped to the ground with a thud.

He stood straight up and lifted his hands to his mouth.

And the faces of the grave robbers turned his way, clear in the shining silver light, and vivid for the first time. Their eyes were locked on his. Their teeth were wet as they displayed grins of triumph. And…

"Holy shit!" he cried, turning to run…

Directly into the person standing behind him.

12

"The cemetery!" Sheriff Conway shouted, slamming down the phone and looking up at Cooper with an expression of rage and terror. "Goddamn it, I shoulda known!"

"The cemetery?" Cooper exclaimed. "You gotta be kidding!"

In a flash, Conway moved around the room, waving his arms and explaining, "They're diggin' him up, boys," as he unlocked a cabinet and started handing out long guns to the men as they moved past in an impromptu line.

"Get a coupla trucks, fast! We gotta stop 'em 'fore they turn it loose again!"

"Who?" Cooper shouted, pressing through the excited crowd and feeling instantly absurd. "Who're you talking about?"

"Norris!" Conway hissed, jutting his face so close that the detective could feel the heat of his breath. "Now, get a coat and cover yourself."

"No!" Cooper said, stubbornly planting his feet and crossing his arms over his chest. "Tell me, or I stay put."

Conway's eyes seethed as his lips quivered and men moved around him. The door opened and men ran into the night, and a truck engine roared somewhere close.

"It's Woodie's father," Conway said, low and hard. "They're gonna break the charm."

Cooper shook his head, saying, "That don't do it, Sheriff."

"Listen," Conway explained, "I was a young man. I didn't know shit about nothin', or about almost nothin', anyway. Old

Man Dunning was sheriff back then. I was just his boy. He let 'em do it. They couldn'ta done it without his okay. Mrs. Norris threatened lawsuits up the ass, but Dunning convinced her that a lawsuit wouldn't fix a house that burned down with one of her kids in it, like what might happen if she raised any more fuss. So's her and her new man shut up and left. Like, that day. Never came back."

Cooper ground his teeth.

"They buried him the magic way," Conway said. "The first Norris was buried by his son, someplace nobody could ever find. Matthew Norris was lost in the woods, and nobody ever found him either. Robert Norris was the first one that folks could get their hands on, and they weren't gonna let that chance go by."

"What the hell did they do?" Cooper whispered.

"Nothin' that no dead body would mind." Conway shrugged, lifting a tweed jacket that had belonged to Emil off a chair and handing it over as a man called for them to hurry.

"They just buried him like a Vyrmin's supposed to be buried to keep the land safe. They cut off his head and laid it at his feet, and turned his body so that it was on its chest. Then they nailed his hands, palm down, to the box, and covered him with wolfsbane leaves."

"My God," Cooper mumbled, absently accepting the coat that sheriff offered. "You people are…"

"Scared?" Conway asked, eyes narrow.

Cooper shook his head. The scars on his stomach burned. His mind went quiet.

Crazy, he wanted to say, but didn't.

Instead, he allowed Conway to lead him out to his Ford, and listened as an anonymous man in a pickup truck shrieked, "*Yeeee-haaaaaa*! Let's go git 'em boys!"

And the sheriff said, "I wish I had me some silver bullets," as he started the car.

What in the hell have I gotten myself into? Cooper thought as the car started to move. *What in the righteous Hell did I get myself wrapped up in this time?*

13

There was an ancient apple tree near the grave, and its naked branches hung low, squirming with unnatural light. Luther didn't even struggle as he was led to a spot near where the girl was standing, hanging her head in despair and apparently unaware of the presence of her intended rescuer.

The light around the grave was bright and phosphorescent. It pulsated in a misty, bone-chilling haze that seemed to seep right through Luther's flesh to make him tremble. A ring of people in big down overcoats and heavy hiking boots stood shoulder-to-shoulder around the hole, while two more dug, first with shovels and then, after loud pronouncements of impatience, with their hands, like dogs. At the head of the grave was the woman—that gorgeous lady in white with whom Luther had been so taken—standing next to the skinny, long-haired man, whose mouth hung open and who swayed as if at any instant he would tumble forward, headfirst into the freshly dug ditch before which he stood.

Luther froze.

The light, that queer, silver glow, was radiating out from the thin man's open left eye, falling like a searchlight beam on the hole before oozing up to illuminate the faces of the people so expectantly poised with their shovels and…

Chains.

They were horrible, these people. And as Luther's gaze moved unwillingly from one face to the next, he gasped with revolted fascination. They seemed to be from another planet, or another time: heavy, sloping brows, beady animal eyes, large canine teeth, and dark hair and skin, all behind thick dripping clouds of frozen breath, grotesquely combined to make them look retarded—it was the only word he could think of...developmentally stunted, twisted, distorted...like Neanderthals, some of them, so deformed as to be closer to some species of ape, or prehistoric tribe, or...God...some circus sideshow-throwback-to-an-ignorant-time-when-people-who-weren't-quite-normal-were-displayed-like-animlas-to-be-jeered-at-because-"normal"-people-were-afraid and...

His amazement numbed him through. He felt soft inside, like he could just melt. He felt alien, lost, and trivial. He watched as a tongue licked heavy lips before a voice, thick with spit and ire, grunted out its approval.

The captive girl raised her head and looked him straight in the face from across the hole, her eyes screaming silently, "Do something!"

And Luther did.

He began to cry.

Then he threw all his weight into the man—or thing—holding him, giving him just the slightest of spaces through which to run as his mind fixed itself on the idea of dragging this out for another minute, two minutes, three—any number that brought him closer to the twenty he thought it would take for the sheriff to come, because the sheriff was coming, but he needed twenty minutes.

And, with unbelievable quickness, the man who had been holding him turned, snatched out with his hand, and grabbed Luther's hair, yanking him backward so that his feet left the ground and something snapped in his neck and made a pain shoot down his left arm.

A clattering of steel snaked through the branches overhead as someone threw a length of chain up and over a stout limb. The girl screamed as the man holding her began pulling at her clothes. In the hole the sound of digging had transformed itself into the sound of scraping, and soon shovels were thumping in a rain of muddy blows on an echoing coffin lid. Eyes gleamed in the dark. Figures emerged and danced beneath the hazy moon. Luther's arm wouldn't move, and when he tried to lift his head, bones ground together in his neck. Painfully he slid to his knees, seeing out of the corner of his eye a hand explode up from the hole holding an ivory-colored something that he instinctively knew was a skull.

And all hell broke loose.

The entire group burst into a chorus of howls and gibbering, insane exclamations as some jumped down into the hole and others tore at their jackets. Some were dancing now, really dancing in whirling, snakelike tornados of beating feet and screaming mouths. A flash of white that Luther sensed was the woman at the head of the grave suddenly shot into the air, circled the ground, and then retuned in the wink of an eye. There was singing. There was barking. There was the sound of cloth being torn and...

The girl clawed, cried and beat at two huge men who were stripping off her blouse and bra as they lifted her, like a sacrificial lamb, over their heads toward where the chain hung from the tree, gleaming in the silver light, which had grown to an absolute rage.

A knife flashed.

A foot flew and kicked the side of Luther's head.

He rolled on the ground, bones grinding away beneath his jaw, his legs fluttering uselessly in the mud.

The girl struggled hysterically.

Big black legs blocked his view of her for a moment before moving away to reveal a scene of such horror that, despite his neck, which he knew was broken, he overrode the paralysis of his damaged nerves and willed himself to move, willed himself...

To close his eyes.

He'd seen the girl, dangling over the hole. They'd stripped her naked and, with the knife, cut two holes in her side into which they had forced the hook at the chain's end, securing it around a rib before slashing her wrists and hoisting her up so that she spun and struggled, her arms and legs twitching and her head convulsively turning as she screamed, and bled, and spun around and around and...

Bones flew out of the hole.

Luther saw them...his eyes were open again.

Bones flew up in a grotesque spray, and monsters laughed, and feet stamped, and chunks of rotting casket landed with wet sounds...

And there was the face of a horse.

And then someone lifted Luther's body and hurled him into the grave.

14

By the time they got there, it was over. At least for Luther. They ran in like the cavalry, waving the rifles the sheriff had just given them and calling out their approach enthusiastically, as if overjoyed at their opportunity to act. As they came, things scattered before them in the dark. Big things, little things, things with tiny yellow eyes that had come up from the Valley for some reason in a great mass, as if drawn to this place. Badgers, raccoons, opossums, cats, and dogs...lots and lots of dogs. They shot blackly from the dark, across the path of the charging men, rustling leaves and disappearing like phantoms.

There was no light: not in the caretaker's shack, not on the grounds. So it was almost a half hour before their searching turned up anything unusual in the dark. After their initial charge, they had to stop, regroup, go back to the truck, and get flashlights. When they started again, their mood was somewhat muted. When they finally stumbled on the violated grave, their mood fell into a solid gloom.

Silence overtook even the most boisterous of the new deputies as Sheriff Conway pushed his way to the front of the crowd and aimed his flashlight square on the face of the girl's now-still body, hanging limply over the new-dug hole.

"It's Lefty Zimmer's daughter, Linda," he said to Detective Cooper, who, clutching the too-big mackinaw that Conway had provided for him back at the jailhouse, was standing directly to his right.

The girl's face was a frozen mask of agony; blood ran from her nose, mouth, and hands, the rib from which she hung had been pulled up through her torn skin so that little white licks of cartilage clearly gleamed through a fibrous mass of muscle that ended in a terrible curve of bloody steel.

The flashlight's beam moved from her to the ground, where huge black eyes stared up blankly from the bottom of the grave, dripping blood lay in sticky puddles on a long, chestnut-brown snout.

"And that's Linda Zimmer's horse, Ginger," Conway said, fixing the light on the horse's face.

The horse's remains were positioned so that its nose faced the foot of the grave. Its legs were bent to embrace the curled body of a man who lay with his upper portion embedded in the shattered wood of a casket lid, and whole legs were weirdly twisted into a kind of cockeyed X. Blood dripped over the entire macabre arrangement, and large clumps of seeping mud had pulled themselves from the gnarled, root-and-rock embedded walls and piled themselves in wet, lumpy mounds inside the empty casket.

Slowly the flashlight beam moved up, and over the remains of a rectangular tombstone where it lay flat in the snow after having been toppled over and trod upon by many booted feet.

Through the ice and mud, etched into the stone, the words, ROBERT NORRIS, SR. were still visible. And the sheriff's light lingered on them as he said, "It was a shot in the dark, the way they buried him, and I think they all knew it. But they did it anyway. They did it to keep the wolves away. As long as his body stayed the way they put it, the wolves weren't supposed to be able to come back here. The land was stained for them."

He paused and lifted his eyes to Cooper's, revealing a terrible aura of fear and defeat.

"But tonight the wolves took it back. That's what this has been all about. They came here and they took the Valley back. They dug him up, killed an animal whose spirit was tamed, and soaked the ground with a lamb's blood. A lamb from the Flock named Linda Zimmer. They took the land back, and now they're here to stay, unless we can do something about it."

"No," Cooper said simply, feeling a weirdly pleasant tingle prickle the sensitive flesh of his new scar. "It's not that way."

Conway moved the flashlight's beam to the detective's face, making the younger man squint and raise a hand as he said, "You can't believe in any of this, Sheriff. You just can't or it'll blow you away."

Cooper couldn't see the sheriff's face in the glare of his beam, but he could feel the man's emotions radiating like heat through the misty cold air.

"It's drugs," Cooper continued, adamantly, gaining strength from the sound of his own voice, and the sudden feeling of being alone that not being able to see the other men gave him. "You read my report. You saw what Woodie Norris was involved in up north. He was a hard core addict, and so where the people he hung around with. He's my friend, but he's still sick. And the people doing these things...they're crazy. Get it? *Crazy*! Not witches! We have to understand them if we're going to predict what they'll do next, second-guess them, and gain control. But if we let ourselves believe any of this, then we're no better than they are, and we'll never..."

"I saw it, Mr. Cooper," the sheriff interrupted, and there was a tone in his voice so completely authoritative that Cooper let his own statement die on his lips. "While you were out chasin' that thing that killed Emil, I saw the Man in the Woods...and something else. Something horrible. So I don't need you tellin' me about belief, 'cause I do believe! I believe with all my heart. If I didn't admit that I believed, then I'd have to admit that I was crazy..."

"That's my point."

"That's where you're wrong."

The light fell from Cooper's face and he saw that, in the gloom, the sheriff's eyes were glistening with tears.

"You stepped outta the circle left foot first," Conway said, very softly. "And you screamed at the wolfsbane kiss. If I had any sense, I'd shoot you dead, right here on this spot, and save us both a lot of trouble. But it's my fault you came here in the first place. I called you. So I can't do it...at least not yet.

"But from here on out, you better remember how close to dying you came right this minute. And you came very close, Mr. Cooper. If I didn't believe I could beat this thing, you'd be dead already. So don't make no more points. And don't let yourself think you got exclusive rights to reality. What you're gonna have to accept is that you don't know everything about everything. If you don't accept that, you're gonna die. It's that simple."

"A bite isn't going to turn me into a werewolf," Cooper insisted. "This isn't a fucking movie."

"The bite won't turn you into anything," Conway agreed. "It'll just bring out what's already inside you. You stepped outta the circle left foot first. That means you don't favor the side that's right. You burned at the wolfsbane touch, and that means that you got the poison in ya. You saw a Vyrmin change when she put on the belt, but still you won't believe. And that means that your eyes are closed."

"It means I didn't see anyone change into anything!"

"That's 'cause the body hadn't been dug up yet."

"Jesus! Sheriff, you can't really expect me to..."

"The change was stopped by the charm on the land."

"Sheriff..."

"They killed the charm," Conway said, snapping off his flashlight and dropping his arm so that his words hung independently in the dark. "Now that Robert Norris' body's gone, you'll see your changes, I promise. Before the full moon sets, you'll see more than you ever thought possible. And I'm sorry for that. I really am. But there's nothing we can do about it now. The Blood Prince will come...and it's you that's gonna call him here."

II

THE KILLIBROOK VALLEY

THREE

15

Do you still have nightmares? the letter read.

And...

Remember how Dad used to study your face when you'd scream in the night? Like he was looking for something, in the glare when he'd turn on the light. Remember how he'd bend over the bed with those big, dead eyes?

Robert Norris, Jr., nodded, remembering the letter, and trying to keep his attention on the ever-shifting, headlight-bright tunnel through which he was guiding his big blue Bronco. The trees overhanging the road were heavy with fresh snow, their tangled branches drooping so low as to scrape the truck's roof as it crept through the featureless, country-dark indigenous to the Killibrook Valley.

When winter came, this land died, he thought, with a frown—and everyone and everything that lived on it died as well. Or at least that's how it seemed. Snow came in twenty-foot drifts that clogged roads and froze so solid that it often didn't melt until May. Inevitably, spring revealed the carcasses of hapless animals, probably months old, all twisted legs, matted hair, and bucktoothed, death-mask grins. Occasionally strange men were even found in those drifts; never locals...locals had more sense than to drown in snow. It was always some outsider: stiff as a board, one hand sticking up from a dirty mound of ice, nameless, no ID. The cops would just have to chip him out and bury him again, once the ground unfroze.

Norris had been in voluntary exile from this sad parcel of Ohio for ten years—a refugee from a bad land and home. He'd made a solemn oath, both to himself and to the Valley that they would never lay eyes on one another again.

And he'd meant it—from his heart.

But tonight he was back, responding to a summons of such urgency that it had rendered his pledge mute.

It was into the residue of your dream that he'd thrust his face, the letter continued. *So close that you could smell the fear rising off his skin like heat. And he'd say, 'Did you wake up before or after?' And you'd answer, 'Before,' just so he'd go away.*

Do you remember his eyes, Bob? Do you remember how his eyes made you tell him that you'd woken yourself up before it happened, whether you had or not? That you hadn't seen the blood in your dream?

Well, I've got Dad's eyes now, Bob...or at least I've got one of them.

Robert Norris...Junior...still had nightmares.

And at three-thirty in the morning, the telephone had rung him from one, right into the middle of another.

☆ ☆ ☆

In his dream...

The woman wanted to cry, but she didn't dare because the sound would draw him back. He enjoyed watching her cry, and he liked to see her suffer.

She was lying in a small, cramped room with whitewashed walls and a big, flowered easy chair in one corner. Her nightgown was torn. A silver moon hung motionlessly in the sky outside. And thin, milky light bled through the parted drapes, forming an elongated pattern of glowing windowpane rectangles and shadowy crosses on the floor. There were four thick blankets covering her trembling body, and water was running in the kitchen.

He was out there, and every time he cursed, she cringed.

How it had started this time she wasn't sure. She'd gone to bed early, as much to get away from her husband as anything else, leaving him alone in his chair where he was looking out the window at the snow falling in the parking lot, a half-empty mayonnaise jar of liquor on his lap. He was in one of his moods again...one of his quiet, sullen tempers when he didn't talk, or even look at her. She put on her nightgown, climbed under the covers, and huddled herself into a ball, dreaming, as she did every night, of the day she'd wake up to find him dead next to her, his face bruised black from the heart attack that would end her misery.

Sometime after eleven he got into bed, wearing, she saw when she caught sight of his silhouette against the glowing window, his tattered flannel shirt, and nothing else. He lay next to her, breathing roughly and tossing drunkenly until the doorbell rang. Then he went away, spoke to someone a moment, and came back angry.

Maybe it was because a customer had come so late. Or maybe it was just because he was awake. But his quiet mood had fled before a rush of unfocused rage he seemed to always carry with him. Ripping off the blankets, he roared something about how the way she slept made him crazy, dragged her out of bed, and punched her with his fist, five times, ten. Then he went back out to the kitchen to wash his hands, leaving her to cower, first on the floor and then on the bed, sitting up with her back against the headboard, crying noiselessly to herself and waiting for the sun to come up and save her. He'd be up all night now, she knew. That was his pattern: drink, try to sleep, beat her, then drink alone in the living room until he fell asleep on the couch at sunrise. He'd stay on the couch all day, and she'd sneak out to clean the rooms and do the work that kept the motel going.

She didn't know why she stayed with him. Probably because at the age of sixty, with no living relatives, she didn't have anywhere else to go. She'd sped her day working, avoiding her own home, until dinnertime brought her back to cook his food. He'd eat, start drinking again, and the whole lurid scene would play itself out in the night, as it had since their third year of marriage.

Or maybe it wouldn't.

Maybe he would just go to sleep.

And that was probably the worst part: the not knowing.

Sometimes she thought she could stand it better if she'd just know!

God, she hated him! She hated him, feared him, and for the life of her, couldn't remember a time when things had been any other way.

The water ran in the kitchen sink for an incredibly long time. And, through the window, red lights flashed. People were moving around outside, and once or twice, the crackle of police radios buzzed faintly through the thin walls. Wiping tears from her cheeks, she glanced up and thought about asking him what was happening in the parking lot. But she didn't move. Whatever it was, it wasn't any of her business, and he'd probably hit her again for asking.

So she just sat here, wrapped in her blankets, listening to him wash his hands and talk to himself—he'd been doing that for the last week or so, and it worried her. He'd ask questions out loud and then answer them, grunting or laughing as if someone were in the room with him until his conversation turned ugly and he'd get himself worked up for another beating.

"Not again!" she whispered, terrified.

The water stopped and she heard a low, tense tone of voice mumbling in the next room. He was moving again and a tiny groan of despair escaped her swollen lips.

And then the door burst open and he was there.

Outside, the first tint of morning softened the darkness, and in the room's gentle light she saw him, leaning with his back to the door, his scrawny, hairy legs bowed beneath his hanging shirt and his heaving chest. His eyes were wild, glazed, and aglow with a hideous light of fury so intense that she clenched her fists at her sides and tired her best not to grimace. Remaining perfectly still, she watched him through eyes almost shut, hoping that he'd think that she was asleep and leave her alone.

"More!" he whispered.

And she noticed for the first time that, in the darkness behind his left leg, he was dangling his shotgun.

She gasped, choking the sound by biting her tongue.

"There should be more!" he said.

And then he left the room.

She sighed, and felt the tears come.

He was gone for nearly an hour, and when he came back, the sun was up.

Still, she didn't dare move.

Closing the door gently, he paused before turning and displaying a leer so genuinely insane that it made her bolt straight up in bed and cry, "Ernie, no! What did I do? Oh, Ernie. . .please! No!"

He swung the shotgun up so that it pointed at the ceiling, and ran his hand along its barrel, smearing a glob of Vaseline over the blue-black rod. Up and down his hand moved, obscenely oiling the steel as he stepped toward where she pumped her feet on the sheets and pressed herself hopelessly into the headboard, screaming, "Help! Oh God…HELP ME!"

"It's down deep inside and we'll bring it out," he growled, advancing toward the bed and cocking the gun.

The woman opened her mouth.

The gun came forward…

✡ ✡ ✡

And Norris screamed in his bed. Twisting madly, he tore himself up and swung his eyes furiously around the room. He was holding something black against his head, and in his ear a voice said, "Bob?" Clattering around on the nightstand, with ebbing visions of what the woman had seen, he searched for the light switch and listened as the voice in the black telephone receiver said, "Bob, it's Woodie. You better come down."

Pause.

"Bob?"

"I'm here," Norris said, squinting at the clock and gasping as sweat rolled down between his eyes.

Three-thirty.

"Bob?"

"I'm here"

"Woodie's had an accident."

"Woodie? Who is this?"

"Jesus, Bob!"

"Mike?"

"You better come down. I'll tell you where. But you better come 'cause, man, it's bad. It's really bad."

Bad?

Mike Cooper never talked like that. He was a very special kind of cop; he was a friend; and he was emotionally flat—or at least that's what he wanted everyone to think. "If you let yourself get all wired up over the shit I see every day," he'd once told Norris over drinks in a bar near the county morgue, "you'd spend all your time going, 'How could anybody do something like that?'—which is just what these creeps want—and you wouldn't be any good to anybody…not the victim, the department, or yourself."

So as a direct result of his unshakable desire to be "good," he kept his voice even, his tone soft, and his word choice confined to "interesting," "suspicious," and, in extreme cases, "regrettable."

At least he had until this morning.

Something "bad" had happened to Woodie, Robert Norris' younger brother, and the author of the letter he had received on Monday.

Dear Bob, it read. *I'm sending you this because it's too risky for me to try to see you face-to-face.*

That was Woodie, all right: Mr. Dramatic., Norris thought as he carefully slid his car off the road and onto the bouncing gravel of the Lexington Motel's parking lot.

His dream was all but gone. By a familiar act of mental discipline he'd banished it from memory. He'd been having nightmares for so long that he had learned to just shake them off and to file them away. They came and went like mist, and since there was nothing he could do to stop them—no therapy, drugs or magic—he had, in his stoic, almost painfully practical way, taught himself restraint. They came, he screamed, and they disappeared: coexistence in the same body…an uncomfortable compromise.

The motel was an L-shaped building, one floor, studded with yellow light bulbs that made it shimmer a sickeningly familiar green. It had an office at one end, and rental units running window/door, window/door, around the back. Just about every window was dark, except for one at the south end, which glowed a cheap, feeble amber. That unit's door stood open in the cold, and amid the oddly staggered cluster of cars and pickup trucks parked nearby was a Harpersville Sheriff's Department cruiser.

There was an ambulance backed up close to the door, but it was dark inside and one of its uniformed attendants was leaning up against its great, flat side, smoking a cigarette.

Silhouettes moved back and forth across the amber window.

Norris felt as if his car were rolling toward the light completely of its own volition, carrying him somewhere he sincerely didn't want to be.

The letter was the first time Norris had heard from his brother since the cemetery episode. (Woodie—who had been very drunk at the time—had been arrested the previous Halloween for trespassing in a graveyard. The police report stated that he had given "Waiting for the Great Pumpkin" as his reason for being on the premises after midnight.)

After rambling around for a while about the Norris family history, which had been Woodie's obsession for the past few years, the letter finally settled into its most disturbing, and, yes, Norris thought, pushing the gearshift forward and turning off the car, its craziest part...

The part about death.

It said:

Listen: I know how you are, Bob. You won't believe me. Just because it's me, you won't believe. But you've got to hear anyway. One of my eyes sees what I see. And the other sees what Dad missed. Understand? When I die, will you understand?

A uniformed policeman stuck his head out of the open motel room and then pulled it back. As Norris climbed from his car, a figure emerged and made its way over, so that, just as he slammed the door, a pair of strong hands touched his chest and Detective Mike Cooper's earnest face—outlined by the light behind his head and fuzzed by a cloud of frozen breath—thrust itself boldly toward his.

"Mr. Norris," Cooper said, gripping Norris' coat and pulling him sideways, away from the ambulance. "Thank you for coming."

Norris shuffled his feet and lifted one hand. But before he could speak, Cooper had hustled him past the ambulance to a spot between two sheriff's cruisers that was dark, and, he suddenly realized, out of the smoking paramedic's hearing.

"Real quick, Bob," Cooper said. "I didn't want to do this, but it's gotten out of hand, so listen.

"Woodie's been mauled. I mean it, Bob. Mauled…and bad. You're not supposed to be here. No civilians at the C.S., period, department rule, no exceptions. But it's Woodie, for Christ's sake! So we'll say that you're consulting; you're a CCMP animal behavior specialist. Okay? Can you handle that?"

"But, Mike," Norris sputtered as Cooper dragged him around the cars and toward the open motel room door from which three men had so recently appeared.

His mind was working with the words Cooper had used: mauled, C.S.—crime scene—animal behavior.

Animal?

Mauled?

"My God," his lips mimed silently as Cooper introduced him as a representative of the Cuyahoga County MetroPark System's Criminal Consultation Division.

I'm a fucking park ranger! Norris protested in his mind as, over a fat man's shoulder, he caught a glimpse of the room's interior. There was something dark splashed on the walls in there.

"Mr. Norris," the fat man said, sweeping his hand before him. "Right this way, sir."

As a member of the Park Services Division—stationed in Berea, south of Cleveland—Norris was familiar with the animals that populated Ohio's wilder areas. He'd seen foxes, raccoons, and opossums; even a wildcat or two. He'd seen groundhogs, badgers, beavers, dear, the odd coyote, and even a bear, once—way down south where sighting one was about as common as spotting Elvis in the mall. But he'd never seen a lion, tiger, or wolf running free at the fringes of civilization's backyard, and these were the beasts that immediately leapt into his mind as he stepped, full face ahead, into the room where his baby brother had met his sudden and horrible…demise.

"Oh, God," he whispered as his knees went rubbery.

"Keep it together," Cooper's strong voice said close behind. "And then tell us about it."

"Oh, Jesus!" Norris said, louder this time, feeling his head swim and seeing the room in tight little flashes of detail that were interspersed with long moments of blurred, tear-filled confusion.

"You…" he said, turning and feeling bile burn the back of this throat. "You…you left him here?"

Then his mouth fell open.

Cooper, the fat man, three guys in grey uniforms, and two in blue coveralls were standing, blocking his way to the door. There were bright lights on tall aluminum poles, and there were cameras. There were faces, intense, careful faces, studying him, watching him, aiming the collective weight of their expectant gaze at him as he swallowed back the urge to vomit and searched out Cooper's familiar features.

"You set me up!" he moaned, bewildered.

Flashbulbs popped, dazzling his eyes and making him throw his hands over his face.

"Bob…?" Cooper's voice asked.

"Somebody grab him!" another man announced.

Norris stumbled away from the group and into the middle

of the room, which was so small that its one, single bed, tiny four-drawer dresser, and TV-try nightstand—broken and scattered as if by an explosion—made it feel cramped. He half turned, rolled his eyes, and groaned, waving his arms and reeling back to shake his head as he barked, "You fucker!"

More flashbulbs popped.

Cooper touched him.

Norris pushed him away, slipping on the blood-soaked carpet in the process so that the next thing he knew, he was on the bed.

"Goddamn it! He'll fuck it all up!"

"Jesus, Mike!"

Hands were coming at him again as Norris rolled, and slid to his knees at the bedside—like a child saying his prayers.

On the mattress before him...right before him...inches from his face...was part of what was left of Woodie...real name, William.

(He called himself Woodie because he said two brothers named William and Robert—Billy and Bobby—sounded like Norman Rockwell's version of the American family. And Woodie always wanted to be different.

"Christ!" Norris gagged, and then his stomach locked up. Something—not someone, even in his shock he knew, instinctively, that it wasn't a human being who had done this, but something—had torn Woodie apart.

If it was Woodie.

Which was hard to tell.

What was on the bed resembled an insect more than it did a human being. A good portion of a man's rib cage—complete with red muscle and white cartilage—was half propped against a soggy pillow. Jutting from the end of the basketlike arrangement was a shattered length of spinal vertebrae that ended in a lump of meat that was part of a leg, to the knee.

The sheets were puddled with blood, and across the floor, walls, and even the ceiling, great splashes of red dripped and congealed. The arms, head, and other leg of the body had been torn off, leaving little strings of skin hanging from the gaping, pulpy ruins of neck, shoulder, and groin. And huge, crescent-shaped chunks of flesh had been bitten from the corpse, leaving jagged, deep gouges that roughly matched those that had been bitten into the walls.

Over the bed was a broken window and its glass sparkled madly as Norris felt his body being lifted from the floor. He struggled, kicked, and shouted, but there were too many arms, too many men, pulling and hustling him out, away from the light, away from the blood, away from Woodie's face, which was the last thing he'd seen, on the floor, under the splintered wood of a broken dresser drawer. The head was on its side, the face torn into unrecognizable pulp, one eye open, and one eye gouged out…

One eye…

Sees what I see!

Norris felt a terrible fist form under his ribs as his heart seized itself into a knot.

And one eye…

Sees what Dad missed!

Snow was falling…and so was he.

There was an awful crack when his knees hit the pavement. He heaved once, and then again as he hung his head and gurgled, spit, and then growled…no words…and he didn't know why he did it. But he growled…and it felt good.

It felt better than good.

It felt *right*!

The sound came from deep inside his chest, and swelled in a rumbling surge that made the whole of his throat vibrate. He did it once, on his hands and knees, there in the slush and snow and steaming vomit. He growled once, whipped his head up, and leveled his hot, red eyes on Cooper's face, and then he growled again, with his teeth exposed and his fists clenched.

"Goddaaaaamn you!"

The sound came, dripping with threat.

Cooper, stretched tall by perspective and silhouetted by the light from inside the motel room, nodded gravely—as if some secret suspicion of his had been confirmed.

Then he said, "Clean him up."

16

From a window at the other end of the motel, Ernie Cray, the Lexington's owner, watched Robert Norris vomit, and laughed.

"So the big shot brother's a wimp," he muttered, less than sympathetically, craning his neck as Norris was dragged behind the ambulance. 'What an asshole."

Ernie was standing in his kitchen, bathing his wounded hand under a stream of cold water, and looking out the window over the sink.

He was feeling surly and mean.

The cut itself wasn't bad; what bothered him was the he couldn't remember how he had gotten it. All he knew for sure was the his injury had something to do with Woodie—that's how he had signed the register book, Woodie Norris, big block letters—and, by extension, with his park ranger brother. Together, these two had dragged something strange into Ernie's life; something so peculiar that it hung like a smell and affected his mind.

"I knew I shoulda sent that creepy son of a bitch packing," he added, glancing down and examining his wound.

It started at the crown of his right hand's middle knuckle and zigzagged its way back to the bump on his wrist that was the end of his ulna. At the knuckle, it was a craggy, raw-looking tear, but after about an inch, it branched out into little, neat slices that filled with blood as soon as he moved his hand out from under the water.

It hurt like hell.

And God...the blood!

It was all over the place—dribbled over the countertop, the faucet fixtures, the floor—and no matter how long he kept the hand under the water, there still seemed to be more coming.

"Dumbass," he mumbled, turning on the light over the sink.

Suddenly a pallid white puddle fell on his face, transforming the window into a black mirror. Shadowy forms moved within his floating reflection, punching it through with stabbing flashlight beams, and silently blowing chunks of his head away with red and blue bursts of police car emergency bubbles.

"Shouldn't have given him a key," the eerie, insubstantial man, clad in an unbuttoned, red and black, lumberjack-style flannel shirt said from his place inside the window pane.

I shoulda told him that we was full up," Ernie agreed.

The reflected man's expression was dour. His eyes were deep-set and dark, his head shone bald on the top, its sides overgrown with bushy white hair that prickled as if it were electronically charged.

"I shoulda known. I felt it soon's I saw him. But it was snowin' so bad...and, shit, I don't know..."

His reflection shrugged.

"Too late now."

✲ ✲ ✲

What Ernie had felt when he got up to see, "Who the hell's banging on the door at twelve-thirty in the goddamn morning when the sign ain't even on?" was a strange sensation of vertigo that seemingly had as its object the spaces beyond the walls of the room he occupied. He didn't know how to put it any better than that, and he was sleepy anyway.

As he got out of bed, a funny, head rush overcame him, making him lurch. Putting his hand on a dresser to steady himself, he suddenly knew—just knew—that the motel wasn't where it had been when he had gone to sleep. Things had changed. Maybe he was still groggy, but he sensed that an alteration had taken place, a twisting of things that directly involved him. Such sudden knowledge was irrational, of course, but its impact was so powerful that it made him pause and hold his breath. In that silent, intimate moment, he was sure that he could feel the building floating—the whole goddamn thing, floating—in some dreamy space that was as dark and cold as all creation.

His wife didn't stir, even when the pounding started again. She never did: selective hearing. She just went right on snoring, the hulk, a crocheted bedspread tangled over the four blankets that she insisted she needed to stay warm.

"She nests like a bear," Ernie complained, his voice shattering the moment as he pulled on his slippers and growled, "I'm coming. Jesus Christ!"

But when he snapped on the hallway light, it hit him again: a twinge; a real, physical flutter in his chest that made his heart skip.

There was something...*serious* going on here tonight. Something, really...Lord, it sounded crazy...but there was something *big* outside.

And whatever it was, it was knocking on his door.

When finally he did open that door, after glancing over to see that his shotgun was still leaning against the wall, Ernie half-expected to see the President—or the Queen of England, or some other personage of remarkable distinction—standing in the harsh gleam of his porch light. But instead he found a man...a thin, long-haired man, shuffling his feet in the cold and holding one hand over his eyes in a salute intended to keep the blowing snow from frosting his lashes.

"Got a room?" he asked, and his voice was strained, nervous, and...was it vaguely desperate?

Against his better judgment, Ernie gave the man a key, briefly perfunctorily explaining the house rules, and collecting his twenty dollars, which the kid handed over with trembling fingers.

He's on the run, Ernie thought. He'd been in the motel business long enough to know trouble when he saw it. The thin timbre of the kid's voice, the way he wouldn't look Ernie in the eye, and the skittish, almost flighty way he moved—he was running all right. But from whom?

Cops?

Jealous husband?

Drug dealers?

When the kid went back to his car, Ernie watched him through the window and saw that there was another person sitting in the passenger's seat. He couldn't tell if it was a man or a woman—and nowadays it didn't really seem to matter—but he would have bet woman.

Jealous husband, he decided…or angry father…letting the drapes close and turning from the window as he felt that dreadful sensation of unease move—like a patch of fog or a cold draft—following the young man away from the office and down to the south side of the motel. Whoever he was, the kid exuded a…a vibration, an aura that irritated Ernie's skin, making it feel itchy, like there was wool in his arms and cotton in his mouth. It made him feel like squirming, pointlessly, like kids do when you show them a worm. And it made him thirsty.

So he got himself a shot of moonshine and went back to bed. He intended to sleep, but the sight of his wife…just lying there—good-for-nothing, son-of-a-bitching…

When the beating was over, his hands were bloody, and his wife was crying. He stared at her for a moment, feeling a physical wash of relief ebbing the frustration in his guts, and heard a great crash of shattering glass outside. Without even thinking—and in a weird display of detachment that focused his attention on events outside this little cell of space he thought of as his own, impenetrable fortress against the laws and logic of the world—Ernie went to his kitchen and called the sheriff.

✡ ✡ ✡

That wormy, itchy feeling was worse than ever now, and Robert Norris was its source. He, like his brother, made Ernie's skin crawl.

"Fucker," he said, returning his attention to the sink and rubbing his hand over his wound to clear away some of the blood so that he could see if he needed stitches.

So much blood for such a little cut.

Just a little cut.

And then Ernie Cray noticed something that made his eyes grow wide and his heart go cold. Grabbing his wrist and lifting his bleeding hand closer to his face, he stared at it, transfixed and confused, as a police car slid past his window, its light revolving.

"Cops," he hissed, his reflection's eyes twinkling red as it mimicked him in the glass. "Right outside! There's an ambulance, right outside!"

With an inarticulate cry, he lunged for the door…

And locked it.

Leaning his back to the wood, he studied the wound again, watching as his skin seemed to swell, right before his eyes, as if his hand were suddenly full of some thick, lumpy liquid. Wiping the blood away, roughly, he began probing at the cut's ragged edges with his fingertips, ignoring the pain as the room around him disappeared.

Finally, he pushed the bloody slice open and stroked it, carefully moving streaks of red until the things he'd seen were laid out: moist, dark, and fine.

Hairs.

Ernie grinned.

There were hairs protruding from inside his hand: long, black hairs, growing on the underside of his skin.

No wonder there was so much blood, splashed, from the bedroom—where his wife still reclined—to the sink, where he had just been standing, washing his hairy, bloody hands.

No wonder there was so much blood.

Blinking, he whispered, "There should probably be more."

And then Ernie Cray checked the lock on his front door, lifted his shotgun from its place in the corner, and headed back to his bedroom.

17

After he had been "cleaned up," a process during which he stood mute, implacable, and zoned, Robert Norris was placed on a bed that was identical to the one upon which his brother's body had been found, in a room three doors down from the murder scene. There, he remained for what could have been an hour—maybe more, maybe less; he couldn't tell, and he really didn't care—trembling violently and trying to summon from somewhere inside himself a sliver of steel, or a single, cold slice of nerve, that would make the awful gagging sensation in his chest go away. He felt battered and weak. He was repulsed at his own frailty and ashamed of the sweat on his palms. He was Woodie's big brother—and he wanted to do…

Something…

Anything.

But what?

Woodie was dead.

Terribly, obscenely, irreversibly…

Dead.

And vaguely, Norris felt that somehow it was all his fault.

Trying to trace the logic of such a conclusion was pointless, he knew. But his conviction was unshakable. Somehow, Woodie had died because of him. He'd been doing something that had to do with the dreams that had plagued both their lives. He'd said so in his letter. Those dreams were the same ones that had terrified Norris' father and had, years later, fascinated the psychologist his mother had ended up marrying.

✲ ✲ ✲

The first time the young Robert Norris ever saw Dr. Datch, his soon-to-be stepfather (who to this day insisted that Norris call him "Daddy-O"), was in the hospital room where Woodie was lying after the car accident that had killed their dad. A lot of people he knew—his mother, grandparents, and even a couple of crotchety old aunts—were all standing in a circle around the bed. There was also a bunch of people he didn't recognize, all dressed in white, sprinkled through the group. And among them was a man with longish brown hair, glasses, and a soft belly, standing with his hand on his mother's shoulder.

"Where's Daddy?" Woodie asked, weakly.

And they told him Daddy was dead.

"That's not true," Woodie said, making his mother cry.

"You were right," the man with the glasses said to her with a frown. "He's pretty banged up."

"What happened?" a lady in a white smock asked. "Can you tell us why you were out so late?"

Woodie replied that he couldn't.

And Dr. Datch then proceeded to explain to everyone present how normal it was for a person to block traumatic events from memory. It was his contention that buried memories often found their way into the shadowy corridors of a man's soul, where they wandered for years, being twisted by darkness and neglect until they reemerged years later as a full-blown neurosis. To prevent that from happening to Woodie—and with his mother's approval—he proposed initiating a series of therapy sessions with both boys involving hypnosis. Those sessions ended up lasting for the whole year before he married the boys' mother and for all the years leading up to the day that Bobby Norris finally got away, by going to college. During those years, Dr. Datch lost interest in Woodie, but he kept coming back to Bobby, and their sessions often lasted well into the long hours of the night. The doctor kept everything Norris said while "under" in a big, black binder that he guarded like a secret.

Growing up with the knowledge that there was a part of his brain that was hidden from him—like a waterproof space inside a ship that no one could open—Robert Norris felt strangely compelled to be by himself. Thus, he was drawn to the woods—these very woods—the anonymity of the Killibrook Valley. When he was alone among the trees he could forget his stepfather's black book. He could remove himself from the sidelong glances his parents both seemed to be perpetually sneaking his way. And, most of all, he could forget the dreams…

Which were another thing his stepfather seemed to be interested in.

Many nights, Norris would wake up with a start, clawing his way back from the midst of some wretched, awful nighttime vision, only to find Daddy-O sitting on a chair beside his bed, writing in that imposing black volume.

"What's in that book?" he asked him once.

"You," came his reply.

"No, I'm not," the boy insisted. "No one has me locked in any book."

As he got older, he went even deeper into the woods each day, until finally he decided that it was time to stay there and never come back. He went to college, far away, leaving his mother and Daddy-O behind.

They still lived down there, in Mist County, just south of Harpersville. He wondered how long it would be before they learned of Woodie's death. Thinking of his mother, he allowed himself to mentally drift back to the modest brick bungalow surrounded by a rolling lawn in which he had been raised. The Killibrook Valley State Park started like a barricade at the ridge about a hundred yards from his bedroom window, and as a child he had stared for hours at the brooding line of oak, ash, and evergreen, yearning for the embrace of its shadowy depths so deeply that he was often impervious to the fall of night. In the morning, he'd awaken with the forest still in his eyes.

✡ ✡ ✡

"One of my eyes sees what I see," Woodie's letter had said, and Norris thoughtlessly slid his hand under his jacket pocket and found the small, hard thing he'd picked up in the room where Woodie's body lay. It had been on the floor, and he'd seen it after he'd slipped on Woodie's blood. "And the other sees what Dad missed."

He lifted the object to the light, and a deep, smoke-grey sparkle, intricate and real, danced near a shiny black dot. He didn't have the slightest ideas of what had possessed him to pick it up in the first place. But when he saw it, his only thought was to hide it from the men around Woodie's corpse. When he fell, he splashed one hand down atop it. He held it in his fist as they dragged him out of the room. And he stuffed it into his jacket when they hustled him down to "clean him up" as Cooper had ordered.

Now it was his alone.

And he didn't know why he wanted it, or what he was going to do with it.

He moved his hand, and the light sparkled from grey to a clear milky white.

Eyes…

They were so significant in his life—the one truly constant image in the symbology of his persistent dreamscape. Vivid pictures of them, hovering overhead, staring into his soul, and filling the sky, had come to him almost every night for as long as he could remember. There was so much expression embodied in the eye, so much knowledge filtered through its lens. So much of a man's mind could be seen reflected in the eye. And so much information could be read there...

But the one he held, Woodie's glass eye, simply stared at him: silent, cold, and impassive.

Woodie had worn one since the accident that had killed their dad. Some arteries were ruptured when his head hit the windshield. There was an infection, and soon there wasn't an eye they could save anymore. Few people could tell that the eye was artificial, unless they really looked, which not many ever did.

But Norris knew.

He'd held Woodie in his arms as the boy cried in his hospital bed, half his face covered with bandages, and his good eye squeezed tightly shut. He had held his brother as he cried and cried. They'd just brought the eye in for him to see. The first of many he'd have over his growing years. They thought it would make him happy.

And now...

"One of my eyes sees what I see."

Norris closed his hand over the little, cup-shaped piece that was all he had left of his brother.

"And the other sees what Dad missed."

What the hell could Daddy-O possibly have missed?

When the motel room door opened, Norris shoved the eye back into his pocket and looked toward the wall to hide his guilty expression. Without a word, Mike Cooper stepped inside, closed the door, and settled himself on a chair near the foot of the bed.

Norris waited a long time before he finally asked, "Why?" without turning his head or moving his hand.

In his pocket, Woodie's eye felt warm.

"Because we've got a real blue-ribbon winner here, Bob," Cooper responded in what Norris had come to identify as his "official" voice.

That voice was meant to create a distance between the cop and his subject; to establish a relationship in which Cooper asked the questions, and the subject answered, because it wasn't just a man looking for information, but the symbolic weight of authority.

"And because it's standard procedure: brother killed? Suspect the brother. Cain and Abel."

"I thought I knew you," Norris said, disgusted by the official voice, and almighty pissed that his friend had chosen to use it.

"Woodie called me yesterday afternoon," Cooper countered, his tone softening. "He was scared, vague and virtually incoherent. He was in a gas station off Route 36, just north of Columbus, in the Killibrook Valley Reservoir area. He said he was heading out of Harpersville, and that I should meet him in Akron. . .if he made it out alive."

Norris heard a door open and sat up. Accepting the coffee handed to him by the deputy who had just walked in, he swung his legs over the edge of the bed and put his elbows on his knees so that he faced away from Cooper, who started talking again as soon as the deputy was gone.

"Woodie wasn't calling me as a friend, Bob," he said, noisily slurping his own coffee. "He was calling me as a cop. He talked about you, mostly. There were some things on his mind. Mostly about you. He said that he'd found things out about you that would bring the 'beasts from the woods'—those were his exact words."

Norris heard the pages of a notebook being flipped.

"Let's see. . .yeah, here. 'From the past's settling dust, I've unearthed a truth so terrible that it'll bring the beasts from the woods to my door.'

"I wrote it down, Bob. I never heard him talk like that before, so I wrote it down. Then I went and waited where he said he'd meet me: the McDonald's off I-77, just south of Akron, at midnight. That's when he said he'd get there. I went. But before I did I measured it on a map. And you know what I found?"

Norris frowned.

"It's roughly ninety miles from where he said he was to where he said he was going to be. Now, on a highway, ninety miles is what, an hour and a half? Two hours, max? But Woodie wanted me to wait seven. He called at five, scared, almost panicky. He was alone, and apparently on the run. But he didn't go to the local cops, and he didn't want to meet me for a full seven hours.

"Now, you and him pretty much grew up down here, Bob. What was he doing? Where would he go?"

Norris steadied himself before saying, "Fuck you, Mike. I want a lawyer."

"Why?" Cooper asked, his voice sounding genuinely confused.

"Cain and Abel," Norris said, standing and turning to face Cooper for the first time since their interview had begun.

What he found was startling.

Cooper was a short, heavyset man in his mid-thirties, with dark hair that was perpetually cut in an almost military fashion, closely set eyes that were usually moistly pink around the edges, and bushy brows that nearly met over his nose. His personal appearance was a source of pride to him, and he was meticulous about keeping himself neat and organized.

At least he had been until this morning.

What Norris found when he turned to confront his friend was a Mike Cooper unlike any he had ever seen. His face looked pouchy and bruised. His back sagged. And around his mouth, the deep wrinkles that some people called laugh lines were emphasized to absurd prominence by his coarse morning's worth of unshaved stubble.

He didn't shave! Norris thought. That's impossible. It's like the Pope taking a leak in the Fountain at Lourdes!

Cooper's shoes were thickly encrusted with fresh mud. His hair was dirty and uncombed. And the overcoat he was wearing—some kind of tweed thing that looked as if it had been dragged through a corn field—was buttoned right up to his neck. If Norris didn't know better, he would have sworn that Cooper wasn't wearing a shirt under that coat. He couldn't see the tips of a collar, and Cooper always—absolutely always—wore stiff white shirts with button-down collars.

"Whatever killed Woodie bit the walls, Bob," Cooper said. "What would bite the fucking walls?"

"You don't get it, Mike," Norris replied, not allowing the shock of seeing his friend in such a disheveled state disrupt his train of thought. "I'm not answering any questions without a lawyer in the room. I'm not letting you set me up again."

"Jesus," Cooper returned, placing his coffee on the TV tray next to him. "You're the one that doesn't get it. I 'set you up' to save your ass. Even though I was looking for Woodie all up and down Route 36, these good-old-boys found him before I did. You saw 'em when you got here, didn't you? They guys with the tan shirts and sunglasses—at night! Woodie had a notebook in his car, Bob. And your name's in it. I pulled you in as a favor, *old chum.*"

"You knew I wouldn't handle it," Norris said, softly.

"I knew you'd puke. Shit. So would I...I mean, if it was my brother, for Christ's sake."

"And they were there taking pictures..."

"Of you pukin' your guts out."

Norris was silent.

"Now, as far as these guys are concerned, you're a candy-ass Roger Ranger without an ounce of balls who couldn't possibly have anything to do with violent murder. Or at least I hope that's pretty close to how you're going to start out with most of 'em. But they aren't dumb, so you're gonna have to watch yourself. Keep as much distance between them and you as you can the whole time you're down here."

"The whole time I'm down where?" Norris asked, feeling a sinking sensation settling on his stomach.

"Do you want to know who killed your brother?" Cooper asked back.

Norris nodded.

"So do I," the detective said. "Now, sit down. You just got recruited."

"Into what?"

"Into the Church."

Norris didn't even breathe. With his left hand, he searched behind himself for the edge of the bed, found it, and settled his weight down on the squeaking mattress.

He was still in shock, and he knew it...he had to be.

Cooper apparently knew it too, so he went slow.

"I've never explained the department to you because it wasn't any of your business," he said, his face registering Norris' every move as tiny flinches in the muscles around his cobalt-blue eyes. "Officially, we're called the Division of Behavioral Comparison. But we spend so much time praying that the Church joke stuck. We do the bad ones. The ones nobody else wants."

Norris swallowed.

"We started in 1984 after an eleven-year-old girl was snatched and dismembered in this same Killibrook Valley," Cooper continued, lifting a briefcase from the floor and laying it across his knees. "They finally nailed the asshole who did it—and yeah, I called him the asshole, not the unsub, or perpetrator, or any of that shit...since I hate these guys...I hate them with all my heart. Anyway...they finally caught up with him in Minnesota, but only after he got three more kids.

"So, as a way to try to prevent such a thing from happening in Ohio again, our illustrious governor set up the Church to identify and track unsolved, violent pattern crimes nationwide. We're supposed to spot known creeps when they wander into the state, and warn the local cops involved. We don't have any real jurisdiction to make arrests, so no one has to listen to us. Which means that what usually happens is that the local cops just let us lay out what we know and then tell us to get lost; like a certain county sheriff named Conway did to me this morning in no uncertain terms...what a bastard."

From the briefcase, Cooper withdrew a sheet of newspaper and held it up. On the page, streaks of charcoal lightly defined a grey oval into which a darker, more sinister pattern was tattooed.

"Now, the Killibrook Valley's been pretty prominent in the Church's history so far. We were first organized because of a murder that happened here, and we've been back God knows how many times since.

"On the surface, that might not sound so strange. Any wooded area's bound to be a tempting spot for an asshole to dump a victim. And every state park in the country's got the same problem. But the Killibrook Valley's got it worse. And what's more, it's got this."

Norris felt a bead of sweat crawl down his spine as he mentally estimated the length of the imprint as...

"Two feet?" he gasped. "This thing's huge!"

Cooper nodded. "That bite was seven feet off the floor."

"There's nothing in Ohio...there's nothing in the country this big!" Norris said, "I don't think a grizzly bear's jaws span two feet open. And a bear's jaw wouldn't open like that even if they were. Those look…unhinged…like a snake…though snakes don't really unhinge their jaws. They have…well…"

"Your animal background's just one of the reasons I called you in this morning," Cooper said, his eyes narrowing. "Your experience with Woodie's the other. When he called me yesterday, it was only the last in a series of calls that started about six weeks ago."

"You make that sound suspicious," Norris interjected with a frown.

"It is."

"Are you telling me that Woodie knew something about this," Norris said, indicating the rubbing in his hand, "and that he came down here anyway?"

Cooper nodded.

There was a terrible pressure building up in the room that Norris was hesitant to disturb. If its subject would have been anyone other than Woodie, he might have just gotten up and walked away. But it was his brother's life they were discussing, and ruefully he was compelled to say, "Let's just have it, Mike. No more dramatics. Just lay it out."

Cooper seemed to understand.

Taking a deep breath, he released it slowly before saying, "Woodie told me that you were going to kill him."

Norris blinked.

Cooper's expression was relentless.

"It started in Cleveland. In a place called the Institute of Metaphysical Research."

Norris sighed.

And Cooper spelled it out…

18

"Woodie was into drugs."

That's how the detective began, and this came as no great surprise to Robert Norris. He already knew what his brother was like: he was into drugs, and booze, and losing sleep. He was into dreams, and ESP, and just about anything else that offered him a chance to "glimpse that weird section of reality that lurks in the corner of our perception." He believed that for everything the natural world presented, there was another, deeper meaning that was hidden so long as the observer was limited to a single, stable reference point. By altering the way a person saw things, he reasoned, it was possible to discover the true nature of the world.

That was Woodie.

He was nuts.

He was so nuts that Norris wasn't really able to communicate with him. After college, they had drifted apart, their contact with one another growing more infrequent as Bob pursued his forestry career, and Woodie followed the urgings of his persistent inner voice. Finally they didn't see each other at all anymore. From what Norris heard from mutual acquaintances, his brother had found a group of people who shared his way of looking at things, and from that moment, about a month from the time of his murder, he had disappeared, lost to anyone but his friends at the Institute of Metaphysical Research.

"I ran down that Institute of his pretty carefully," Cooper said. "I was worried about him. You know...I wanted to see what he was getting himself wrapped up in. What I found was that the place was run by a man named Green. That's all: just Mr. Green. He paid cash for an old titty bar in the Heights part of town and started what he called a learning center.

"He used advertisements in newspapers and magazines to invite the curious to free public lectures on shit from out-of-body projection to the prophecies of Nostradamus. At first attendance was sparse. But after every meeting there were always a few people intrigued enough to stick around and talk to him personally. Pretty soon, the Institute had twenty-some paying members, and private, invitation-only, Friday night meetings were added to the public, Sunday afternoon lectures.

"On Fridays they discussed *phenomena,*" Cooper said with a disapproving frown. "Woodie would go there and *discuss* these *phenomena* until he could hardly talk and had to go home to sleep it off.

"Peyote's what they did. It's a hallucinogen often used by Native Americans in magic rituals, and Mr. Green always had plenty. Woodie said that when he ate these peyote buttons, he experienced the most profound intellectual insights he'd ever had. And he wanted me to come and see for myself. We smoked a little shit together in college..."

This was a lingering sore spot between Norris and the detective.

"So my being a cop didn't prevent him from inviting me along. I guess he must have thought that I missed getting stoned or something. I didn't go, or course, but I did check out Mr. Green more carefully after hearing about his little parties."

Spurred on by his personal interest in the matter, Cooper described how he went all out in his investigations: Social Security numbers, credit check, police record, the whole nine yards. But every avenue he explored came up empty. Zero. Mr. Green was a blank, not so much as a library card. Becoming worried that there was more to the man than his happy bullshit sessions, with a little weed thrown in for his friends, he went to Woodie's apartment early one Saturday morning.

And what he found was frightening.

"He really looked like hell," he said, readjusting himself on his seat. "Really. I mean it. Like, bad. He'd lost a lot of weight, and the place looked like a dorm room: dirty clothes all over, dishes piled in the sink, crap everywhere. But his eyes were the worst. They were wild, like he was looking for something, searching, all the time. His real eye was red…and, I swear, his glass eye looked like it was red too…like it wasn't artificial anymore. Like it was a part of him, somehow…it was weird."

"Why didn't you call me?" Norris asked.

"Because you'd have beaten the shit out of him," Cooper responded.

Which was probably true.

What both men knew so well that neither had felt the need to mention it was that Woodie was the only person in the world that Robert Norris loved strongly enough to physically injure. He was notoriously straight-laced when it came to drugs, and he'd often beaten his brother bloody trying to straighten him out. In college, when these beatings failed, he went after the people supplying his brother's bad habits, so that, in the last year that Woodie was on campus, not one dealer would sell to him for fear of his brother's wrath. It was this great love that finally drove Norris from Woodie's company. He couldn't bear to see him killing himself, so, in defeat, he gave up and left him alone.

"I know you meant well," Cooper said. "But Woodie didn't need an ass-kicking. If I thought one would have helped, I'd have given it to him myself."

Norris half smiled. He knew Cooper was telling the truth—the detective loved his brother almost as much as he did.

"What he needed was help," Cooper continued. "Something was affecting his mind. Not just the drugs. Peyote's like pot. It gives you a sense of expanse, makes you feel like you're perceiving things on some deeper level. I knew that was just the kind of thing Woodie was looking for. But it wasn't enough to change him like that. No. There was something else happening to him. Something heavy."

Slowly, Cooper described the lethargic frenzy in which Woodie had let him into his apartment. The young man was jittery, and hardly able to contain his excitement. Forgetting any polite preliminaries, he explained that he looked the way he did because something "amazing" had happened to him the previous evening, something that was still happening, but which he couldn't yet explain.

They sat down, Woodie in an armchair and Cooper on the couch. A cluttered coffee table separated them, and in the air hung the heavy sweetness of old incense. Without prompting, Woodie had started talking about Mr. Green.

The man was awesome, he said. He was the most formidable personality he had ever come across. At first, he'd just thought that he was a typical crackpot, screwing around with psychic bullshit for the fun of it. But he was wrong. Mr. Green was the genuine article, and he'd taken a personal interest in Woodie after learning that the Norris family lived in the Killibrook Valley.

It seemed that the Valley was Mr. Green's major preoccupation. There was something about it, he said, something very important. As a matter of fact, he'd started the Institute with the very intention of assembling a first-rate investigative team that he could use to discover the secret hidden in those impenetrable trees. With Woodie on the team, there would be no stopping them. Together, they'd flush out the "evil forces" at work in the darkest recesses of the Valley's soul.

Hearing Woodie talk like this had frightened Cooper even more than the look in his eyes, and he sat rigidly silent as an intricately woven system of what he took to be delusions spewed from the young man's mouth.

"We need your help," Woodie had said, finally, fidgeting in his seat, hardly able to stay still. "We need you to use the Church's computers to chart the incidents of animal-related violence that have happened down home over the years."

He always called Harpersville, "down home," as if he were referring to Georgia or some other part of the Deep South.

"You've got to let us use your eyes, Mike," he said. "It's all about the way you see things. Understand?"

In his seat near Norris' bed, Cooper's face looked distastefully grim; as if remembering the urgency in Woodie's voice still unsettled him.

"I asked him how he knew the Church had facilities like that, and he said, 'Mr. Green told me. He knows all about what you guys can do. I told you, he knows everything. You can't get anything past Mr. Green. You wouldn't believe the things he's capable of.'

"Like what, specifically, I asked," Cooper said. "Which was exactly what he wanted."

The bluntness of the detective's questions had seemed to irritate Woodie, and a devious look came over his face. It was as if broaching so serious a subject as the powers of the great Mr. Green somehow diminished their importance, and yet, it was the very opening for which the young man had been so obviously waiting.

"You've been checking up on him," Woodie said with a cockeyed grin. "He knows all about it, but it doesn't bother him. He says that there's always a price to pay when one steps over the boundaries of everyday experience into the realm of 'apparent reality's' hidden truths. He accepts this. He's that kind of man.

"But if you want me to answer your question, you'll have to do what I ask by conducting the research Mr. Green needs to complete his studies. He could do it himself, but it would take time, and by cooperating you could save him years of work. If you do that for me, I'll tell you anything you want to know about him."

Cooper hesitantly agreed to this deal, saying he'd run Woodie's questions through the Church's computers on the condition that Woodie not see Mr. Green again until he returned with whatever information he could find. Woodie promised that he'd stay away from the Institute for a week, which was a lie and Cooper knew it. But he hoped that playing along with Woodie's request would buy his friends in the Narcotics Division enough time to dig up something with which to nail this Mr. Green and shut down his Institute for good.

During the following week, the guys in vice went over the area with everything they had, putting pressure on local dealers, a few users who had talked to the cops in the past for dope money, even the pimps who seemed to know everything about everyone in the neighborhood, but on every attempt they came up dry. The Institute of Metaphysical Research was clean. No one had ever supplied anybody associated with it with drugs of any kind, and no one had ever even spoken to the mysterious Mr. Green. Other than Woodie's verbal insistence that peyote was being used on the premises, there was nothing that anyone could identify that would physically link the place to illegal activity.

Cooper knew that he'd need more time to get to the bottom of this problem. He also realized that he'd have to produce the information for which Woodie had asked or risk angering him into future silence. So the Friday before he was supposed to see Woodie again, he spent a late-night session on the Church's computers. And what he discovered was, quite frankly, a revelation...

"Whoever this Mr. Green is," Cooper said, leaning forward in his chair, "he's apparently right about his assertion that there's something seriously wrong with the Killibrook Valley. The place is like a killing field: murders, rapes, mutilations, all stretching back as far as police records go, and all scattered around without a pattern or a focal point other than the one provided by the actual forest itself. The area's so big that unless you were specifically looking for it, the concentration of these episodes wouldn't be apparent. And the number of reports is low enough that the time between each one would allow for a cooling-off period that would erase any apparent connection in the local cops' collective mind.

"But when I set up a search parameter using the park as the confines of the search, and allowed for an association of episodes that happened miles apart, in different jurisdictional districts, the computer constructed a neat little graph showing a distinct, seasonal relationship between reported violence and the boundaries of the Valley—a graph exactly like the one you'd expect to find if you had a full-fledged, completely functional homicidal psychopath calling this area home."

"Which means what?" Norris asked, against his better judgment.

"Which means that, whether I liked it or not, Woodie seemed to be getting himself caught up in something that looked, at least on the surface, like it was real. This Mr. Green character looked like he might actually be onto something. There were even a few moments there when, looking at the printout of all those killings, I could actually imagine some kind of 'thing,' human or otherwise, running around loose down here...or even a whole family of...whatevers...given the extended time frame of the data-points."

"So, what did you do?"

"The next morning, I showed Woodie my report."

Norris' expression betrayed what a mistake he thought that had been.

"I thought that it might scare him off," Cooper continued after a guilty pause. "But it had exactly the opposite effect. When he looked at those numbers his eyes went wide and he got all excited.

"'This is fantastic!' he yelled at me, jumping up from where he'd been studying the file I'd spread out on his coffee table. 'It's just like Mr. Green said! Oh, Mike, man, you're a saint!'

"That morning was the last time I saw him alive."

Cooper finished his story in cold, precise tones that proved just how deeply he felt his responsibility for what had happened to Woodie.

"I waited a couple of days, and then I called his apartment. When I finally went over there, his landlady said that he hadn't been home since Saturday, and that nobody had seen him around. I checked his job, and he hadn't been in there either. So I went down to the Institute, but the place was boarded up tight. Shut down. Gone. I ran every check I could but it was no soap. Woodie had disappeared and I was scared.

"At ten last night, I'd just gotten my nerve screwed up enough to call you when my phone rang. It was Woodie, and he was in trouble.

"'Mike!' he says, real close to the phone. 'I figured it out, and now it's gonna kill me! You gotta help me, Mike! It's Bob! For Christ sake, I never would've believed it, but it's Bob! He's gonna let the beasts from the woods come out! He's gonna kill me, and he's gonna kill you too if we don't stop him! He'll kill everybody, and the worst thing is that *he won't even know he's doing it!*'"

Cooper looked into Norris' eyes with naked contrition.

"His voice was panicky, really flipped-out. But he was alive! And for a second, I was relieved. I tried to calm him down, listened to what he had to say, and was just about to hang up the phone when he said the two things that have been sticking in my mind like thorns.

"The first was that he had a diary with him, right there in the phone booth. He said that he'd put it together so that I'd have an explanation, even if he never got out of the Valley. He said that it would explain everything and that once I saw it, I'd understand.

"'Be careful with it,' he said. 'It cost me my life to write.'"

"Was that his diary in the car?" Norris asked curiously.

"I guess so," Cooper replied. "But it's really more of a theory, I'd guess you'd call it...a lot of rambling bullshit about some kind of energy linking different members of your family from one generation to the next. Crap like that.

"But," Cooper continued, seriously, "the second thing he said he had with him was much more important. It was a girl. That's what he called her. Just, 'the girl.'"

"'I've got the girl with me,' he mumbled near the end. 'So they'll be after me for sure. Without her, it's no good. None of it! It's no good! They'll do anything to get her back, so if you don't come—like right now, Mike—I'm dead meat!'

"Whoever *the girl* is, she's a witness," Cooper added, clenching his hand. "Together, she and Woodie were running for their lives. But he still stopped the car long enough to call me and talk like he was crazy...totally spaced-out. Even though I was sure that he was stoned, there was still something in his voice that told me that whatever was happening to him wasn't just in his head. So I hung up and took off.

"I was careless, Bob. I guess that's what it all boils down to. I guess that's what I wanted to say to you, face-to-face. I should've called the cops down here and had them run him down. I should've taken precautions. I should've treated it more seriously. But I didn't. I just told him to take it easy, and that I'd meet him wherever he said. But he never showed up. I'm really very sorry."

Norris lifted his hand as if to wave the apology away as unnecessary.

"I waited for him for over an hour," Cooper continued, softly. "And then I started driving up and down Route 36, looking for his car. Apparently he ended up here at the motel at about midnight.

"At one-fifteen, Sheriff Conway responded to a disturbance call, notifying the local hospital and calling for a pretty hefty backup. I just followed the noise on the radio. As soon as I heard that 'man down' call, I knew I had fucked up royal."

He sighed and stared at the floor for a moment. Then he looked up and added, "Sheriff Conway had to get a key from the motel manager before he could get in the room, so Woodie must have locked the door. This animal, unless he opened the door for it—which I doubt he'd do—must have been waiting for him inside.

"Supposedly this was a random stop, at a random motel. He got a key to a random room, walked in, locked the door, and found something waiting that tore him apart and then jumped right through the goddamn window, since the glass was all blown out, not into the room...leaving his female companion to disappear into the night—or carrying her off. If it didn't take her, she can't be far since Woodie's car is still here.

"So when you're ready," he concluded, handing Norris a large yellow envelope, "here's everything I've got so far: photographs of Woodie's body, detail shots of specific wounds, body position, schematics of the layout of the room, pictures of footprints, and an outline of events as I know them.

"Study it. Work on it. You know the people down here and the lay of the land. These local cops think you ain't got a backbone so they'll probably leave you alone. Sticking around to ask a few questions, maybe tagging along behind a deputy or two to see if they're any closer to finding out who killed your brother, and why, won't be seen as terribly unusual. Especially with you being a park ranger, which I'd imagine is like being in the National Guard to these boys…like playing Army. They'll leave you alone, and you can find the girl."

"Why me?" Norris asked.

Cooper snapped his briefcase shut, placed it on the floor, and rested his elbows on the arms of his chair.

"Listen," he said, seriously. "I don't know what Woodie stumbled on down here, but according to my computer's profile, whatever it is has been around for a very long time—like over a hundred years. It can't be a single man working alone, that much is clear. We may have a family of psychopaths who, for generations, have been tearing people to shit themselves, or breeding some kind of dogs to do it. Or maybe it's a fucking family of man-eating bears. Maybe it's anything…but whatever it is, a dope peddler named Mr. Green sent Woodie down here to find it, and it killed him while I was driving around with my thumb up my ass.

"Now a bunch of Tractor Pull enthusiasts is going to try to sort things out. I've got a platoon of really good people, and a truckload of state-of-the-art equipment waiting to help me back at the department, but I can't use any of it because I don't have the jurisdiction. But that's not going to stop me this time. This time, I'm getting involved. This time I'm making the arrest…and you're going to help me do it.

"This is your neck of the woods, and you're a hunter. I'd do it myself, but I'm a realist. I was born and raised in the city, and I don't even have a real pair of boots. I'd be lost in ten minutes. While I was fucking around, precious seconds would be ticking away. I could let Conway handle it, but I want the collar for myself. So that leaves you.

"Find the girl for me, Bob!" he concluded, rising from his seat. "Get out there and do what you know how to do better than anybody down here. Get out in those woods and find that girl."

"But, Mike," Norris protested, weakly, looking up at his friend. "I'm not a cop."

Cooper's lips were bloodless when he answered, "You are now."

And then the sound of something exploding ripped through the morning air so abruptly that it made both med jump.

The sound was a harsh one…

A blast of concussion close by.

The sound was a deadly one…

Like a shotgun going off across the yard.

19

As Norris emerged into the new-morning sun, he expected to find policemen running toward the sound of shouting. What he didn't expect was an angry sheriff, waiting for him in the snow.

But that's what he got.

The transformation of the motel from a nightmarish, mist-enshrouded oasis of eerie, flashing lights to an unassuming barracks squatting beneath a bright blue sky, had occurred during the time he had spent locked in his room. The sun was up, and a luxurious layer of new-fallen snow reflected its vivid rays, making the yard a painful glare in which four men stood shoulder-to-shoulder in a single, dark smudge not ten yards away.

It took his eyes a moment to adjust to the light. But once they did, the sheriff's face became unmistakable.

Norris knew him.

And the man knew Norris.

Sheriff Conway was short and thin, with blondish-grey hair. He stood with his feet firmly set on the ground, his back erect, and his eyes, which were little more than a pair of black slits against the sunshine, were riveted on Norris' face. His left hand was hidden in the pocket of his tan vinyl jacket, and his right held a notebook that was apparently Woodie's diary.

But where the sheriff's visage remained statue-like and unmoving, the three deputies who accompanied him—two to his left and one to his right—reacted to Norris with animated expression of…

Fear!

He was stunned.

To a man, the three dropped their jaws and stared at him, taking a single, reflexive step back and moving their hands nervously over their arms as if, beneath their heavy coats, their skin had begun to itch.

Somewhere behind them, shots were fired: sounding like tiny pops cracking off the frozen Valley.

Neither the deputies nor the sheriff reacted to the sound. But Cooper moved his head back and forth a couple of times and shouted, "What goes on here?" which seemed to break the spell. Blinking, the deputies stumbled backward, turned, and ran toward the motel's office: the apparent source of the original shotgun blast, as well as the subsequent pistol reports.

Other men were running.

Cooper drew his gun.

And Sheriff Conway pointed a lean spike of a finger at Norris' face, saying, "I won't let you do it. This time, I'll kill it."

These words made Norris' blood run cold, because, somewhere beneath the veneer of his conscious mind, he seemed to understand what they meant. In that instant, a brief, almost mystical contact seemed to occur as this old sheriff reached into Norris' soul and touched it with a threat so chilling that it made something physical happen inside his skull. Suddenly he felt the echoing reverberations of some haunting, distant knowledge—some memory long hidden, and yet complete—calling out to him from the misty haze of forgotten years. It seemed familiar, in a disturbingly insubstantial way that reflexively he tried to ignore...

But couldn't.

No more than he could ignore the sensation of heat—real heat—throbbing at the center of his fist. Without his having thought to do so, his hands had sought out Woodie's eye and was squeezing it in his pocket, protectively containing the warmth that was now climbing up his arm.

Whatever expression he wore, it was apparently the one for which the sheriff had been searching because, before turning to follow his men, the older man smiled and snapped his fingers as if to say, "Gotcha!"

Then he was gone, and Cooper had Norris' arm.

"Stick close, Bob," he said, leading the way. "I don't like the sound of this."

Together the two men approached the motel's office, Cooper clutching his gun and Norris walking stiffly against the tugging on his jacket sleeve. Around them, all motion ceased as the last deputy disappeared inside the motel and a strange stillness settled on the yard. The only sound was that of snow crunching underfoot.

At least until they reached the office door.

And then things started up again.

The door's lock had been smashed, leaving broken, splintered wood. Just as Cooper was about to step through the door, a series of shouts made him freeze, and two white-faced deputies burst from inside, one holding a hand over his mouth, the other brandishing a hunting rifle. They rushed past the detective, stuttered on the ice, chopped their feet a couple of times, and then split up, one breaking into a full run for the patch of parked cars at the lot's south side, while the other remained, slack-jawed and staring at Norris like a kid at the zoo.

In seconds they were followed by more, even less organized officers.

"Goddamn!" someone shouted from within the depths of the motel.

"Sweet Lord Jesus!" someone else said.

"I wish Emil was here with his dogs," yet another man observed.

A truck's engine fired up and tires hissed as the first deputy maneuvered his pickup out of the lot.

Men thundered down the office's three wooden steps and dispersed into the yard.

"Fucker hauled ass!" someone said, laughing, raising a hand to his brow, and watching the pickup disappear in a roiling, snowy ball down the road that connected Harpersville with State Route 36.

"I can't say as I blame him," someone responded, darkly. "But Conway'll have his balls for sure."

Another car started.

And the sheriff appeared, squinting.

"Get out and find it," he said to the deputy standing closest to the stairs. Then he turned to Norris and added, "You…park ranger. This way."

Norris could feel the eyes of the sheriff's men on his back, and Cooper's presence at his heels as he followed Conway into the gloom…

And into the smell.

The air was heavy with it: a swirling mix of gun smoke and gore that wafted from a hall that was even darker than this living room/kitchenette, with its stained linoleum and ragged carpets. It permeated the place in sweet-and-sour waves, insinuating itself deep into Norris' stomach by climbing down his throat, nauseating his body while stimulating his mind with the first specific memory in that faceless group that had been teasing at him from the past…

He'd seen this already!

He'd dreamt it!

This had been the dream from which Cooper's telephone call had summoned him not five hours before. This room, this place, and this fear—all were familiar…all were as they had been when…

"No," he whispered, his feet stalling on the floor and his

hands working out before him.

There would be eyes next!

He'd seen them!

Eyes!

Conway's face filled his vision.

"He said that you'd *know without knowing*," the sheriff said, holding the notebook under Norris' nose. "What did he mean by that?"

The younger man's lips moved, but no words came out.

Two very large deputies emerged from the hall at the sheriff's back and stood, bouncing their rifles in their hands and staring at Norris with expressionless eyes. Their presence seemed to add a new and more immediately threatening atmosphere to the room that motivated Cooper into taking a step forward and saying, "Listen, you can't just threaten this man like a criminal."

But Conway cut him off by raising his open palm and looking Norris straight in the eye.

"I knew you were coming," he said, inflecting his words with a tone of conspiratorial menace that seemed to color the very air. "I could feel it. When the first of it started, I knew, like I do sometimes. We lost some animals...and then we lost a lot more than that. It weren't like a normal winter comin' on, when the dogs out in the Retreat get all starved and go a little crazy, maybe get a little mean and start killing food, 'stead'a waitin' for it to die on its own. Something told me that this time things were different, right from the first. Something told me that *this* time Bobby Norris was coming home."

Norris' hand returned to his pocket.

"And here you are," the sheriff said. "And here we are...and there Mrs. Cray is, lying in her own blood. What done it to her, Bobby? In your brother's book, he says you'd know."

Norris could feel his face beginning to twitch. It was a condition he had suffered since childhood: when he got really upset, the muscles around his mouth and eyes tensed up and started to spasm, producing little puckers in his expression that looked as if he were about to cry. He could feel those twitches starting now, but he couldn't stop them. He couldn't even bring himself to try. Instead, he squeezed his fist around the hot ball in his jacket pocket, felt a wire of heat twist up his arm, and saw, in the pit of his brain, a brilliant white flash that seemed to detonate when that heat hit the base of his skull.

"He used the shotgun," he stammered, unthinking, as a sudden blare sounded in the parking lot, followed by the roar of a truck's engine leading to a terrible crash. "He put it…in her mouth."

The two deputies at the bedroom door lunged forward, brushing past Norris on either side and knocking him back. He bobbed like a puppet, his eyes fixed ahead as his lips moved and the sheriff's expression darkened to a deep, almost purple red.

Outside, men were shouting.

Someone ran past a window.

Two shots were fired.

And Cooper turned to follow the deputies out of the room.

"The shotgun," Norris whispered, taking a zombie-like step forward as the eye in his pocket pulsated and the light in his head obscured everything but the images dancing there.

Sheriff Conway nodded fiercely, his fixed attention livid as he spit, "It's true! After all these years, that son of a bitch was right: *you can see it*!"

Norris wasn't listening—he'd entered the hall leading to Ernie Cray's bedroom…the hall, so dark and threatening, through which he felt as if he were passing from one world to another, like a birth…

Or a death.

Which is how the roomed smelled inside: like death.

"Go ahead, then! Look at what you did!" Conway said, quite loudly, as he ran out the door and into the yard, where all hell had broken loose in a din of screaming tires, shattering glass, and men shouting and shooting their guns...

But the noise didn't matter...not to Norris...not here.

The noise...

There was always so much noise...behind him, where he had already been. Memories were the noises that he carried in his head. They followed behind as he blundered forth into the silence...

Into the trees.

He was standing alone in the doorway of an eight-by-ten room that was almost identical to the one in which his brother had died. On the bed was another body, but unlike Woodie's, this one didn't interest him. He'd already seen it...seen what had been done to it—in his mind, when the wire of heat emanating from Woodie's glass eye had found his brain and brought back his dream.

He'd already seen old Mrs. Cray, in her pink flannel nightgown, her hair knotted into a hundred tiny curls that were fastened to her head by a perfect cross of two plastic-tipped bobby pins each. He'd seen the way her fat arms flopped unnaturally over the sides of the bed, all the skin between the shoulder and elbow gone on them both, and the exposed muscle thick with blackly clotting blood. He'd seen the torn flesh hanging in ribbons, and the way her eyes bulged from their sockets, seemingly fixed in death upon the crucifix hanging on the wall. He'd seen the angle at which her head was held by the barrel of an old shotgun: rammed down her throat so far that the trigger guard smashed her nose to one side. And he'd seen the incredible, insane mess that had been made of her stomach and thighs when the shotgun had been fired.

He'd seen all this earlier, and it didn't surprise him now.

He'd seen it all…

And he'd seen the eyes!

As he moved forward, tiny pieces of something soft oozed underfoot, and a breeze disturbed the layer of smoke where it hung about four feet from the floor. The bed was on his right, and a window was on his left, its glass shattered, its view full of trees: nothing but snow-covered trees. There was a flowered chair lying on its side out there. That's what had broken the glass: a chair, being heaved through it. There were a lot of footprints in the snow around the chair because the cops thought the killer had fled that way.

But they were wrong.

Because the killer had eyes…

Eyes that filled the sky and followed a man everywhere he went in shadowy, fleeting slivers of half-imagined memories. Eyes that seemed to define a man's mental landscape, watching from behind the eyes of others: friends, lovers, brothers. Eyes that knew everything, but that revealed nothing.

The killer had eyes…

And the killer had not fled.

Norris stopped at the foot of the bed and watched as, three feet before him, the closet door swung open…slowly.

"Hail!" came a voice, gurgling, soft, rumbling from the depths of darkness contained in the coffin-like confines of the closet space.

Something was in there—something big, and hunched, with half of its form hidden behind limp tongues of hanging garments, and the other half obscured by shadow. All of the beast that was truly visible in that blur was the twin, matching flashes of its terrible, yellow eyes.

Those eyes burned.

And seemingly in response to their fire, the eye in Norris'

pocket burned as well—so hot that he had to grit his teeth and concentrate on not letting it go.

"Hail to thee, Blood Prince!" the voice growled. "Hail to thee for thine kin!"

With these words, Norris' knees abandoned their charge, and for the second time since his arrival in Harpersville, he collapsed.

At almost that same instant, there came a rustling, followed by a smear in his vision that he knew was the thing in the closet, moving. It happened fast—so *fast*! The voice—mucus-thick and bloody-slow—sounded like the auditory equivalent of a gnarled root, buried in mud. But it bore absolutely no relation to the way its possessor maneuvered itself from its hiding place. In a flowing, watery motion that, in his retched posture, Norris couldn't even follow with his eyes, the thing was out of the darkness and up on the windowsill, where it squatted like a gargoyle, its hands gripping the frame on either side of its face, and its head thrust boldly forward.

"At last you've come!" it leered with an obscene grin. "And bearing the stone!"

Norris' head jerked up, and from where he knelt, he saw the twisted figure of what had once been a man, perched in the window. Darkened almost black, and fuzzed all around by the harsh, silver blades of winter sun, the creature's limbs were thin and knobby, its skin wrinkled and strangely unfocused, as if a layer of soft, downy hair covered it in some place, while patches of a more coarse, bristling fur dripped wet and hot in others. There was something...wet...something wet that was twisted and pale on one side and red on the other...like skin...the skin from Mrs. Cray's arms, braided around its waist like a belt, with the knot positioned just below the thing's navel. The hair on its head hung low. Its testicles dangled brazenly between its legs. And its face was a nightmare...

It was Ernie Cray's face.

Norris had known him, once, a really long time ago.

It looked like Ernie Cray...

Turned inside out.

"Bring out the stone," the thing demanded, a thread of saliva crawling down its chin. "Bring out the stone, and show it to the sun."

The twitching in Norris' face had infected the rest of his body, and there, on his knees, he trembled uncontrollably. Inside his head an eruption was building. He could feel the molten mass of his thoughts boiling at his brain's core, and the pressure it created crushed his lungs. He could feel his body shake, and the tears on his cheeks. He could feel his hand, withdrawing Woodie's eye and holding it up to the light.

And he could feel the thrill of it!

The charge of sheer power!

He didn't understand its source, or its purpose, he wasn't even sure that it was directed at him. All he knew was that suddenly, he was in the presence of *something big,* and that just its proximity was enough to change him, and the world, forever.

Held between his thumb and index finger, Woodie's eye came alive in the light, reflecting the sun's rays in sharp, hypnotizing flashes so pure that they positively demanded attention. They burst and died in a kaleidoscopic torrent that expressed itself in unfathomable geometric patterns as he altered its angle to the light by rolling it between his fingers.

And then one reflected ray caught Woodie's eye just right and a light-beam bridge was formed to Norris' left pupil, driving what little breath he had left in his lungs out in a gasp and filling his head with a dazzling brilliance in which he saw...

A woman.

As if her image had been seared directly onto the tissue of

his brain, he saw her face and body with such clarity that no detail went unmarked. She was tall and statuesque; beautiful, in a vaguely European way, with high cheekbones, milky skin, and incredibly long blond hair that fell down her back in a wave as thick as a horse's tail. Her spine was arched, her feet were planted wide on the rampart of some great, old house, and her arms were at her sides, palms forward as she lifted her face to the sky. Overhead, a full moon hovered eerily in purple mist, dripping effervescent layers of light that seemed to fall from space, directly onto the woman's skin and into her eyes.

At the sight of her, Norris felt a tremendous swelling of pure desire.

Never in his life had the image or thought of another human being affected him so completely with such a blinding, physical lust as did this woman, with her flowing grace and light-trapping flesh. He wanted her, needed her, longed for her so desperately that an ache grew in his groin that he was certain would kill him if she should elude his advances. He could feel himself reaching across the featureless depths of space itself to find her, to hold her, to possess and enfold her in himself, for she was meant to be *his!* and he would kill anyone who tried to keep them apart.

But then, in a staggering flash of insight, he knew with absolute certainty, that she would not elude him. That one day he would consume her, every bit—flesh, blood and bone. He'd take her into his belly and drink of the moonlight in her place, just as she was drinking now...

Because...

She wasn't human.

She was an illusion, an artificial female shell born of evil and ripe with a violent potential that was the very essence of the animal. She radiated an aura of danger, attracting what invisible spirits there were in the surrounding air unto herself like a magnet.

And suddenly, Norris knew that the air was full of such spirits.

They danced on the moonlight, giving to his vision a sense of wholeness—an inexorable unity that made the sky, the moon, and this lady in the woods all separate pieces of one, single entity, fused solid by the milky light that tainted everything it touched in ways still secret after eons of its influence.

The moon was evil!

Beneath its silver glow, the landscape became enlivened with a dreadful feeling of foreboding, a powerful directness of purpose simple, and yet beyond Norris' human ability to contain...

He saw all of this in a single heartbeat...in a single, gleaming instant during which one beam of sunshine caught the smooth, hard edge of Woodie's eye and shone into his own, straight on, so that his arm locked where it was, and his mouth dropped open.

And somehow he saw that too.

He saw himself, holding something...and it wasn't an eye anymore. It was something old and beautiful—something that other men had held before him, for almost as long as there had been light to catch its facets. Perhaps it was a gem. Or just a stone made special by perfect polishing. Perhaps it was a piece of the brilliance it so magically reflected, a chip of the sun itself, made solid by some miraculous mistake or design and sought for centuries by men who wanted nothing more than to hold it, and to *see*!

And then the thing in the window aid, "Now come!" in a voice so personal that it intruded on Norris' thoughts and left him feeling violated in some brutal, intimate way.

He blinked, and his head spun.

He drew breath, and the room swayed.

He lowered his arm, and the beast in the window pointed down at him and said, "Come to the trees, Robert Norris. You know the way. Come to the trees, and find yourself!"

Then it was gone.

Norris didn't even see it go.

It simply disappeared, flowing with a grace and purpose so much beyond the human as to be almost absurd.

"He said that you'd 'know without knowing,'" Sheriff Conway had said Woodie wrote in his book, and Norris suddenly understood exactly what those words meant.

If there would have been anything of substance left in his stomach, he'd have lost it in that instant. As a matter of fact, he almost regretted his inability to vomit now. He would have welcomed the sense of cleansing, the feeling of removing everything from inside himself and being left empty. Because this moment was the beginning...he knew...

Without knowing.

It was coming back.

He could hardly make himself move.

But his will was strong, and calling on every bit of it, he rose from the floor, and without so much as glancing at it again, he replaced Woodie's eye in the dark folds of his jacket pocket. Then he surveyed the room for a moment, and crossed himself over the corpse of Mrs. Bernice Cray, his second victim...

Woodie had been his first.

"Blood Prince," a shadowy face hovering over his head seemed to say in his mind.

He frowned.

Blood Prince.

Madness was a terrible thing.

Without another word, Robert Norris left the room and headed out to where he had left his Bronco...in the motel's parking lot, where men were still shouting, shots were still being fired, and all the noise of memory remained, draining him back from the impenetrable silence of the trees.

20

"'It can't be true!' you said!" Sheriff Conway shouted as he caught up with Detective Cooper, halfway across the yard. "Well, do you believe it now?"

Cooper didn't respond.

And how could he?

Around him, men were running toward where a pickup truck was smashed into the side of the ambulance containing Woodie Norris' corpse. In the snow behind the truck, tire tracks led directly across the lot to the wreck, without so much as swerving, as if the driver—who was presently slumped over the steering wheel—had maneuvered his vehicle into the ambulance *deliberately.*

Cooper was concentrating on that man's profile and trying to ignore the rush of thoughts flooding his mind. But inside his skull, he was hearing the insane, impossible things the sheriff had told him about Bob Norris, and the one, screaming sentence that would not stop running itself through his consciousness, over and over again.

He'd read it on the first page of Woodie's diary. He'd read it while the awful wound on his stomach burned, and Sheriff Conway stood, aiming a flashlight and making steam in the cold night as he whispered the words that still rang in his head as the harbingers of evil.

They said:

"For you, whoever you are, this is my *die*-ry. Read it and *die*, for soon *the moon will be full!*"

He'd known, at that instant in which he had raised his

eyes to meet Conway's steely gaze that the sheriff knew so very much more than he did about Woodie Norris. He could see it in the man's expression, but even now he refused to really believe all of what the sheriff had said…

Until the man behind the truck's wheel snapped his head and turned to face the detective, stopping him in his tracks. For a split second their eyes met, and then the man made Cooper believe everything by grinning madly, slamming the truck into reverse and swerving backward, right into a pair of approaching deputies who screamed and tried vainly to dive out of the way.

"You fucker!" Cooper shouted, raising his gun. "You meant to do it!"

The two men kept screaming while one crawled on his hands and knees in the slush toward where a police car was parked, and the other rolled in a ball, back and forth, pressing his forehead to his knee and leaving a terrible red stain on the snow beneath him that glistened almost black every time he moved.

Conway was waving his arms.

Cooper drew his sight on the pickup's cab.

And the driver turned to face him again, frantically working the gearshift through a gale of laughing howls.

He's crazy! Cooper thought, involuntarily holding his shot. He's completely out of his mind.

Just like the sheriff said.

A man leapt onto the back of the pickup, and his body tumbled in a flail of waving arms and legs as the truck lurched forward. In an instant he was up again and moving toward the front compartment, his gun drawn and his balance unsteady.

The truck performed a perfect doughnut, settled into a roaring charge, and then made a beeline for a gaggle of deputies huddled close together near the motel office.

The man on the back of the truck had on hand on the cab, but to Cooper's amazement, once he was settled, he turned and began shooting back at the deputies they had just passed. He went right on shooting until the truck slammed into the side of the motel and his body was thrown over the cab and onto the Chevy's hood.

Someone grabbed Cooper's shoulder just as the truck's rear window exploded into a million glittering chips and more shots echoed from around the yard. Before his amazed eyes, the truck was overrun with ugly black holes as deputies poured round after round into its sheet metal and, apparently, its driver.

The hand on his shoulder was Conway's, and roughly Cooper shrugged it off. There was a roaring in his head and when he spoke, he screamed.

"How can it be?!?!"

Conway's expression betrayed his utter bewilderment.

"What difference does it make?" he shouted, waving his arms as if to indicate everything around them as one, complete example.

Then the truck was moving again.

With a grunt, Cooper threw himself into the sheriff, knocking the older man back. Rolling over so that he came up on one knee, Cooper locked his pistol arm and braced its elbow with his other hand. The truck roared past not five feet to his right, and as he held his breath and focused his complete attention on the driver's bobbing head over his gun's sight, it swerved abruptly backward, toward where the wounded man still rolled in the snow.

"You're gone," he hissed, feeling his arm slam with impact two times...

Then four...

And six.

The truck's windshield went white with insane, lightning bolt patterns of splintering glass. Almost instantly, its front wheels turned hard and its body lurched up as if it would leave its chassis, careening within inches of the man in the snow and ending its assault where Cooper had seen it begin: rammed into the side of Woodie's ambulance.

The impact was anticlimactic, but a split second after it happened, the man on the ground screamed, "Fuck yeah!"

Cooper's hands were shaking, his neck was sweaty, and his heart was singing in his chest...but it skipped a beat when, with his arm still upraised, he saw, close to the blur of his gun, Robert Norris, his friend and—at least according to Woodie's book—the cause of everything that had happened so far, step unsteadily from the motel's office, squinting in the sun. He paused, surveyed the lot, and began walking, with single purpose, toward his truck.

Upon seeing Norris, Cooper's skin seemed to go into immediate convulsions and, mindlessly, he began scratching his arm.

Conway was heading toward Norris' Bronco.

Cooper ran behind.

In his mind he was going over it: his arrival in town, his first meeting with Conway, the things the "witness" had said...

And the sheriff's solemn announcement that "this ain't exactly the first time I had trouble with the Norris family, especially the boys."

Cooper hadn't been surprised to hear that the Norris boys had been familiar to the sheriff of the town in which they had been raised. Woodie was wild, and the detective imagined that he had probably gotten into quite a bit of trouble when he was younger.

But he *was* surprised to hear that Conway wasn't talking about Woodie. He was talking about Robert, the other brother...the woodsman, college graduate, and member of every animal protection and ecology outfit in existence: the good one, in other words.

"He practically made me crazy, him and his father, for years, when I first got on the department," Conway had said, his eyes sparkling a weird, iridescent red as the light of an ambulance revolved through an open door, making Woodie's body appear to squirm on the floor. "His father told me that the boy's got the woods in his blood—that's he's wild. Not like his brother's wild: boozing it up and chasing girls. Bobby's father said that he was *really* wild, like an animal. Or at least that's what he said."

And that's what the sheriff believed, as it turned out: that Robert Norris was somehow dangerous, just being himself. That just being near him could prove harmful.

"That's why I was so goddamn glad to see him move north," he had explained while they waited for Norris to arrive after Cooper's call.

"That's it!" Conway was screaming as Cooper reached him. "We're gonna finish it *now*!"

Norris didn't hardly even seem to hear him. He was calmly rummaging through a pile of stuff in his truck's front seat, apparently moving things from one bag to another, as if he were packing. His movements were easy, and his expression placid. He looked very much like a man who had made a decision.

"Goddamn it! Talk to me!" Conway screamed, reaching out as if he intended to spin the younger man around.

In midair his hand stopped, and standing behind him, Cooper could feel the tension that stiffened the sheriff's body.

Norris straightened himself up and turned around.

"Bob," Cooper said, hoarsely. "What is it. . .I mean, really. . .?"

"It's bad," Norris responded, sliding a rifle from off its rack behind the driver's seat and picking up the backpack he'd just filled. "Believe me, if you only knew the half of it. But there's nothing you can do or say, Mike. You're going to have enough trouble while I'm gone just keeping things together here. I'd imagine that they'll make it very difficult for you now that it's begun."

"Now that what's begun?" Cooper found himself shouting.

Conway began running his hands over his upper arms.

Norris' face took on a sadness unlike anything Cooper had ever seen. It was an emotion so deep that it seemed to alter everything about his features, making him look almost completely different than he had...as if he'd been changed: really changed. In his eyes there was a jumble of hidden responses that seemed to be arranging themselves for some kind of reaction. But just when Cooper believed that his friend would let it out, that there was something there to release that he could understand, a darkness fell over his face and he said, "Lock yourselves inside."

Then he headed back out across the lot. Pausing at the wrecked pickup truck, he glanced inside and motioned with his head.

"See?" he asked.

And Cooper, following behind, looked in to find that the driver was gone.

His mouth fell open.

Men scattered as Norris approached the woods, swinging his knapsack and resting his rifle on his right shoulder.

Cooper had never really seen him so much in his element before, he realized, amazed at his perception and the fact that he'd had it now. But Norris looked...well, he looked *good.* He looked like a man at peace with his surroundings. His tall, lean body, dark, piercing eyes, and sandy, soft hair, all flowed together seamlessly as he ambled along. The closer he got to the trees, the more alive he seemed to grow, until, when he reached the very edge of the woods he turned, and Cooper found in his expression the logic of their relationship: Cooper could follow no father because he didn't belong where Norris was going.

"It's a woman, I think," he said, as if fulfilling an obligation. "I've seen her, and I think that she might even be Woodie's 'girl.' Although I can't be sure."

His narrow eyes drifted, far away.

"It's all coming back to me, as I think it was intended from the first. It doesn't make a lot of sense right now, but I suppose that it doesn't have to."

Cooper's composure was all but ruined. He could feel himself quivering in his spot, and to his amazement, an almost unbearable urge to fall to the ground and to avert his eyes nearly overcame him. It was a reflexive, innate sensation, and he had to consciously force himself from succumbing to it.

Norris' cheeks flushed a little as he lifted his arm and waved it at the motel yard saying, "Hide them from the moon."

"Bob...oh, Jesus, Bob!" Cooper stammered, straining to take just one step toward his friend.

Norris' expression squeezed in tight.

"I thought I knew you," Cooper said—as Norris had said an hour before.

"I guess that we were both wrong," Norris responded. "Now listen: you said that these are my woods. And you don't know how right you were. Whatever has to be done here, I'll have to do it alone. You can't help me. No one can. So you'll just have to do your best here. If I'm not back before the sun goes down..." His voice wavered. "If I'm not back...then leave."

He's crazy, Cooper decided, silently, experiencing a sense of loss so deep that it nearly choked him. *He's crazy just like his brother. Just like the sheriff said he'd be.*

"I can't let you go, Bob," the detective said, trying to

summon up his *official* voice. "I've got to explain."

"It's too late for that, Mike," Norris responded with a sad shake of his head. "Now, go back to your kind while there's still time."

Cooper raised his hand.

In it, he held a gun.

"Good bye, Mike," Norris said, turning.

"You're under arrest," Cooper said, feebly.

Norris took two steps into the woods, threw his knapsack over his left shoulder, and skipped over an icy log.

"Stop!" Cooper begged, trembling.

Norris didn't respond.

Cooper squeezed his teeth together, drew his sight squarely on a spot between Norris' shoulder blades…

And watched him disappear into the gnarled tangle of the silent, frozen trees.

He just watched him go.

And then he turned to face the parking lot, where Sheriff Conway was waving into the woods two big men wearing heavy, white-and-green splotched jackets. They carried knapsacks and rifles, and each had a walkie-talkie dangling from his belt. The sheriff watched them carefully slide into the tree line moments after Norris disappeared, and a grim look of satisfaction hardened his expression. Lifting a walkie-talkie of his own, he gave the one-word command that would send two more two-man teams—one stationed about a half mile due north, and the other waiting an equal distance to the south—into the woods. These teams would use radio contact with the lead team to triangulate Norris' location. Then they would follow him, even though they all had a pretty good idea of where he was going. They would follow him, and he wouldn't even know they were there. From here on out, he would be under constant scrutiny, no matter where he went.

He wouldn't escape.

With a sigh, Cooper realized that, despite a couple of unforeseen complications, everything was going more or less according to Sheriff Conway's plan. He didn't know how he had done it, but the man had apparently arranged things perfectly.

21

After saying *the words,* Ernie Cray launched himself from his bedroom window and plunged into the welcoming embrace of his beloved forest. At almost the exact instant that his feet hit the snow, the process of transformation that had begun while he was still in bed with his wife started into its next phase. He stopped, lifted his head, and smelled the air.

Blood.

The aroma delighted him, and he nearly succumbed to his desire to chase, tear, and kill. He could feel the urges welling up from inside of him like a fever. It seemed as if there were a spot—behind his heart, maybe—that was sending out pulsating, sonar blasts that vibrated the fluids in his brain and made it hard for him to think…hard for him to do anything but listen to the demands of his nature…

Which were Wild!

Before the transformation, he'd been a louse…a real low-life bastard—even by the relatively relaxed standards of a mind-your-own-business town like Harpersville. His sins were basically private ones, directed at his wife, who he treated like a dog. The only time he did anything out of order in public was after he'd been drinking the moonshine he bought from some of the boys who made it up in the woods. Store-bought liquor was easily available, and in some cases even cheaper than the homemade stuff, but Ernie was of the old school, and preferred good, solid, corn "squeezins" to anything that came in a bottle with a fancy label. There was a mystique about moonshine, a special essence that started with it name.

They called it moonshine because it was made at night by

men who used the moon for light. And because, when swirled in a cup outdoors in the dark, it shone that same whitish-silver pale of the moon itself. The story went that good moonshine liquor, the kind made by special men taught by their fathers, was more than just alcohol. It was liquefied moonlight. . .the pure, untainted tincture of night that reached to a man's soul and withdrew the pieces of his most carefully concealed personality in a way that nothing else could. Not even "white lightning," which, to a connoisseur, was a different proposition altogether.

Moonshine was an almost holy thing, and the men who drank it were devout. Not everyone could handle it, both because of its strength, and because of the things they might discover about themselves under its influence. When Ernie drank it, the ugliest foulness of his soul emerged in full flower, and for a few glorious hours he wallowed in the depravity that was at the heart of his being.

For Ernie Cray was one of those not-so-rare people: a born brute, a throwback to an earlier time when mankind was a little closer to the woods and depended more heavily on the tooth for survival. Once, men like him, possessors of the *blood spark,* were valued for their ferocity. They were the hunters, the killers, the warrior princes. They were the beasts in disguise that protected the tribe, or fought for the king, and the appetites that came with their fierce natures were tolerated. . .and fed.

But that was long ago.

In modern times civilization constrained men like Ernie, confining their Wild natures with stringent laws that threatened punishment and death for any who engaged in behavior that just a few hundred years ago had been valued and encouraged. Cowed by overwhelming odds—because in nature the sheep always outnumbered the wolf—the ancestors of those who had once ruled by the fang became society's frustrated, secretly angry outsiders: watching with red, predatory eyes from behind the obsequious placidity that marked the Flock's members. But inside, these people were like raging furnaces, just waiting for the proper fuel to send their flames burning out of control. Fuel like good moonshine liquor, made right, that would let a man do what was in his soul, and then enable him to deny responsibility for his actions because the booze had made him *a little crazy*.

But that was all over now—at least it was for Ernie Cray. What was inside him was coming out, literally and physically. Something had come to Harpersville—something so powerful that just its proximity was enough to change him, to alter him in ways that he had never thought possible, and to release his animal's soul. Whatever had come was so powerful that it would have made the change possible even without the belt he had made from his wife, he realized. But he was glad he'd made it anyway.

For a moment the blood smell intoxicated him, and he wavered in the trees like a drunk, gripping a branch so as not to fall. In this posture he paused and listened for the voice that had come into his head when he had perched himself in his former bedroom's window—he'd never sleep indoors again—and spoken the words he had been compelled to utter to the great man kneeling on the floor.

Suddenly a spasm overran his limbs, and he quaked with its impact, grinding his teeth together and squeezing his eyes shut as a powerful surge of energy ripped through his body. Its source was the same place from which the words that had filled his mind had come—a specific location, transmitting invisible waves from deep in the forest that reached out and worked a kind of magic on his body that fully brought his insides out.

He groaned, released the branch he'd been holding, and clutched his stomach. Staggering in a knock-kneed circle as a sticky stream of viscous black bile spewed from his lips, he dropped heavily to the ground and rolled in the snow, smearing himself with mud and his own waste beneath the sun, which blazed maddeningly through the dark, tangled branches that swirled overhead. His mind exploded…not with the sequenced progression of impulses that he would have called thoughts before the onset of the change, but with a shattering miasma of sharp, vivid images, like snapshot pictures of frozen moments in time. There was no logic to this flood, no unifying theme that might link them together and create one identifiable impression. It was as if he'd been sucked inside another, greater consciousness, and was seeing the most violent contents of that being's memory, piecemeal, and all at once.

Its impact was even more profound than the convolutions wrought on his body, and, face pressed firmly into the soaking mud, he screamed through a gurgling, nauseous wretch that scissored his torso nearly in half and bent him into a tightly held fetal position.

When his scream died, the second part of his transformation was complete, and lifting his head he saw the world through new eyes…

And was dazzled.

Every movement, down to the most minutely insignificant detail, attracted his attention with a reflexive speed that was as fast as the firing of a nerve. No integration of information occurred, no filtering of impressions through a complex, distracting system of human preconceptions muddied the simple purity of his sight. He saw his surroundings as an animal would see them: precisely as they related to himself. He was one with his environment, as if external reality had ceased to be the incomprehensible puzzle that he, in his human egotism, had striven to manipulate, becoming instead an extension of his own, physical being. Moving through these trees would be as natural as breathing, and just as easy.

Though he was still lying on the ground, his head suddenly jerked up as a movement snatched his attention. A man in a ragged tan uniform appeared, stumbling from tree to tree as if in a daze. The human portion of Ernie's mind recognized him as the deputy who had driven his pickup truck away from the motel earlier, only to return when his own transformation had begun—but the animal part of him instantly identified the man as not yet altered...he was still essentially human, and as such, he was prey.

Ernie lifted himself into a half-crouch and snarled threateningly at the man, focusing his attention on his soft, white throat, but holding himself back from the attack until he saw in which direction the man's nature would turn.

The man froze when Ernie growled, his face slackening into a rubbery, twitching mask of comic confusion as the air seemed to swell with the renewed push of the energy pouring out from the trees.

As Ernie watched, the man doubled over and yowled through the metamorphosis that he, himself had so recently endured.

If there had been more humanity left in him, he would have been repulsed at the gush of black fluid running from the man's mouth. He would have been awestruck at the viscosity of his skin as it quivered over him in startling ripples that contorted his face and locked his muscles in a crucified posture of sheer rigidity. He would have been horrified at the thick, crushing sound of flesh being literally vomited up in a bloody, bulging bubble that swelled the man's throat and pulled his stomach into a concave cavity that made his ribs stand out beneath his wet shirt like the skeleton of some twisted, broken ship.

But the part of Ernie's human nature that might express such feelings was dead, and he watched impassively, unimpressed with what he saw, save for its being the proof he needed that this man was not to be feared, but welcomed as a Brother in the Blood.

The deputy gurgled as the transformation progressed. He swayed and clutched at himself, ripping his shirt to ribbons in blind agony and twisting his head forward as a huge black membrane burst from his mouth and rolled his face back over his skull, exposing a bloody red pulp of raw meat, overrun with an intricate map of gorged, blue and red veins and arteries. He fell, as Ernie had fallen, pulling himself into a thrashing ball as the exterior of his body turned itself around, revealing a moist skin of prickling hair while finger- and toenails thickened and cracked. He writhed in the muddy snow until finally the change was finished, and tentatively he raised his head, as Ernie had done, to sniff the air.

The human in him had been pushed back, but had not fled his form altogether...not yet. Even more power was needed for that final change. And that power was yet to come. So, for now, his limbs and body still resembled those of a man, though overall he was heavier and more thickly muscled than he had been before. At his groin, a carpet of black fur surrounded his dangling penis, and that hair seemed to spread out, over the rest of his form, thinning as it went until, along his back, it degenerated into a sparse sprinkle that dotted his still moist flesh. Hanging off him at his elbows were ribbons of tissue, like a ruined placenta, and when he moved, there was an animal surety to his limbs that was dangerously free.

But though his body might have still retained is essential humanity, his face revealed the extent to which he'd been transformed. When he stood, his head hung heavily at the end of a deeply matted neck, his face's features were swollen with bloody hair, and his mouth was wide and strong. Beneath his black lips ran a row of long canine teeth, stretching, it seemed, from one ear to the other. His eyes blazed yellow beneath a heavy ridge that sloped straight back to a crown of segmented bone from which ropes of muscle ran to the jaws. Everything about this new arrangement seemed wholly designed for the act of efficient and powerful biting. And as if test their purpose, the man snapped has jaws three times before focusing his eyes warily on Ernie, as if he were waiting for whatever might happen next.

Ernie didn't keep him waiting long.

In a rush he was on his feet, moving with such incredible speed that the forest around him blended into a single blur. Just as quickly, his newfound brother leapt aside, and in an instant they were circling one another, growling, snapping their huge jaws, and breathing deep of the musky aroma of wet fur and blood. There was an exuberance to their investigations that was pure and innocent. Like two dogs they barked at one another, attacked and jumped back, muzzled and bit—all playfully, but with a deadly earnestness that Ernie sensed could explode into true combat in an instant.

After a time, the other man broke and ran, and Ernie followed. Silently they skimmed through the woods with a nimble precision that took them a mile and then back before they stopped, their tongues lolling and their noses running behind great puffs of frozen mist. The end of their run had deposited them about a hundred yards behind the Lexington Motel, and through the trees they watched as a third creature, freshly changed like themselves, worked his way down the ridge.

When the three were together, a closeness was created, and they knew, without speaking—for words were now alien to their thought processes—that they were the first...after hundreds of years...the first to return to the Wild.

Ernie was the largest and oldest of the males, and as such he instantly assumed a role of dominance. Throwing back his great, hairy head, he emptied his lungs in a roar that shuddered his chest and exploded through the trees like thunder. The others watched him quizzically for a moment and then offered their own voices in a chorus of howls that blended into a music so chilling that animals for miles froze in their tracks and urinated where they stood.

The Singing had come again!

After generations of silence, the ancient Song of the Wild was again floating through the forest while the singers rejoiced in the knowledge that they had finally become together what they had always secretly been apart...

When the Singing stopped, Ernie Cray glanced at his companions and, in that telepathic way of animals communicating with their own kind, made his wishes known: there were men at the top of the hill...men in the motel. There were unwitting, fleshy members of the Flock within striking range...probably huddled together, as was their nature when startled by the Song...

Imagining them so—for that human quality was still his to enjoy—Ernie, the leader of this small, dangerous pack, suddenly found himself bursting with a gnawing, overpowering hunger that marked this morning, and this moment, as that time when, after countless peaceful nights, the Hunt would begin again.

And then the pack moved in.

III

DIE•RY

FOUR

22

As Cooper turned from watching the sheriff's men enter the woods in pursuit of Robert Norris, the events of the previous evening were vivid in his mind.

It's really amazing that so much could be so clear, and so little really revealed by it all, he thought, realizing that if things hadn't gone so seriously wrong, the idea of six big, armed men following a single, unwitting park ranger into the woods so they could stop him from becoming the werewolf king would have struck him as being very funny.

But not now.

Now he was scared.

After the cemetery episode had come the discovery of Woodie's mangled body in the Lexington Motel, and Cooper had been swept from one scene of bloody murder to another, stubbornly protesting, both verbally and in his mind, that what they were witnessing was the acting-out of a violently deranged group of insane people, and not, as the sheriff insisted, the resurrection of an ancient and frightening evil.

Everything he saw, from the weird, ritualistic motif of Lefty Zimmer's dog's-head soup, to the outlandish explosion of violence aimed at Woodie Norris' dead body, all served to verify his theory about drugs being at the heart of some delusional construct that was impelling the members of the Institute of Metaphysical Research along their dizzying spiral to madness.

But those same ghoulish signals, so clear to the detective, simply fueled Sheriff Conway's belief that there were real Vyrmin running around the town, and that they only way to fight them was some ridiculous plan of his that had something to do with behaving like a dog.

"'Cause see, a dog's really the way you gotta look at this," he had said in a room next to where Woodie's body lay. "'Cause only a dog's smart enough to protect the flock in a pinch."

That was after midnight.

And by then, Cooper was pretty well shot…

✡ ✡ ✡

He'd nearly frozen to death at the cemetery, poking around for "clues" with the other deputies, and finding a shitload. But nobody, least of all Sheriff Conway, seemed to have the slightest idea of what to do with any of them. It was like a silent comedy, all shot in jittering black-and-white, with jerking movements and an outlandish plot that not even its participants could possibly take seriously.

Somebody would find something and shout, "Hey! Look'it this!" And the sheriff and Cooper would jog over and Cooper would say, "Great! A boot print; make a plaster cast of it and we'll see if it matches up with any of the ones we found around the horse's carcass at the Zimmer farm."

And Conway would shrug it off and say, "Fuck it. We already know it'll match. And besides, a boot's a boot. What we really need is the print of a bare foot so we can see if they're still human at all."

And Cooper would roll his eyes and hiss under his breath and just go on, weaving between the tombstones, in the mist and snow, with a silver moon poking through the clouds overhead and a sinking, deep-gut feeling settling in his bowels that no matter what, things couldn't possible get any goofier than this.

Only to discover that he was wrong…

Because, shortly after midnight, a red-faced yo-yo that Conway had sent back to his office to "man the phones" came squealing the tires on his van up the path to the caretaker's shack and shouting out the window, "We got us another one! Holy shit!"

Which of course turned out to be Woodie.

The sheriff's reaction to Woodie's death was surprisingly reserved. Especially after the way he'd huffed and puffed at the cemetery. Cooper expected him to turn purple and have a stroke when they walked in and found Woodie splashed all over the walls. But instead, the murder of Woodie Norris seemed to have an almost calming effect on him. It was as if by dying, the younger Norris had somehow put something into focus for the sheriff, making him less confused and therefore, more rational.

But Cooper reacted quite differently. While Conway was calmly examining the room, the detective, until now the sole advocate of sanity and deductive reason in the bunch, broke down and cried. He just stood in the doorway of that motel room, clutching his wounded chest and bawling his eyes out for what must have been a good ten minutes. It wasn't until the sheriff literally led him out by the arm that he was able to stop.

Twenty minutes after that, sitting on a cheap motel bed and sipping coffee that tasted like lacquer thinner, he listened to Conway drop his bomb.

"I want you to call Bobby Norris down here. And when you do, I want you to tell him this," he said.

And then he proceeded to tell Cooper, word for word, a story in which Woodie made a terrified call from a phone booth, raving about beasts chasing him, and everything being his brother's fault.

Cooper, after ten respectful seconds of stunned silence, laughed in his face.

And the sheriff, with all the reserve of a priest, reached out and slapped him so hard that it made his right ear buzz.

"Now we'll go over it again," he said, as Cooper raised a hand to his burning cheek.

And they did.

Again.

And again.

Until Cooper finally made the call, at three in the morning, that brought Robert Norris rushing down to his old hometown, because something bad had happened to his baby brother, and his good old pal Mike Cooper was on his side, and doing him a favor.

As Cooper hung up, the sheriff put a hand on his shoulder and smiled, saying, "That was good. That was real good. I 'specially liked the part about it being 'bad.' That made it sound authentic."

And Cooper shrugged the older man's hand away, suddenly feeling a little sick at his touch.

After that, Conway seemed to think that he owed the detective an explanation. It would take Robert Norris at least two hours to arrive, and the sheriff apparently wanted Cooper on his side when he finally did show up. So he sat the young man down, folded his hands, and said, "While you were fuming back at the jailhouse, I made a coupla calls. One was to the man who married Bobby Norris' mama. His name's Datch, and he's a head doctor."

"I know," Cooper said, disinterestedly. He was quickly coming to the conclusion that he didn't like Sheriff Conway…not one, single bit.

"Dr. Datch wasn't none too thrilled to hear from me," Conway continued, despite, or maybe because of, the detective's tone. "I asked him about Woodie, and he was a little evasive until I kinda spelled things out for him. Gave him some bits and pieces. Maybe hinted that there might be trouble."

"You threatened him."

"Okay." The sheriff shrugged. "If you wanna get technical…but it verified something I already knew, and put some things in perspective."

"Like what?" Cooper asked, despite himself.

"It wasn't Woodie in that car the night his father was killed," the sheriff answered, with all the appropriate dramatic candor. "It was Bobby."

"You're nuts," Cooper replied, sloughing off even the suggestion as absurd.

"You're wrong," Conway insisted. "I was there, remember. I pulled that kid out myself."

"But Bob told me that Woodie lost his eye in that accident."

"Woodie's eye came out two years later. He fell off a bike."

"But Bob told me…"

"According to his stepfather," the sheriff interrupted, "Bobby Norris is about the most remarkable case of defensive memory loss he's ever seen. He even kept a notebook on the boy. Used to hypnotize him and everything. Called it 'screen memories,' which, as far as I can tell, means that the boy subconsciously rearranged his life to hide a painful event instead of dealing with it."

"I know how a screen memory works. I had a professor who called them *scream* memories. And they are notoriously unreliable."

"Maybe so…but they're logical, when you think on 'em a minute. Supposedly Bobby was the reason they were out so late in the first place. Datch says that Bobby sees his daddy's death as being his fault...'cause of his dreams."

"Dreams?"

"He's always had bad dreams, since he was born, it seems. Used to wake up screaming, night after night. Went on for years. Finally, according to what Bobby's mama told her second husband, his daddy couldn't take it no more. He started trying to find out what was wrong with him...started taking him to doctors."

The way the sheriff inflected the word "doctors" caught Cooper's attention and made him frown.

"But they weren't regular doctors," the sheriff went on, apparently aware that he had hit the detective a little closer to home.

"According to Mrs. Norris, her husband was afraid that there was something seriously wrong with the boy, something maybe, inherited. See, Robert Norris, Sr., he didn't know too much about the Vyrmin or such like. Like I told the boys before, his daddy disappeared up in the woods when he was just a little guy, and by the time he was grown, there hadn't been anything funny going on for so long that he didn't hear too much about his family's curse. Oh, he got it a little from the kids at school, but that went away over the years, and the next thing you know he's a normal, everyday kind of guy with a wife and two sons, one of which has an occasional bad dream like a lot of kids do, while the other never sleeps a single night through without screaming himself awake.

"Not a single night. Not a one.

"So he starts to study on it, and he finds out that, yeah, his family did have a history of being a little odd. Matter of fact, his mama, who wasn't all that old then, told him that she had met his dad in Columbus, but that he had brought her back to Harpersville just after they got married. Told him how folks treated the family like lepers. Told him all the stuff about his daddy that she probably swore to herself she'd never tell, but that she knew she would someday, because someday he would ask. He'd have to.

"So he found out and got worried. There had been plenty of signs by then. Started about the time of his sixth birthday. But he never paid it no mind. Other folks did, a little, 'specially the older ones. But he never paid it no mind...until his boy started to slip. And then he did everything he could think of to help him. But he couldn't just go to a regular doctor and say that he thought that maybe his son had inherited the family curse. So he started sneaking out at night, sometimes driving from sundown to sunup to get to doctors way out of town, barging in at all hours and paying crazy amounts of money for them to look at Bobby and say what they thought.

"That's how he ended up gettin' killed. It was on a night like that."

"How did Datch find all this out? About the doctors, I mean," Cooper asked, genuinely interested now.

"Bobby told him."

Cooper's eyes narrowed.

"Datch hypnotized him and he told the whole story. Mind you, if you'd asked him while he was just awake and normal, he'd know nothing about it. But when the doctor put him under, he told it, in detail: all about his dad's drinking too, and some of them doctors who weren't all that on the up-and-up...about some of the awful things they did to him while his daddy sat drunk in a dark waiting room. And about the last doctor he saw, on the night his daddy was killed...it was that last doctor who told him what he was."

"Yeah? And what was that?"

"The Blood Prince."

"He said that?"

The sheriff nodded.

"He said that. . .in those words?"

The sheriff nodded again.

"I don't believe it."

"Datch don't got no reason to lie, and he says he's got tapes of the kid sayin' it when he was eight or nine years old. He took it to mean that he had developed some kinda guilt complex over his father's death that ended up gettin' twisted into a kind of buried megalomania where he confused his own actions with the impact they have on others. Somehow, he ended up deciding that he's capable of killing people, just by thinkin' 'bout it, 'cause—and this is the kicker—the dream he'd been having the night they went out was about his daddy dying when his head hit the windshield of his car. I guess that when Datch asked him to describe that dream, even while he was in his trance, it made the kid cry. That's how bad it was."

"So he thinks he killed his own father?" Cooper said, draining his coffee cup and, at least for the moment, forgetting that there was a dead body in the room right next door.

"Not 'thinks,'" the sheriff corrected. "Subconsciously he's convinced he did."

"So to screen that, he came up with this artificial memory in which it was Woodie in the car, and not him," Cooper mused aloud. "I never even though to question it. I mean, why would I? He never really talked about it. And Woodie never mentioned it at all. Christ. . ."

"Now you wanna hear about the Dr. Green who his daddy had taken him to see the night he died in that accident?"

"Dr.—"

'Green."

Cooper stared. "Coincidence" he said after a pause.

"Description fits," the sheriff nearly whispered, leaning in very close. "The boy's description of that last doctor fits exactly with the one you gave me of the Mr. Green from Cleveland, and the one I could give you of the Mr. Green who brought his Indian Diggers into my town. It fits, Mr. Cooper, right down to a hair."

"So what's it mean?"

"It means that, when Bobby gets here," Conway replied, "we better have our stories straight if we're gonna use him to get to the bottom of this thing."

So they got their stories straight, and Cooper repeated the scenario about Woodie's midnight run, calls from the phone booth, and eventual murder to his friend both over the phone and in a motel room later that morning. The only part that was not completely fabricated to roughly match the evidence Norris would see was the part about Woodie's diary. That was real. They'd found it—a half-filled spiral notebook of spaced-out ramblings—in the backseat of the Pinto, written in a shaky, apparently hurried hand. Its contents were convoluted, at best. But having heard everything he had about werewolves and Vyrmin legends from the sheriff, Cooper recognized at least a portion of what Woodie had written down. And he had to admit to himself that, whether he liked it or not, the sheriff seemed to be on the right track. So he went along with the lie. He repeated the scenario as his emotions ebbed ever closer to the boiling point until his temper broke, as Cooper had known it would, and he picked up his gun and headed out to find his brother's killer.

Just like Conway said.

"That's the key, Mr. Cooper," the sheriff had emphasized. "We gotta think like dogs. We'll give the wolf some runnin' room, and then just let him lead us right back to the pack's lair."

"That's assuming he knows where it is," Cooper cut in.

"He knows," Conway assured him gravely. "Believe me, Mr. Cooper. He knows."

☆ ☆ ☆

But now that the deed was done, Cooper couldn't stand himself. He stood at the edge of the parking lot, watching the trees sparkle with freshly settled snow beneath a brilliant, white winter's sun, and the shadowy, closed-door conspiracies and archaic bogeyman stories of the wee morning hours all took on an aspect of absolute fantasy in his mind.

And worse.

They took on the aspect of betrayal.

"Let me explain," he shouted into the hole in the woods where Robert Norris had disappeared. But there was no reply. "Bob! For Christ's sake, listen!"

And then he turned.

"Goddamn it!" he spit, slamming his revolver against his thigh when he found Conway, standing about thirty feet away, near the center of the motel's parking lot, holding a walkie-talkie near his mouth.

His attention was fixed on the older man's face, and a sneer crept over his upper lip.

"You son of a bitch," he hissed, lowering his head and aiming his eyes forward from beneath furrowed brows.

The sheriff, too far away to hear Cooper's words, still seemed to catch something from his expression because, as the detective began walking his way, he lowered his walkie-talkie and stared.

Cooper took five steps, froze, and turned back around.

"We'd better get inside," Conway called from across the lot.

"Wolves?" Cooper asked the air, astonished, straining his ears to pick up every bit of sound. "In Ohio?"

The call from the Retreat was unmistakable. Even a city boy like him recognized it. From the trees, it coiled like an auditory serpent, moaning in a single, baleful voice before falling, only to reemerge as a chorus of howls that chilled his blood.

Conway was suddenly at his side, taking his arm.

The howling went on a moment longer and then stopped.

"Wolves?" Cooper mumbled again.

There weren't any wolves in Ohio. And there hadn't been for over a hundred and fifty years. Sure, one was spotted in New York State, or Michigan every now and then. But those were just wandering down from Canada. On the eastern half of the continental United States, the wolf had been hunted to extinction as a pest. The last one to be killed in Ohio was in 1832. He'd seen a microfilm of the newspaper article about it when he was in college, complete with an accompanying photograph of the proud hunter—baggy pants, handlebar mustache, and those dark, beady eyes that everyone in old pictures seems to have—standing with his musket next to where the animal hung by its hind legs from a tree.

The howling stopped.

Cooper felt Conway stiffen for a split second and then hiss, "Shit!" before pulling him by the sleeve.

The detective stumbled, half fighting the tugging on his jacket and sensing the motion, speed, and imminent, unstoppable approach of something in the trees. It was a feeling of undeniable momentum, of natural, animal power, and in a weird, inappropriate way, he found it beautiful. He couldn't see, hear, or smell anything. It was just a tingle in his gut and a shudder up his spine. It was something electrical maybe…

But whatever it was, Conway apparently felt it too, because he became frantic.

"Move, damn you! Can't you see the Hunt's begun?" he shouted in Cooper's face, making the young man turn and examine him as if he were an exhibit.

"What did you say?" he asked.

And the sheriff suddenly looked as if he'd forgotten the

entire English language—just now, this second, forgotten it, the whole fucking thing.

"I..." he began, standing perfectly still. "I...don't know."

And then they were both running. Their minds didn't have any say-so anymore. Their bodies took over, and they were running across the parking lot, screaming for the remaining deputies to grab whoever was wounded and get them the hell inside the building because...

The "because" burst into the sunshine at that instant, and as members of the Flock have done for thousands of years, when confronted with the wolf in the flesh, every man in that little courtyard stopped what he was doing and started with his mouth open, paralyzed by fright, just long enough for the hunters to begin their attack.

23

When Robert Norris heard the howling, he too stopped in his tracks. But for him, it was a very different experience than for the others, because…

He understood what the wolf song said.

Not in words. It wasn't exactly words that he heard. Instead, it was a kind of instinctual, natural sound, like the patter of falling rain or the moaning of the wind that, without articulate definition, described an event so intrinsic, so acutely attuned to the logic of the wilderness, that the imperfection of human language stood as a feeble approximation by comparison. This sound emerged from that wellspring from which all language, or the very concept of language, had been drawn. This simple, animal howl said more in its modulated way than all the words he had ever been taught, and communicated with a part of his spirit that he had suspected was there only in those most perfect moments when he would stand amid the trees and feel the presence of God in His works.

It stalled his forward progress and took command of his senses, driving from his mind every intention he had developed, replacing them with a pure and crystalline confusion that expressed itself most eloquently in the stunned silence of his limp, gaping mouth, which hung open in a breathless O. It chilled him to the bone, and he listened, enraptured, as that first solo voice fell off and a chorus of three voices took its place—primitive, timeless, and in an equally wordless way, expressive of a simple, yet complex concept that he would have thought of as *harmony* if his mind had been capable of pulling that word from the dictionary in his skull.

Three-part harmony.

He closed his eyes.

Three, acting as one.

As if in a dream, he reached into his pocket and withdrew the vibrating ball of heat that was his brother's artificial eye. When it hit the light, a weird, tranquil stillness descended on his thoughts, radiating up, through the very bones in his arm.

He heard the wolf song shimmer through the blackness in his mind, and in a vague, echoing way, the sense of it came clear.

Joy.

The song celebrated.

Joy...at a return.

Joy...at simply being.

Joy...at release.

When he opened his eyes, he found that his right arm had lifted Woodie's glass eye up over his head.

"Let me explain," his friend Mike Cooper had shouted after him as he first entered these woods, and there had been a moment, a brief, flashing instant, during which Norris had considered turning around and giving the man his chance. But that had been a red moment, an instant of passion when he was still a furnace of vengeful hate, seething at a fever's pitch with images of his brother's dead body, and a moment of purpose—a purpose unlike any he had ever felt before in his life. He had been about to turn and give the man his chance, but the wolf song had interrupted it, and now it seemed that that moment had occurred a million years ago. For now he was locked in a tenebrous place between the song of the wilderness and the pulling—no, the absolute demand—of his body. He wanted to lift his eyes to the thing he held aloft in his hand and feel, as he had felt before—in the room in which a woman had lain, dead below a cloud of sulfurous smoke and supernatural dread—that contact with...something...he didn't know what...

But it was something...big!

He could feel the eye in his hand, screaming to his most secret placed to *look at me!*

And he wanted to look.

But a part of him was terrified at what he might find should he actually do it.

He wanted to look.

And despite it all, he did.

And as sunlight hit the eye, he was suddenly somewhere else.

But more...

As the sunlight hit the eye, he was suddenly *someone* else...

And a woman was crying.

24

The first beast emerged from the Retreat in a flurry of perfect motion and energy. The sight of it staggered Cooper where he stood, and he had to reach out and take Conway's arm so as not to fall. His knees felt weak, but worse, his brain was protesting in his head, squirming, as if it wanted to get out, as if it wanted to just push itself through his ears and go scurrying across the parking lot in a mad rush to return to the place it had been before it had ever heard of Harpersville, Ohio, and the terrors that seemed to give the place its own horrendous identity.

Conway's brain apparently was performing similar convolutions because, in that same instant, the sheriff reached out and grabbed Cooper's arm and, together, they stood, tentatively supporting one another as reality itself seemed to slip into memory.

"It comes in bloody rage and deadly grace," the sheriff said. And Cooper, despite his already overloaded mental switchboard, recognized the archaic diction of the man's pronouncement, and was intrigued by it.

"Why are you talking like that?" he asked, and he meant more than the words inferred.

He meant, "Why is your voice so calm? Why do your words sound so right, so appropriate, so fucking natural? Why, and this is the big one, Mr. Sheriff of this shit-box town, oh yes, this is the big, sixty-four-thousand dollar question, why, with all of it, do I believe they're true?"

"I don't know," the sheriff said, and somehow that was no more than what Cooper had expected.

Then he turned his head and saw the first of the Vyrmin

emerge into the sun glare of a December morning, bursting forth from that shadowy wilderness that was the Killibrook Valley, into the hard truth of a new, serious reality in which the things that howled in the dark suddenly were make flesh in the light and...

Conway and Cooper hugged one another and stared.

They were standing at the edge of the Retreat with the trees at their backs. The first figure darted up from a patch of brush about twenty yards to their right. From their vantage point they saw the parking lot stretch for about forty yards before it ended in the steaming wreck of the ambulance and pickup truck. There were five or six men clustered aimlessly around a body lying on the ground there, and one man was leaning against the ambulance, his arm crooked in a bloody, improvised sling. Before anyone could make a sound, the group scattered like birds, dark against the white snow, and another creature appeared, moving in next to the first from the left. A third soon followed, and the three formed a line between the deputies and that place where Conway and Cooper stood like a pair of embracing lovers, startled by an unexpected porch light.

They're impossible! Cooper's mind screamed.

No!

No-no-no-no-noooo!

They looked kind of like apes: their legs were short and muscular, covered with hair and tipped by what looked like paws, but with fingers. Their arms were heavy and started at hunched shoulders. When they moved, their heads, shoulders, chests, and arms all swung as one in whatever direction they wanted to look, pivoting on those tiny legs as if brain and body were one single spring, looking for something at which to snap. Their hands, as big as shovel blades, hung dangerously at their sides, the fingers opening and closing, opening and closing, and...

"*Noooooooo!*" Cooper screamed, shattering the moment and making Conway jump. "Oh, Christ in heaven…that face!"

The creatures glanced at one another ever so briefly, and then, as if perfectly choreographed, the one in the center leaned forward and growled out a hideous warning toward where the sheriff and detective stood, while the other two turned and chased after the fleeting deputies. Finishing his howl, the center creature hesitated just long enough to see Conway lean back and drag Cooper behind him into the woods, before turning to join his companions.

The creatures had to be a good thirty yards behind the deputies, but an instant after the first two turned, Cooper saw a bright red flash and knew, as the ground beneath his feet disappeared and he felt himself tumbling backward, that one man had already died.

How?

How could they move so fast?

How?

"That face!" he shouted, struggling against the strong arms that gripped his coat as he stumbled, fell, tumbled, and then scrambled for his feet. "The one in the middle! My God, it looked like that old man…"

"Ernie Cray," the sheriff offered.

"Yeah!" Cooper said, pulling himself free and rolling suddenly in a ball.

The Retreat was very steep at this particular place, and without Conway's steadying hands, Cooper went sliding on the ice and frozen ground, crashing into brittle, sapling trees and bouncing off larger trunks until he was able to get a hand around a substantial elm and arrest his untethered motion. Breathing hard, he hugged the tree, closed his eyes, opened them, and tried to get to his feet again as a scream—a very human scream this time—shrieked from overhead.

But, before he could lean into his climb back up the way

he had just slid down, Conway came duck-shuffling from tree to tree and grabbed him by the collar, pulling him down again.

And someone else screamed.

And Cooper took a swing at the sheriff's head.

And the next thing he knew there were stars flying and he was falling again and when he landed and looked up, the sheriff's face was about two miles wide in his vision and a voice that sounded as if it were coming down from heaven itself boomed in his ears. "Don't fight me, Vyrmin. Your destiny lies in these trees!"

And Cooper found this sentence uproariously funny, and, there on the ground, staring up past Conway's face into the sun, he laughed, loud, hard, even while the sheriff slapped him, two times, and three, and…

He kept right on laughing.

As he brought his knee up into the sheriff's groin…

And then Conway wasn't slapping him anymore.

25

There was a woman crying, there, in the dark, although he didn't know if it was dark where she was crying. All he knew was that it was dark where he was hearing her cry.

Because of that sound, but even more so, because of that darkness, Robert Norris suddenly felt a strange surge of order come muscling its way into his thoughts, through the jumbled mess of impressions he had been bombarded with since first seeing Woodie's body in that motel room, and for the first time in hours, he actually tried to understand what had been happening to him.

That process of thinking settled him silent.

"What in the righteous hell is going on here?" he thought, in the dark,

He was in the woods, for Christ's sake! Cooper had tried to stop him with an explanation, but he had ignored the attempt and had gone sauntering into the woods to...

What?

Find Woodie's girl?

Find Woodie's killer?

Find...

"Come to the trees, Robert Norris," the thing in the motel window had said. "You know the way. Come to the trees, and find yourself."

Find...yourself?

If he had had eyes, he'd have blinked. But he didn't have eyes. He couldn't have. If he had had eyes, he would have seen more than this blackness. Even with his eyes closed—if he had had eyes to close—he would have seen more than this blackness. This blackness was total, complete, and suffocating.

It filled him, and surrounded him, and gave him only one thing...

The sound of a woman crying.

He knew he was standing in the woods, not more than a half mile down the south side of the Retreat overlooking the Killibrook Valley. He was holding a hunting rifle in one hand and his younger brother's glass eye in the other. He was wearing his park ranger's uniform: light tan pants with a forest green stripe down the side of each leg, big hiking boots, and a forest-green jacket. And he knew he was holding Woodie's eye up to the light again—although he didn't know why. But he was doing it...

Out there.

Somewhere.

But that "out there" was in a different place, somehow. Because, in here, wherever "here" was, *what*ever "here" was, there was only darkness, and a woman's sobs.

And then a voice.

Muffled.

He couldn't make out what it said.

Mummmbla-mummmmbla-mummmmm.

What was it?

Listen.

Listen hard.

God!

Suddenly it was as if the darkness had changed its very nature from black to absolute white. It made him want to scream and slink back, cringing away from the light in terror and pain. It blinded him and...

Blinded?!

He could see!

But what did he have to see with?

Darkness.

Then light.

Darkness.

Light.

Fuzzy images swimming in a blurred liquid gold of radiant glow and bulbous swollen shadow.

Darkness.

Images…less fuzzy…a shape…like a man's…head.

A face!

Darkness…

Blink.

The face…a stranger's face, and yet, Norris had seen it before.

Watching now, looking hard, seeing…who was it?

The man was old…ancient almost. He had longish white hair and skin of an ashen grey, overrun with a shattered pattern of a million wrinkles. His beard was thick and seemed to mask his mouth entirely. He was leaning in close. Norris could see the way his shoulders turned into arms, which approached, only to get lost in distortion when they got too close for him to focus…

Point of view…

Perspective!

It was like looking out a hole…

No.

A window!

It was like looking out a window from inside a dark room. He couldn't see any of the room around him, all he could do was sense it, sense its darkness. It had been so dark in here before the man with the beard—*God, he looked so familiar*—opened the window and let the light in…

No, that wasn't quite right.

It had been so dark in here before the man with the beard took the bandages off and allowed the eye to open!

Norris felt his entire being pucker with the thought of

it. . .the revelation. It washed through him in a cold wave that iced over his most minute impressions and silenced him, so that, while the woman went on crying in the background, he watched without further comment as the man unwound a long rope of terry-cloth bandage from around someone's head. . .

From around Woodie's head, he finally allowed himself to think.

It's Mr. Green, and he's taking bandages off my brother's head.

I'm inside my brother's head.

I'm my brother's eye.

But my brother's dead.

So I must be dead.

How can I be my brother's eye?

The sound of a woman's grief went right on, even as Mr. Green's head moved to one side and the face of the woman Norris had seen on the rampart of that spectral house in the woods became visible behind him. Her hair was long and golden. Her eyes were blue. Her face was young, sweet, and so painfully innocent that it made him ache just seeing it so close.

She was sad, but she wasn't crying.

Her grief was all inside Woodie's head as a thought, or a memory, or maybe even a wishful dream. Soundlessly she watched what went on with solemn attention, her entire posture revealing just how badly she wanted whatever was happening to work. She wanted that very, very much. Norris thought that her own need might have frightened her a little. And he knew that it definitely frightened him.

Mr. Green, the bandages looped over his big hands and his eyes steady, leaned back in his chair, smiled, and asked, "Can you?"

The room bounced up and down as Woodie nodded his head, slowly at first, and then more rapidly.

Mr. Green's smile turned into a grin, and behind him the blond woman burst into tears.

"Well, my boy," Mr. Green said, lifting the bandages up higher as if displaying them. "How's it feel to see with an 'artificial' eye?"

Woodie said nothing.

Mr. Green leaned in close, whispering, "And you said that there was no such thing as magic."

Then he laughed, making something snap inside Robert Norris. Suddenly, he wanted more than anything to be out of this body, out of this mind, out...

Because he remembered Mr. Green...

And his magic.

He remembered Mr. Green...

Almost.

Magic...or madness?

Intellectually, Norris supposed that they were probably one and the same but he couldn't afford the time to ponder it fully because Mr. Green's face was wrecking his ability to concentrate. That face called out to him from what seemed a time tunnel of memory, teasing at his deepest fears and revealing itself only in a simple, one-dimensional invocation of emotion: this face had been with him in his dreams. It was the possessor of the eyes that watched him from the sky, and it was the master of his nightmare world. But what it had done specifically, and to whom it belonged, though significant, he knew, were beyond his ability to name. He knew this man, but he didn't *know* him.

Magic.

Or madness.

What was the difference?

Suddenly, the distinction seemed so extremely important that it could potentially be the difference between...

Magic or madness.

Weren't they both simply an acknowledgment that, under the proper circumstances, the impossible could occur? Didn't they each describe a state in which reality was suspended and the line separating the mundane from the remarkable was blurred? Wasn't just saying one or the other often enough to explain away the most profoundly off-center event?

As in:

"Oh, I *don't* understand it because it's magic."

Or...

"Oh, I *can't* understand it because it's madness."

And weren't they both equally true in those cases?

Didn't they, by not explaining a thing, each serve to explain the universe to anyone willing to accept "not knowing" as a form of knowledge?

Didn't they make anything possible?

"No!" Robert Norris screamed, hearing his own voice echoing somewhere far away in the dark.

"This isn't happening!

"This *can't* be happening!

"I don't believe in magic...

"So then, I must be mad."

That silenced the screaming in the dark, and for a very quiet moment he made no sound, allowed himself no thought, and didn't try, not even a little bit, to understand anything. He just watched as Mr. Green reached out his hand and led him... Woodie... him... them... through what looked like a darkened hallway and into a room full of people who were all huddled in a bunch, dressed in some kind of weird, baggy robes.

As they moved, details came clear in the gloom. The building they were in was shabby, dirty, and at least judging by the condition of the concrete-block walls, very old. They started out in a small room with a lot of pipes and valves which he assumed ran to a couple of hot water tanks, and ended up in a very big room that was easily the size of a small theater. The entire place was lit with the flickering glow of at least a hundred candles, and on the walls were hung leaf-covered branches. In the unsure light, it was difficult to tell if the branches were real or plastic, but the leaves all looked so fresh that he assumed that they had to be artificial. But something made him sense that he was wrong. He didn't know what it was, but he had the distinct feeling that someone had cut the branches off a bunch of oaks and evergreens and stuck them on these walls, where they had just continued growing in the dark.

The strangest sensation of touch tingled...something. He couldn't quite get a grip on whether he had a physical body or not, but ghostlike shivers ran through his consciousness that hinted at some kind of contact with something—maybe not firm, but developing.

Trying to ignore the people in the robes, he concentrated on those shivers and found that they were coming from all directions, up, down, back, front, and they were brief, but distinct: a hand brushed against skin and was warm, wood-smoke stung a watery eye, someone's lips touched...

What?

Woodie moved his head and Norris saw that the woman who had been standing behind Mr. Green in the small room had moved around to the front of him, knelt down, and while all the hooded people in the big, woodsy room watched, was kissing his hand.

Woodie looked up, and Norris thought, *Oh, Woodie, you fucking basket case, what the hell did you get yourself involved in? Is this that Institute of yours? Is this what you were doing all this time I thought you were sitting around and getting stoned while the Stooges were on the late late late show like you did in school?*

A sliver of sound crept in and then retreated, only to come

back more boldly.

Singing.

Pieces of a song.

And then a voice....

Mr. Green.

"...of you," it said, somewhere close, and Norris strained to hear. "Won't be long. Soon the stone will be so much a part of your body that it will feel as if you had been born with it."

Stone? Norris thought as Woodie took stock of the room. *What stone?*

They looked up...

And that's when he saw it.

His first reaction was a stunned silence. His second, was fear. And his third, anger. He moved through each swiftly, without much thought. The thing didn't require a lot of pondering, and it wasn't designed to motivate it. It was designed to elicit an emotional response, and in the end, that's just what it did.

"Jesus!" he thought, studying it for as long as Woodie gave him. When Woodie decided to look away, Norris tried to make him keep his eyes aimed up, and in so doing discovered an important fact about his condition: he was strictly a passenger here. An observer. He could see through Woodie's eyes—eye—but he could do nothing to influence his brother's actions. So while he had the chance, he looked, and what he saw explained a lot.

Someone had painted a figure on the ceiling, and it was as big as the available space would allow. Done in such a way as to hint that it was actually larger than even its rendering would suggest, the figure seemed to command all perspective with its sheer size. The night sky had been depicted in black and purple, with a smattering of white stars reflecting the constellations as they would have been seen near the end of

November—Norris was a woodsman after all, so picking out the Big Dipper was no great trick.

And the moon was full.

It was that full moon that was the focus of the entire arrangement because it served as the eye of the creature hovering in the sky.

Its figure was cast as little more than a shape of a darker darkness than even the night. It looked down into the room, which, given the leaves on the walls, suddenly felt like a clearing in some distant forest, its head roundish, dark, and sullen, its thick neck, pointed ears, wild hair and horns silhouetted against the sky.

And then Woodie looked away.

But Norris had seen enough.

Satan.

Woodie was a fucking devil worshiper!

"If I had arms, I'd kick your ass!" Norris roared in the dark. "Can you hear me? You little shithead son of a bitch!"

But Woodie couldn't hear because he, like everyone in the room, was listening to Mr. Green.

"Hearken unto me," the man suddenly announced, and all eyes turned his way. "For on this night it is done. The moon's final phase has begun, and the stone has come home to its place. The Blood Prince is balanced at the precipice of his rise!

"Behold!"

And with this, the man moved a lever on the wall and a grinding sound drew Woodie's attention back to the ceiling where he found that the moon in the painting had disappeared. A cool draft descended from the opening where the moon had been, flickering the candles and swirling smoke.

A window, Norris thought. Or a skylight in the roof.

"The stone draws its own," Mr. Green said in a tone more powerful than this frail demeanor would have seemed to permit.

And a light rolled above.

It started as a sliver of silver, disappeared, and then gained strength. It was brighter the second time, and lasted longer, eliciting a collective gasp of anticipation from the group. Its third appearance flared like a match and stretched into a perfect silver beam that wavered not an inch as it slid down and dazzled Norris' sight.

His first reaction was to cry out. But he didn't because, this time, the light didn't hurt as it had when Woodie had first opened his new eye and unwittingly blinded his brother. This time it was warm and luscious, and he could feel it caressing him and spreading out, filling the inside of Woodie's head so that things became known to him…Woodie, to him…Robert, to him…them…

They.

"Jesus!" a voice pronounced an instant before an immense hand loomed up and blocked the light. "Oh, Christ!"

A voice?

Whose?

Inside his cell, Robert Norris was reeling with it. As Woodie removed his hand, the room blurred into focus before him and he wanted to turn away, but he couldn't, because this wasn't his head, wasn't his life. He had to look, had to see, had to watch as his brother pulled his hand away, lifted his head, and made them both *see*, for the first time in either of their lives. Made them *see* like neither of them had ever imagined they could, beyond the physical and into the balance, the truth, the reality of what was before them.

Over everything a glittering miasma of sparkling silver pinpoints drained like falling sparks, but Norris assumed that this was simply an afterimage produced by tingling nerves in Woodie's head. The show lasted for about ten seconds before its glow diminished sufficiently for shapes to come into focus.

And, as if he too where inside Woodie's skull, and had chosen that exact instant when sight began to return, Mr. Green said, "Call out their names, for you know them now!"

And a figure stepped forward, lifted its hands, and pulled back its hood.

It was dark inside Woodie's head again, so Norris saw only the man's face when the hood fell. But in the next instant, a murmur began far below where he seemed to hover before the window that was the eye socket of his brother's skull, and suddenly he felt as if he were suspended on a scaffold about a hundred feet over an immense crowd that stretched forever in every direction below him. That crowd had apparently begun mumbling to itself because a sea of rolling sounds swelled twice before a single note of agreement came rushing up toward where he hung, gained momentum, and finally exploded past him into the outside air as "Galltar?"

It was Woodie's voice, and it reverberated as if filling a valley, making the man who had just removed his hood grin and throw back his head in a harsh and boisterous belly laugh that nearly drowned out the rest of Woodie's statement.

"Your pack once ran in the north lands, where the snow is deep, and the night falls hard," he went on, raising his voice to be heard over the man's enthusiastic bellows. "Your fathers were few, but hungry. And in some villages where the past is not so long ago, their names are still sung in hushed tones of fear and respect."

The laugh from the man in the hood had finished, and his deep, black eyes glistened moistly at the last of Woodie's statement. His features, so rough and primitive—all jaw, tooth, and muscle—softened into a reverent frown, and he knelt to one knee and said, in a deep, growling voice, "Hail."

And the next figure stepped forward, showing itself to be a woman.

The crowd below murmured again, but for not nearly so

long before another meteor of sound rushed past Norris in his place and Woodie said, "Zonoria," making the woman smile dangerously.

"Your pack was fierce, and the blood it spilled on the steppe of the Black Sea turned the soil to red clay. Your fathers were many, and were among the first. They spread across Russia before it was called that. And when the Romans were new, you were already old."

Ruefully, it seemed, the woman knelt and said, "Hail!"

And the next figure took one step.

It went on like this for nearly an hour. Each and every person in that room, twenty-three in all, removed his or her hood and listened as Woodie said their names and told them of the history of the family from which they sprang. They each were the last of their line, Norris realized as the parade marched on, and many were hearing about their lineage for the first time. Each had come from somewhere far away, having been summoned by some force that had been using the Institute of Metaphysical Research as its disguise. They came from Europe, China, Africa, and Canada, South America, India, England, and places that Norris had never even heard of. But despite the distances involved, they all resembled one another to a startling degree. Their features bordered on the brutish, and even in the women, there gleamed an implied strength and a savage intelligence that was silently intimidating.

Finally, when the last hood had dropped, Woodie turned from the group and looked Mr. Green in the eye.

"You killed my father," he said, and the old man studied him carefully. "I thank you, O great one, for he had forgotten the trees and, had he lived, I would never have found myself."

And this time it was Woodie's turn to kneel.

"Hail," said Mr. Green, reaching down and taking Woodie's hands.

When Woodie looked up, Norris saw something happening that, even after all the rest, he could not accept: Mr. Green became younger. Just a couple of minutes before, the man looked so frail that it appeared as if it were difficult for him to even speak, and yet, here he was, not young, but definitely younger. As Norris watched, wisps of his white hair crawled over his forehead, moving independently, like his beard, which was fuller, longer, whiter…

"No!" the man said, quickly, raising one finger in front of Woodie's face in warning, but maintaining his good-natured grin. "Not yet. Look not upon me in that way. Use not the stone for me, or your bride; for you have culled but the surface of the memory that is your birthright. What is yet to come will prepare you. But for now, be content, and let only your human mind see when you look upon me, and her."

It was then that Mr. Green presented the girl to Woodie. He'd been seeing her at the periphery of the night since his new eye opened, but now she became the focus, as he had wanted her to be all along.

Woodie was in love with the girl, but before this moment, she had not responded.

"He did this for her!" Norris said in the dark. "She caused it. Whatever this is all about, it was her idea, and he did it to please her because…"

She was positively ravishing, and something else…

She was a part of that which was now a part of him.

The references were complicated and, Norris realized, spinning around him so quickly that he really wasn't following what was happening because he had only bits and pieces of what he needed. Unless he got some of his brother's memories straight in his own mind, he would grope along as things happened around him and miss their significance. So, as hard as it was to do, he pulled his attention away from the window that was Woodie's eye, and aimed the essence of his being into the darkness that he had no other way of describing other than being "behind" him.

At first, nothing happened.

There was darkness there, impenetrable and deep, but positively livid with a feeling of terrific size and teeming life.

There were voices and lights behind him now, and it was all he could do to resist the urge to turn back around and see what was happening to his brother…and to him. But resist he did, and finally he was rewarded with a tingling sensation of something soft caressing…something soft.

He felt suddenly as if he were lying on a bed, in the dark, while millions and millions of spiders crawled over his naked body, searching for a way inside.

Revulsion was instant and instinctive.

This wasn't right…not the way it was supposed to be. No one man was ever intended to share the mind of another in this way, and in so doing, Norris was ignoring the very balance of nature that he had dedicated his life to preserving.

And yet…

It was his brother. They shared the same parents, the same genes. Didn't that count for something?

It came in tiny, almost imperceptible flickers at first. Just the briefest glimpse of a face here, a hand there…off to one side in the dark, so that Norris jerked one way and then another as…

"Mom?" he asked.

"Dad?"

The darkness wasn't nearly so thick now, he realized, and all around him he sensed the undulating, slithering tangle of a pressing mass of dark, wet flesh. Suddenly, he felt as if he had been submerged in an immense bowl of worms, and was seeing light filtered between a hundred feet of their surging bodies. Between those bodies, in the shadows that formed and then disappeared, there were images, locked and fleeting, that, when taken individually meant nothing, but that, when allowed just to come and go, left distinct impressions on his consciousness.

It was suddenly relaxing, seeing things this way. It was suddenly so easy just not to think.

Giving himself over to the dark, he allowed a frightening thing to happen: his sense of self suddenly drifted away, floating apart from where he now hung...back there, somewhere.

He was back there...

And yet.

He let himself go.

And then there was the girl. But this time he wasn't seeing her through the window of Woodie's eye. He was seeing her in the eye of Woodie's mind. And she was sick.

And...

* * *

He'd been coming to the Institute regularly for about eight weeks. At first it had only been for the Sunday lectures, and after the first he hadn't been so sure that the Institute of Metaphysical Research was his bag. Mr. Green, the man who operated the place, was fascinating, that was true, if not a little weird—he looked like death dropped by for an ice-cream cone, his skin was so white and his eyes so sunken. And the topics they discussed were kind of neat: the first time it had been Atlantis, and the second, telekinesis. But the audience made him a little nervous. Mostly there were just housewife types, and squirrelly little people who probably spent most of their time reading science fiction paperbacks and watching reruns of *The Twilight Zone,* over and over again. But scattered through the crowd there were the foreigners, the dark-skinned, dark-haired, quiet types who smelled funny and who sat so silently at every lecture Woodie attended—the same ones every time, plus one or two new ones on any given Sunday—and they seemed to color the mood of the place a sinister grey. They added a seediness to the proceedings that tasted so bad in his already paranoid mind that he had pretty much decided that every meeting he attended would be his last.

But that was before he spotted the girl.

Once he saw her, he knew he'd keep coming back for as long as she was around because he fell in love with her instantly, and every additional sighting just fueled that fire. So instead of just Sundays, he ended up knocking on that gnarled old door on Friday nights too, paid his forty-dollar membership fee, and became a card-carrying psychic researcher. But no matter what he did, his lady love ignored him, and he soon realized that she was going to remain beyond his reach as long as he stayed on the "plane of consciousness" he presently inhabited…

Because that was how they talked on Friday nights.

At first, he giggled listening to people use terms like "collective unconscious," "alternative evolutionary theory," and "distinction of psychic species," but after a while—and a good deal of the peyote floating around the room, free for the taking on silver serving trays—he started picking up on things. Pretty soon, he was having a good time, and those foreign members who had given him the creeps before turned out to be really nice people, if still a little on the quiet side, especially about the girl.

She didn't have a name, it seemed. Or at least none that anyone would reveal. But somehow that didn't seem so important anymore. All that was important was that she was there, in the flesh, and he could admire and love her from afar in ever-increasing heights of private passion as he got more and more stoned, more and more comfortable, more and more accustomed to the vocabulary and logic of the Institute and its members.

During the meetings he watched her hovering near Mr. Green—never more than a few steps from him—her golden hair hanging down to partially obscure her face, and her frayed white gowns looking shabby and uncomfortable. She hardly ever lifted her eyes from the floor, and once or twice she even had a length of rope tied into a hangman's knot dangling from her neck, marking her as separate, special, and a witch, if he understood the symbology correctly.

"Weird," he thought. But weird seemed to be the thing on Friday nights, and besides, who was he to judge? So he just mingled, helped himself to more peyote, and stole glances at her from across crowded, smoky rooms.

Then, one night in the "big room," which was the Institute's auditorium—it had been a bar area when the building was known as the "Ride 'Em Cowboy Lounge: Go-Go Girls to Go-Go"—Mr. Green took the stage and announced that "the girl" was deathly ill and needed a special kind of "healing" that only one specific Friday night member of the group could provide. Her soul was wilting and would soon die if that one did not come forward to make contact with her body's "life essence."

Well. . .Woodie certainly wouldn't have minded a little life essence contact, although this "soul sickness" stuff made him a little nervous. But the girl just looked thin, and a little too wasted most of the time, so he figured it wasn't anything a good meal and a couple of weeks off the drugs wouldn't fix—AIDS or cancer never so much as entered his mind—so he stood up and said, "I'd like to do whatever I can, if she'll have me."

And the room fell cold.

A few weeks before, Mr. Green had gone out and gathered up a bunch of tree branches someplace and arranged them on the walls of the auditorium where they had hung ever since, without losing a single leaf. Woodie noticed that things—like bugs, maybe—seemed to be moving among those leaves that should have died but hadn't, creating a rustling sound that should have been ominous, but wasn't.

Mr. Green was up there on the stage where the go-go girls used to go-go, and the girl stood behind him, the rope around her neck again, and her face still pointed to the floor.

"Are you sure, brother Norris?" he asked.

And Woodie nodded.

And that's when Mr. Green brought out the "stone."

He produced it from a fold in his own white robe and held it in his fist over his head.

"The magic required is powerful, and will change you," he said.

Woodie smiled and said, "Okay."

"Come forward."

And Woodie did.

When he got to the stage, Mr. Green explained.

"I am not who I seem to be, and the girl is a part of me. By helping her, you will be helping me, and by helping me, you will be helping yourself because you are but one of the fingers on my hand. Do you understand?"

"Not at all." Woodie smiled, still looking at the girl, who refused to return his gaze.

"I have always been, and I will always be. Your father knew me, but denied my right to his children," Mr. Green continued, and the reference to his father made Woodie turn his head.

"This is for thee."

And the next thing he knew, Woodie was looking at a perfectly formed glass eye lying on Mr. Green's open palm.

He swallowed.

"We knew your love for her would bring you forward, for

loving her has been your way for a million years," Mr. Green said, softly, and everyone in the room seemed to inhale. "You are the vessel of the moonstone, the wolfstone, the bloodstone power that has secured your family its place at my right hand since the stone was warm from its fiery fall down from the heavens. She is your vessel. The stone will be in you...and you will be in her."

Woodie was listening, but he really wasn't. He heard pieces of what Mr. Green was saying, but it didn't make the slightest bit of sense.

"The iris in that eye is exactly the color of the one I'm wearing," he said. "How did you know? Who made it?"

"When you take the stone into yourself, you will see through it more clearly than you have ever seen before," Mr. Green said, lifting the stone up close to Woodie's face. "It will be the first time in three thousand years that a Nurrenvelt has seen through the stone, and it will set the world free."

Woodie swallowed. His head was swimming...but that was the peyote...wasn't it? Well, wasn't it? It couldn't have anything to do with the musky, almost furry smell Mr. Green seemed to exude, or the warmth radiating from the girl's body. She was standing a good twelve feet away, so it was impossible for him to feel the vibration of her flesh or the power of her heart, beating invisibly in his head.

"Without nourishment, she'll die," Mr. Green added, indicating the girl. "She is not of this earth, and only you can give her the bread that will save her life."

"Why me?" Woodie asked, dryly.

"Because it was your blood that called her up that first time, so long ago."

"And what bread can I give her that she needs?"

"First the stone."

"And then?"

"The stone."

☆ ☆ ☆

Robert Norris turned back to the light shining through the hole in his brother's skull and let the memory go because he could guess the rest. The moonstone—or whatever Mr. Green had called it—really was magic. He'd put it in Woodie's head, and now both he and Woodie were actually using it to see. Robert Norris, whose body was standing in the middle of a snow-covered glade, was seeing things that his now-dead brother had seen, first person, from inside that dead brother's skull.

Magic lantern show, he thought, for no reason.

But the analogy felt right.

Magic!

☆ ☆ ☆

He was back in the auditorium, but Woodie was on the stage. Before him the rest of the room was still lit with candles, and all the people—the foreigners who had come so far to gather here—had put their hoods back up so that their brutish faces were obscured by peaked shadows. Mr. Green was leading him by the hand, and the girl, looking far less frail then she had when the bandages were first removed, was waiting, her head still hung down, and the rope again adorning her neck.

There were branches on the walls and ceiling in the little alcove holding the stage, forming an artificial tunnel, like a clearing in a thick wood overhung with foliage.

There was grass on the ground.

And there was a bed.

"From the eye of the sky comes the Lover of Man's Blood, reunited with the Lady of the Night," Mr. Green was saying, but Norris' attention was on the girl. "Behold their union, all ye last of the First. The Wild have not died! This brave gathering shall mark the end of the exile of those whose fathers once ruled the forests as Masters of the Hunt. The

Blood Prince comes, and with him, the new Dark Times."

A roar erupted that nearly deafened Norris in the dark.

"Behold the Demon Lover!"

And the girl looked up for the first time.

Somehow, lost in the anticipation of what he felt could only turn out to be an example of his brother's drug-induced exhibitionism, Norris found himself looking forward to the girl and the bed. It was crazy, but so was everything else, and for a split second he had unconsciously allowed himself to savor the sight of her soft flesh and luxurious, flowing hair. Seeing her—just her—almost explained Woodie's actions, almost justified the lengths to which he had apparently gone to secure his chance to love her.

But when she lifted her face and met his eyes with her own, it all blew away, and in that instant he understood the truth behind what she, and Mr. Green, and every person in that room represented. Suddenly he felt trapped, kidnapped, and alone; suddenly he exploded with a rage so terrible that it felt as if he would burst into a single flame of anger and go rushing through Woodie's mouth and eyes as licks of surging fire. He hurled his attention around in the dark, found no way out, and no way to act, trembled with frustration, and folded himself in on himself as, in a final desperate expression of his helplessness, he screamed out an inarticulate cry that shook the blackness inside his mad brother's skull, but did nothing to stop him from taking that first, inevitable step toward the bed.

After that, all Norris could do was watch.

When she lifted her face, he saw her eyes first, and, despite the panic electrifying the darkness—panic that he realized was both his and his brother's, intermingled so intimately as to be practically indistinguishable—they reached down and touched a part of his being that he had never felt stimulated before. The distance from the surface of his fearful thoughts to the soul of his murky desires seemed great, but for one, timeless instant, a haunting call echoed through the mist of what could only have been centuries, speaking in a language that the earliest and most primitive pieces of his personality understood. He felt a stirring, there in the dark—a deep, subterranean rumble that felt as if something old and big were awakening from an unfathomable slumber in some hidden chamber of his heart. He felt a maneuvering in his consciousness of things long denied, shadowy bits of hunger suppressed by instinct since…

When?

He paused, his attention fixated on the girl's eyes, which were a deep, vein-mapped yellow, bisected by vertical black slits that swelled and narrowed like a cat's—or, more accurately, like something vaguely reptilian gazing up through the eons from the beginning of a feline's ancestral chain.

Woodie's hands worked their way over the robe he was wearing, searching for some fastener or hook, found none, and began tearing fabric as if his body were impervious to the convolutions of his mind. His breathing was labored and quick, producing a thick, gurgling rattle that served as a counterpoint to the thunder of his racing heart. And his thoughts, thrilled through with terror for his own safety, were suddenly laced with a very different kind of thrill that seemed to find its source in his own surging blood.

"Woodie!" Norris screamed with one half of his mind, while the other half asked, "When did this start? Oh, God, how long have we been like this?"

"Don't do it, Woodie! Please! She's not even human!"

The golden-haired thing was crouching now, hands held loosely before it and fingers curled into claws. Its yellow eyes blazed hatefully as it moved to its left, circling the bed and pulling back its lips in a snarl that revealed teeth that were long, perfect, and needle-sharp.

Woodie's heartbeat was suddenly augmented by the abrupt syncopated rhythm of a drum, pounding somewhere close, yet invisible.

The branches hanging all around swayed suggestively, rustling and crackling as things moved among them, positioning themselves for a better view and sparkling into the shadows like a thousand tiny eyes.

Woodie tossed the tatters of his robe aside and circled to his right, crouching, dripping sweat, studying the girl's eyes and exposing his own teeth as he growled out a response to her snarl.

"As it happened a million years ago," the voice of Mr. Green narrated, as if for the benefit of some attentive audience, "the human finds the beast and discovers love."

Whoever Mr. Green was addressing, they were certainly nowhere to be seen. The people in the robes weren't listening because they had begun dancing, off in the shadows thrown by the wildly flickering candles. A drum practically flooded the air with a horrendous din, punctuated by the dancers' wordless grunts—so much like a chant, and yet expressive of no concept other than a growing anticipation. When the man spoke again, his voice fell from above, as if he had climbed a ladder or was speaking through the window in the ceiling that had been painted up to resemble the moon...which was the eye of the creature in the sky.

It was as if he had *become* the creature in the sky!

"The stone arrived from above, one dark night, on a barren, snow-covered clearing in what they call the Black Forest today. It fell through the darkness leaving a tail of red fire that stretched back up to the moon, from which it had originated. A creature was drawn by that fire and followed it to the blackened hole in the earth from which wisps of smoke swirled to make the air smell like lightning. That creature was important because it was the first of the Fathers, the sire of the

Breed, and the original Blood Prince."

Robert Norris heard the words, and somehow was able to perceive their meaning, despite his own protests and desperate struggles to keep Woodie from doing what he was about to do.

The girl's robe had slipped down one of her shoulders, and the skin revealed was maddeningly seductive.

"The First Father came wrapped in animal fur and armed with a sharpened bone," said the voice that was no longer Mr. Green's because it was bigger, deeper, and less focused. The walls shook with the sound. "He was shunned by his tribe and driven from any gathering of his kind by thrown rocks and shouts. He was strong, smart, and dangerous. He took women when he wanted them and ate children when there was nothing else. And sometimes he ate them even when there was something else, because he *liked* the meat of man. He liked the taste of it...he was the Lover of Man's Blood.

"His hair was golden.

"The modern word for him is *cannibal*."

The girl lunged to one side quickly and then altered her course back around the way she had come. Woodie followed her movements, skillfully skipping one way and then the other with a smooth grace that seemed impossible, considering how much dope he had consumed, and the way his vision doubled and then refocused as he tried to keep himself centered directly in front of her. A laugh that was more of a grunt escaped from him the second time the girl tried to evade his circling approach, and that laugh stimulated a din of cruel merriment in the crowd that swelled into a surge of laughter that was undirected and sinister.

"The First Father had been roaming the plain for nearly three years," the voice continued. "Alone and dirty, he lived on the periphery of the wilderness, watching the humankind that had repelled him, and taking them as his food when he needed to because they were the easiest prey, especially the woman who were pregnant with their infants.

"When he saw the stone, glowing red in the charcoaled earth, he was not afraid, for there was a sliver of bile in his nature that made him bold. He stepped up and took it in his hand, screamed out, and dropped it as his flesh blistered with its heat. He looked at his roasted skin, smelled it, and smiled. The second time he picked it up it had cooled, and he raised it to this eyes and, looking through it, saw something on the other side of the hole. When he lowered the stone, the image disappeared. But raising the grey, glasslike rock to his eye again, he found that he could recall the form, or smear of solidity, he had seen, hovering over the ground like a tiny, glowing moon.

"For a moment he was confused, and repeated his experiment. But he was a creature of action, not theory, and soon his attention was arrested by what he saw. His confusion gave way to joy as the form of the Lady of the Night took shape. It was she, the same as she is here now, who came to this ancient ancestor of all the Wild, and it was she who was to show him the path that has led us all here tonight.

"At first, her figure was like a liquid, moving, changing, fascinating the Man-Beast, First Father, Sire of the Wild. It swayed with the breeze and showed him many kinds of creatures, many shapes and sizes, combinations and arrangements, some familiar, and some unseen by any man before or since.

"The First Father studied the Lady of the Night, and when she assumed a form he liked, he laughed his loud, enthusiastic roar, and she noted his pleasure and marked it. His tastes were predictably primitive, but efficient. He was attracted by the form of a human female, as well as the forms of the more animal primate females he was accustomed to, and by them both, he was aroused. But at the same time, as a killer, he admired the wings he had seen bats use to fly—not the feathered ones of birds, but the fleshy ones of furry creatures like himself. He envied the big cat its claws, the lizard it tough skin, the elk its speed, and the wolf: over all and above any other, this man whose intellect we might at first be tempted to find suspect admired the wolf its unparalleled cunning. He also liked hair the color of his own, blond…nearly white—another reason for his being shunned from a tribe in which hair was uniformly black or brown. For this early man was albino, and consequently his light-sensitive eyes make him a creature of the night, much like the wolf he so admired.

"Finally, when the smoke was gone, the First Father lowered the stone and found a beautiful woman standing naked before him. And as might be expected in a man of his nature, he was instantly attracted to her. He felt her perfect harmony with his own being and sensed that, in her, all the other things that he had seen and responded to were hidden, just below the surface.

"What he didn't know—perhaps what he could not have known or even understood—was that he had made her. It was his mind that had given her form. She was sent from above without physical proportion as a gift that would save the world. As the one brave enough to claim the stone, the First Father became her creator and master, as much as any man can be master of a being such as she."

As if cued by this last sentence, the girl moved with blinding speed and tore off her robe. Her naked body revealed so abruptly, stunned Norris inside his brother's head and affected Woodie so thoroughly that, for an instant, his reaction produced a physical vibration that traveled up his spine and quivered his entire body. The girl—or woman, for bereft of her covering there was no mistaking her for anything less than mature—stood still for a moment, as if to give her pursuer an opportunity to study every detail of her figure, and then, in a remarkable, almost absurd transference of roles, she assumed the hunter's stance, and Woodie, despite himself, moved to avoid her advances.

"Oh God!" Norris shouted inside Woodie's skull. "Don't let her touch us! Don't let her do it!"

But Mr. Green was speaking again, and his words were deafening.

"Lovers they were, and lovers they have been ever since. That same Lady of the Night and all the Blood Princes descended from that first, brave man. Lovers they were, and together they built a secret world. Just the Lady's touch gave the Blood Prince the power to keep hold of the stone, and just touching the Blood Prince kept the Lady 'real,' which was all she desired. Together, Lady and the First Father found others like himself, and as their numbers grew, so did their knowledge of the powers they possessed because of the stone. They learned their advantages, marked their limitations, and bonded together in the first and most dangerous pack in the history of this planet, bringing ruin down upon untold numbers of those creatures who had shunned them, and feared them, and hated them in their natural guise.

"But still the numbers of the Flock grew. Whole species of man, for at that time there were many, many types, had disappeared under the fang. But those that remained reproduced quickly, and learned much of their surroundings. So it was decided that, in order to hunt more effectively, the pack would split up and go their own individual ways. Twenty-four killers comprised that nuclear family, and they hung their heads and disbanded, traveling many miles and arranging themselves over the planet. But even so far apart, they could sense the presence of the others and feel the power of the stone, so they never felt alone.

"New packs were formed, with new killers, now called Vyrmin, emerging from the very heart of those civilized sheep as slaves to the original Fathers, who served as the minds and hearts of each hunting unit. For thousands of years, blood ran in rivers, the Flock flourished but was kept to manageable numbers, the wolves flourished and ruled the land, and the Dark Times were the only times. In Europe, Africa, Russia, and even in what was to be called America, the wolf legends were passed from one generation to the next.

"But slowly—so slowly as to be imperceptible at first—the Flock's numbers grew.

"And grew.

"Like rats, the sheep thickened over the planet. Roaming the forests, I myself searched out the Vyrmin among them. But to no avail.

"The Flock just grew.

"We hunted and killed with renewed purpose, gorging ourselves full while finding more and more members to join us.

"But still the Flock grew.

"The Black Plague came, and the Flock was thinned.

"But soon it passed, and the Flock grew again.

"Wars came, and the Flock was thinned.

"We feasted on their flesh, and gnawed their bones.

"But always the Flock recovered...

"For the first time we didn't eat what we killed.

"And still the Flock *grew!*

"It overran everything, destroying all in its path and raping those precious forests that are the very soul of the spirit that energizes this otherwise desolate rock. It swelled to ridiculous size, and the wild nature in its members that fueled the packs dimmed as *civilization* warped minds and softened bodies. It blackened the air, fouled the water, and soured the earth. It pushed out from the original pockets of its home and it grew, and grew, and *grew!*

"As it did, the Wild suddenly found themselves the

hunted. Without eating our kill, we left evidence of ourselves and for the sheep to find and study. They were smart, and for their nature, amazingly willing to become aggressive. Soon, any action violent or natural that did not benefit the Flock was outlawed. The killers they found were locked away, or killed themselves. The weak, strong now because of numbers, imposed their own sense of order and turned the world upside down. And finally, three hundred years ago, the packs were thinned so far as to put the remaining Wild at the mercy of their onetime prey. They scattered and hid, running for their lives, denying their natures in the process.

"As for the Lady of the Night, and the Man in the Woods, we are powerful when the packs are powerful, and weakened when the packs are weak. We shrank from our onetime glory to the pitiful, nearly starved creatures you see today, waiting for that one opportunity, that one miraculous time, when it might be possible to reclaim our power...and our place!

"And that time has come!

"What begins here tonight, with these last descendants of the First, who have come so far to respond to the call of the Wild, will lead us to a new Dark Time for the Flock that will save this planet from the disease that is mankind. The wolfstone will be the gateway to the Wild, and the Blood Prince, as he has always been, will be the key that will throw open that gateway. The sheep are smothering this earth, choking its breath and breaking its heart. We can save this globe. And we shall! By roaming free and reclaiming our place as the Masters of the Hunt, we shall follow the demands of our natures and rejuvenate the natural balance!

"Hail, the Blood Prince!

"Hail, the Lady of the Night!

"Hail, the Demon Lover, bane of mankind!"

And that finished it, Norris realized as the voice

culminated in a crescendo overhead. He didn't know when it had happened, but somewhere during the narrative, everything in the room had gone still. The drums had stopped, as had the dancing. The girl had stopped, and stood naked in her place. And Woodie had just planted his feet and waited. There was something important about what was being said, something so vital and personal that not one person in the room could help him- or herself from listening.

And listen they did.

But when that voice hit its final note, and the sentence of release peaked, the world started moving again, and events rolled on as Norris had been praying that they would not since realizing what the girl and Woodie were going to do.

"Now!" Woodie growled, hunching into a crouch.

The woman snarled back at him from across the bed.

The drums exploded, people danced, and the stars began to move…

"Wait!" Norris screamed. *"The stars can't move! They're painted on!"*

But his words didn't matter.

Stars were moving, clouds tumbled, and that huge, dark thing that was the watcher in the sky that Norris had called Satan—simply because Satan was the word he knew—lifted its ghostly arms and threw back its head in a laugh that sounded like thunder, and…

"Nooooooo!" Norris shrieked.

And the woman touched Woodie's flesh.

It was like instantaneous combustion, and the flash they produced repelled them both backward before a great white fireball. The crowd roared when the sparks flew, but before Woodie could organize his senses, the woman was up and flapping her wings.

"Christ!" Norris moaned as his brother rolled on the

floor, found his hands and knees, and was lifted, straight up into the air so that his perspective dipped beneath him like the view from a movie camera knocked from its tripod.

Then he fell, landing atop the bed and producing a huge plume of dust. Wings flapped, his vision bounced, and his arms and legs flayed as powerful hands grabbed bunches of his skin and squeezed, firing pain up his back and down his legs. When he tried to crawl, he was lifted again, and taking the sheet off the mattress with him, he kicked and screamed as he was turned to face his newfound love in the air.

Norris' cries—echoing through the blackness around him and obscuring all sound inside Woodie's head—were mimicked as his brother opened his mouth and produced a truly audible, simply awful wail of terror. All the passion he had felt was gone. Any attraction he had felt for the woman in the white robe had fled. Revulsion and horror took absolute possession of his senses and convulsed him into a shuddering mass of struggling muscle and sweat...

Almost.

Externally he was that way.

But somewhere inside...

The woman's bat wings beat faster, lifting the pair higher and tumbling them together intimately—she with her arms around him, and he with his fists beating at the sides of her head. From the base of her spine squirmed a scaly, snakelike tail with a spatula head that moved up from between her legs and through Woodie's thighs to flatten itself on his buttocks and press his pelvis firmly into hers. Her flesh seemed to be moving over her muscles, crawling, in a way, and puckering itself into weird, indefinable folds and crevices that pulled, peaked and then split, producing whiffs of steam and a series of noxious sucking sounds, the loudest of which seemed positioned near Woodies' groin.

"Oh Christ, oh God, oh Jeeesssssssuss!" Norris howled as

a wire of heat implanted itself right into the center of Woodies' brain. Norris could almost see it, tangling a fiery red and twisting through the darkness from some point that looked to be a thousand miles away, from a million years ago. It climbed up from the very depths of Woodies soul and invigorated his reptilian brain stem with an electricity so powerful that it stiffened both his legs and his penis in one painful jerk.

"Woodie!" Norris screamed. "Stop it! For God's sake don't!"

But it wasn't really all Woodie's fault, he realized at that instant. As much as he screamed, it would do no good, even if his brother could hear. Woodie was simply reacting in the way his body was built to react. Norris found himself, somewhere deep down inside, wondering if he too didn't have just a twinge of his brother's passion. If perhaps this was not so hard to understand, not so repulsive...

Not so ugly...

Why...

"No!"

The woman had been so attractive—he could see her as she had appeared: all innocence and charm.

The moment passed and her face was back in his eyes, hair hanging in billowing tendrils that hissed and squirmed around her ears, eyes glaring coldly, having lost all hints of any humanity they might have ever possessed, tongue flashing out, six inches and then a foot, long, black, and forked, from between the lips of a snout that suddenly looked as if it had once belonged to a baboon. As she turned over in midair to pull Woodie on top of her, she snarled so savagely that foam flecked the gleaming points of her wicked teeth. Her lizard eyes squeezed shut, and her clawed, clutching hands tore into Woodie's back until one finger actually hooked itself through a slab of muscle and caught the back of one of his ribs.

Woodie screamed as he entered her…

No, not entered.

Was pulled into her.

The sensation was sickening and fierce. Lips closed around his penis, and immediately a sucking sound, louder than those Norris had heard before, and even more insistent, began lapping as a pressure like a vacuum drew him inside. The force of it was agonizing, and for an irrational instant, Norris feared that Woodie's entire body would be crushed through the opening of the woman's vagina, folding in on itself and following the bruised head of his erection like a rat into a snake's patient jaws.

Woodie went limp as the sucking grew louder.

And images swirled through Norris' mind, stunning him with indecipherable eddies of confused hallucination, and dancing, damaged-nerve sparkles. Time seemed to peel away before his eyes, and somewhere in the incredible, volcanic distance of an eon's breath, he thought that he might have glimpsed the very edge of a place where that monstrous thing that hovered with the moon in its eye sat behind a veil of rolling storm clouds, on a throne made of stars, smiling as it held the world in one hand and Norris' heart—a hundred million miles across and pumping in explosive bursts of dry thunder—in the other. As he watched, the wondrous, black thing, all size and silhouette, turned its one, pale grey eye his way and nodded its towering head and…

Woodie's orgasm tore up through his body, locking every muscle from his jaw to his heel and staggering Norris' thoughts into a spinning, insane vortex of pleasure.

The woman raked one clawed hand down Woodie's face…

And then there was a beautiful white sun shining in a pale blue sky, over trees that were frosted with a glaze of gleaming ice. A hand was holding something small and hard just overhead, and a plume of frozen breath rose from the bottom of the viewer's vision, right from where frozen breath is supposed to rise when the eyes with which a person is seeing are where they are supposed to be.

Norris blinked, shook his head once, and felt his knees go weak beneath him. His mouth was hanging open, so he closed it. His spine was stiff, so he loosened it. Warm tears were running down his face, and they felt so good that he did nothing to stop them. Inside his head there was total silence—not so much as a single thought or distinct impression. He was stunned and empty. His vision was over. And as he lowered his arm and glanced around himself in his little snow-covered glade, he didn't even react to the things he found lying in the snow. He just ran his eyes over them once, collected his bearings, aimed himself directly into the woods, and started walking...

Right over the churned, bloody snow that encircled him.

Right over the gnarled remains of a tweed jacket.

Right over the Korean War-vintage Colt .45 automatic, lying in a pool of dark brown, half-frozen mud, gleaming in the sun and pocked with a pair of deep gouges in its steel—gouges that looked very much like the impressions of some large animal's teeth.

26

"H.W.? Jesus! What the fuck, Sheriff? Come on, anybody! I got fucking lightning bolts down here!" the walkie-talkie dangling from Sheriff Conway's belt buzzed as Conway dropped to his knees and then over on his side in the snow, clutching his groin and grimacing as his face turned first red and then a frightening shade of blue.

"H.W.?" the voice intoned desperately. "This is unit one, I mean…Oh, fuck it! This is Buddy, Sheriff. I got trouble here with that ranger and I'm gonna grease 'im if you don't' say otherwise. You read that? I'm gonna grease his ass! Count o' three. One…"

Detective Cooper watched Conway gasping for breath as his radio squawked in the mud. But there was a weirdly insignificant cast to his impressions that he couldn't explain, preventing anything he saw or heard from making any real impact on him just now. The only thing that he felt was truly important at that moment was the sensation of strength surging up from his gut and invigorating his entire body.

"Two. I ain't shittin', goddamn it! Come in, Sheriff, 'cause I swear this fucker's dead meat otherwise!"

"Nnnn…" was the only sound Conway was apparently capable of producing, and he did it through clenched teeth while forcing his right hand to leave his injured testicles and move, ever so slightly toward his belt.

The trees are so crystal clear! Cooper thought, moving his eyes across the vista of the Valley below, and then back up, toward where there was still screaming in the motel's parking lot. *So perfectly beautiful! It's like I'm seeing them for the first time! Like they're new…or I'm new, and all this was just waiting for me!*

As he watched, a loud roar erupted into a physical projectile that surged up from the parking lot's horizon in the shape of a man. As if he had been launched from a catapult, the deputy, whose face Cooper could not see because of all the blood covering it, climbed into the air in an almost lazy arc, his arms and legs twisting slowly and his cry of fear pitifully thin compared to the wild-animal roar that accompanied it. He seemed to hang, suspended in powder blue for a surprisingly long time before his descent turned him completely over and he crashed into a very tall, almost naked white ash tree. He hit about three-quarters of the way up the trunk, headfirst, producing a terrible *clunk!* that echoed over the Valley an instant before his limp body's slide began tearing branches that snapped and broke like bones until he stopped, entangled upside down and dripping about thirty feet from the ground.

Amazing! Cooper thought. *Really remarkable!*

"Three!" the walkie-talkie announced. "Okay, he's history."

"Don't!" Conway hoarsely barked, bringing his radio to his lips in a jerking rush that banged his front teeth with its plastic top. "Leave him be! Read it? Leave him be!"

"Sheriff?" the deputy named Buddy said, his voice gasping desperately up from the cheap little speaker. "You oughta see this shit! I mean, goddamn and Christ Almighty!"

"Leave him be," the sheriff said again, relief softening his shoulders as he worked his knees back under him. "Leave him be…leave him…"

He's a wreck, Cooper thought, shaking his head. He was standing only about ten feet from the older man, with his hands on his hips and his eyes slightly squinted because the sunlight was just so goddamn bright at this spot that it made him want to turn his head away.

"Leave him..." Conway whispered again, as if his mind were unable to form any other sentence...

And then, in a rush that Cooper had not expected him capable of performing, the sheriff's left hand, the one still on his balls, moved to his holster, drew his weapon, pulled it up, and held it there as the end of the thing disappeared behind a flash so bright that at first the detective thought it was just its silent blaze that had knocked him back.

"Uggggg!" his lungs made him say as all the air in them rushed up through his throat.

Then the gunshot flash changed into a thunderous report that masked the detective's cries as he landed hard on his tailbone, bashed his head against something that was really fucking remarkably hard, and slid—his arms and legs flapping like rubber flippers—down the bouncing, sharp and slick side of the Retreat.

27

The shot had to be a good one because Conway knew he wasn't going to get another try. *One and out!* he thought, hardly able to move because of the pain tracking his nerves outward from his groin. His heart was hammering, and a funny, acrid taste like sour lemon seemed to be boiling up his throat and out his nose.

One and out.

Ka-blam!

His .45 roared at the end of his arm, which had magically appeared just where his brain had wanted it to be. The recoil almost knocked him over. But it looked like the bullet had knocked the detective right out of his shoes.

"Yeah!" he wheezed, realizing that the front of his mouth felt funny, and then saying, "Ouch!" loudly when his probing tongue found a place where his right front tooth had been before he had knocked it out with his walkie-talkie.

It was then that he realized that he had spoken into the radio...was still speaking, as it turned out, saying, "Leave him be," over and over again.

He made himself stop.

Two minutes later he climbed painfully to his feet, staggered a little, said, "I'm comin' down," to the guy on the walkie-talkie, and moved toward where he had seen Cooper's body tumble, intent on finishing the job he should have done back at the cemetery, but hadn't because...

"I'm just too fucking softhearted," he whispered, his balls throbbing like blips on a radar screen. "But not no more. No-sir...not one fuckin' bit more!"

28

The pain was fabulous, and for long moments it completely stymied Cooper's ability to think coherently. Lying in a heap at the bottom of the hill down which he had just slid without, amazingly—perhaps even impossibly—breaking any bones, waves of agony swelled up from the spot on his left shoulder where the sheriff's bullet had hit.

Fucker was aiming for my heart! he thought.

And then…

He growled, low, and under his breath, rumbling his chest and shuddering his throat.

And that scared him even more than the idea of having just been shot.

Bob growled like that, he thought, excitedly pulling himself up the side of a bent tree and using it as support until his wobbly legs seemed ready to hold his weight. *When they dragged him out of that room where Woodie had died, he puked his guts, looked me right in the eye, and growled like an animal, like he'd rip out my throat if I got close enough. Not too close. Close enough. It was only a second or two that he did it, but God, he did it, and I did too! What the fuck's going on with me?*

His shirt was sticky, wet, and, in the frigid air, kind of stiff. His entire left side, from his hip to his neck, was ablaze with aching tendrils of fire. And his belly…

Felt great.

He frowned, and poked himself through his shirt, right where he knew the worst of his bite, and consequently, the worst of his wolfsbane scars were hidden. The sensation that he created was intensely pleasant...

He swallowed.

And saw the light.

It was falling from the sky in a single, silver shaft, pale, eerie, almost invisible. But with his eyes so sensitive—*When did they get like that?* he thought—he could make it out, pointing directly to a spot in the trees that looked to be about a hundred yards ahead.

Without thinking any more, since it was just confusing him anyway, he moved to follow the light, pleasantly surprised to find that his legs felt strong and his steps were sure.

When he found the clearing, he burst out of the trees without ceremony, startling the two men standing off to his left so badly that one of them—the one not holding the walkie-talkie—jumped at least two feet straight up in the air before spinning to swing his rifle around in front and aiming it right at the detective's gut.

Cooper raised his hands, simultaneously fighting down the urge to charge the man and bite him with his teeth.

"Jesus!" the man with the rifle said, smiling stupidly and lowering his weapon. "It's that city fella. You tryin' to get yourself killed or what?"

The second man didn't even turn around. He just stood there, displaying his back, watching something in the clearing and speaking into the radio. "I ain't shittin', Sheriff. There's real lightning bolts down here."

When Cooper moved his eyes from the rifle, he saw what the man was watching, and he also froze in his place.

Robert Norris was standing in the center of the clearing, holding something over his head, with his extended right arm stiff at the elbow. The sunbeam Cooper had seen from above fell from the sky and hit whatever it was Norris was holding, bounced off it, and proceeded, as if purified into a single laser beam, straight into the man's left eye. The beam looked white-hot and swirled with sparkling aerials that entwined it like smoke. Flashes occasionally erupted form Norris' palm, cracking outward and decaying in the air silently as twisting, multi-branched webs that glowed a vivid white...as if reality were actually a movie, and the film was splitting apart so that the projection bulb could briefly shine through. From his open mouth, an eerie, golden glow radiated brightly, as if the entire inside of his head were filled with light.

His whole body was rigid. His left arm hung limply at his side. And his face gleamed with reflected light from the beam shining into his eye.

"What'ya think of that?" the man with the rifle said, cocking his head.

"It ain't natural. We oughta blow him away for it," the man whose back was turned said into his walkie-talkie.

Cooper was about to speak when a voice shouted, "Freeze!" from behind him.

He turned, saw Sheriff Conway aiming his Colt at his face from less than twenty feet away, and without thinking, dropped to the ground.

The sheriff's gun fired and the deputy with the rifle flew back in a flurry of waving arms and goofy "Wa? Wa?" sounds. The second deputy, finally roused from his meditations, spun uselessly and threw his radio straight up in the air while he swung his own rifle up and fired in response, blasting the tree next to which Sheriff Conway was positioned in his straight-armed, two-handed firing crouch.

Cooper rolled, bobbed up once, and then dove for the tree line, a puff of snow and mud splattering nearby as the sheriff, apparently oblivious to the near miss his deputy had sent his way, tracked the detective's intended escape route and sent first one shot and then two more in pursuit.

Cooper made it to the trees unscathed, drew his own weapon, raised it, and was about to fire...

When an arm came down gently on his wrist, making him look up fearfully...directly into the blazing red eyes of an old man, with a flowing white beard and tiny bones tangled in his hair, who said, *"Not that way, my son. Thus is not the way of the Wild."*

And then the man was gone, and Cooper's gun was lying in the snow, unfired. He stared at it for a moment, and the words racing through his head took on a jumbled, useless quality that disgusted him.

So he ignored the words...

And took off the tweed jacket the sheriff had made him wear, back at the jailhouse, a thousand years ago.

There was a hole in its left breast side, charred a little and positioned at the very center of a thick, bloody stain that soaked through its worn material and was already turning brown at the edges. Taking the coat off seemed to take a long time, and Cooper experienced a sensation like removing a very heavy object that he had been carrying on his back forever without even realizing it was there. His body seemed suddenly buoyant, and his spirits lifted.

But a darkness was hanging over his him as he examined himself.

Out there, in the clearing, he heard footsteps, first moving together, off to his right and far away, and then, as if the two men had met, made their plans, and accepted their individual responsibilities, moving apart, one to the left, one farther right.

But he didn't care.

The Man in the Woods, he thought, shaking his head and running his tongue along his teeth, which felt funny in his head.

They seemed so sharp, and so...sensitive. That was the

only word for it. Running his tongue along them created a sensation… as if they weren't just enamel anymore, but had nerves in their flesh, as well as at their center. Unwillingly he imagined what it would feel like to bite something now, to feel the spongy texture of *meat* covering every inch of his teeth, to feel the moist juices of *meat* glazing every part of his long, sharp teeth as they penetrated deep into…

He pressed his jaws together and frowned.

I've seen the fucking Man in the Woods! he thought, lifting his eyes and glancing around himself. *I've seen the creatures—the werewolves that hick Conway warned me about. I've seen magic, right before my eyes, and I still don't believe it. I've been bitten, burned, shot, and chased, and I still don't believe it!*

He put his finger through the hole in the fabric of his coat and wiggled it.

I can't believe it!

He finally looked at his naked chest.

I won't believe it!

A weak whimper escaped his trembling lips when he saw what he looked like without the coat. He had suspected that something was happening to him, but he hadn't allowed himself to think about it…

It's impossible! that civilized part of him down deep in his soul shrieked as some even deeper part, some part that seemed to stretch back and embrace the irrational like salvation, nodded its invisible assent in a silent *I told you so. But you never listen to me, because you and your wires, beeps and buttons know everything there is to know, and the old ways are all wrong and naïve.*

He didn't know which was worse, the bite or the bullet wound, so he started with the bullet and groaned.

It was right there—the end of it. The little black spot of a .45 caliber automatic slug, dark, dull, and bloody, was protruding from a terribly swollen mound of scarred flesh that was an intense shade of purple, splattered with blood, and just a couple of inches from where his chin ended when he looked down and to the left.

Impossible.

It hadn't gone in! The goddamn bullet hadn't gone in. It had hit him straight and dead to rights, broken a bunch of blood vessels, knocked him on his ass and then down a hill, blown all the wind from his lungs, and nearly broken his collarbone—judging by the ache in his back—but it hadn't penetrated his body. His skin had stopped it. It hurt like hell, but his skin—just his *skin*—had stopped a bullet from damaging his insides.

Impossible.

His eyes moved from the bullet to the mess of tissue that flowered over his stomach, lower chest, and down, God knew how far, into his pants.

The woman had bitten him, and the remnants of her teeth were still there, like four little black spiders nestled in the center of their deadly, spreading web. Sheriff Conway had thrown some kind of magic potion made from wolfsbane on him, and his skin had bubbled when it touched him, and those marks were still there, dark and splashed. But it was the color and texture of his skin that were so appalling, for in every spot the scar tissue was, the flesh had turned into a deep, angry blister. It looked as if some soft, fleshy sea creature, like a starfish filled with curdled milk and possessing twenty or thirty feelers, had adhered itself to his flesh. He could almost see through the skin on the surface of this awful development, and inside, just barely visible, he saw something that made his heart turn to ice...

Hairs.

They were there.

He took his right index finger—knowing what would happen when he did it, and just how it would feel—and pushed the nail through the center of the blister, closing his eyes and experiencing the pleasure and power of an orgasm. Warm fluid was running down his legs. And when he opened his eyes, a large flap of dead skin was peeled back over one of the puncture wounds near his navel, revealing a tuft of dark, wet hair spreading out from the hole.

"Impossible," he whispered, hopelessly.

And even while he said it, he knew it was a lie.

"It would have been better for us all had I killed you over the Vyrmin's grave," a voice said, and Cooper looked up from his wound to find the barrel of Conway's Colt a scant inch from his nose.

"Why is this happening to me?" he asked, moving his eyes along the sheriff's arm and settling his gaze on the man's face.

It was a horrible face, he decided in that instant. He didn't know why he hadn't noticed it before, but there was something about the arrangement of the thing, the way the features were constructed, its lack of any real hair, the beady, listless eyes and flat, obscene mouth, that made him both angry and hungry at the same time.

Hungry.

"Do it," he whispered, lowering his head. "I don't want to be what I apparently am. Just do it and save me from myself."

"Well spoken," the sheriff said…

And then he fired.

But by the time the gun exploded through the forest air, the sheriff's aim had been ruined, and Cooper watched in stunned amazement as a creature, even more remarkable than the ones he had seen in the parking lot, materialized from the trees and pounced, saving his life.

It was a vital, powerful animal, unlike those still howling overhead, in that it was silent, and so much faster than the others that it was blinding. It swooped up from the bush in a blurred streak, and the next thing Cooper knew, it had the sheriff's gun hand in its mouth and was raising itself to its full height, which lifted Conway off his feet by one arm as the Colt, which had its barrel protruding about an inch from one side of the monster's jaws, flashed making the beast appear as if it were spitting fire.

Conway screamed as the animal flipped its head and sent him tumbling in a rag-doll flop over its shoulder and into the trees to disappear beneath a crackle of branches and a cascade of powdery snow. In an instant, the beast turned its attention to the deputy who had come up behind Cooper with the intent of offering the sheriff covering fire. He was standing near the edge of the clearing, starry-eyed and dumb, his rifle lying at his feet and his face sheet-white. He would have offered no resistance, had he had the opportunity, which he didn't, because, the beast, all nine feet of it, covered the distance between the two of them in three quick steps and tore off the deputy's head in a single motion that happened so fast that the man never had the chance to scream. All the detective saw was a spray of pink out of the corner of his eye, and then it was over.

Almost.

Cooper was trembling, and the front of his trousers was wet. He didn't know if that was from the fluid he had released when he'd broken his blister, or from urinating when his bladder let go—which he though it had, about forty seconds ago. And he didn't care. Moving his entire body to face the towering thing that had just saved his life—with the probably intent of making him lunch now that the smoke was clearing—he looked up into the things face. . .and felt the earth shudder beneath his feet.

"I don't believe it!" he meant to scream, but his voice was

weak, and the words were barely audible.

Around him there were other things approaching, rustling brush and closing in, but he didn't pay any attention to whatever they were at all. He just went right on staring into the savage, primitive face of something so big, and so perfectly awful, that, even when a voice said, "So you don't *want* to be what you are?" he didn't respond, but went right on staring, and shaking his head, "No, no, no!"

"Well, we'll just have to see what we can do to change your mind," the voice continued, and still Cooper wouldn't' acknowledge it.

Slowly, he turned his face from the creature that had just killed the deputy, and found himself staring right into a hairy stomach, rising and falling at his eye level. Moving his gaze up, he found two breasts the size of medicine balls, also covered with fur, and above these, a face similar to the one of his savior, but female, and grinning. It was this face, with its animal's eyes and wild mane of black, tangled hair, and pointed ears, that had spoken to him. And in awe he watched as the thing revealed teeth as big as steak knives, and flicked out its arm, slamming the back of its hand into the side of his face and snapping his head around. His body flew, right into the arms of the first creature he'd seen…

The one with the bloody jaws.

And the length of sharpened bone in its hand.

The one with the dirty blond hair…

And the single, glaring eye.

Then then he was out.

FIVE

29

Norris walked through the woods like a zombie, but despite his external appearance of oblivion, his senses were working hard, and he was acutely aware of everything he encountered. Not much of it made any sense, but he was beyond trying to impose his own conceptions of order on things. He was only concerned with finding the "Holy Ground," because that was where Mr. Green had said they were going...although he couldn't place the instant that he had heard the old man use the term. There were a lot of things he just seemed to know without having any reason to know them. And where and what the Holy Ground was seemed to be one of those things. He thought that perhaps he had always known...or maybe...

No.

There was a time when it had happened.

But when was it?

The night Woodie lost his eye in that car wreck that killed Dad and changed the rest of our lives, he thought, stopping to wipe the sweat off his forehead with the back of a trembling hand.

"Oh, Christ," he whispered, not knowing why. "Something about that just isn't right."

Blinking, he glanced around and tried to get an idea of exactly where he was in the woods. He knew he'd been moving pretty fast for at least an hour, and if he hadn't allowed himself to get completely zoned-out while doing it, he should have been heading due north, which would put him roughly two miles from the Killibrook River, which at this section of its run was really more like the Killibrook Creek.

I've got to cross the river, he thought, sighing and starting out again, crunching snow underfoot and feeling a strange sensation—like eyes at his back—following him through the stillness. The woods felt funny here, and he'd picked it up right away. Things were wrong with them, and he'd been noticing what those things were all along, but he hadn't been allowing his mind to dwell on them.

The plants didn't look right.

And the trees were weird.

"The Holy Ground," he said aloud, just to hear the confirmation of his own voice.

And Woodie's eye pulsated in his pocket.

The Holy Ground was the Indian burial grounds...it had to be. About four miles past the river and to the west was a clearing that bore no trees or bushes. It was roughly circular in shape and dipped down, like a bowl, in the center. Some folks said that it was the crater from a meteor that had hit the earth millions of years ago, but there wasn't any scientific evidence to prove it. All that was there was a circle in the woods, two or three hundred yards across and scooped out to a depth of about thirty feet in the center so that when it really rained like hell, the thing would eventually start filling up. It didn't happen often, but it happened—no doubt about it.

The story went that the Native Americans used to bury their magic dead down there when the bowl was full of rainwater. They'd float them out in a canoe, weigh them down, and dumped them over the side. Only the medicine men went that way, it was said. Only the medicine men and the Tatawambie, or spirit bodies. Those were the crazies, which was a rough, white-man translation if there ever was one. The

Tatawambie were people who had committed murder—and that was one big deal in the Indian tribes indigenous to Ohio then. They didn't go for that...at all.

Of course, most of what Norris knew of the Indian burial grounds was gleaned from stories the old guys told around the barbershop and general store when he was a kid. Looking the area up in the library while he was in college years later, he had discovered that most history books didn't even mention the place. And those that did simply referred to it as a local curiosity with many unsubstantiated legends attributed to it. Whether it was actually even a burial ground, or just a hole, no one had ever really proved.

It just *was*...whatever it was.

At the river, he hesitated and studied the sky. Blinking, he decided that, according to the sun, it was at least five o'clock in the afternoon. Evening was coming on, and before he knew it, darkness would fall.

He turned around.

Behind him there was nothing but miles of trees and snow. In the distance was the imposing slope of the Retreat. And atop that, Harpersville, or at least the very edge of it. Between here and there, something was moving...and he could feel it.

He'd always believed in his ability to read the woods. It was something he had been able to do since he was a kid. All he needed was a little quiet and he could touch the forest with his heart.

Trying to explain something like that was a pretty tall order for a kid, especially when the kid's dad was somebody like Dr. Datch, who was constantly scribbling things in a black book that supposedly had "you" inside it. So Norris had never bothered to tell anyone, not even Woodie. It had remained his private secret—just between him and God. Which was kind of who he felt he was talking to when he did it anyway. Maybe some people prayed. But Norris just stood quiet in the woods and felt the perfection of the entire system…and that feeling of perfection, he sensed, was the closest he'd ever come to knowing God. Which for him, was plenty close enough.

But this time he didn't feel God when he studied the trees. This time he broke off even trying seconds after he started and pulled Woodie's eye out of his pocket as if he intended to throw it away. He glared at it, and a veil seemed to flutter over his mind, somewhere near the back of his skull.

He'd seen things the last time…

Brushing snow off a nearby rock, he laid the eye atop it and brought his rifle's butt down with a harsh snap that cracked the eye and sent pieces of it flying in a spray. Stooping, he probed through the splinters until he settled on one, smoky-grey object, no larger than a microchip that he held between his thumb and index finger, gingerly turning it over and over again with somber interest.

"Proof," he whispered, rolling the stone and feeling its smooth edges on his skin. "It's really there."

Why did it excite him so? Why did he suddenly feel relieved to see it, as if he had feared that his visions had in fact been delusions, and not the truth of what had happened to his brother? Given the implication of what he had seen, wouldn't it have been better if he was just out of his mind, and this threat was therefore limited to just himself, and no one else? Wouldn't it have been the altruistic thing: wishing the agonies of insanity for oneself in an attempt to spare one's friends and loved ones from sharing the horrors of those lunatic visions? Shouldn't he hope that it was all a lie, and none of it was true?

"Yes," he thought. "I should hope that. But I don't. I want it to be true."

And, with his honest feelings thus spoken, he lifted the stone, this time only to the level of his forehead, aimed it at the sun, and waited for…

* * *

This transition wasn't nearly so hard to take as the first, probably because he knew it was coming. One minute he was standing by the river in the frozen woods, and the next he was driving a car along a very dark road in the middle of what looked like a blizzard, which the weatherman, who was on the radio at that moment, was saying would get much worse.

Woodie shouldn't have been driving, that much was obvious almost instantly. His head was lolling on his neck and the car was drifting perilously toward the road's shoulder and back. He was stoned on his ass again, and Norris wondered what part of his brother's life he was seeing this time. It had to be after the episode in the Institute of Metaphysical Research, and before his death in the Lexington Motel, which, according to Cooper's description of events, was a period of just three days. He was about to turn around in the dark and try to gather up enough of Woodie's memories to pinpoint their location when his field of vision swayed giddily and the person in the passenger's seat of the car swung into view.

She'd changed quite a bit since the first time he'd seen her, through his brother's memories, about a month ago. Then she had been frail, thin, and sickly. But now she was better. Her contact with a human—specifically Woodie—had apparently done wonders for her constitution, because her skin tone was healthy, and her eyes sparkled with energy and intelligence. Even her tattered white robes looked better. And her hair was superb—like sunlight made solid.

But Norris couldn't' stand it anymore. In one abrupt jerk he moved his attention away from the window of his brother's eye and studied the memories he found, nestled in the darkness of Woodies' skull, which were distorted, confused, and nearly indecipherable, probably because of all the drugs he had ingested…

Which was one of the things Norris saw:

Woodie was on a bed—the same bed over which he and the demon had made their union—and, as a group of very rough, very strong hands held him down, other hands were forcing great quantities of peyote, raw and juicy, into his mouth.

"*Not so much!*" Woodie was screaming in his mind, writhing on the bed and doing his best to choke the stuff back up. "*Never so much!*"

But no matter what he did, there was more coming. And all the while the Lady of the Night—nude, and very human now—straddled him and rode his bucking body, screaming out as she achieved orgasm after orgasm.

The people feeding him the peyote were eating too, off in the shadows…but it wasn't a plant they were consuming. Gagging and retching, they were pushing lumps of something that dripped in oily streaks into their mouths. Some were able to swallow on the first or second try, while others didn't seem able to keep whatever it was that looked so juicy and red down before their fourth or fifth attempt.

As bad as all that peyote was, Woodie sensed that he was lucky that they were saving the dripping red stuff for themselves, and that somehow, he was getting the better end of the bargain…

At least for now.

Then he was crawling over concrete, on his hands and knees.

Then he was lying on a bed, staring at a perfectly normal white plaster ceiling over which a tiny black spider moved from right to left.

Then he was trying to talk Mike Cooper into doing something that Cooper didn't really want to do, because Mr. Green said that it was important that Cooper get involved with whatever it was they were trying to achieve, which was the salvation of the planet by the genocide, or controlled slaughter, of the Flock...which meant mankind...

And then he was driving a car again.

And then they were digging up a grave...and that's where Norris' attention settled and he allowed Woodie's memories to unfold from there:

* * *

At the instant Galltar hurled the young sexton into the empty grave, the stain on the land was broken, and a new and powerful force surged up from the earth to invigorate the descendants of the First Father. They tore off their clothes, and Woodie looked up to see that they were already changing in ways that seemed to take them back in time, and down the evolutionary scale, closer to what their ancestors must have looked like when the First Father, clothed in animal skins and carrying a sharpened bone, found the moonstone and let the genie out of the bottle with his mind.

"Only you can break the charm!" had been their urgent, insistent refrain. "We'll go down to Harpersville and prepare everything. We'll cultivate the people, find the grave, see if there are any Dogs with teeth in the area, and make all ready for your arrival. But it must be you. Only the stone will allow us to move the bones.

"And we must move the bones!"

Move the bones!

The words echoed in his head.

So much peyote.

Move the bones!

At first he didn't think it would work. Mr. Green disappeared immediately after Woodie and the Lady of the Night were first joined, and eventually he and she had driven down to Harpersville to work the "powerful magic needed to reclaim the Holy Ground."

Maybe it was all that peyote…Woodie wasn't sure just how much dope he'd taken into his system over the past few days, but he was sure it was a lot. He even had vague memories of people making him eat the stuff…and of other people, his friends, eating horrible things…but none of that sat right in his head.

He wasn't sure about anything.

His brain was just so fuzzy, and there were so many little *voices,* as he had taken to calling them, although a more accurate word might have been "urges," tugging at him from deep inside that he really didn't trust himself anymore. There were things he wanted to do—awful things that beckoned to him from the recesses of his being—and mostly they were centered around the woman, the demon, his Lady of the Night.

So, on the way down to Harpersville, he drove—which he shouldn't have—and he didn't know how they arrived alive, especially with the woman doing the things she did in the car with her hands and tongue.

Then there was that business in the street near the city jail when the lights went out, but he attributed that to the dope again.

And then they were at the cemetery and she spoke to him for the first time…

And that was weird.

Before that instant he hadn't noticed her silence. But when she finally did say words, he realized that it was the first time he'd heard her voice in any other way than a snarl or a moan. She had a strange, moody tone, imbued with a rich, reverberating timbre that seemed to radiate up more from a tunnel than a throat. It was such a soothing sound for him to hear that immediately his attention fixed on it, and he felt as if she had found some special frequency that matched perfectly with that one, sober area of his brain that was not too confused by dope to function.

"I don't know how it will be done," she said, assuming the form of the girl in white again as they got out of his Pinto at the graveyard. Before the overhead light came on she had been more reptilian than human—a lizard-like silhouette in the dark, sending over a skilled tongue at least three feet long that had unzipped the fly on his jeans and done things to him that had kept his mind off the screaming he had heard when she had left him in the car to go inside the jail for a few minutes.

"But whatever you do, know that it will be correct," she continued, taking his hand and leading him to the grave side. "For the Master has decreed that thou shalt lift the curse of thine father. And so it shall be done. So it must be done, and quickly, for they have a Dog here—a very powerful Dog. And without moving the bones, the Blood Prince will never make his rise."

And we certainly can't have that, Woodie thought humorlessly, swaying on his feet.

The rest of the people from the Institute were there, lined on either side of his father's grave. He hadn't seen some of them in a couple of days and he wanted to stop and say hello, but a strange sensation suddenly overtook him, starting as a tiny hum in his head and blossoming into a real sound that...

He froze, his eyes wide and staring at the ground.

He could see right through the dirt!

He could see into his father's coffin!

And what he saw infuriated him.

There he was—his father—lying in his box. He'd been in the ground for twenty-five years, but he hadn't changed all that much from the way Woodie remembered him. His eyes were still brown, his hair was still curly. And he was wearing that same blue, pin-striped suit that he had kept in a plastic zipper bag in the cedar closet for when someone got married or died. He was looking up as if he could see Woodie, and his lips were forming the words, "Help me! Help me!" over and over again, weakly, and with trembling effort.

Which wasn't surprising, because his head was lying between his knees.

A flash that came from the corner of his eye obscured Woodie's vision for an instant, and then he lifted his arms and said, *"Dig!"* in a big, commanding voice that was confident and sober.

"But, sire," one of the people standing close responded formally. This ground is sealed against our touch. We can disturb it not."

And Woodie spun, fired out one hand and grabbed the speaker by the front of his robe. With terrible force he hurled the man to the ground and pointed saying, "*Dig*!" as the first movements of the dirt began.

The man, on his hands and knees, looked down in surprise. Beneath him, snow-dusted grass churned, swaying as if it were responding to some swirling current before rocks rolled themselves over and disturbed worms twisted their dismay. From deep inside the moving dirt, flickers of something bright flashed, glancing up as cracks formed in the ground and a rumble vibrated below.

The man looked up.

And Woodie told him to dig again.

He needed no further prompting.

In moments there were three big men with shovels scraping frantically at the glowing dirt, and, with the very first gouges they produced, the light burst forth.

It hit Woodie in the eye and blinded him, filling his skull and drowning his thoughts with a brilliant silver glow that obliterated everything for what seemed like only a second and then…

A hand touched his and the Lady of the Night said, "Hail. It is done."

And he blinked.

The light was gone, and the grave was violated. His knees felt liquid when he saw the empty coffin, the horse's head, and the body. They almost gave way when he looked up and found the girl dangling at the end of her chain. But when he looked down at the object he was holding in his right hand, his revulsion was complete.

He was going to drop it, but his fingers didn't want to move. It was a long bone, white and heavy. A thighbone, most likely, belonging to a man—to his father.

He tried to drop it again, but I seemed to adhere to his palm.

In his mind, his father's desperately pleading face, which Woodie had so recently seen in its coffin, ceased its begging and looked him calmly in the eye.

Free, it seemed to say. *At last my son has come to end my shame. Take it as a gift. From a father to a son. Take it, and use it well.*

Woodie looked at the bone again, and suddenly something about its cold hardness in his hand made him reconsider. He bounced it, admiring its weight. He swung it before him a couple of times and it cut the air with a satisfying *ssswwish!* He tapped its end on his father's tombstone, and it produced a solidly ominous *thunk!*

His father's face smiled benevolently in his mind.

And Woodie decided that he'd just wait and see before he threw the bone away because, who knew, maybe it would come in handy sometime.

✡ ✡ ✡

And Norris turned from the memory and faced the window of his brother's eyes socket again, just as the Pinto pulled off to one side of the road and a figure, fuzzy in the blowing snow, came trotting up to the driver's side window.

The thighbone was lying across Woodie's lap, telling Norris that this event was happening after the cemetery. The woman was speaking as Woodie rolled down his window.

"The final stage," she was saying, but Woodie didn't seem to care. "He will be your key."

Norris was confused by all he had seen—by the events themselves, but, even more, by his brother's strangely flat, seemingly emotionless response to it all. Since the joining over the bed at the Institute, the people that he was with had been keeping him very drugged, but even that didn't explain his apathy. Norris sensed that something fundamental had changed in his brother—perhaps had even died—and that such an alteration could never have been performed by an outside source. Whatever had happened to Woodie's mind, it had been drawn from inside him. It had been there all along, just waiting for the proper circumstances to release it into the world.

And when Woodie spoke to the young man at the side of the road, Norris' suspicions were confirmed.

"Hey, man!" Woodie said, and remarkably his words did not slur at all. "Wanna ride? You're gonna freeze walkin' in this shit."

When the boy got in, Norris saw that he could be no more than eighteen years old, and suddenly things began falling into place for him. Suddenly he sensed the truth, and in silence, he watched his suspicions bear fruit.

They went to a bar. Norris even recognized which one it was. Woodie kept glancing at his watch every few minutes, and because he did, Norris was able to keep track of the time without hardly trying. He remembered what Cooper had said about Woodie calling him and saying that they should meet at a McDonald's in Akron at midnight, but judging by the way they were drinking, they weren't going to make that rendezvous, which Norris already knew they had missed.

I'm watching him spend his last few hours on earth,

Norris thought as Woodie bought another round of beers for himself and the guy he had picked up on the road just outside of town. The woman in white wasn't drinking, but staring silently at her hands, which were folded on the tabletop. And Norris thought, *He doesn't know it, but it's all winding down to a close, and he's just sipping away the time, downing beers and doped out of his mind, just like he spent most of the rest of his life.*

The kid they picked up was called Raymond. That's all he'd say. He was about Woodie's height, and just as thin. His hair was blond, not as blond as Woodie's, but a fairly light shade of brown. And he was wearing jeans. But beyond that, any resemblance between the two disappeared. Once he took his coat off, Raymond revealed his arms to be tattooed from wrist to shoulder with a variety of snakes, knives, and flowers, all done in gaudy reds and blacks and connected by strings of words that said things like "Helmet laws suck, and "Longhaired country boy." Raymond lived in Mist County and was up in Harpersville because Mist County was dry—you couldn't buy beer. His old Oldsmobile did fine in regular weather, but as soon as it got cold and damp, well, sometimes it didn't work so good. It had died about a mile from where he had been walking, and, well, "It was awful nice o' ya ta pick me up 'cause I was 'bout to freeze my balls off. What's with your girlfriend, anyway? Don't' she talk?"

And they were quickly becoming friends.

And, "Jesus, man, where you getting' all this money for beers? Wish there was something I could do to pay you back."

And of course there was.

Just as Ernie Cray was later to relate, Woodie pulled his Pinto up to the office door of the Lexington Motel at almost exactly midnight. By then it was snowing very hard, Raymond was very drunk, and Woodie was very quiet.

"I ain't never seen nothing like this," Raymond was mumbling in the backseat, his head down so that someone looking out of the motel would only see Woodie and his girlfriend, and not him, because then they'd have to pay more and there wasn't any sense paying extra if you don't have to.

That made no sense at all, but Raymond didn't argue because the broad was a fox, and her boyfriend like to watch her do it with other guys, and...

"I ain't lyin', man! I only read 'bout shit like this in them magazines they keep behind the counter at the drugstore so's you gotta ask for 'em special and everybody in the place can hear. Never thought it was true...tell you that for free!"

"Just relax," Woodie said, his voice even as he withdrew his wallet and glanced over at the woman. "It's not so unusual."

The look she returned was one of confidence and even pride. Her eyes had taken on their yellowish, reptilian tinge again, and somehow that seemed appropriate because they were Woodie's favorite. He liked the way the centers opened and closed in response to the light.

"Be back in a minute," he said, and he was.

The motel room was small, but that was okay. The woman held the door open while Woodie helped Raymond inside. He talked a good game, but when it came to holding his alcohol, he didn't seem to do it very well.

They dropped him on the bed, and he lay still so long that Norris began to suspect that he'd passed out. Then he roused himself a little, half scooted up toward the headboard, and, with a bleary, anticipatory grin said, "Okay, who's got the whipped cream?"

As Woodie stood staring down at the young man, the girl made a perfunctory reconnaissance of the room, opening the little bathroom door to his right, and closing the curtains on the window to his left. Over the bed hung a portrait of Jesus: one of those ones where he's depicted as being a young

Caucasian, long-haired type, crowned with bloody thorns and looking mournfully skyward with big soulful eyes. *Lamb of God,* Woodie thought for some reason, and it made him smile.

"For the others, it happened before they came down here," the girl said softly into his ear, and Woodie tensed. He'd been so intent on the boy that he hadn't heard her sidle up beside him. "The first is always the hardest, but it must be so."

"Just get on with it," Woodie responded breathlessly, and inside him, Norris sensed more than anticipation. He felt his brother's excitement. It was a feeling that he had watched evolve from the Institute to the cemetery to the motel, and it had nothing to do with the peyote. Woodie was fully participating in all that happened to him. He was not an unwilling innocent, but a conscious, acting conspirator in his own fate. He wasn't fighting at all, but rushing headlong into what Norris knew would be his own doom.

"There a radio in this place?" Raymond was asking as he fumbled with something on the little black TV tray that served as a nightstand. Norris noticed that there were three mallard ducks in flight pained on the thing and that one of its legs was bent.

Without a word, the girl moved toward the bed.

It began in silence, and Norris squirmed inside his brother's head. At once he winced, and wanted to pull back and avert his attention from this because it made him feel dirty, as if he were contributing to it somehow by being its witness. But there was also that part of him that could do nothing but watch—wide-eyed and clinical—as the girl became suddenly so seductive that, even from where he was seeing things, Norris couldn't help but respond to her himself.

She apparently could turn it on like an electric light. And that was a good analogy, Norris decided. One minute she was just what she was: a young girl with long blond hair wearing an innocuous white dress/gown type of thing that had turned some heads in the beer joint earlier, more because it was so inappropriate for a cold winter's night than because it was particularly sexy. And the next minute her whole body seemed to radiate a veritable pulse of prickling, animal power.

She lifted her arms up over hear head, bunching her hair in her hands and letting it fall as she curved her spine and closed her eyes with a sigh that was deep and luxurious in a way that was all acceptance and invitation. Her gown clung to her breasts and stomach, moving as if animated to outline every detail of her form as the one light from the scrawny lamp by the bed seemed to dim and the shadowy triangle between her legs showed every so subtly through the whispering white material.

Raymond became, if not sober, then at least interested, and he followed the girl with his eyes as she moved over onto his left side and began undoing the buttons on his flannel shirt.

Woodie positioned himself behind where Raymond was lying so that the girl stood directly in front of him with the open bathroom door behind her. His breathing was heavy and ragged, and sweat was moistening his forehead and gathering in his eyebrows in quivering, oily beads.

Norris strained to see Woodie's face in the mirror behind the girl. She blocked his view most of the time, but if she turned just right, he could almost see what Woodie looked like, and for some reason, at that instant it became very important to him that he see his brother's face because, he realized, at any moment something was going to happen and Woodie was going to die. Either the "stranger" named Raymond was going to do something to him, or the girl was going to do it; but whoever it was, Woodie was not walking out of this room alive. Norris had seen his bloody, dismembered body, a door that was locked from the inside, and the broken widow with its single line of tracks leading away and into the woods. Woodie's death was imminent, and it was suddenly of the utmost importance to Norris that he see his face at least one more time.

When the women dropped her gown, he got his wish.

And his world turned upside down.

The way they were positioned, Raymond didn't see it. That was why they had done it that way, Norris knew in a rush. Just as the girl's dress slid off her shoulders, the boy on the bed said, "Holy Jesus on a bicycle," and started to turn over toward Woodie. It was a strange reaction: turning away from a naked woman, but he was probably doing it to make sure that Woodie really did want him to go ahead and screw his girlfriend, right here, while he watched. But before he could look over his shoulder, the girl had dropped to her knees, put her hands on his chest, and was kissing him.

When she moved, the view to the mirror was suddenly cleared, and Norris saw his brother's face...

And was amazed.

"Woodie!" he gasped, unable to think, and feeling something that was very much like a cold breeze blowing through his awareness. "Oh, Jesus! Woodie!"

Woodie's eyes were wide. His hands were clenched into fists and positioned one on either side of his chest so that his elbows were high behind him. His mouth was open and a long stream of saliva was hanging from his lower lip, dripping with running beads and reaching in a stringy line past where the edge of the mirror ended. It may have touched the floor for all Norris knew. But spit wasn't his concern. It was his brother's teeth that held his attention, because, with his lips drawn back as they were, those teeth seemed to grow.

"Oh, my my!" Raymond said as the woman undid his fly. "You do know how to do things."

His shirt was off, and in a moment his trousers were

bunched at his knees. He had his head resting on the palm of his cocked left arm, and he was stroking the girl's head with his right. In any real sense, he was now alone with her in the room, and the danger hovering behind him could have been on the other side of the sun, for all he knew.

Woodie was looking down, at the back of Raymond's neck.

Norris was looking at his brother's face in the mirror.

And the woman looked up as her face…

Changed.

The sounds that followed happened so close together that they may as well have been simultaneous. As Woodie bit him, Raymond shouted, and when Raymond shouted, Woodie growled. It was almost funny, really. Or at least it would have been if Norris didn't know that this had been the moment of truth, the act that led directly to his brother's murder.

And even though he thought that he'd look away when the time came, he didn't. He kept right on watching, as Woodie stood up, and his face came into view in the mirror.

It had been the look in the girl's eyes that had made Woodie move. She had looked up, and her eyes had gone yellow again, and there had been something in her expression that all but screamed, "Now! Do it now!"

And with a grunt, Woodie had plunged his face down and bitten Raymond's neck so hard that when he jerked his head back up again, he left a gouge in the boy's skin that was already filling with blood.

"What the?! Hey….*Owwwww!*" Raymond yelled, lifting his hand to his neck and rolling…or trying to roll.

But the girl was holding him as easily as if he were a child.

Woodie swallowed on his first attempt, roared triumphantly, and stretched his face into a wide-eyed look of madness that glared in the bathroom glass with streaks of blood crawling down his chin.

Raymond was screaming.

And Norris knew that he'd been wrong.

As the change happened, it suddenly all made sense to him, and he was flabbergasted with himself for having been so wrong about everything. He'd had all he needed to know right in front of him, but he had clung to the preposterous story that Mike Cooper had told him when he first arrived on the murder scene, and its false chronology had confused him totally.

Now, seeing events unfold, he realized that Cooper had lied to him—that Woodie had never asked for a meeting at any McDonald's in Akron, or anywhere else. That Woodie hadn't begged for help to get out of the Institute of Metaphysical Research. And that his brother's diary wasn't really a notebook thrown carelessly on the backseat of his Pinto.

This was his brother's diary.

This eye...this stone...this moment.

His brother hadn't died in this motel room...it had only been his brother's humanity that had perished.

The body they had found belonged to someone else.

As Raymond rolled on the bed, Woodie stared at his own face in the bathroom mirror. Both he and his brother, who was inside his head, watched as first Woodies' face and then the rest of his body underwent a transformation of staggering proportion. It wasn't like Lefty Zimmer's, which had been a transformation of the mind, but not of the body, because, at that time, Woodie and the girl had still been on their way down from Cleveland and therefore the power for a physical change hadn't been available to him. And it wasn't like Cheryl Lockner's, which had been the first physical manifestation, but had been limited because the bones hadn't yet been moved and the curse was still on the land. And it wasn't like Ernie Cray's, which, when it would happen the following morning, would be the closest thing to a real change yet, because the power would have come...but the moon still wouldn't be full, so it wouldn't be complete.

This was a full-blown alteration that moved Woodie Norris from one plane of being to another in a matter of seconds. It seemed to swell up from inside the man so that, for one terrible instant, he stood perfectly still, as if waiting, and then it hit him with all the force of a blow.

The first thing to change was his hair—it grew, on his head and everywhere. In a wink it reached to his waist and spread over his jaws and neck. His face stretched as did, simultaneously, his fingers, until his lower jaw hung low and bristling with sharp, canine teeth and his hands had become wicked, claw-like arrangements that sported mean, sharp nails at the cap of each finger. His brow pushed itself out over his staring, animal eyes—which were pocketed like a gorilla's amid pouches of dark, wrinkled skin—and his forehead sloped back to a peaked ridge over pointed, wolfish ears. Suddenly his nose was moist and sensitive, his arms hung low, and his clothing tore away as he grew bigger and bigger, his head virtually touching the ceiling as soon as he became...

Nine feet tall.

He towered over the bed, trembled, and then, with a shudder that made him clench his huge fists, and an effort that watered his eyes, he looked directly down at where Raymond lay—awestruck on the bed in a bloody fetal position—and expressed his newfound power and rage in one long, agonizing howl that shook the walls and made the terrified man lose what little was left of his composure, and his mind.

Norris watched it all in the bathroom mirror. He didn't miss a detail, and finally, when the change was nearing its end, he said in a voice filled with wonder, "Neanderthal."

For that was the word he knew.

He had heard Mr. Green's story of the first Blood Prince, heard how he had found the stone after it fell from the moon millions of years ago. And here was the proof of it, the logical extension of its events: Woodie Norris, as least according to Mr. Green, was a direct descendant of that first, primitive man who had taken the magic from the sky and made it a part of himself. He was connected, by some invisible umbilical, to a time before history had begun, and now, with the stone's help, and apparently released by his first taste of human flesh, he had *become* that ancestral forebear! He *was* that primitive cannibal! Time had ceased exerting its control and was suddenly meaningless—at least for now. At this instant the Wild had returned, and all the changes, evolutions, developments, and discoveries that mankind had experienced over the course of countless generations were rendered insignificant. All that mattered now was all that had mattered from that first instant of life's inception on the planet: there was life, and it needed to be fed.

Survival.

The Hunt!

It was suddenly all reduced to that because Woodie Norris and a man named Green, who was, Robert Norris suddenly understood, everything he claimed to be!

Norris?

Woodie...and Robert.

They were brothers!

If Woodie was a direct descendant of that first, banished primitive who consumed members of his own species and lived the wild life even at a time when behaving in a civilized manner was as easy as sleeping in a cave, that meant that Robert was also thus related. He shared the same genes with his brother, and in truth, he was the eldest son. Wasn't he as much a part of the Wild as Woodie...or had he been ignored?

Norris stopped his thoughts with a conscious effort and said, "Listen to yourself! Ignored? You're acting like you feel left out! Like you want to be a part of this! Look at that thing! Look at what your baby brother's become!"

Just as he did, the final few convolutions contorted Woodie's skull and altered its shape and size so much that the glass eye he wore—the one through which Norris was witnessing this entire event—no longer fit into its socket. As Woodie jerked his head around and aimed his snarling face at the boy on the bed, his eye flew out, making Norris involuntarily scream as his perspective went tumbling through a dizzying spin within which he was trapped without so much as a hint of stability. Reflexively he tried to hold on to something...but he had no hands. Desperately he tried to look away...but outside Woodie's head there was no dark place of memory and dream in which he could hide, and everything he saw spun and rushed at him from every direction, so that finally he felt as if he had been launched into a terrible world of immense objects and pointless motion.

The eye landed on the carpet, bounced, rolled, and settled near a chair leg, cockeyed, so that Norris found himself looking up at an odd angle, into the room. From this floor-bound perspective, Woodie's hairy body loomed even larger than it had from above, his legs stretching as tall as an office building in a room of fun-house angles and endless depths. Bereft of its contact with Woodie's being, the stone seemed to lose some of its life, and Norris realized that he was deaf inside it: he no longer had the use of Woodie's ears through which to hear. All he could do was watch as Woodie reached down to the bed...so far down it seemed...and picked Raymond up...so, so far up...and...

All the violence that resulted in the carnage that Norris found when he was thrust into the room—*would find* when he was thrust into the room hours later, he tried to remember in a vague attempt at keeping some kind of handle on at least a piece of reality—happened in less than one minute.

Woodie's fury was complete, and his strength, staggering. He held Raymond up, straight-armed out from his body so that the boy's head touched the ceiling, looked at him for a moment, and then, in an explosion of brute force, simply pulled both his arms off, allowing the now screaming body to drop onto the bed.

Raymond was rolling frantically in the sheets, bleeding steaming sprays from the stumps of his shoulders and marring the walls on either side while Woodie *ate* his arms.

Ate them!

Norris felt nausea sweep through him in gasping waves, but without a body he had no way to express it.

When the last of Raymond's hand disappeared into Woodie's mouth, he swallowed and threw his arms out on either side, bellowing exuberantly before bashing himself into the walls around him, as if suddenly realizing that he was indoors. He punched holes in the plaster, bit through wood, railed at the air, and tore gouges in the ceiling with his fingers. After a pause, he ripped Raymond to pieces with three deadly sweeps of his hands...fingers like knives...knives like mercy.

"Thank God he's finally dead," Norris whispered when Raymond stopped struggling.

In an instant the body's head was off, as was most of his face. His chest was open. And what followed, the feeding, numbed Norris through.

When Woodie finished, he stood for a moment with his huge chest heaving, glanced over to the bathroom mirror, and became suddenly very interested in it. He stepped closer, stared, and then lifted his hand to touch the cheek under his empty eye socket. He studied it for a long time, his brows working until he finally turned, looked over the floor, and spotted the eye on the carpet.

Norris saw relief spread over his brother's face as he

leaned down from what looked like a thousand feet up to retrieve his eye. But strangely, with his hand no more than a few inches away, Woodie stopped, cocked his head as if someone were speaking to him, and stood back up, leaving the eye where it lay.

Then Norris saw the woman.

She was standing, beautiful, virtually glowing with radiant light, her long white robes unmarked and gloriously clean in so awful a place as the motel room had become. She was looking at Woodie without a trace of fear or concern for herself. If any word could have described her expression, it could only have been "satisfied." She was looking at this immense, slavering beast as a mother would a child who had performed some simple task correctly for the first time. And when Woodie returned her gaze, that childish attitude became his own.

He cowered a little, pointing to the eye and moving his lips as if he were speaking…

Speaking, Norris thought. *Can that ape speak?*

The woman listened and then shook her head.

Woodie's face twisted with anger, but he did not make so much as a single move forward. Instead he spoke faster and Norris strained, desperate to hear but relegated to a view of shattering silence. Woodie's words were coming hard and fast, and all the while he continued pointing down at the eye, so that Norris saw his face balanced miles away at the end of an arm that looked as big as the space shuttle's solid rocket booster.

But despite his impassioned argument, the woman still refused to let Woodie retrieve his eye. Finally, as if in compensation, she produced the thighbone that she had apparently retrieved from the car, and Woodie fell silent looking at it. With solemn purpose, he listened as the woman apparently described the object, holding it out for him to take and smiling benevolently when he finally did.

When the bone was in Woodie's hairy hand, the woman

tossed back her head with a laugh and threw her arms out wide. Woodie rushed into them and picked her up off the floor, reminding Norris sickly of some old movie musical when the boy finally gets the girl. But when he released her, the girl had become something that no old movie musical would ever have featured: she had her bat wings back, and she was only about three feet tall, and she had a tail...

And Woodie leapt right through the glass window, disappearing into the night.

And the girl flew through the hole he had made and up, into the darkened sky.

And Norris suddenly found himself alone, in that horrible room, to await...

"Myself," he said, feeling his thoughts spinning at the brink of collapse. "I'm going to arrive in a few hours. I'm going to lie here, in the blood, and wait for myself to come and put me in my pocket!"

In a little while red and blue lights were spinning outside, and the door was forced open. In stumbled Sheriff Conway and Detective Michael Cooper together!

He did lie, Norris thought, feeling excited on the one hand that he was in fact beginning to put things into perspective, and vaguely apathetic about anything these silly creatures were doing. *He no more followed the police radio here than I did. He and Conway have been in on this all along.*

The two men looked over the room and went away, leaving Norris alone for a while.

Then the door opened again and a bunch of guys with cameras and such came in.

Then the door opened a third time, and Norris fell silent as he watched himself come into the room, stagger, and fall, looking like the biggest asshole to ever ride a horse. He couldn't believe himself. He was suddenly appalled and embarrassed. He was so puny when compared to his brother. He was so weak, and frail, and slow, and senseless when compared to Woodie, with his broad shoulders and powerful hands.

He was so…ugly.

The revelation hit him while he was watching himself slide off the bed and onto the floor. He realized in that instant—the one just before the deputies lifted him off the floor and threw him outside to vomit—that he was doing the exact thing that Mr. Green had warned Woodie not to do: he was looking through the stone and seeing what was there as the stone would see it. He was seeing things from a perspective that was alien to his own human viewpoint. He was becoming part of something…*big*!

"I'm…" he began to say, starting off a very important thought. "I'm…a part of…"

And then his own hand—the hand of the Robert Norris who was human and normal and who would never have dreamed of anything like what he had just seen—came down on the eye and grabbed it in his fist…

And the whole world went dark.

But the thought was still there…the idea had come.

Norris was left spinning through that darkness with nothing but a growing sense of his own place, position, and purpose. He was left tumbling through a nightmare space that seemed to rush from darkness, toward a light that emanated from an eye…an eye that had been watching him from his dreams since he was a child…his dreams…the eye…they were together…he was there…they were there…the dreams had a man with an eye…two eyes…and a beard…

And he was a child.

And his dad was drunk.

And it was nighttime.

And there was a man with a beard…

And terrible eyes…

Mr. Green.

And Norris was only five…

And his father was drunk…

And Mr. Green was there…

And Mr. Green said, "Now sleep, until the wolf in thine heart it born."

And the next thing he knew…

"Now, sleep…"

And the next thing he knew…

He remembered it all.

IV
BLOOD PRINCE

SIX

30

"I'm going to tell you about it, boy," Norris heard an echoing voice say from the shadows of his own past. "I'm going to tell you, and you're going to keep it hidden until again we meet, many years from now."

The old man's face was thrust up close to his own, and the hand was holding his chin so that he could not look away or remember anything else. The words climbed up like living things from the vault of his mind and tore his life into two separate parts: those five brief years before Dr. Green had "examined" him, and everything that had happened since. He hadn't known it, but for twenty-five years he had simply been marking time, waiting for the moment when that hidden door in his head would fly open, and these words would pour forth like poisoned darts into his awareness.

And pour they did, verbatim, as if he weren't remembering at all, but hearing them again, as he had heard them before, so long ago…

"You won't speak of it, or think of it, or remember it until the day I summon you unto myself," Dr. Green said with quiet confidence. "On that day, you'll remember…*and you'll come*. No resisting will prevent it. You'll come. And together, we'll change the world. Now, listen:

"The man who brought you here tonight isn't your father, and the place you live isn't your home. You are of the trees and the valleys. Your nature is green, and your essence earthen. In your heart there's no concrete or steel, but forests and open skies. In your soul resides the flame of freedom, lost to all but a precious, dwindling few.

"For you are Wild.

"There are others of the Wild, but you…oh, you will be their prince, because you have been born a Sender! Your dreams will be the key to the future of your kin. *Your* gift will open *their* gate. And as the Breed's emancipator, you will be revered!"

Oh God, Norris thought, his fists clenching before his face as his head dropped and his eyes squeezed shut. *What is this? Oh, Jesus! What is it?*

His posture was agonized, his body trembling. As he struggled to keep his knees from buckling he felt tears running down his face and saw a faint glimmer of some glowing spark, hovering close to the front of his mind.

The light of reason, he thought, watching that spark fade precariously before the darkness of his memories.

He wanted to reach out and draw back its comforting glow, but instead, he watched helplessly as a curtain of even darker images rushed in and extinguished that light for good…

And then something snapped.

Without reason's light to blind his mind's eye, he saw things afresh. He heard the word *Sender* and thought about his dreams. He remembered that feeling of terror he had become so accustomed to over the years: the sensation of huge, pressing dread that descended on him every time he went to sleep, the overpowering horror that had driven him kicking and clawing his way out of bed as if the sheets were ablaze each and every night, and he realized that, somewhere in the back of his mind, he had always suspected that there was more to his dreams than just nightmare chills. He had always sensed…

No!

"Sensed" was too weak a word.

He had always *known* he was special in some way. He had never verbalized it, of course, but he had *KNOWN* it, as surely as he had known that the little house with the sagging roof and cockeyed shutters hadn't been nestled back in the trees off the old dairy road before that night that his father had scooped him out of bed and said, "We're gonna get to the bottom of this 'fore you do any more harm!"

* * *

Norris opened his eyes and stared straight ahead, seeing the memory so vividly that it was as if there were a movie screen in his head. Superimposed over that screen, he saw that he was still standing on the south shore of the Killibrook River, and that the forest on the other side looked dimly flat—like a two-dimensional approximation of reality washed in lifeless, running shades of grey.

He blinked.

And realized that the day had slipped away.

Around him, the nebulous, transitional period between the setting of the sun and the coming of the moon had fallen, and twilight shadows haunted the darkening trees with twisted, murky stillness. The sky—still bloody with the last vestiges of a fading day—was perfectly clear. And the air was cold. Not as it had been earlier, when it was just at freezing, so that the snow that fell was wet and heavy. But really cold, almost bitter. Soon the Valley would crack underfoot, and slushy mud would turn to ice.

He hadn't seen Dr. Green's house in twilight. He'd seen it in full dark. His father's face—stained an alien green by the glow of their Rambler's instruments—had hung expectantly over the steering wheel as he navigated the winding path of the old State Route 6. It was Bobby himself who first spotted the sign, bent and pointing in the antiseptic glow of the car's headlights, reading "Doc," at the end of what he thought might have been a road, but that was actually a gravel driveway. And he remembered thinking that the place looked a little like the gingerbread house in that old fairy tale as they pulled through the trees and saw it, built right into the side of a hill, where neither of them had known a house to be before.

"Well," his father had said, "let's give this one a try. Maybe he won't throw us out."

In the wake of such memories, and beneath the cold shadow of approaching night, Norris gazed across the river, feeling as if time itself had begun to fade from his consciousness. There didn't seem to be any difference between what had been and what was anymore—the present had become a constant. Maybe he had stepped into a warp in the fabric of reality, a pocket of existence that never changed. That might explain it. But he was certain that, if he didn't move, he could stay here forever—right in this spot—caught in a permanent now. If a mastodon wandered up beside him at that instant and dipped its trunk into the stream for a drink, it would have surprised him no more than if a Civil War soldier had appeared to fill his canteen.

He lowered his arm, the muscles in his jaw working beneath his skin, his eyes fixed on the tiny, smoke-grey chip he held between his thumb and index finger.

"My life was in two parts," he said to the stone. "And you made it one again. But what's it all mean?"

The Man in the Woods was standing on the other side of the river, and Norris sensed him before he saw him there.

Lifting his eyes from the stone once more, he studied the figure he found, half hidden in the forest, about thirty feet away. In the shadows, the man's form was somewhat vague, ill defined, and dark. His face was constructed more from the negative impressions of patterns created by tangled foliage than anything solid. His body seemed comprised of the spaces between two trees, or three.

If you didn't know he was there, you might have missed him. If you didn't expect to see him, you probably wouldn't. If you wanted to touch him, you'd have to do it with your heart, because your hand would find only frustration.

In that moment, Norris appreciated just how much effort it had been for this creature to take on the substantial, human shape it had for so long. He realized how painful it must have been, how...demeaning. That was the word! For this being to coalesce itself into the body that various people had seen over the years, it would have had to deny its own true form...its own true identity. It was a creature made entirely of the spaces between things! To see it required only that one know how to look.

Woodie had said that!

Or something very much like it.

He believed that for everything the natural world presented, there was another, deeper meaning that was hidden so long as the observer was limited to a single, stable reference point.

Like the Man in the Woods: see the trees with your eyes, see the Man with your heart.

By altering the way a person saw things, it was possible to discover the truth about the world.

Norris swallowed, and squeezed the stone beneath his fingers...it had certainly altered the way he saw things.

So what was the truth?

That a piece of the moon had fallen a million years ago and was found by a caveman to whom Robert Norris, twentieth-century park ranger and nature lover, was directly related? That because of that rock, a demon had been drawn into the real world from the imagination of that man, and that now that demon was willing to do the bidding of the stone's keeper in return for sex? And that, also because of that rock, a group of cannibal kings had come together and had been imbued with the power of drawing a man's or a woman's most secretly hidden urges to the surface, thereby turning that person into a werewolf slave?

When Norris looked back at the trees, he found that the Man in the Woods had moved, and was now to his left, and back nearly a hundred feet.

Norris felt compelled to follow. Wrapping his fist around the stone, he lifted his rifle across his chest, set his jaw, and stepped into the stream thinking, *Why the fuck not? And besides, you've only got two choices here, sport. One is that you believe that Woodie did all the things you saw him do and that he left his eye on the floor of that motel knowing that you'd come along and use it the way you did. You can believe that your brother consciously opened the way for you to follow him into the woods, or you can believe that those nightmares you've been having all your life have finally started coming while you're awake, which means that you can't tell the difference between what's real and what's not anymore. The word for the last one there, is "crazy."*

They lock crazy people up, don't they? They put them in big grey buildings with rubber rooms.

No way—not me.

So what's the choice?

The woods, or...

Some choice.

If it's all true, then, well...Christ!

But if it's not, then the Valley is as good a place as any for a park ranger to blow his goddamn brains out.

So Norris crossed the river.

And when he did, the Man in the Woods disappeared.

31

At the same time that Robert Norris was splashing his way across the still unfrozen Killibrook River, Sheriff Conway was just coming back around from unconsciousness. When he first opened his eyes, he saw nothing but a kind of whitish-grey fluff, piled up close to his face. A chilling numbness made his jaw and the whole left side of his head feel as if some grainy mass had been poured into the opening of his right ear to run like sand in an hourglass into every low spot it could find. The light was bad, but in it he could still see the fluff closest to his eyes swirl when he exhaled. For a long moment his brain was as dry as that fluff—whatever it was.

And then the last image he had seen before his gun had gone off—and his own light had gone out—came rushing back in on him like a runaway freight, and he bolted up to find himself sitting waist-deep in a perfectly smooth sea of glowing white snow. There were dark shapes mounded around him in the night. And overhead, the sky pressed down in a purplish, mottled bruise that made him involuntarily think of skin seen in dim light.

This must be how things look to a fly when a boy does that old trick of snatching one out of the air so that he can hold his fist up to his ear and hear it buzz, he thought. *This must be what it looks like inside a fist.*

Thinking of a fist reminded him of his own arm, and if he could have screamed, that's just what he would have done. Instead, his voice came out as nothing much more than a whimper.

From where he was sitting, he could see a dark, bristling

line of shadow encircling his glowing field of vision. It was as if he had been dropped into a very large bowl of sugar sitting on a table in a dark room. The area around him was perfectly flat—except for those two dark mounds—so that when he raised his right arm, he saw its silhouette as the most starkly defined object of any available to him. Even in the dark, he could see how badly his jacket sleeve was torn—shredded, more like—and the irregularity of his skin's surface, which at first he took to be attributable to lumps of half-frozen mud, adhering to him as he moved.

But that dark length of numb shadow hanging off his lower knuckle wasn't mud.

No!

Christ Jesus, that dark thing about the size of a caterpillar wasn't mud. It was a finger—his pinky! The pinky of his right, pistol-drawing, pencil-pushing hand! And it was hanging there, six inches from his staring eyes, by a thread of what he suddenly understood was his own skin!

He jumped at the realization, clutching his left hand over his mouth—because he had to keep the right hand away from his face—and feeling the spot where his tooth had been knocked out scream with pain. In response to the shudder that ran through his body, his pinky fell off.

"God!" he croaked through his fingers as his stomach spun inside him. And then, "Poison!" he said, trying to get to his feet but achieving only a drunken stagger up on one leg before falling back, straight down, face-first into the snow.

When he hit, his mind gave the rest of him a gloriously detailed and mercifully brief replay of those last few seconds of consciousness before he had awakened in this sugar bowl…

Detective Cooper was kneeling before him, at the business end of the sheriff's .45. And an instant before the flash of detonation erased him from view, a face simply materialized and swallowed the sheriff's arm.

He remembered how the thing's black lips had looked, flexing as they pressed against his jacket. He remembered the plume of frozen breath that had curled from its glistening snout. And he remembered, most of all, its glaring, hate-filled eye, staring deeply into his own as the beast snapped its neck back and tossed him over his shoulder and into this hole...

"No!" a voice in his head piped up, contradicting the rushed chronology of his impressions. "I'm not anywhere near that spot. I've been carried, or dragged, miles into the Valley. This is the Indian burial ground. I've seen it. Never in winter. Never covered in a blanket of fresh snow. But I've seen it, and there's no other place like it..."

He stopped, and even through the bubble of panic he felt struggling to burst his racing heart, he forced his thoughts into enough order to say, "There's no other place like this on earth."

And then he was moving...

It was like crawling over the surface of the moon. The air was cold, the night was quiet, and the white fluff around him puffed into tiny, drifting clouds as he struggled on his hands and knees toward the black mound closest to him.

It was a man.

And he was still warm.

Conway laid his hands on the man's back and turned him over and...

The man's teeth snapped, and his eyes flashed...

And Conway was on his feet for an instant before he fell, rolled, and came up with his dripping hands before him and a cloud of steam obscuring his face.

The man looked at him for a second and then writhed in on himself in the mud, squirming, naked from the waist up, and horribly scared. It was Detective Cooper, and as he moved, his jacket—which had been carelessly thrown over his upper body—was bunched into a ball and ended up tangled around his legs, which kicked spasmodically in an infuriatingly slow rhythm that looked as if he were dreaming that he was riding a bicycle.

A voice drifted in on the sheriff's consciousness, and soon he realized that someone was laughing...softly...little more than a giggle, but insistent.

"Ha ha ha!"

He turned, and the remaining mound was sitting up in the snow.

"What's funny?" Conway asked.

And the man hung his head as his shoulders rocked gently and he said, "Us. We. You and me. We're funny..."

His voice was soft and empty.

"They're going to eat us," he continued, giggling between the words. "We haven't got a chance. You and me. Any minute. They're going to eat us alive."

And Cooper kept squirming on the ground.

"Perkins?" Conway asked.

"That's right," the laughing man said. "Deputy John R. Perkins. That was my name before you sent us into the woods after that park ranger. Now my name don't matter. Nobody's name matters no more. Now, we're just meat...nothing else. We're all just meat, and they're gonna eat us alive, soon as the moon comes. They'll eat us both, and there's nothing we can do no more to stop 'em."

Somewhere along the way, the laughing man's laugh had turned into a series of sobs.

Staggering up, Conway tried to get the deputy on his feet, but after a brief struggle he just left him sitting where he was, shaking his head and preparing to die. When he leaned over and took the man's gun out of its holster, he didn't even seem to notice. And when he stepped up to Detective Cooper, the sound of the hammer being drawn back was loud in the night.

Cooper stopped rolling and looked up at the gun's barrel. In the gloom, his face was smeared with mud, and his eyes glistened white. He stared for a moment without expression and then he broke down and laughed, weakly, pulling himself into a ball as pain seemed to rack his body and his voice said, "Christ, you never give up," before a gurgling sound choked him and made the rest of his sentence nearly unintelligible.

"No," Conway agreed, grimly. "I don't."

"You…c-c-can't kill me…like…th…that," Cooper hissed through clenched teeth. "Wish you…could. But it's not the way of the…Wild."

Conway looked at the gun and then back at Cooper, seeing the terrible marks on the man's chest and studying the bullet wound near his left shoulder.

"Guns don't work," Cooper added.

"Why?" Conway asked.

"How…should I know?" the detective suddenly shouted, his strength seeming to increase in a rush. "They just fucking don't! You shot me once, and it didn't work! It just hurt. And now…God…I can feel something inside. Go….God…it feels like it's getting bigger."

"It's who you really are, who you've always been, coming out."

"I'm not like this! I was never like this before now!"

"It's always been there."

"I'd like to kill you, Conway! I'd like to rip your goddamn heart out!"

I'm sure you would."

"Gggggrrrrrr!"

This last came out as a gob of spit and steaming breath, spraying from between the detective's teeth as he squeezed his eyes shut and clutched at his stomach.

Conway raised the gun.

And the laughing man suddenly jumped up and said, "That's it! That's what we can do! As he bumbled over and grabbed the sheriff's shoulder. "Do me, Sheriff! Please. Do me first! Shoot me, Sheriff! Shoot me, then shoot yourself. It our only way out!"

The man was crying again as he slid to his knees and pressed his forehead to Conway's thigh.

"For the love of Christ, Sheriff!" he sobbed. "Shoot me before it's too late!"

Conway shrugged the deputy off but he ended up hugging the sheriff's knees and crying like a child. Conway was tempted to kick him away, but he didn't. Instead, he disengaged himself as gently as he could, looked down at Cooper again, then up at the sky.

Then he froze.

There wasn't any moon up there.

He was standing beneath a perfectly black sky, sprinkled with starts and clear as a bell.

But there wasn't any moon.

"It's over," the crying man said. "Just face it, Sheriff. They won."

Conway's body went rigid when he heard this. His spine tensed but he became suddenly very hard where he stood. Without another word he lifted his arm and shot the whimpering deputy once through the head, sending his body over with an anticlimactic plop and making Cooper howl with delight. He then turned and, with a grunt, kicked the detective in the stomach as hard as he could. The sound of the blow was dull, and wet, and Cooper buckled around the sheriff's boot for a second. This person-to-person contact seemed to make an impact on the detective's body, and when Conway drew back as if to repeat the blow, Cooper flinched.

"Fight it," Conway demanded, and there was something in the black spots of the detective's eyes that made him think that maybe he was getting through. "You told me that you didn't want to be what you are. If that's true, then fight it now because I *need* you!"

"You don't understand..." Cooper hissed with obvious effort. "You don't realize..."

"I do understand," Conway interrupted. "I can feel him coming."

"Then...you should know," Cooper snarled. "Then you should..."

"Don't tell me what I should do!" the sheriff exploded, kicking out again and connecting so hard that the sound of his boot on one of the detective's ribs was like that of an echoing home run in a major-league park.

Then he was squatting with the detective's hair bunched up in the remains of his right hand's fist, pulling his head up at an odd angle and screaming into his face, "*Fight it you son of a bitch*!"

And then a series of dark shapes stepped onto the stark whiteness of the field's edge, emerging from the trees like specters.

Conway saw them almost at once, but he didn't react. His mind was whirling too fast, and his body was trembling. Releasing the detective, he remained in his crouch, thinking, *It's come to this. It's me and them...and I'm alone.* It dawned on him at that moment that he was seeing people—though they were awfully big to be just ordinary people—moving almost sixty yards away, in the dark, without any moon for light, at night. Curiously he sifted a handful of snow through his fingers and watched it sparkle as it fell. It looked like neon dust, glowing an electric white, yet cold to the touch. Its light was eerie and sterile in an almost alien sort of way that reminded him of...

Frozen air...

Stars in space...

Sandy smooth dunes beneath lifeless dark.

His head swam with it, and he imagined/remembered astronauts bouncing comically away from a landing craft to position a stiff American flag on a stick.

Placing one hand on the ground for balance, he let himself see how the burial grounds must have looked from above: the perfectly white circle of snow surrounded by the darkness of the forest...and he realized that, from this perspective, the area would resemble...

A full moon.

"Why?" Detective Cooper suddenly asked.

And when Conway looked down, he noticed that the man was staring at the remains of the sheriff's gnarled right hand.

"Why just me?" he asked, gripping the wound on his stomach with a grimace. "It bit you too. So why's it just me that's changing?"

Conway didn't answer. But in his head his grandmother's voice said, "Everybody's got some o' the evil in 'em...and everybody's got some o' the good. Only the saints are all one way, and only the Vyrmin are all the other."

"Saints?" he thought.

And then the detective screamed, and the sheriff's whole body went tense.

"*Gooooood!*" the man howled, and Conway couldn't tell if he meant "Good!" or "God!" But it didn't matter either way because the tone of his voice could only have meant one thing: the change was coming.

He was on his feet and standing over the writhing man in an instant. Though he knew it would do no good—"Not the way of the Wild"—he aimed down and shot the man twice, directly in the left eye. The sound of his shots cracked in the night and echoed sharply over the Valley. To his surprise, blood flew and the bullets slammed into Cooper's skull, gouging out great dark holes that sent a black spray over the glowing white snow and tore his eyes and chunks of bone into pulp.

Encouraged, the sheriff placed his right boot on Cooper's throat and held him still as he pressed the barrel of the gun into the bleeding hole in the side of the detective's face and fired again, sending the bullet toward the base of the man's spine.

His body stiffed and then went still.

But the sheriff was cautious. While more dark forms joined those that already encircled the burial grounds, he remained poised, gun at the ready, boot still on the dead man's throat, studying the bloody mess he had made of a face he'd come to know so well.

In the air he could smell gun smoke, blood, and urine. His own sweat tinged his lips, seeping into the corners of his mouth and making him taste salt without so much as moving his tongue. The stump of his right pinky throbbed in time to his heart, producing no actual pain but a steady series of ghostly twinges in a finger he knew he no longer had. Because of those twinges, he involuntarily imagined the face of the beast that had bitten him again, and wondered where the poison from the creature's teeth had gone. He could almost see his arm mapped with veins that were progressively turning black as the hateful venom moved toward his heart.

And then Cooper's head jerked…

And Conway leapt back two feet.

"Jesus Christ!" he whispered, amazed, and yet not really surprised. He'd almost expected it. He had been too late to stop it, but it had been worth a try.

"I'm sorry," he added, speaking to the Mike Cooper he had known before he'd been bitten by Cheryl Lockner in that alley. That Mike Cooper was gone now, and all that was left of him was...

Growling and writhing on the ground in a puddle of churned-up mud and bloody snow.

As the sheriff watched, amazed, and yet resigned at the same time, the man squirmed so hard that his arms and legs looked as if they would break apart at the joints as they dragged his shattered head around like a wet paper bag. The broken jaw was moving, emitting gargled, half-human groans as a black form emerged like a membranous bubble from between the man's jutting teeth.

Conway took another step back, but could not take his eyes from the man's face.

The body arched up on the ground at that moment. All motion ceased and the throat went hard. With his spine locked, Cooper fell silent for nearly twenty seconds. Then the flesh around his mouth began peeling back over the remains of his skull, and the sound of bones crackling filled the air.

Conway felt his stomach locking and unlocking under his heart, and his left hand went up before his face, as if trying to ward off a blow.

It looked as if the man were simply turned inside out. As if a person might reach his hand into a sock, and pull its toe through its end so that the inside would suddenly become the outside, the man's flesh rolled back and great gobs of wet hair and bristling bone glistened, moved, and rearranged themselves into the shape of...something...lying on its side in the snow. It seemed to go on for hours, but in fact it took less than a minute. When it was through, the thing that remained lay panting for a time, as if exhausted after its exertion, its tongue lolling from its mouth and its eyes starting as...

Conway staggered back another step.

Which he shouldn't have done.

Because the thing lifted its head in response to the motion, and in that second, for the first time in three centuries, a member of the Flock, Sheriff Conway, locked eyes with a fully formed Vyrmin wolf—a former homicide detective named Michael Cooper who the sheriff had only knew for a few hours—and shattering the silence of civilization, the sound of a wolf's panting breath recalled the most primitive of all emotions in the sheriff's heart…and…

Seeing the Hunter, the Hunted was afraid.

For most of his life, the woodcut image of Jean Grenier, that old French werewolf who was forever heading back into the woods with that bundle of rags that so upset the stick-waving crowd at his heels, had haunted Sheriff Conway. It had been his own personal bogeyman, his own personification of the dark side. He'd first seen it when he was probably four years old, and as will happen to people who are deeply impressed with something at so tender an age, he had carried it with him ever since. It had become a part of his psyche, his soul. It had been real to him in a way that other "realities"—like love or marriage—had never been; and it was specific.

The beast that was lifting itself from the ground now was in every way just as specific as that old woodcut image. In truth, it could almost have been that woodcut, pulling itself from a pool of grainy, age-yellowed paper and taking substance from the air.

Its humanity was gone.

It was a wolf.

It stood nearly five feet high at the shoulders and had a thick coat of shining fur that looked black in the night light. Its angles were sharp—in what Conway had taken to be the German style from Grenier's picture—and its eyes flashed as bright as cigarette coals in the dark. Silver spit dripped from jaws that seemed to grin as the beast panted out its frozen fog. And its teeth were just immense.

But even seeing it so close was not nearly so shocking as

the sound of it speaking. When it did that, Conway's whole brain turned over in his skull.

"Hail!" the thing said, and when it did, the muscles in its throat knotted, and its tongue danced in its mouth, as if the effort of speech approached the very limits of its audible capacity.

"Hail!" it barked again...

And then it moved.

Conway didn't mean to do it, but he screamed when the thing came at him. His hands went up before his face, and despite his courage and his resolution to die in the defense of the world and the balance he had known, he cried out in terror as his mind filled with pictures of teeth and ribbons of bloody flesh, all peeled from his own throat.

But the thing didn't touch him.

Instead, it simply ran past him, across the field and right up to where the big figures of things that looked very much like people, but that obviously weren't, were waiting...

When it arrived, another wolf, slightly smaller than the first, bounded into sight, and together the pair ran in great, snowy circles, jumping and barking and nipping at one another as the sheriff numbly turned to watch.

Cheryl, he thought, vaguely. *She's come for the mate she made for herself when she bit him.*

And then Conway saw the glow in the trees: the pulsating bluish-white haze of twilight illumination that was moving down from the hill beyond where Cooper and Cheryl Lockner were frolicking in his sight. Seeing that light, he knew that the Blood Prince had finally come.

And overhead, the darkness parted as a glowing circle, like an eye opening in a face as wide as the heavens themselves, flickered out the first tentative sparkle of the new full moon.

32

With every step, Robert Norris saw things more clearly, until he was practically running—as if his pounding boots could settle his screaming mind.

With the memory of Dr. Green came a sense of perspective and order that he had never had before. He suddenly understood why he craved solitude in the woods: God was there. God wasn't to be found in the buildings of mankind, in his choking cities of concrete and pollution. God didn't reside in the gilded cages called churches by pompous humans, camouflaged by false piety and fully prepared to destroy everything around them because this world didn't matter. To them, the heaven they imagined they'd find after death was much more important…

But they had it wrong.

Because this world did matter.

Maybe not to them so much, but they were not the only creatures on it. The perfect balance of the system, its unique symmetry and indomitable, self-contained harmony, was an instrument in the concert of the universe. It was one piece of the whole that was *being*. By simply following its course, it was contributing its own part to the song of the planets, the "music of the spheres," the melody that, taken together, was what humans had christened "God."

So it damned well did matter.

It mattered a lot—to the system, to the animals, to the stars.

And humans had no right to ruin it.

They had no right!

The thought stopped him dead in his tracks.

"It's not theirs; who told them that it was theirs?" he said, breathlessly, staring down at the rifle he held. "The world belongs to us all...it belongs to the stars. They have no right to kill it."

He pitched the rifle to the ground, aiming it away from his body and feeling a shudder of sudden revulsion moisten his gut.

In his pocket the moonstone was warm, and he pulled it out. When he did, its glow filled the trees around him and made everything he saw beautiful.

"Think," he said.

But that didn't seem to work.

"Then just feel," he whispered.

And that was the key.

Raising his eyes to the heavens, he let the vibrations of the forest slide into his body, let all the visions he'd seen seep gently away, and watched as the first flicker of the moon glanced down at him from above. Surprisingly, he wasn't afraid...not really. He wasn't even startled by the moon's apparent willingness to shine just for him. The moon had been following him wherever he went all his life...he just hadn't realized it before. He just hadn't known.

The Man in the Woods was out there somewhere, and he wished he could speak with him. She was out there somewhere as well, probably keeping Woodie company, keeping him calm. Woodie had always been so excitable. They had all been excitable...Galltar, Zonaoria, Lozella, Slett...

He blinked, and almost made the mistake of thinking. But he fought it, preferring instead to just let things *be*.

The original "tribe" of the Wild had not been Neanderthal any more than the original modern human on the planet had been any one specific species that had survived all the rest. Mankind was a mix of a series of primates that ultimately produced the hairless, big-brained being that so dominated the planet now. At the time the moonstone fell there were at least twenty different species of man wandering the plains of earth.

Norris smiled, remembering how that wilderness had looked: the lushness of the greens, the abundance of life and its smells.

There were two energies in the world: the light and the dark. Properly balanced, they were the only energies anyone could ever need. But humans had chosen the light to the exclusion of everything else. They had turned their back on the dark side of themselves, and after generations of denial, had changed themselves from one thing, which was a natural member of the earth's system, to another, which was an adversary to anything not like themselves.

Norris remembered what it had been like when he first found the stone…

He trembled, but he kept his peaceful expression pointed at the moon.

When he—not Woodie, not some faceless ancestor, but *he*, the man who stood beneath the moon now as much as any man anywhere—when *he* found the stone, he was so lonely. He had been driven from the company of the tribe for the crime of acting like an animal. They were better than that. They didn't want him around. They knew everything.

Arrogant fucks!

But the stone gave him the power. The stone gave him sight. The stone brought them together—the last on the planet—the only creatures to ever walk the earth that were completely in balance between the light and the dark: they were animals, who could really *think*.

They were the First.

They were the Wild!

And they were out there now, waiting for their Prince.

He wanted to go to them, to establish a new dominion and start the Dark Times again...to take revenge for the indignities the Wild had suffered over the centuries. He knew that was why the Man in the Woods had brought them back together. After three hundred years during which he had faded nearly to nothing and had almost disappeared, the Man in the Woods had given it one last shot.

And this night was it.

There might not have even been this night if the Apollo team hadn't brought those moon rocks back in the seventies. They weren't as powerful as the one that had been burnished by the flames caused when it plunged through the earth's atmosphere, leaving it purged of impurities and as solid as glass, but they emitted enough low-level energy to keep him going. So he hung on until the stars were lined up right, and Robert Norris was of an age where his feelings and mind were balanced.

And then he had risked it all.

But Norris knew that he could never do what the Man in the Woods wanted...that poor old spirit. He was a throwback to a different time, a period of magic and spells and the rack. A time of creaking wooden wheels and rusted hooks when hot irons sizzled the flesh of "witches" and "vampires" and the Church doomed everyone to the madness of its "reason."

Alas...the old spook's day had passed.

But the night had come. And with it the moon's light. The moon took the energy of the sun's heat and reflected it down...changed the way the world saw it, the same way the moonstone changed the way Norris saw the world. In that reflected light, he understood his dilemma: ignore his ancestry and save the species known as man from the horrors of the werewolf—which it had already experienced for longer than anyone alive could realize because most of the real carnage had occurred before people recorded history in writing—or he could ignore the Wild and let mankind kill the earth, which is exactly what the species would do, given time and free rein.

Norris was a man...but he was also a man who loved the wilderness, who lived for the trees...

"Come to the trees...and find yourself," the beast that was Ernie Cray had said.

Find yourself...

And doom a generation.

He saw Woodie dismember a boy named Raymond again, and cringed when he realized that the sight didn't bother him anymore. He remembered the blood, and the grave, and the woman on the chain, and wondered why it had all been necessary. Why did they have to eat human flesh to make the change from human to animal? Why did they need Woodie to bring the stone before they could move his father's bones? And why did they want to move them in the first place?

It all had something to do with the way you saw things...it was all involved in perspective.

It was all...

And then he understood...and the ground actually shook.

33

Conway felt the ground tremble an instant before he sensed the approach of something powerful from the trees. Whatever it was, the force of it felt as if a tornado were pushing a wall of air out from the distance to churn everything it touched.

As the line of figures at the edge of the burial grounds turned to watch, the black trees on the horizon swayed, and dead leaves swirled. The hair on Conway's head rippled, though his skin registered no wind. And the snow around his feet ran in skimming eyelets that skipped into tiny, sandstorm funnels. Cooper and Cheryl Lockner stopped their prancing and stood frozen on the snow, their long, pointed snouts lifted high in silhouette as if to catch some scent. And the stump of Conway's lost finger sang with tremulous sensations that were not pain...but that were by no means pleasant.

This must be what animals feel right before the coming of a tidal wave or the eruption of a volcano, the sheriff decided, more with his body than with his mind. It was like the occurrence of some great natural event, and it instilled in him the same sense of awe and fear that every human in history had felt in the face of any similar, unknown force.

It was that feeling that made Conway understand.

This was old, he thought, forcing down the persistent screams of terror from his spinning guts. This was something eternal, a demonstration of a power that had existed forever. And mankind had faced it before—and had won.

The key was to think! To reason it out and not let the mindless, merciless waves of nature wash you away. Man had logic and imagination. That's what separated him from the animals. He could control his environment and determine his own destiny. He had done it before...and right now, Conway would have to do it again.

If he could.

Because, right now, *only* he could.

He was the Flock's Dog.

And the Wolf was coming.

Pound for pound, a dog can't beat a wolf in a fair fight. But who said a fight had to be fair? When an animal risks losing an eye, or its life, it fights any way it can, and uses every tooth and nail at its disposal along the way.

At that instant, the sheriff was sorry that he had killed the deputy. He'd done it as an act of mercy. Knowing that the chances of either of them ever seeing the sunrise was nearly zero, he had acquiesced to the man's pitiful pleas and ended his life in a swift and painless way: a bullet to the head. Far better, he had reasoned, than the horrible finale of being eaten by so perfect a predator as that thing he had seen Detective Cooper become.

But now he wished that he would have stayed his shot. If only so that he might have a set of human ears to hear his own final screams. It would be awful, dying alone with only the beast that was killing you for company.

Again, the ground shook, and Conway's attention snapped back to the tree line. The glowing light was closer, brighter, and moving steadily now. The creatures near the rim of the burial grounds were drawing back to either side of the field, and Cooper and Cheryl Lockner were motionless near the trees. Overhead, something seemed to move—something vague and dark, swirling in the unmarred night sky to concentrate itself around the moon. Cooper glanced up, and the movement seemed to stop...perhaps it hadn't really been there at all. But when he looked back at the trees, the sky went right on changing.

And then the trees parted, and a man stepped into view.

At his appearance, a peal of thunder rocked the Valley, echoing powerfully so that by the time the last of the rumble faded, it had bounced over the trees so many times that it sounded like ten thunderclaps instead of just one. From the spot where the man stood, a ripple, like a wave, ran in a crescent shape, out across the snow, frosting the sheriff's skin as it passed him, and filling his eyes for a moment so that, when he looked, everything seemed to come back to him from a blurry mess of watery dark.

The big shapes near the tree line were kneeling.

The wolves that were Detective Cooper and Cheryl Lockner dropped their heads, pulled their tails up between their legs, and tentatively approached the figure from the woods, who was…

Encased in light.

The glow was silver, strong, and steady. It rose thirty feet over him in a dome and illuminated the area around him for an equal distance, making him look like a man-shaped spot of black at its center. From what Conway could see, he was unremarkable—at least when compared to the hulking beasts that were now kneeling before him—and he was holding one arm up over his head. That arm ended in a bright blur where his hand should have been, and the sheriff realized that the silver glow that was now bleeding down to travel across the snow of the burial grounds, making it pulsate as if electrified, had, as its source, something in the man's invisible hand.

The man stopped, and Cooper and Cheryl Lockner inched their way toward him, paused, and stood waiting. The man looked down at them briefly before reaching out his free hand and petting first one and then the other on the head.

Conway's first, reflexive reaction at this point was to say, "No! Watch yourself! They're killers!" But he didn't move and he couldn't speak because, when the man's hand touched the first wolf, he saw the beast encircled with a hazy, silver glow that erased its wolf shape and left inside it an image of a naked man resting on his hands and knees and allowing someone to rub his head. When the dark man removed his hand and placed it on the second wolf, the first resumed its canine shape and the second glowed inside its own cocoon of light as it assumed the shape of a naked woman.

Conway blinked.

And more wolves slunk silently from the blackness of the forest as if they had been waiting there to see what would happen before showing themselves.

The greeting went on for a long time. At first, there were just the first two wolves to touch, but those two soon gave way to what looked like an endless line. Every time the man's hand came down, Conway saw the animal's human appearance, and over the course of the next few minutes he recognized Ernie Cray, two of his own deputies, and a number of people from town who he had not even known were missing, including the wife of the young sexton who had been murdered at the graveyard. In her wolf shape she held a bundle in her jaws that reminded Conway of Jean Grenier's woodcut image to a sickening degree. And reverently she laid this offering—her own human baby, which made the sheriff remember that she was a mother twice and wonder what had happened to her second child—at the feet of the dark man, who patted her three times, as if in reward.

By the time it was over, the dark man had touched twelve wolves...

Twelve? Conway thought. There were twelve people, living in our little town, who were so bad inside that they just changed as soon as the bones were moved? Out of the tiny town of Harpersville, there were twelve people who dreamed of killing, and who were cruel enough to run to the woods the first chance they got? Twelve Vyrmin in my little Flock?

It was amazing—awesome, in fact. If that ratio of Vyrmin to human held true over the whole state, or country, or world, then soon—if nothing was done to stop it—there would be no place to run, nowhere to hide. There'd be wolves everywhere, in every crack and under every rock. It would be a virtual war, a hell like in the old days when the fairy tales had been written. There'd be killings every night and executions every day. There'd be people trying to hide and inquisitors asking questions. Everyone would suspect everyone else, and no one would be safe.

It would be like the descent of a plague.

It would be like the Dark Ages.

It would be…

"A new Dark Time," he whispered, and just the feel of the words on his tongue…

Made him grimace.

Just the feel of the words on his tongue…

Made him move.

As the dark shapes of the creatures kneeling rose to approach the man from the trees, Conway was already stepping forward. As he watched the figures converge before him, he realized that he had been right: whatever those twenty or so things actually were, they were huge, because as soon as they were arranged near the dark man, they towered over him by a good four feet.

"Think!" he was saying to himself as he approached. "Work it out! Don't' fight fair!"

He hadn't gone ten feet when the dark man looked his way, freezing the sheriff with the simple force of his glance. Suddenly there were twelve sets of fire-red eyes fixed firmly on Conway's face. Twelve sets of jaws worked themselves into twelve dripping grins. And a line of wolves all crouched, as if ready to spring.

Conway's flesh crawled.

The dark man raised his hand, and the wolves lifted their heads in response.

Conway lifted his gun.

And the dark man stepped into the snow of the burial grounds.

When his foot came down, a whole string of things happened, and Conway's head reeled trying to sort them out.

First, a flash of light shot across the snow and blasted up, creating a bright circle that was exactly as large as the burial grounds, but that ended in a dome-shaped roof overhead. It was as if the grounds had suddenly been covered by a glass bowl, with the dark, night sky above.

In that sky, the undulating form that the sheriff had sensed but had not seen before darkened and took the same shape as the one that had briefly appeared over the jail when the Man in the Woods had disappeared after Emil Lockner's death: that immense, half-human silhouette of an unimaginable being with the moon in its eye. Its shoulders dropped down below the horizon. Its substance was a darkness just this side of complete, which appeared solid when compared to the lighter dark of the natural sky. And its silent attention was focused on this one bright spot in which the sheriff realized he was suddenly trapped.

As if guarding the glowing burial grounds, the surrounding woods seemed to press in close, animated and moving in the windless night. The trees and bushes, tangled briars and leafless brambles, all huddled into a squat, forming, in each place the sheriff looked, the yawning, dark impressions of watching faces. It wasn't one single face anymore, not one specific being. The Man in the Woods had split into a thousand identical beings…had apparently become the woods, because in every shadowy, ominous expression, Conway saw that exact same face of the bearded man who had said, "He's their dog," to a thing that…

Now fluttered overhead.

Conway almost broke his neck jerking his head up when he noticed the demon above him. It circled twice in its bat-like shape after emerging from the night sky as if taking flesh from the dark air itself. When its reconnaissance was through, it settled itself like a vulture, resting on the surface of the light-dome that encased them all, as if the light were solid—which, at least in this creature's estimation, it apparently was. And peering down, not at the sheriff, but at the dark man whose presence had altered things so profoundly, it folded its wings and curled its tail up over its shoulder.

There were other things that happened when the man's foot touched the snow…

Animal screams shrilled from the forest.

Dogs barked in the distance.

The stars blinked and then became brighter, moving in the sky until their patterns were familiar, but different.

But these were all peripheral when compared to the depth of Conway's emotion at seeing the dark man's face for the first time.

"Bobby Norris," he said to himself…to the man…to the goddamn night itself. "I knew it was you, but I wouldn't let myself believe."

Norris stopped about ten yards from the sheriff, with his entourage of hulking, hairy followers spread out behind him on either side. The twelve wolves from the village positioned themselves in a circle, back, about sixty feet, grinning and dangling their tongues. And the demon sitting on the light moved herself over to get a better view of the proceedings.

The gun in the sheriff's hand felt suddenly very heavy, while at the same time, very small, like a lead ball-bearing.

Norris's eyes were gentle and his face pleasant as he said,

"Hello, Sheriff Conway. It's been a long time."

Conway opened and closed his mouth three times before he was able to sort out, "Hello, Bobby," from the rest of what was in his head. "So what happens now?" he added, sounding like a robot.

On the other side of Norris, the huge, hairy creatures that looked so much like gorillas, while also looking like men, hung their faces, side by side.

"Well..." Norris began with an almost imperceptible shrug. "I was thinking about that on my way out here tonight." He paused and, as if a thought had just occurred to him, asked, "Do you know where we are?"

Conway shook his head, slowly.

"It's one of the dead places," Norris said with an easy smile. "You should know that. Because of irregularities in the mineral content of this area's bedrock, and a concentration of certain metals in one, circular spot, the earth's magnetic field is disrupted in such a way as to make this location a kind of fish-eyed lightening rod, particularly conducive to the moon's energy. That's why my great-grandfather chose this spot when he was running from his home in Germany. It drew him here—drew him to itself. It has that power. It's been drawing people here for a long time. Centuries, in fact. And I just found out about it.

"There are only a few places like this on the whole planet, and we've had one right here in Harpersville all these years and nobody ever realized it—probably because Ohio's perceived by the rest of the country as being such a boring place. I mean, how could anything interesting possibly be in Ohio? In reality, it's actually quite a big deal. And I just found out about it myself. I found out a lot of things in the past few hours. And they've changed me, Sheriff. They really have. And whether you know it or not, they've changed you too."

"Me?" the sheriff mouthed, silently.

Norris nodded.

"I know that you don't understand, so I'll explain it to you," he said, in a tone of voice that hinted at a cold rationality that frightened Sheriff Conway as much as the implied irrationality of the monsters standing around him. "Most of this has been a load of shit anyway, so we may as well dispose of it now.

"You see, you're responsible for most of the silliness that's been happening in town—you, personally, and your kind, your species, in general. You'll deny it, of course, but you are. And you didn't even realize it. And don't think that I don't know what's been going on, because I do. I'm a Sender, as it turns out; that means that, when I sleep, my spirit travels to others of the Wild and I see what's happening to them and what they're doing. It's all been so brutal, so incredibly human. It's got to stop."

At the word "stop," Conway's heart skipped, and for a second he allowed himself a brief stab of hope.

"It's all in how you see things," Norris continued carefully. "I mentioned perception before—how people see Ohio in such and such a way. But the interesting thing is that because of the perception of others, many people in Ohio see themselves in a like manner. They make their lives, and the place they live, conform to the expectations or the perceptions of others. They make a thought, a reality."

"And that's my whole point: perception's everything. You've got to believe that, Sheriff Conway, or you'll never understand. It sounds like philosophical bullshit, but it's true. Our senses are our only link to the world outside our bodies. If you change perception, you essentially change reality. That's why the Wild have been moving bones, and the Vyrmin have been boiling dog heads, and you have been cooking wolfsbane tea. You've all been acting on assumptions that are based on outdated perceptions."

"I saved your life," Conway said, he didn't know why.

Norris nodded his head.

"That's a perfect example," he said. "You saved the life of a small, human child by pulling him from a burning car. Or, more accurately, you saved the life of the young innocent you perceived that child to be. If you had known then what you know now about me, you would have let me burn."

"That's not true," Conway said, with little conviction.

"That's an interesting statement, coming from a man who just shot a deputy in cold blood."

"I was trying to save him from a lot of pain."

"Your motivations don't change the facts: you shot him."

"He asked me to."

"You see, Sheriff? Your human mind insists on trying to manipulate reality be altering the way you perceive things. I didn't make any judgments about your act. I merely made the observation that you did it. And, after having seen you do it, I get the feeling that, given your personality, you wouldn't *flinch* from killing someone if you thought that that person was a danger to you or others."

"That's self-defense," the sheriff cut in.

"Killing is killing," Norris countered. "That's the difference between the Flock and the Wild: we don't explain it, we just do it."

"So you're on their side, then?"

"You gathered everything you know about dealing with werewolves from old European stories and legends," Norris continued, ignoring the question. "The Wild gathered here today got their information about *being* werewolves from the Man in the Woods. And he's literally as old as the hills. His information came from the perceptions of a primitive, unsophisticated barbarian who just happened to have the luck of finding the moonstone before any else did. And who also happened to be my original great-grandfather."

"What's the moonstone?" Conway asked.

"This," Norris said proudly, holding up the stone between his thumb and index finger. "It makes thoughts come to life."

Conway said nothing.

"I don't blame you for being skeptical," Norris said. "But believe it, because it's true.

"But back to the original question. What's supposed to happen next is that I should announce the resurrection of the Hunt and make these creatures gathered here very happy. They'd tear you apart and offer a piece of your meat to me to eat, and the blood would set my Wild side free...which is perception creeping in again: all these violent acts of mutilation and eating of raw flesh, they've all been designed to shock the participant's perceptions into a new arrangement. They're horrendous because the alteration of the person's point of view is so significant that only a really incredible experience could achieve it."

"Like cutting a horse in half?" Conway asked.

Norris nodded

"Or hanging an innocent girl on a chain," he added, glumly.

"Anyway, after I ate a piece of you without vomiting it back up, I'd turn into a creature just like my companions here...only better. Then we'd all go off into the hills again and start ripping out the throats of unlucky travelers...like good little werewolves have been doing for centuries. We'd start up the packs again, recruit Vyrmin from the Flock, and spend a great deal of time howling at the moon. At least that's what's *supposed* to happen."

Norris paused, and his eyes narrowed.

"But I've got other ideas. As disappointed as my friends might be tonight, instead of being the first installment in what everyone probably hoped would be a nightly blood feast, just like in the old days, and all the rest of that shit, tonight, we're going to see the last evening in which the Wild will allow archaic perceptions and nonsense rules to dictate our behavior. We have work to do, Sheriff Conway. Important work. This world is on the brink, and I intend to bring it back.

"So..." he said, stepping forward. "There will be no more mindless slaughter. No more random acts of terror for the fun of it. The day of the slavering beast is past, and the day of the *thinking* killer has come. It's been happening anyway. All those serial murderers and psychopaths that are so popular nowadays. All those tin pot despots and corporate assholes...they're all just Vyrmin who haven't discovered their true natures yet. But their methods are right on target. And we're going to *improve* them."

"What are you saying?" Conway asked, almost as a whisper.

"What I'm saying,"—Norris smiled—"is that the time has come for the werewolf to enter the twentieth century. If we just went back to creeping through graveyards and howling at the moon, mankind and all his wonderful technology would wipe us out in six weeks. We wouldn't stand a chance.

"But we're human, too...after all. Actually, we're probably the most human animals on the planet. We have the capacity for abstract thought; we've just been ignoring it because it's easier...and more fun...to let ourselves go and do what comes naturally. What we need is organization. A system. We need to kill large numbers of people quickly so that we can get a handle on the Flock's size again. So we can get ourselves in control again. Then, after we've trimmed the planet's human population to a manageable number, we can ease off, let the Flock recover a little, and hunt in any way we please."

"Like stocking a pond for fishing," Conway said.

"Exactly," Norris agreed. "But don't think that I take human life lightly. This is a serious business."

"If that thing you're holding can make wishes come true," Conway said, "why don't you just use it to change things the way you want and be done with it? Why go to all this trouble?"

"You still don't get it." Norris frowned. "And that surprises me a little. The stone alone doesn't really change anything. We do that. The stone is just the doorway through which a person must pass on the road to becoming what he envisions himself to be. It lets you be what you are, or what you think you are, anyway. It let my ancient great-grandfather become the monster that he and his tribe thought he was, and therefore laid out the ground rules for every werewolf that's ever been since."

"And that's why my gun didn't kill Detective Cooper," Conway mused aloud.

"That's right," Norris agreed. "Guns are new. There's really no place for them in the system, since they were unheard of when the original father started it all. They cause damage physically sometimes, but they aren't integrated into the lore beyond the old silver bullet routine, which I think was probably a fluke. Someone must have gotten lucky once, and it stuck. Maybe whoever did it didn't even shoot a real werewolf. Knowing the way humans do things, that wouldn't surprise me at all."

Conway wasn't looking at Norris anymore. He was looking at the .38-caliber Policeman's Special that he was holding at the end of his arm, pointed at the park ranger's face, and thinking, *Will it do the job? If I shoot him, will he die?*

And the sheriff saw it: up, over Norris' head, on the black slope of the Retreat. Norris' back was to it, as were the backs of all the Wild and the twelve new Vyrmin wolves. But Conway was facing it…

And he saw it!

Think! his mind screamed. *There's got to be something you can do!*

But when Norris spoke again, the words almost shattered Conway's spirit.

"Ah, you've finally noticed the torches," he said, still smiling. "They've been busy in town since you left. The witness made quite an impression on them, and all those juicy bits of evidence you left at the graveyard really blew on the embers. Also, two of those deputies you sent into the woods after me doubled back and headed for town. They stirred up a real firestorm, and the mob will simply follow the light"—he raised his arms and indicated the glow around himself—"until they find us, here. But by then, we'll be gone, and what's left of you will only serve to inflame their frustrations."

"Gone where?" Conway asked.

But Norris ignored him. "First things first," he said, turning to the one-eyed beast standing to his left.

Behind and up, Conway could see the sparkling prickles of yellow and pink working their way down the side of the black Retreat and disappearing below the fuzzy tree line. *How many villagers were coming?* he wondered. *And how many were already working their way through the woods? How long would it take for them to arrive? And what would happen when they did?*

The beast to Norris' left bowed its head and grunted, "Hail, my brother. Hail...to the...new...way," as it held out the bone it was holding in its huge hand.

Norris took the offering and examined it for a moment before finding a spot that seemed to catch his interest. One end of the bone was rounded and natural. But the other had been sharpened and notched—like an arrowhead. After testing the point with his finger, he fit the moonstone into a pit in the bone near the apex of its tip and raised it high over his head.

At first nothing happened. Every creature standing near him studied the bone without so much as moving. Conway ran his eyes over the expectant faces, looked at Norris' calm smile, and then looked at the place in the bone where the young man had lodged the moonstone just in time to see a sparkle emanate from there, die, and then grow.

"It's happening," Norris said, softly.

Conway swallowed.

The beasts in their line began to stir.

The bushes and trees surrounding the grounds rustled, making the sheriff think that the first of the villagers had arrived before he realized that it was the Man in the Woods who was making the sound.

"My dear!" Norris announced, not really as a shout, but loud and confident. "Come to me!"

And from overhead came the flapping of wings.

Conway looked up just in time to see the demon drop. It glided down on wings of leather, settled itself on the ground close to Norris' feet, and looked at him, hard.

Norris returned that look and screamed, "Behold!" as he thrust the bone higher into the air and seemed to command the very stars to obey him.

It should have been ridiculous.

But it wasn't.

Conway was sure that the young man could do whatever it was he intended. He was sure that he could make the moon move if he so wished. And, as the sheriff watched, that' just what the moon appeared to do.

In a flash like lightning a beam shone down from the moon, reflected off the end of Norris' scepter, and engulfed the demon where it stood. The creature disappeared in the light for an instant and then reappeared when the light faded—just as quickly as it had come. In the place where the hairy, apish little monster had been, there now stood a woman of regal proportion—no longer a blond European, as her previous incarnation had rendered her, but a brunette American. She could have been anyone, but whoever she was, she radiated an aura of competence, intellect, and—incredibly—honesty.

The grin on Norris' face was truly evil for the first time. His eyes sparkled when he saw the naked beauty before him, and extending his hand, he spoke to Sheriff Conway without taking his eyes off the woman.

"Now, that's more like it. Beauty and the Beast, all rolled into one. Who would suspect her of anything unkind? Who would look at her and say, 'I'm afraid'? What man could deny her anything she asked for? And who wouldn't be surprised when the moment of truth arrives, and she makes someone bleed?"

The creature stepped forward and took Norris' hand. The instant their skin touched, a sparkle of bluish light crackled around them and made the hair wave on their heads.

Norris smiled, "The old spark's still there."

The woman said nothing, but studied him with deep, blue eyes so filled with suppressed energy and desire that there seemed to be a physical bridge through the air from her to him as she took her place at his side.

There was a sound in the forest, not far away.

Shouts.

Human voices.

But where?

Norris turned his head in response to the call and then looked at the sheriff.

"What's next, eh, Sheriff?" he said, lowering the bone and brandishing it before himself. "How will I use the stone to change the world? Isn't that what you'd like to know? Because that' exactly what I'm going to do! What's next? Well, just for argument's sake, how about this?"

He turned then, abruptly, pointing the bone out before him as his spine bowed and his neck thrust his head forward. Aiming the bone directly at the one-eyed beast next to him, he shouted, "Meet the future Archbishop of the Roman Catholic Church in the United States!"

From the bone's tip shot a ray of the purest silver light that Conway had ever seen. When it hit the beast, it literally knocked him off his feet, creating a sound like a sonic boom, and a flash that blinded the sheriff, making his hands come up before his eyes automatically.

When the light faded, and Conway could again see, a beautiful young man was lifting himself to his feet from the spot where the ape-thing had fallen. The fellow's hair was auburn, his skin was a rich, creamy white, and his physique was perfect. Involuntarily the sheriff imagined him in the robes of a priest and realized, in an instant, that he would cut an awesome and convincing figure.

The young man blinked and ran his hands over his chest. He looked like Woodie Norris, a little, but this Woodie Norris could have easily been a movie star.

Norris grinned and pretended to blow the smoke off the end of the bone, as if it were a pistol and he a matinee cowboy.

"Get it, Sheriff Conway?" he asked as an aside.

The trees rustled harder, and Conway couldn't tell whether it was the villagers or the Man in the Woods this time.

"Or how about the future head of the United Nations Security Council?" Norris asked, spun, and let fly with another silver bolt.

A lovely woman of obviously African descent appeared where there had been a female beast before the flash. She was nearly as beautiful as the demon woman had become, but without the sensuous lips or heat-radiating eyes. She was professional-looking and had a demeanor of the natural-born leader. She was examining herself and she looked up with a smile that appeared as if it were crawling out of her skull through her mouth and spreading over her face.

"She understands," Norris announced. "Don't you, my dear Zonoria?"

The beautiful woman nodded and said, "They'll *trust* me."

Norris laughed. "They certainly will. And why not? You're not ugly anymore. And everyone knows that beautiful things are never bad. Only ugly things are bad! Isn't that right, Sheriff?"

Before Conway could respond, a rustling in the trees stole his already divided attention, grew louder and deeper before it peaked, and then settled. The Man in the Woods stepped from the shadows, arrayed in his full beard, flowing white robes and grim-faced frown.

There were bones dangling in his hair.

The sight of him made every muscle in Conway's body feel as if it had turned to wood.

The spirit and the Blood Prince regarded one another for a long, silent time before Norris finally observed, "You don't approve, oldest of us."

The Man in the Woods was standing only about ten feet away from Norris, which placed him almost an equal distance from the sheriff. From where he stood, Conway could smell the odor of the thing, the musky, woodsy scent of animal fur and raindrops that called to something deep inside him, while at the same time repulsing another, equally important part of himself.

"No," the Man in the Woods said. "I don't approve. It's not as it has been. It's different now."

"I made it possible for us to win, to triumph, to overcome and to finally dominate forever."

"It's not a question of winning. There is no triumph...no final...no end. It's a question of being. We need only to survive. Forever is nothing if forever is our prize."

Norris raised the scepter and pointed it at the old man, who stood stony and still.

"I carried your secret and answered your summons," he said, softly. "I accepted the memories of my birthright and took the stone to myself. I am what has been, what is, and what is to come. I am the Nurrenvelt, and older. I am the Blood Prince, as it was your wish for me to be. I am the future of the Wild, and without me, there will be no being. We cannot survive without this change.

"Now, decide."

"I will remain as I am," the Man in the Woods said.

And Norris nodded. "As is your right. But you will not ruin this for the rest of us. We've earned our chance."

"They're coming," the Man in the Woods said, offhandedly.

And Conway heard the voices in the trees again...closer this time...much, much closer.

"I know," Norris said.

"How will the others escape?" the Man in the Woods asked.

Norris said nothing.

"Shall I make the shadows to hide them?" the Man in the Woods asked. "Shall I make the trees to bend, and the darkness to mask their retreat? Shall I dazzle the eyes of the Flock with sights and make them afraid? Shall I protect them, as it has been my pleasure in the past? Or does this *new* way discount the love of centuries?"

"We will do without your help, for now," Norris said, sternly.

And the voices in the trees almost formed words.

"So be it," the Man in the Woods said, raising his arms. "Although I weep at the thought, I will bid thee farewell. But if thou should find a need for that which I have given in the past, call unto me, and I shall give of myself again."

"I know," Norris said. "And I love you for it, my father."

Something very important was happening at this instant, and Conway knew it. He suspected what it was but could not yet identify it exactly. Something more than the surface event was going on, but he didn't have time to sort through the details for the truth because, as the Man in the Woods turned and sent one last baleful glance over his shoulder at the spot where the Blood Prince stood with his bride, the first flickers of torchlight danced in the darkness.

The old man was gone before Conway knew it, and Norris was now looking his way.

"It's time," the young man was saying with tears in his eyes.

Conway raised the gun.

Norris didn't smile this time.

With every ounce of will he possessed, Conway was searching his mind for some hint, some clue, as to what he might do to hurt this monster—this beautiful, muscular, handsome monster with his ravishing companion. He was literally tearing through the pages of all the stories about the Vyrmin he had ever heard. Ripping through the words of his grandmother and others. Searching for just one indication of what his course should be, because he knew that this was his last chance. Get it wrong and it was over…get it wrong, and *everything* was over.

"Don't play fair," his mind said.

And Norris looked into his eyes.

There was light everywhere by this time. It was almost funny to be standing in the forest at night, and yet to have your eyes filled with so much light that they could hardly handle it all. There was so much light, radiating up from the snow of the burial grounds—the dead spot, as Norris had called it—that the sheriff hardly saw the first faces of the frightened villagers emerge from between the trees with their torches, and axes, and knives, and pikes.

In that moonlike glow, all the objects that the people carried shone eerily, as if their edges had been coated with…

Silver!

Conway was amazed.

The people had coated the blades of their axes, their kitchen knives, their harvesting scythes, with silver. They must have melted every silver dollar, every silver chain, every set of grandma's silverware and silver plates in Harpersville to come up with enough of the stuff to do the job. They must have talked it through. They must have listened to Emil Lockner, the witness. They must have believed the old stories.

They must think they knew what's happening.

And that's when it hit him.

That's when the sheriff really saw, and his rage boiled up from inside like a volcano.

"You lied!" he screamed, silencing everything and making the whole world hold still for an instant.

"You fucking bastard!" he cried, trembling now and holding his gun with both hands. *"It's not just you!"*

And, having said it, the sheriff fired his gun.

34

He could feel the power climbing his legs, up from the ground. He didn't really understand it, but he didn't need to. All he needed was the knowledge that what he had been told was not the whole truth, because, he suddenly realized, it wasn't just Norris who could do things with the power around them. Anyone in the circle was part of that power, though how much control someone else could exert, especially someone who had only realized the truth within the last couple of seconds, remained to be seen.

When Conway fired his gun, he wasn't thinking about killing Bobby Norris. As a matter of fact, Bobby Norris was probably about the farthest thing from his mind. What he was thinking about was the stone. He was concentrating on it, seeing it in his mind to the exclusion of everything else and making it a part of his consciousness. When he squeezed the trigger, the stone was the only reason he had for doing it. And the power vibrating under his feet—the power that the burial grounds possessed, and the power that responded to Norris' moonstone energy—ran up his legs and into his brain and over his whole body as the gun exploded...

And the bullet flew true.

Norris was screaming even before the bullet hit...

That was physically impossible, Conway knew, but that didn't matter here anymore. Norris was screaming as the end of the bone he had been using to channel the moonstone's power exploded with impact, and then he was crying and holding a hand over his face as the shattered scepter fell and blood shot from between his fingers.

A terrible, swelling sound rolled up from the forest, like the approach of a thousand horses rumbling the Valley's floor. It shuddered through the air until Conway could feel it in his bones, in his brain, in his bowels, and it made him drop his gun and clutch at his head, covering his ears with his hands as he watched Norris stumble around with both bloody hands covering his face, and the demon woman—who had looked so beautiful before, but who was allowing her true nature to show through in licks of vision that disappeared as quickly as hallucination—opened her mouth to scream.

And then Norris crouched, gathered his strength, and tore his hands away from his face, looking Conway directly in the eye.

And the sheriff knew that he had made a terrible, terrible mistake.

The bullet had hit the moonstone. That was what Conway had been imagining it doing when he pulled the trigger. Somehow, all that energy in the circle had climbed through his body and made it possible for him to shoot so straight that he had hit something that small with one shot. When the bullet hit, it shattered the stone, sending pieces flying. One of them had struck Norris in the eye…

A piece of the moonstone had put out his left eye…

And now, as he looked up, it was changing his face.

"Oh my God!" Conway whispered, staggering back until his knees gave out beneath him. "Oh Jesus! What have I done?!"

The ground itself swelled and buckled as Norris raised himself to his full height—six feet, seven, nine, twelve. The powdery snow went hard and then was overrun with cracks that emanated out from where the Blood Prince stood, and, from between those cracks, the power of the earth responded to its sister moon and bled light up in sharp rays. But unlike the moonstone rays, the light coming up from the ground was not silver—it was golden, bright and hot. It punched holes in the clouds of blowing snow around Norris' body and continued up, through the moonstone's dome of light, shattering it and washing everything in a dazzling, radiant color.

Conway tried to hang on to his balance, but it was impossible, and with a cry and a futile flurry of his hands, he fell backward and rolled as the burial grounds went from being a depression in the earth to a mound one hundred yards across, rising higher and higher, as the new Blood Prince, clothed in spectacular glory, climbed his way to the top.

When he reached the summit, Norris threw out his arms and howled. From where Conway lay, his back against the stump of a tree and his face lifted to the shining night, he saw the man—or thing, for now he was huge—silhouetted against the blazing moon. His arms were as long as his entire height had been just moments before, covered with long, flowing hair that rippled with invisible wind. The mane around his head was magnificent, thick, and billowing to a tapered point that would have easily reached to the pit of his back, had it not been standing straight out from his head behind him. His teeth gleamed, his throat strained, and a billowing plume of steam rose from his stretching mouth as his voice filled the sky, shook the trees, and reached deep into Conway's soul to touch something that was so old that every thought he was having simply shriveled and fell away from his mind like scabs. Lying there in the snow, hearing the Blood Prince singing the Song of the Wild as only the Blood Prince could, the sheriff understood what it must have been like a thousand years ago, or a million, when the flickering glow of a campfire was the only thing that created any distance between a man's mortality and the wilderness, with all its power. He understood the

Hunt, and how natural it was…

And he understood where the Wild came from…

He saw his own soul.

And he was afraid.

He was so….so afraid!

Thunder rocked the Valley when the Blood Prince concluded his song. Scrambling around on the mound that served as the Prince's throne, the others of the Wild and their new Vyrmin servants, tried to approach their leader, but simply fell to their knees and averted their eyes as the sky convulsed and Norris began singing again.

More thunder pealed, ripped, and then pounded down from above as the thing that had the moon in its eye…

Moved!

Conway saw it, and his skin prickled over with icy beads of sweat. His bladder let go, and warmth ran over his crotch and soaked his legs, but he didn't care. It couldn't have mattered less to him at that moment. All that mattered was what he was seeing in the sky…

The form around the moon was moving, turning, swelling itself up as if it were inhaling the universe into its lungs and was about to blow it out into a jumbled roar that would rearrange reality in some new and totally random way.

"Noooooo!" Conway screamed, lifting his mangled hand before his face.

He didn't hear it, but his voice had joined a chorus of insistent denials created by the screams of every human near the burial grounds. Every villager, and by this time there were a lot of them amid the trees, lifted his or her head up, saw, if not the same thing that the sheriff did, then something very much like it, and screamed out their own *"No!"* as if the collective force of their voices might have some impact on that which had chosen to act.

And then, with an explosion of rolling sound that

deafened all present, the figure around the moon expanded, first out, blotting all light from the sky and blinding everyone and everything with a blanket of absolute darkness that swallowed the stars and the moon, and then it focused itself into a single bolt of pitch-black power that shot down and hit the Blood Prince where he stood howling on the hill, erasing him from sight and leaving a smoking hole in the snow where he had been.

All was silence then.

All was pressure.

All was anticipation because there was more, and everyone—the new Vyrmin wolves, the Wild, the humans, and the Flock's Dog, Sheriff H.W. Conway, who was wet with his own piss and crying full tears now—knew that what they were witnessing was not yet over…

It was not an end.

It was a beginning.

Not a whisper marred the perfect, held-breath stillness of the moment before the Dark Times returned. Not a stirring touched the anticipatory tension of that time-before.

Everyone waited…and watched the top of the hill as, from the blackened ground, an arm emerged and was clear beneath the new full moon.

In the sky the awesome figure of the creature in the heavens had disappeared. The stars were arranged in their old, familiar pattern, and clouds were boiling up from the horizon, as if a vacuum so powerful that it had drawn them from the other side of the world had been created when the black lightning bolt touched the earth.

The arm wavered and then pulled itself into a shoulder. Mud crumpled and rolled. Soft earth squishing sounds were loud in the silence. And more of the creature came into view.

The Indians used to bury their dead here, Conway

thought, his mouth hanging limply from his skull. *They'd float them out in canoes when the grounds were flooded and they would dump them. And when the waters went away, the bodies would be gone.*

More earth crumbled, and a head emerged from the ground.

Where did those bodies go?

The thing was on its knees.

They were the bodies of the mad!

It was on its feet.

They were all mad...now.

It was turning its face from one side to another, scanning the trees as if drinking in its domain.

When it settled its attention on the sheriff, his fear melted into a kind of resolved despair—he was lost...dead...doomed... damned. So he got to his wobbling feet, threw out his chest, balled both hands into the best fists he could make, and stared right back at the thing on the hill. Looking up, jutting out his jaw, working the muscles under his ears, he stood defiant...and prayed that his death wouldn't hurt too badly.

The thing regarded him coolly as the sheriff's eyes adjusted to the available light. There were no more glowing rays from the earth or silver beams from the moonstone. There were no more dazzling explosions of power emanating from magic sources. There was just the moon, and it was shining its own brand of magic light—cold, cool, and natural.

The creature's face was unclear in the moon-glow. It looked insubstantial somehow. As if it weren't real at all, but instead was a hole in the air. It moved, and breathed, but there didn't seem to be anything detailed about it. It was empty.

At least it was until it opened its eye...

Its left eye.

The eye that had received the moonstone chip.

When it opened that eye, a split second of light gleamed therein, and then the creature's silhouetted shape—with its tangled hair and horns—disappeared, and was replaced by the naked, shimmering figure of Robert Norris.

"Thank you," Norris said, looking down at the place where Conway stood. "Thou hast done what no other could do. *It is as it has never been.*"

There was a strange, reverberating hollowness to the man's voice that was haunting and empty. It seemed to be echoing up from a great depth, and when the words faded, they didn't so much seem to die as they did to move on, farther away, like television beams disappearing into space.

"Take your life as payment for my own," the Blood Prince continued. And Conway saw the glint of the horns growing back up from his forehead. "We shall meet again, when the world is mine."

From behind Norris' back, wings spread up, as if growing from his hips and climbing into the air over his shoulders. They were huge, moist-looking things, with veiny, taut skin stretched between weirdly pliable ribs that reminded Conway of the stinging whip-barbs on a catfish. For an instant the sheriff was certain he could see something snake-like flick around the man's legs from behind, like a spatula-tipped tail, but he blinked and it was gone. With a great rustle, Norris' wings flapped twice, as if he were testing their integrity, and then again, harder, and then in a rhythm that lifted his feet from the ground.

Conway lifted his gun, but his hand was empty. He just couldn't' bring himself to take his eyes from Norris to look for the tiny weapon, and in the back of his spinning mind, he knew a bullet would have been useless now anyway.

From somewhere, appeared another flapping object in the sky. And as Norris rose higher and higher, the demon woman circled him playfully, as if unable to contain her excitement at having another of her kind for company. Together, the pair increased their altitude until Norris' figure was no larger than an inch long in Conway's view before it stopped, and hung, flapping still in one spot. A glint sparkled up there in the nightmare sky that the sheriff knew was Norris' hazy silver eye, and for a moment, he imagined the immense figure that had used the moon for its own eye, feeling giddy when, in his imagination, that figure shrank to exactly Norris' size in one, liquid motion.

The figure hesitated, and then a voice filled the air and said, "Let it begin."

And then the sky was empty.

35

Conway swallowed twice before he could pull his eyes from where he had last seen Bobby Norris' body. He blinked, and blinked again. Before him, on the hillside, the Wild still stood in their ancient, hairy forms, and the Vyrmin cowered as wolves. From deep inside him welled a loathing sense of disgust that nearly paralyzed his thoughts, and tugged at some tiny bell inside his mind that finally peeled into a specific, pronounceable word...

"KILL!" he suddenly heard himself shouting, as if he were an observer to the event.

"KILL!" he screamed again, and the feeling of it became more right.

"KILL THE VYRMIN!

"KILL THE PEST!

"KILL THE EVIL AND SAVE THE FLOCK!"

In response to his call there came a second's hesitant quiet, and then a roar as the people surrounding the hill with their torches shouted out their anger and moved to obey.

SEVEN

36

The change in atmosphere was almost physical in its impact, and every creature on the hill seemed to feel it at once.

As soon as Conway stopped yelling and the aggressive roar of the villagers in the woods filled the air, the monsters each did something different. Some of them, in apparent shock or outrage, reared up, showing their teeth and plunging to the attack. Others apparently deemed it appropriate to dig in and defend themselves at the top of the hill. Still others just ran, without any obvious destination. And the Vyrmin wolves, to a creature, seemed thrilled by the opportunity to kill.

Conway was filled with an overpowering sense of dislocation. Watching the progression of the villagers with their torches and wavering weapons, he saw, briefly in his mind, the woodcut prints of his childhood: the angry villagers of fourteenth-century France and Germany chasing beings that were depicted as precisely the ones he was seeing in the flesh at this instant. It was unsettling, and shoved his already spinning seed of self totally off balance, so that he could feel in his heart, the emergence of some new facet of his personality that he had not known existed before.

He was filled with a sudden sense of purpose and power.

Shoving his way past the crowd that had washed over him in its enthusiasm to obey his command to kill, he wrested an ax from a man whose face he never saw. Around him came the first sounds of the battle: screaming men, screaming women, howling wolves, and the vigorous, bloodcurdling snarls of the Wild. The din was incredible…growing louder and louder until, with his head filled with it and his eyes filled with the sights of flying blood, Conway thought it could get no worse. But it did. It was like a drug that made him spin. It was like a blast of pure oxygen chasing the vessels in his brain. It was like stepping into a dark room, only to find bright lights and a full-length mirror in which your reflection has been awaiting your arrival.

To his left, an immense beast lifted a man off the ground and tore his chest wide open with a sweep of one clawed hand as another man, looking only about half as tall as the creature before him, brought as ax whistling down into the monster's knee.

There was a horrible scream.

To his right, a wolf was chewing the stump of a woman's neck as blood bathed its jaws.

Ahead, a towering creature toppled over under the weight of ten men, all clutching its fur and pulling as others stood in a ring with knives.

And Conway worked his way through.

The ax felt deadly in his hands, and his heart was bursting with pride for the people around him.

"Fight!" he screamed, as if to spur them on.

But they ignored him.

"This is our chance!" he encouraged, more for himself than anyone else.

And this *was* their chance, he knew in his heart. The Flock *had* to fight, had *learned* to fight over the centuries, and had gotten *good* at it. If it hadn't, then there would have been no need for the Blood Prince to try and change the progress of the Hunt. There would have been no reason for the Man in the Woods to follow him from childhood, through his life, and to this night, when the Hunt was to begin again. They could have let things go. But the Flock had grown strong.

"WITNESS THE END OF THE WILD!!!" he screamed.

Who am I? Conway thought as he stalked through the echoing crash of conflict. *Where have I been all my life? Have I lived this before? If so, how many times? What the hell is happening to me?*

But all questions left him when he spotted the thing for which he had been searching.

Hefting his ax up in both hands, he ran at the creature, howling out his intent and charging with all speed and recklessness. The wolf was busy with two other men, one of whom he had grabbed by the groin and was shaking, while the other crawled on the ground, blindly searching with pulpy, blood-running eyes, for his lower jaw. It didn't react to the sheriff's charge in time, perhaps because it was occupied, or perhaps because it mistook his shouts for just so much more noise in the crowd. But for whatever reason, it didn't drop the man it was shaking until Conway had already delivered his first blow.

The ax struck with a sickening thud, and the force of the blow staggered the sheriff and jarred his bones. But the silver coating, despite what Norris had said about there being no magic in silver, apparently did have some special value when dealing with these creatures because, instead of just slashing out a hunk of flesh, or gouging into bone, the ax head seemed possessed with its own sense of purpose and, to the sheriff's amazement, continued on through the wolf's shoulder and into the ground beyond it.

With a terrible scream the animal pivoted, stumbled, and plunged into a pool of its own blood as its right front leg fell away from its body and turned into a severed human arm on the ground. Madly, its neck twisted as its back legs pumped.

Without hesitating, his face speckled with running droplets of blood and his mouth pulled into an awful grin, Conway heaved the ax up and struck again. The wolf tried to avoid the blow, but the sheriff's arms seemed as if they were being guided by some invisible force that made his aim unerringly lethal, and the bloody ax blade bit into the screaming creature's left shoulder and severed its other front leg before it could roll its body up and bring its teeth to bear.

The wolf, minus its two front legs, writhed on the ground in a growing puddle of muddy blood, splashing itself dark as it pushed with its back legs and tried to snap its jaws at Conway's feet. Flickering changes were happening to it, eyes transforming from one color and size to another and back in milliseconds that registered more on the sheriff's nerves than his mind, alterations in the size and shape of the thing that could have been optical tricks, had Conway not understood what was happening.

As three men came up behind, holding torches for him to see by, the sheriff calmly stepped around the struggling beast and brought the ax down again. But his blow was intended to maim, not to kill, and at the knee, the creature's back right leg was lost.

And then his left.

And then the wolf wasn't a wolf anymore.

It was Detective Michael Cooper, lying on the ground, helpless, staring numbly through debilitating waves of pain, bleeding to death.

Conway sensed the eyes on him in the sky. He knew he was being watched. It wasn't the moon this time, as it had been before. It wasn't anything that unfathomably big that he could not hope to defeat it. This time it was a man-sized observer. A thing with wings, and a tail, and a lover that changed its shape and could tear a man's mind and body apart. But it was man-sized, and it had two names.

Blood Prince was one.

Robert Norris was the other.

Conway could intellectualize that. He could crystallize it in his mind and hold onto the image in his heart. He could reach out and touch a name like "Bobby Norris." He could point to it and say, "That! Right there! That's what we have to do. That's what we have to kill! It's right there, and if we try, we can take it!"

It was like a revelation. Like breaking the surface of the water and breathing for the first time after nearly drowning.

He was the Dog!

He was *meant* to do this!

He was *born* to do this!

He was *made only* to do *this*!

He was the Dog that would save his Flock!

"Watch me now, you son of a bitch!" he spit, transferring his ax to his left hand and grabbing a torch from one of the men standing at his side.

"You thought you'd leave me to die," he continued, stepping up to where Cooper lay, twisting on the ground. "Well, it's not over yet."

Even though he was only half-conscious, Cooper screamed when the sheriff thrust the burning torch into the stump of his right shoulder. He tried to roll, shrieked, bit bloody dirt with this teeth, and then passed out, without ever once looking into the sheriff's eyes.

Had he looked into those eyes, he would have found nothing that even resembled mercy. It was probably best that he didn't see what was in there, at that moment, as the flames of the burning ash and kerosene-soaked rags cauterized his pumping arteries and scorched the raw flesh of his wound closed. For had he seen the depth of hatred, anger, and power imbued in the sheriff's eyes at that instant, he very well might have died of sheer terror. For Conway's single purpose in life had come clear to him in that instant, and he would never again sway from it for as long as he lived...

He would never falter...

He would never fail...

He would *never* be without his ax!

With calculated precision, he moved the torch from one bleeding wound to another, until the torso lying on the ground was charred and motionless.

Then he looked back up at the sky, smiled grimly, and turned to watch the rest of the Vyrmin and their masters die in an orgy of bloodletting and an explosion of the Flock's collective power.

It went on all night.

And in the morning, they lit the fires.

EPILOGUE

The guy was a pain in the ass, but he was from Cleveland, had a badge, and was holding a photograph of Detective Michael Cooper, who had come down to Harpersville a week before and had not come back. So Conway listened sympathetically while he asked his questions, and waited for a full thirty seconds, thoughtfully studying Cooper's picture before handing it back.

"Are you sure, Sheriff?" the man asked, knitting his brow. "I've been all over the area, and this is where he said that he was heading. We would really appreciate anything you can do to help us."

Conway glanced at the man from Cleveland and made a show of reexamining the photograph before saying, "I'm sorry. He just don't ring no bells."

The man looked thoroughly disappointed. But without further protest, he packed up his briefcase and went away.

As his office door slammed—and the thin swirl of snowy air died before chilling the room—Conway didn't move from his seat behind his desk. Instead, he watched the detective from Cleveland stomp through the deep snow and climb into a running Ford Fairlane, where another man was waiting. The second man shook his head, and soon the Ford was heading out of Harpersville, probably headed to the next town along the State Route.

They'd been looking for Michael Cooper for nearly the whole time since that night at the burial grounds.

But they wouldn't find him.

No one would.

After the Ford was gone, Conway glanced down at the

great, black volume upon which his bandaged right hand was resting. The stump of his finger didn't ache that badly right now, but it would tonight, when he was lying in bed, alone with himself and his wound. The book was as thick as a Bible, and in a way, that's exactly what it was: Conway's Bible. It was the black book Dr. Datch had kept of his sessions with young Robert Norris, twenty-five years ago. In it were all the details of everything that was to come, spelled out as a little boy's nightmares. Dr. Datch couldn't be blamed for not believing that Bobby was the Blood Prince that he claimed to be under hypnosis. He couldn't be blamed for taking such statements as "Woodie will try. But I will prevail. For the time of the beast has passed, and the time of the great struggle is yet to come. Only a new way can save the Wild from extinction, and I will be that way!" as examples of his stepson's mental problems and not the very accurate predictions of the course of the child's life that they actually were.

No, Dr. Datch couldn't be blamed for missing the signals or, more accurately, interpreting them in a more traditional manner.

But the good doctor did blame himself, and Conway was glad that he did.

On his way downstairs, the sheriff turned on every light in the dingy, concrete-block stairwell. The steps were loud and creaked under his weight. There were spider webs in every corner.

They had killed twenty of the descendants of the First—which left four alive out there somewhere. They had also killed eleven of the twelve Vyrmin wolves that night. And Conway had been the overseer of the slaughter. Sixty humans had either been killed on the spot or had died in the days that followed, but the losses were small when you considered just what the people of Harpersville had been up against.

The people of Harpersville…

Conway felt a lump of pride in his throat every time he thought of them.

Every damned man, woman and ambulatory child had answered the witness' call that night. Every one. They'd all come, en masse—a solid ring of flesh and blood, armed and ready to fight for their world, their life, and their future.

And they had done what they needed to do.

When the killing was over, the chain saws roared over the Valley, and the bonfires blazed. All the charred bones that were later collected had been buried in the magic way, all around town, in a continuous circle of power. Theoretically, Harpersville was now werewolf proof. Conway hadn't said anything to dispel the people's confidence in their own safety. They'd earned a little peace of mind…

Even if it was unfounded.

The cellar door opened with a prolonged squeal, drawing the attention of one of the men in the damp room. From where he sat, an elderly gentleman in a grey suit and a red tie lifted his head and peered at Conway over the tops of his half-rimmed reading glasses. His grey hair was wispy and cropped short. His middle displayed a pronounced paunch that he had carried almost all his life. And his features were knotted with concentration.

"Well?" Dr. Datch inquired, without rising from his seat.

For a moment, Conway ignored the question, his attention focused as it was every time he entered this buried room of dripping sounds and ill-lit, dancing shadows, on the figure in the wheelchair. Dr. Datch had made this man his personal prisoner and had taken to spending almost every waking minute with him, studying him, watching him, talking to him, and listening on those rare occasions when the man chose to speak.

"That's the second one in the last two days," Conway

said, without taking his eyes from Detective Cooper's face. "Things are getting pretty hot out there."

"But are there any indications that we can start?" Dr. Datch asked, placing the copy of Woodie's diary he was reading on an empty beer case next to the recliner a couple of deputies had lugged down to the cellar for him, and standing up. It was against that recliner that the sheriff's ax leaned, close at hand should the doctor need it.

"Yeah," Conway nodded. "This time there are."

If he didn't have to, Conway would have never come down to this room at all. But he felt that he needed to do it...needed to subject himself to it, just to keep it all fresh in his mind, just to keep it focused.

Datch was saying something, but the sheriff wasn't listening.

He was looking into Detective Cooper's eyes.

Cooper was strapped to the wheelchair with leather belts. He shit through a hole in the seat and pissed through a tube. Without any arms or legs he couldn't move, but that didn't stop his captors from securing his head with a neck brace, because he could bite, and he had proven it by trying several times. He was wrapped in a blanket against the cold, but underneath he was nude. His hair was tangled and dirty—they hosed him off a couple of times a week—and he had lost a great deal of body fat because they didn't feed him anything solid anymore...

Too risky.

They had IVs running into arteries in his neck and there was a tube that they were considering ramming down his throat to his stomach...though they hadn't worked up the nerve to try that yet...

If they ever would.

Cooper was staring into Conway's eyes with sheer,

unblinking hatred in his gaze.

"Sheriff?" Dr. Datch asked, startling Conway by placing a hand on his shoulder. The sheriff had not heard him approach.

"What happened that makes you say that we can begin?" he asked, gently.

Conway blinked, and moved his attention to the doctor. He regarded him for a moment, pushed Detective Cooper's look out of his mind, and said, "This last detective was from the Church itself."

At that, Cooper snorted in his chair and tried to squirm. The belts holding him didn't allow so much as a flicker.

"He was really scared," Conway continued, moving Dr. Datch closer to the stairs, as if a few steps' distance from the wheelchair would make him feel better.

"The increase in random-pattern violence in the past five days has been incredible," he said, his voice low. "They've got FBI agents coming now, and they've been turning the whole lower half of the state upside down looking for him." He nodded toward Cooper. "The coincidence of his asking questions about the Institute of Metaphysical Research and my calling him down here on an animal-killing case makes the Church think that he's tied up with something big. Animal killing are their number one priority right now. But there's more going on too."

Dr. Datch looked interested. "What does a Church representative asking questions about the Institute have to do with animal killings?" he asked.

Conway looked grim. "They found a lot of bodies in the building's basement last week," he answered, softly. "The smell's what did it. It got to the bums living in an alley behind the place, if you can imagine. There were a lot of things in that building that's got them thinking that they might have a connected case of some kind of cannibal worship, if they can just find Cooper.

"Also…and this is the big one. They want to find him fast, because there's been reports of cannibal killings in Michigan."

"North," Dr. Datch said.

"Uh-huh," Conway agreed with a nod.

"It's the first indication we've had that one of *them* has made a move," Datch mused aloud. "It's not necessarily Robert." He still called his stepson Robert, even after everything that had happened. "In all likelihood, it's one of the others following the draw of his energy. But at least it is a direction."

"North," Conway said again. "There's a lot of woods up that way."

Datch frowned.

And both men shared a brief mental image of the great white north of Canada, looming over the United States.

"He's probably already up there," Datch finally said.

Conway sighed. "That's what I've been thinking," he agreed, heading for the stairs. "He's been saying that he went up into the sky since he was a kid. I read it in your book, and then I saw him do it with my own eyes. Said that something 'big' was waiting for him. If I was him, and I wanted a little time to get myself together, north's the way I'd head. And if I could fly, I'd be wherever it was that I was going by now."

Dr. Datch put out his hand and touched the sheriff's sleeve, halting the man on the third step up the stairs.

"When can we be on our way?" he asked, looking up into the man's eyes from below.

Conway looked at the doctor for a long time, and then glanced at the wheelchair over the man's shoulder. Cooper was watching him coldly, and his mouth was twitching around the corners, as if he were about to grin, but was trying to keep himself from doing it. Finally, the detective said in a voice like that of a horror movie demon, "Yeah, Fido. When do we go to the park?"

Conway looked back at the doctor. "It's gonna be a bitch," he said unnecessarily. "If there was some other way than taking *him* along."

"We need him," Datch returned. "The closer we get to Robert—to the Blood Prince—the more symptoms he'll exhibit. He'll be like a human divining rod, pointing us to the right path. It'll be hard. But it will be worth it in the end."

"The end," Conway said, admiring the determination in the old man's eyes. He didn't really think that they were anywhere near the end. "Tomorrow," he said, finally, turning and heading back up the stairs. "Ready or not, for better or for worse, we'll begin our Hunt tomorrow."

And below him, Detective Cooper was softly laughing, expressing his delight at the promise of the new day's dawn.

THE END

ABOUT THE AUTHOR

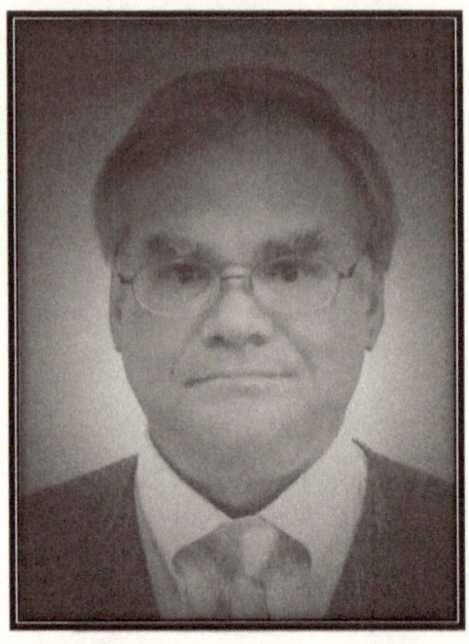

A native of Cleveland, Ohio, Gene Lazuta was introduced to dark stories of fear and the supernatural by his grandmother, who cultivated his taste for fright and fascination with a never-ending stream of folk tales from her native Slovakia. Following college, where he studied literature and psychology, he worked as an undertaker for nearly thirteen years before finding a professional home as a communication specialist at one of the nation's most recognized and respected healthcare organizations.

He is the author of ten novels (six horror-based and four murder mysteries), numerous journal and trade publication articles, and a new non-fiction collaboration. Following the release of the Bloodshot Books edition of *Vyrmin,* he is returning to the supernatural genre by starting work on a story that carries the mythology that *Vyrmin* introduces in a wider, more ominous direction.

Gene lives in Berea, Ohio, with his wife of over thirty years, Sue, his inspiration, his motivation, and the woman to whom every book he has ever written and will ever write is dedicated.

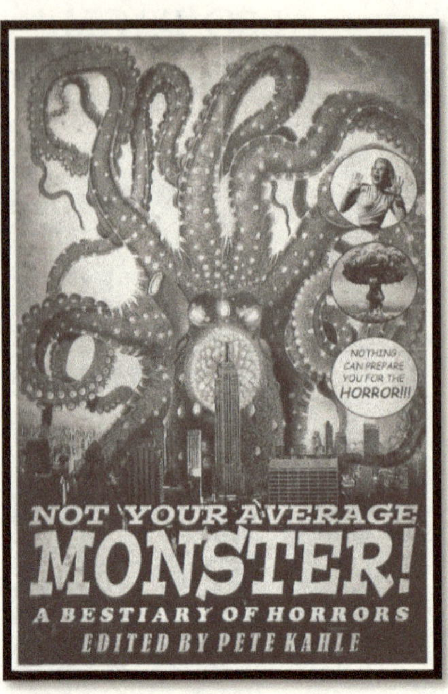
NOTHING CAN PREPARE YOU FOR THE HORROR!!!
NOT YOUR AVERAGE
MONSTER!
A BESTIARY OF HORRORS
EDITED BY PETE KAHLE

JUST WHEN YOU THOUGHT YOU COULD VENTURE OUT OF YOUR HIDING PLACES, HERE COMES ANOTHER HORDE OF HORRORS

Slithering, wriggling, lurking, and creeping. Leaving slick trails of pustulent slime behind them. These aren't your run-of-the-mill monsters populating the pages of this tome. No, these critters feed on the fear that bubbles up inside you when all appears lost and the scent of blood is on the wind. Now is the time to face these demons and read on . . .

NOT YOUR AVERAGE MONSTER, VOL. 2: A MENAGERIE OF VILE BEASTS

THIS NIGHTMARE HAS JUST BEGUN!

Available in paperback or Kindle on Amazon.com

ISBN-13: 978-0692644737

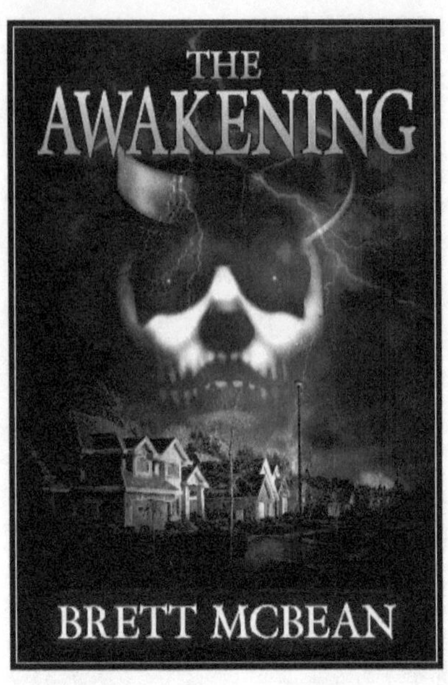

Welcome to the small Midwestern town of Belford, Ohio. It's summer vacation and fourteen-year-old Toby Fairchild is looking forward to spending a lazy, carefree summer playing basketball, staying up late watching monster movies, and camping out in his backyard with his best friend, Frankie.

But then tragedy strikes. And out of this tragedy an unlikely friendship develops between Toby and the local bogeyman, a strange old man across the street named Mr. Joseph. Over the course of a tumultuous summer, Toby will be faced with pain and death, the excitement of his first love, and the underlying racism of the townsfolk, all while learning about the value of freedom at the hands of a kind but cursed old man.

Every town has a dark side. And in Belford, the local bogeyman has a story to tell.

Available in paperback or Kindle on Amazon.com

ON THE HORIZON FROM BLOODSHOT BOOKS

2016

The Frighteners – Stephen Laws

Tunnelvision – R. Patrick Gates

Odd Man Out – James Newman

2017*

Eternal Darkness – Tom Deady

Shadow Child – Joseph A. Citro

The Boulevard Monster – Jeremy Hepler

The Breeze Horror – Candace Caponegro

Abode – Morgan Sylvia

The Raggedy Man – Christopher Collins

Those Who Follow – Michelle Garza & Melissa Lason

Sinkhole – Ken Goldman

Blood Mother: A Novel of Terror – Pete Kahle

The Abomination (The Riders Saga #2) – Pete Kahle

2018*

The Horsemen (The Riders Saga #3) – Pete Kahle

Not Your Average Monster, Volume 3

* other titles to be added when confirmed

BLOODSHOT BOOKS

READ UNTIL
YOU BLEED

www.ingramcontent.com/pod-product-compliance
Lightning Source LLC
Chambersburg PA
CBHW030635260626
47157CB00007B/2340

* 9 7 8 0 9 9 8 0 6 7 9 0 2 *